INFERNAL BLADE

OVERWORLD UNDERGROUND BOOK THREE

JOHN CORWIN

RAVEN
HOUSE

BOOKS BY JOHN CORWIN

THE OVERWORLD CHRONICLES

Sweet Blood of Mine

Dark Light of Mine

Fallen Angel of Mine

Dread Nemesis of Mine

Twisted Sister of Mine

Dearest Mother of Mine

Infernal Father of Mine

Sinister Seraphim of Mine

Wicked War of Mine

Dire Destiny of Ours

Aetherial Annihilation

Baleful Betrayal

Ominous Odyssey

Insidious Insurrection

Utopia Undone

Overworld Apocalypse

Assignment Zero (An Elyssa Short Story)

OVERWORLD UNDERGROUND

Possessed By You

Demonicus

Infernal Blade

OVERWORLD ARCANUM

For the latest on new releases, free ebooks, and more, join John Corwin's Newsletter at www.johncorwin.net!

DEAD IN DAYS

Emily Glass will be dead in days unless she can overcome destiny.

An overlord of Hell put a price on Emily's head and every demon in the underworld wants to claim the prize. She might be the Great Banisher, but even she can't fight off an army of demons. The only way to survive might be to trust an enigmatic Seraphim, and to find the source of her powers.

Where does her demon banishing power come from? How can she rip the powers from vampires? There don't seem to be any other beings with powers like hers, but if they exist, they might help her survive the minions of Hell.

Emily has to solve a mystery even her dead mother couldn't unravel. Otherwise, she'll soon join her in the afterlife.

CHAPTER 1

My funeral was only seven days away.

Provided Aunt Lydia's glimpse into my future was correct, that meant my death was close at hand. To get my mind off such matters, I decided to go for a nice pumpkin spice latte at the corner coffee shop. It was a bad decision in more ways than one, but particularly because today might be the day a car jumped the curve and ran me over.

I twisted the engagement ring around my finger—a habit that had grown more frequent when I worried about things out of my control. That pretty much described my life since discovering the supernatural world hiding within our own.

The left side of my face grew unnaturally warm as I crossed a small road at the intersection. I suspected the heat wasn't a weather-related phenomenon. Especially when the homeless woman with a shopping cart full of odds and ends picked it up and hurled at me with uncanny force.

"Die, Emily Glass!"

I shrieked and dove out of the way. One of my high heels snapped off and I nearly stumbled in front of a bus on Peachtree Street. I fell sideways and rolled over on my bum. The attacker gave me no time to recover from my nasty spill. She drew a rusty kitchen knife from beneath her ragged clothes, raised it above her head, and rushed me with a bloodcurdling scream.

Curse my pumpkin spice cravings!

She was the source of heat I'd felt a moment earlier. The psychic energy emanating from her churned my stomach. I'd encountered enough possessed people to know this woman wasn't in control of her body. A caustic demon pulled the puppet strings, and it was on a mission to murder me.

I froze for an almost fatal instant before trained reflexes activated. When the woman was only a few feet away, I lashed out and kicked her in the knee. Given her full-speed sprint, the damage was disastrous. Her knee made a sickening crack. Knife still outstretched, she fell toward me, a maniacal gleam in her eyes.

My next instinct saved my life. A quick roll to the side removed me from harm's way. The knife sparked and bent as it met unyielding concrete. I jumped to my feet and nearly toppled again thanks to the missing heel on my shoe. They were custom designed, a gift from Tyler, and now they were scuffed, broken, and fit for the rubbish bin.

Are shoes really the priority right now?

I didn't have time to undo the buckles, so I rammed my foot down on the sidewalk until the other heel snapped off. "Who are you, foul creature?"

"The one who will end you, Emily Glass." The possessed woman rose, hobbling on one leg. Her filthy, ragged dress hid the injured knee. Bloody spittle flecked her lips. The bent knife lay abandoned on the sidewalk, but her outstretched hands seemed poised to finish the job. "Domathus placed a lovely price on your head, and I intend to collect."

I should have run, but without the knife, the demon was a lot less threatening. "You can tell him I said hello when I send you back to Hell."

The woman shrieked and limped towards me. Just as she closed to within reach, I gripped her left wrist, ducked and twisted behind her, pinning her arm to her back. My other arm snaked around her neck and tightened the noose. She screamed, other hand clawing awkwardly behind her. I twisted her arm up, drawing another cry of pain. In that instant, a pattern flashed into my mind, and with it, the true name of the aggressor.

"Pistorio, I command you back to Haedaemos!" The woman's hand stopped just inches from my face. Grime encrusted her broken nails; green infection lined the cuticles. Coupled with the caustic aura, she might have left festering wounds on my face with even a scratch. "Pistorio, I command you home!"

"No!" The demonic voice rose in unison with that of the homeless woman. "He will kill me!"

A dark world of violent, shifting shadows and crawling monsters flashed through my mind. A great presence rose up before me, horns curving from the forehead and around the back of the head like a crown. I had seen this monster before and driven his servants back to Haedaemos. It was Domathus, an overlord of the netherworld.

The woman went limp. I had successfully banished the demon, Pistorio, back to Hell, or Haedaemos as those in the Overworld called it.

"Jesus Christ, she just beat up that homeless woman!" A group of teens held their mobile phones toward me, recording the spectacle. Other spectators gaped in horror.

How much did they see? I rewound the brief fight in my mind but couldn't remember seeing anyone else.

"Too often, battlefield vision narrows down to you and the person in front of you," George Walker had told me. "That's when someone else stabs you in the back."

I hadn't been stabbed in the back, but I'd certainly shot myself in the foot. I released the homeless woman and she fell screaming, holding her injured knee. I held up my hands. "She attacked me first! I was just defending myself."

"Rich bitch!" Someone called.

"Liar!"

A man rushed from the crowd and knelt next to the woman. "Are you okay? What did she do to you?"

I was about to retort when I realized something was wrong—terribly wrong. It felt as if heat lamps focused on me from all directions. I cast a wary glance around. The teens stood perhaps twenty feet away, clustered in a group around the phone held by a boy. The warmth seemed to emanate from one of them. The boy glared at me with malicious intent. The flash of yellow in his irises gave him away.

A woman with short blond hair stood behind me, a malicious grin on her face. She was young, perhaps my age. She looked so familiar, I nearly forgot my precarious situation. The demonic warmth emanating from her was different. She held an aura of power. I glimpsed a red glow inside of her, but it wasn't quite the same as the other possessed. It was almost as if the woman controlled the demon, not the other way around.

Is she their leader? Caustics were notoriously unruly unless monitored by greater demons. Domathus had likely sent one of his lieutenants to keep them on task. I couldn't shake the feeling that I'd seen this woman before. But now wasn't the time to satisfy my curiosity.

A possessed woman to my right gave off a sickly caustic aura. I felt more caustics to the left and behind me. The woman added her taunts to those of the teens.

"Someone hold her for the police!"

"Grab that bitch!"

Had these been normal people, I would have gladly remained in place and explained what happened to the police, but this was no ordinary crowd. The possessed encircled me, another noose slowly drawing closed. I had very few choices. I could stay and fight the four or five demonic presences in the crowd. I might even exorcise some of them before they subdued me. Or I could run and look guilty of manhandling an old homeless woman.

Both prospects sounded equally terrible, but one of them gave me much a better chance of survival. Cutting diagonally between the teens and the woman on my right offered a better route and fewer people to navigate. Without further hesitation, I ran for the narrow gap. One of the normal boys tried to grab me. I slipped from his clutches and barged between two women to emerge on the sidewalk.

Pedestrians flocked to the gathering mob, like flies to fresh feces.

A woman stood in my way. "What happened over there?"

"I'm sure you'll hear all about it on the internet." I dodged around her and kept walking.

The demonic presence faded. For whatever reason, the possessed weren't following me. But I felt more pinpricks of heat ahead, and others nearby. I looked across the street and saw an old man leering at me. A group of men who looked as if they'd just stepped away from a golfing resort blocked the sidewalk ahead, every last one of them staring at me.

"Bloody hell." This was getting out of control. I reached into my purse for my mobile. Except my purse was gone, likely lost in the fight. "What a wonderful Monday this is turning out to be." Thankfully, a fingerprint and numeric code protected access to my phone. But my driver's license and other personal effects would be there for all the world to take and see.

So much for anonymity.

Not that I had any to begin with. Domathus had not taken kindly to my interference in his plans for world domination. And now he'd pulled out all the stops to make sure I bloody well never got in his way again.

I had few choices left to me. I might be able to summon a taxi and hope it could spirit me away before the possessed got me, or I might make another run for it in my broken shoes. The three blocks between me and OnTech might as well have been three miles on foot.

The golfer boys strolled my way, seemingly in no hurry to reach their quarry. Two women across the road paced me and stopped when I did, eager grins on their faces. The teen boy and two others left the mob around the homeless woman and walked my way.

The blond woman followed them, leering at me as if this were the greatest game in the world. She called out after me in an accent as British as mine. "Run, run, run, sweet Emily." Then she laughed.

I ran to the curb and looked up and down the street for a taxi. Not a one in sight. An apartment complex and several restaurants lined the side-walk, but if I ran inside any of them, I'd just trap myself. I couldn't very well start screaming for help. The possessed looked like ordinary humans to everyone else. They could pretend to help me and that would be the end of it. So I did the only thing a sane person could do in such an insane situation.

I ran into traffic.

I very nearly ended my life with the first step, but the driver of a silver compact car slammed on his brakes, sparing barely an inch between his bumper and my knees. I dodged a black car and made it to the yellow centerline. Amidst a chorus of honks, shouts, and cries questioning my mental health, I ran down the middle of the road in lunchtime traffic. Thankfully, this was Midtown Atlanta and not a busy highway, or I wouldn't have survived five feet.

Traffic crawled at a steady pace through the gauntlet of traffic lights, meaning the cars paced my desperate jog, giving the drivers plenty of time to ogle the idiot racing down the middle of the road in broken heels.

Had my pursuers been ordinary humans, they might have stalked me from the sidewalks. But caustic demons weren't very good at restraining themselves. They reveled in carnal pleasures, whether that meant sex, drugs, or hunting a woman in broad daylight on a busy road. Howling in excitement, two men and a woman dashed into traffic after me.

The first man had the misfortune to run straight in front of a bus. Though it wasn't going very fast, it slammed him into the back of the car in front of it. With an agonizing scream, one pursuer was out of the chase with broken bones and unaffordable medical bills.

The other two leapt atop cars, running and springing from one to the next like monkeys. Possessed imbued their hosts with superhuman strength and speed, meaning I had very little time before they caught up.

The blond woman paced me from the sidewalk. "Are you frightened, little rabbit?"

I was too out of breath to respond. Given the chance, I'd send her howling back to Haedaemos first. Unlike my attackers, I had no supernatural strength, speed, or reflexes. The Divinity used to bless Templars with supernatural enhancements, but recent revelations exposed her as something malevolent and evil. This fractured the Templar faction, and the Divinity stopped granting blessings before I could claim mine.

George Walker and Mr. Sticks had subjected me to Templar and Custodian training over the past few months. I was a better fighter now, and I'd learned a great deal about the Overworld, but I was still no match for vampires or the possessed.

The light ahead turned red. The cars around me slowed to a stop while cars in the perpendicular street sped across the intersection. The caustics would ensure I swiftly met my maker if I stopped for the light. Then again, the end would likely be just as swift if I kept running. Rather than throw caution completely to the wind, I waved my hands wildly before venturing into the intersection.

Tires screeched. Metal crunched. Horns honked. I flinched at the metallic carnage but continued onward. The male possessed dashed along the top of a bus, howling like a dog. "You're mine, bitch! I'm going to fuck you and tear out your throat!"

"Mine, mine!" the female possessed screeched. "I want to bite off her fingers and hear her scream!"

I wanted to shout a retort, but unlike them, I was out of breath. Despite months of workouts and training, I was not built to sprint nonstop. Two city blocks still separated me from the safety of Tyler and OnTech. A cramp stabbed into my side, and needles of pain shot into my feet. My designer shoes were not designed for athletics.

I can't let these bastards kill me!

I'd conquered a vampire rapist and saved my future husband Tyler from Exorcists. I'd survived a battle with a demon overlord and driven him back to the netherworld. I refused to let these pitiful minions be the end of me. I sucked down another breath and forced my legs to keep moving. But the pounding of feet on car hoods and roofs grew closer and closer with every passing second. Any second now they would—

The possessed man arced overhead and slammed onto the roof of a minivan in front of me. The driver screamed and leapt from the driver's seat. She unbuckled a baby from the seat behind her and ran away, infant cradled in her arms. The female caustic crashed onto an old blue sedan to my right. People scurried from their cars, shouting and screaming in alarm.

I stopped and backed away, gulping ragged breaths. The pain in my side was almost too much to bear, and my knees felt like jelly. I'd nearly made it to within a block of OnTech, but it wasn't close enough.

It seemed Emily Glass would meet her end right on schedule.

CHAPTER 2

The possessed male snarled. "You're gonna pay for making me chase you, bitch." He bared sickly green teeth. Judging from the scars on his arms and his filthy attire, his host abused drugs. It was a wonder he'd driven the body so hard without killing it. The female caustic didn't look any better.

"What good is the hunt without a chase?" It seemed I wouldn't die without my old friend, snark. "I suppose you'd prefer your victims to curl into a little ball first."

He laughed. "Oh, it was fun. But this will be funner."

"More fun." My full British snobbery made an appearance. "Where did Domathus dig up caustics as stupid as you? Are there hillbillies in Haedaemos?" I didn't even know what I was talking about now. Every second I kept them talking was another second I extended my life. "What reward has Domathus promised you?"

"Your soul and a hundred demon spirits." The woman hopped off the car and stalked towards me. "I will become powerful."

"She's mine." The man jumped off the minivan and growled.

"Mine!" the woman screamed. "Mine, mine, mine!"

I caught sight of the blond woman on the sidewalk, leering with glee.

The arguing possessed gave me hope. I looked at the female. "Don't let him steal your reward! He'll probably ask Domathus for your spirit if he wins."

"I will, I will!" The man snapped his teeth so hard, one of them cracked and fell out. "I'll eat your spirit first!"

I was prepared to goad them further but didn't need to bother. The female possessed screamed bloody murder and lunged at the male. Fingernails clawed at eyes. Their bodies slammed into cars so hard, they nearly toppled a red Mini. I summoned all my remaining strength and jogged around the minivan and toward salvation.

With half a block to go, feminine howls of triumph coupled with screams and shouts from frightened onlookers told me the brawl had come to a violent end. I glanced back and saw the female possessed charging toward me, the head of her tormentor clutched beneath an arm like a football. Ordinary humans—noms—leapt out of the way and fled before her.

Just ahead, people walked in and out of the front doors of the shared office building OnTech called home. I wanted to shout for help, pray that someone I knew emerged and came to my rescue, but I couldn't catch my breath. I could hardly put one foot in front of another.

I felt dry demonic heat approaching from behind. Something slammed into my back. I tumbled to the sidewalk. Rough concrete bit into my palms and ripped my jeans. The man's head rolled to a stop just in front of me. I had no more screams to give. This was it. The end.

Chest heaving for air, I crawled on my hands and knees. Strong hands pulled me to my feet. Bodies crowded around me. I blinked the haze from my eyes and saw the faces of strangers protecting me from the killer.

"Mine! Mine!" The woman screamed.

People cried out as the caustic flung them aside like rag dolls. Her bloodied hands reached for me. Something whistled through the air. The woman made an awful gagging noise and froze in place, surprise etched on her bloody face. She grasped at a small blade jutting from her throat before face-planting on the sidewalk. A pool of blood spread out beneath her.

The blond woman stood twenty feet behind the dead caustic, her arm retracting as if she'd just thrown something. She laughed. "This was just for fun. Soon, you'll beg us to end the torment."

"Is this a bloody game?"

"Isn't it all, sweet Emily?" She stepped backward and melted into the crowd.

I didn't wait to give anyone else a chance at my life and stumbled toward the door to the office building. Dazed noms pulled themselves to their feet. Fright and concern showed on the faces of those in my way. I probably looked quite the mess with my broken shoes, torn jeans, and bloody hands.

Shuffling inside, I pounded the call button to the lift, leaving crimson fingerprints behind. I leaned on the wall to remain upright, smearing it with more blood. When the doors opened, I nearly fell inside, but managed to retain some meager dignity. I offered prayers and had them answered when the lift continued to the top floor uninterrupted. The doors dinged open and I was met with a gasp.

"Emily!" Jack Somers dropped his laptop with an unceremonious crash and didn't even look at it. He swept me into his arms, cradled me like a baby, and rushed me through the office. I heard more gasps. Saw Sandra Connors grimacing at me like a poorly done manicure.

"Emily!" Tyler jumped up from his office chair and raced around his ridiculously large desk. "Put her on the couch."

Jack set me down on the expensive leather divan set in the corner of Tyler's office.

"Oh god, Em." Tyler's chiseled face hovered over me. He dropped to his knees next to me and began examining my wounds. "What happened?"

"I'm not dead yet." With that declaration, I closed my eyes to rest them for a moment. I assumed I'd pass out, but my racing mind and thudding heart refused to let me sleep even though the adrenalin had long since evaporated from my veins. I sighed. "I broke my heels and didn't even get my pumpkin spice latte."

Tyler groaned. "You come back covered in blood and that's what you're concerned about?"

"Should I call the police?" Sandra's voice echoed from my left.

"I sincerely doubt we'll need to," Jack replied. "There's a huge crowd on the sidewalk down there."

I groaned and gave up trying to pass out. My hands burned from sidewalk scrapes and my body ached from crown to toe. I opened my eyes and sat up. Sandra hovered in the doorway along with half a dozen concerned office staff. It just wouldn't do for them to hear what I was about to say, so I made something up. "There was a wreck when I was crossing the road. But I'm okay. Please, I just need to rest."

"Sounds good, Em." Tyler shooed everyone else from his office and closed the doors. He walked over and sat beside me. "What really happened?"

"Demon assassins, led by a blond twit."

Tyler growled. "Domathus."

It was a sexy growl, one that shouldn't have even aroused me given my current state. But I felt a welcome heat stirring. *Be a grownup, you ninny.* I cleared my throat. "Yes. Apparently, there's a price on my head."

"Son of a bitch." Tyler's ran his hands along my arms and legs, examining every inch for wounds. "I knew we should have taken more precautions." He took out his mobile and started dialing. "I'm calling a doctor."

"Don't bother." I tapped the disconnect button and ended the call. "I'm only a little scratched up."

"Then let's get out of here right now and go into hiding."

I sighed. "Where would I be safe, hmm? Aunt Lydia saw me in a coffin on October sixth, and I think it's rather clear how I end up there."

Tyler winced. "Are her visions always right?"

I shrugged. "How should I know? I didn't even realize she could see the future until Mum's funeral." I swallowed a lump in my throat. Lydia and my mum, Victoria, were twins, identical in appearance but oh, so opposite in personality. Victoria had been fierce and loyal. Lydia was meek and kept to herself, as far as I knew.

"That blond woman looked so familiar." I tried to place her face but was too tired to focus.

"Maybe she's been following you," Tyler said. "We need to get you into a safe house until this blows over."

"Blows over?" I scoffed. "Do you really think a demon overlord will just let this blow over?" I got up and limped to the medicine cabinet, also known as a liquor shelf, and poured myself a shot of whiskey. I forced it down. It burned like hell and only made me feel worse. "Can you make a frozen margarita in here?"

Tyler laughed. "You're impossible." He went into his office's private bathroom and returned with a damp rag. "Sit down, babe."

I dropped back onto the divan and Tyler began gently cleaning my scrapes and wiping the blood from my arms and legs. His gentleness nearly brought tears to my eyes.

"Thank you, darling."

He kissed my hands and sent shivers up my spine. "Tell me what happened, Em."

I told him the particulars, leaving him gaping in astonishment.

"She threw a head at you?" Tyler grabbed the sides of his own head and paced back and forth. "Jesus, the cops will be all over this!"

"I'm certain it will be quite a media sensation."

Tyler groaned. "And I'm sure the video will be on the line as well."

"Online," I said. "Not on the line." Tyler wasn't the most technological person in the world, mainly because he didn't even try to understand it, despite owning several technology companies.

I went to Tyler's laptop and pulled up websites to look for trending videos. "Nothing yet, but we'll know for sure by morning if they posted the video of me and the homeless woman."

"They're assassinating your character before they kill you." Tyler nodded as if it made all the sense in the world. "That's why that blond woman spared you."

"She made it clear they're toying with me first." My fists clenched. "I'd like to show her a thing or two."

"Demons love to torment their prey." Tyler's jaw tightened. "Domathus doesn't want your death to be easy." He stood behind me and massaged my neck and shoulders, loosening the knot in my muscles. But it didn't do much to ease the tangle of stress building in my chest.

"They got my purse and phone." I groaned. "That's the third phone I've lost in two months." I went to the smartphone maker's website and entered my account information to track the phone. A blip on the map showed it had moved a few blocks from where I'd lost it. Someone had tried to access it too many times and the phone disabled itself. A tap of a button sent a remote erase command and that was that.

"What are you doing?" Tyler looked curiously at the screen.

"Erasing my phone."

"No nude photos for them." Tyler continued his gentle massage.

I groaned. "Unfortunately, they have my ID and wallet. We need to cancel all my credit cards."

"I'll take care of it." Tyler pulled me up out of the chair and held me close. "I don't want to live without you, Em."

I melted in his embrace. "Just promise me you'll commit ritual suicide when I die, okay, love?"

Tyler chuckled. "Of course." He sighed. "Guess I'd better cancel the rest of my appointments today."

"I'm certain the police will be willing to take up the rest of our free time." I looked back down at the sidewalk and blinked. The crowd was gone and not even a spot of blood marred the sidewalk. "What in the world?"

Tyler's phone buzzed. "Sir, there are two men here to see Emily and they refuse to go away." Uma, the new receptionist, desperately wished to be as stern and unmoving has her mentor, Sandra, but she sounded every bit as confused as the day we hired her.

A slight chill emanated from beyond the door and I glimpsed a glowing white sphere in my mind's eye. "Is it a George Walker?" I asked.

"Y-yes. Were you expecting him? Oh, I'm so sorry!"

Everything suddenly made sense to me. "Please send him in, Uma."

An ordinary looking man in a black suit entered a moment later. George wore his brown hair combed to the side. A pair of thin-rimmed glasses perched on his nose today, though they seemed to come and go for no discernable reason. I suspected he wore them to increase his ordinariness, and yet, he and his partner wore black suits that gave them a sinister aura, like that of a secret quasi-governmental agency.

A tall, thin man with a neutral expression entered close behind George.

Mr. Sticks looked somewhat hunched and awkward, but I'd seen him fight a demon spawn and knew he was anything but. In the Overworld, they were known as Custodians—the supernatural cleanup crew. Whenever noms were exposed to the supernatural, the Custodians swept in and sanitized the scene, leaving noms none the wiser.

Uma hovered behind them. "Uh, here they are, Miss Glass."

"Thank you, Uma." I motioned the men inside and closed the door behind them. "I take it you cleaned up the mess below?"

George smiled amicably. "I think we managed to nip it in the bud."

Sticks folded his arms over his chest and stared at us without a word.

George seemed to answer some unspoken communication. "Yes, it very nearly was."

"Is he talking to you again?" I said.

"Communicating, yes." George nodded at Tyler. "Good to see you again, Mr. Rock."

Tyler raised an eyebrow. "How'd you get it cleaned up so fast? Do you have someone watching Emily?"

"Not someone, but something." George held up a small silver marble. "We thought it prudent to assign an ASE to keep an eye on things since the Demonicus Incident. It took some time by mortal standards for Domathus to act, but it appears he's moved the first chess piece in a brutal campaign against Miss Glass."

"He just kicked the table over and sent the chess pieces scattering," Tyler said. "I wouldn't call this assassination attempt subtle."

"Subtler than you might think," George replied calmly. "The video and the chase seemed rather calculated." He flicked the ASE in the air and a holographic menu appeared.

I couldn't stifle a gasp despite having seen such devices in use before.

The recording of the incident started overhead, but George was able to zoom down to a third-person perspective just above the fight with the homeless woman. Tyler's fists tightened and he mimed punching as he watched me fend off the first attacks.

I flinched when I watched myself kicking the old woman in the knee.

"That's my girl." Tyler kissed the top of my head like a proud parent.

I groaned.

"Mr. Sticks and I are impressed with your survival instincts," George said as we watched me run down the middle of the street. "You successfully chose unexpected routes to confuse the enemy." He paused it when the man and woman began chasing me through traffic. "This is where the plan failed."

"Where it nearly ended me," I said. I used my hand to rotate the image until I found the blond woman. "Who is she and why does she look so familiar?"

George blinked and looked from the woman to me.

Tyler whistled. "Damn. She looks like a blond version of you, babe."

"Me?" I stared at her a moment then swiped the image back to my frightened face. My hair and eyes were brown, and my face was pinched with terror. But it was undeniable. The blond woman looked strikingly familiar to me.

"Probably illusion," George said. "Demons love mind games like this. They probably wanted to further confuse you with a doppelganger."

Sticks nodded.

"Make sense." Tyler's knuckles cracked. "Wish I could punch Domathus in the nuts."

George continued the playback, allowing me to see the female caustic strike me in the back with the dead man's head. Just as she approached to deliver the finishing blow, the blond woman threw a dagger and

17

killed her. George grunted. "We flashed the area with a hypnosis spell and adjusted the memories of any witnesses. They'll think the head was a soccer ball and won't remember the body."

"What about all the phones recording it?" I said.

"A static discharge spell erased all phones in the vicinity," George said. "We'll monitor the nom internet for any surviving recordings."

"What about the damaged cars and the chase?" I said. "Surely you can't cover all that up."

"Even now, Custodians are spreading the rumor that it was a publicity stunt for a superhero movie being filmed in the city." George shrugged. "Noms are adept at rationalizing unbelievable things."

"So I needn't worry about a visit from the police?" I said.

"You should be safe for now." George zoomed in on the blonde as she threw a knife at the caustic trying to kill me and paused it. "The first act of your murder is done. Unfortunately, we have no idea what Domathus has planned before his assassins kill you."

CHAPTER 3

Tyler sighed. "Classic demon overlord plotting. Domathus wants to put you through thirteen levels of hell before ending you."

"What a rosy picture you paint," I said. "Unfortunately, my date with destiny is barely six days away, so he hasn't much time to enjoy my suffering." I turned to George. "Unless you have an ironclad way to change the future, I'm doomed."

George turned off the ASE and pocketed it. "We tested your Aunt Lydia's abilities. She predicted future events for thirty-three out of a hundred agents."

"Only thirty-three?" Tyler said.

"Yes, she doesn't have a vision for everyone she meets," George said. "Or at least she professes not to."

"Have those events come to pass?" I asked.

"Twenty-seven have indeed occurred as predicted. The remainder are still in the future." George shrugged. "I'm afraid her precognitive skills are so far one hundred percent accurate."

Tyler slumped. "No. I won't let it happen. I'll take Emily to Antarctica if I have to."

"Where I'll freeze to death?" I shook my head. "Tyler, it's useless. Let's just enjoy the remainder of our time together—"

"No!" He pounded a fist on the liquor cabinet. Glass rattled and only the quick reflexes of Mr. Sticks saved an expensive bottle of scotch from falling to its doom. "I'll go to Hell and kill Domathus myself."

"That's rather unlikely." George shook his head. "You have a better chance here than anywhere else."

A part of me loved the savage, fearless side of Tyler. But I sometimes worried he might not realize his own limits and do something foolish. "Perhaps we can send Domathus to the Abyss," I said. "Can Vallaena help us again?"

"I'm afraid she's quite busy with other important tasks." George glanced at Mr. Sticks and nodded. "Yes, it would be prudent to tell them."

"Tell me what?" Stress tightened in my stomach. I looked at Mr. Sticks and tried to peer inside him. A chill emanated from him as it did from George, though his seemed to operate on a slightly different frequency. "Why don't you ever say anything to me, Mr. Sticks?"

He turned a deadpan look on me and stared.

I stared back, waiting for a voice to speak inside my head. The only voice I heard was my own. I hated not knowing what he was thinking.

"The Templar fracture has worsened. One group follows Daelissa, the Divinity, and the other opposes them. The entire Overworld is on the brink of war, the Synod against the Borathen Templars." George straightened the bottles on the liquor shelf as he spoke. "War is chaotic. It will soon demand all our resources, and I fear we won't be able to protect you."

Vallaena had once described the power of the Divinity. Supposedly she was an angel, but not the kind I knew of from the Bible.

"Whose side are you on, anyway?" Tyler asked. "The Synod's or Thomas Borathen's?"

"As ever, we are on the side of the Overworld." George finished arranging the bottles and turned around. "The Custodians cannot choose a side. We must remain neutral and do what is necessary to keep the noms blissfully unaware of all that is supernatural. If nom governments ever became aware of the Overworld, then we'd truly have an unwinnable war on our hands."

"Don't you rely on the local Templars to assist?" I asked.

"Commander Borathen has continued to help us when needed," George said. "He is an honorable man."

"I certainly like him." I folded my arms. "After hearing the news about Daelissa, I can't believe anyone would willingly follow her."

George held out his hands helplessly. "That isn't for us to decide."

"Oh, I think it is." I caught a glimpse of the white sphere at the heart of his aura. "She gave you a blessing, so perhaps it influences you."

"I disagree." George waved a hand. "But that does bring up another point. You never received a blessing."

"Because Daelissa no longer associates with the Borathen Templars." I raised an eyebrow. "Whatever is a girl to do?"

"I suggest you visit the Templar compound today." George glanced outside the window. "Request a visit with the Clarion."

"The what?" I blinked. "Who's that?"

"Daelissa's replacement." George turned for the door. "Please don't wait, Miss Glass. It may very well save your life."

"If I was a Daemos, I could do a hell of a lot more to protect Emily." Tyler held out his hands imploringly. "Vallaena told me a Daemas named Kassallandra possessed an empty body and became a Daemos. Is there a way I can do that too?"

George shrugged. "I'm afraid you'd have to ask Kassallandra, and I don't know where to find her."

Tyler groaned. "Can you at least take us to the Clarion?"

"Absolutely," George said. "Our car is on the roof."

Tyler's eyes brightened. "Can I drive?"

Mr. Sticks scowled.

"I'm afraid not," George said.

I wished I had my phone. "I need to tell Isabel what's happening. What if Domathus targets her?"

"Anything is possible with demons." Tyler gave me his phone.

I texted her a brief warning. *Demon assassins are after me. Please be careful. They might go after you!*

Isabel's response came seconds later. *Whaaaaaat!? Why are you using Tyler's phone?*

No time to explain. I'll let you know more later. Just be careful!

Love you, sis. You be careful too.

I handed Tyler's phone back and swallowed the lump in my throat. I hoped and prayed Domathus didn't know Isabel existed.

Sandra eyed us as we passed through the lobby to the elevator. "Are you feeling better?"

I glanced at George and gave him a questioning look. "Did you do anything to her?" I whispered.

He shook his head. "No need."

"We're out for the rest of the day, Sandra and Uma." Tyler beamed a wolfish grin at them.

Uma swooned. "C-can I get you anything, Mr. Rock?"

22

Sandra tried to maintain her stony face, but even she melted beneath the glorious rays of Tyler's smile. "I'll keep the office in order."

"Thanks." He winked as the lift doors closed.

I nudged Tyler and chuckled. "Poor Uma will have to change her panties after that smile."

"Did I lay it on too thick?" Tyler asked.

"Always." I squeezed his bum. "But that's why I love you."

Mr. Sticks looked down at me like a disapproving parent to a child.

George hummed something under his breath and ignored our banter.

Though I'd known him for a while, I knew very little about him. "Are you married, George? Have a girlfriend, perhaps?"

"I prefer to keep my personal life private, Miss Glass." George went back to humming.

"I'm certain Mr. Sticks is quite a lady's man," Tyler said. "What woman wouldn't love to be scowled at?"

Mr. Sticks didn't scowl or glare but followed George's example and ignored us. When we reached the top floor, Tyler used his keycard to open the roof access stairwell and we went outside. There was no car visible on the roof, but I spotted the blur just a few feet ahead. Mr. Sticks opened a camouflaged door and Tyler and I piled into the back. George climbed into the passenger side, and Mr. Sticks took the controls.

The vehicle lifted straight up. I looked out of the window, giddy with awe. "This is just heavenly. I wish we could use one of these instead of the helicopter."

Tyler frowned. "I love my helicopter."

"Yes, but it's louder than all hell." I watched the city pass beneath us. "This is quieter than flying on wings."

"Well, until the Templars let me buy a flying car, I'm stuck with plain old choppers." Tyler squeezed my hand. "Maybe we should officially join the Templars and get a company car."

"Doesn't work that way," George said.

"And no one sells them to anyone?" Tyler quirked his lips. "Why have such cool toys if no one can use them?"

"There's an entire network of ASEs in the sky dedicated to monitoring magic usage and transportation." George waved a hand around. "The OTA, Overworld Transportation Authority, allows only specific uses of magical flight."

"Maybe it's time for the Overworld to share some advances with the noms," Tyler said. "Imagine the lives you could change."

"Oh, we can imagine quite a lot of change," George said. "Unfortunately, most of it would be for the worst, given the noms' track record."

I couldn't disagree.

Moments later we set down on the gravel driveway on a horse farm in Decatur—at least that's what it appeared to be to the casual observer. The large barn hid an underground network of tunnels and parking garages for all manner of magical machines. Something looked different from the last time. The old church near the house bore black marks and broken stone.

"What happened?" I asked.

"I'm not sure." George looked at Mr. Sticks and shook his head. "It's been a few weeks since we've been here."

"This isn't your headquarters?" Tyler asked.

"Custodians maintain their own facilities," George said.

Sticks parked the car near the barn, and we got out. Blast marks marred the stone church, and a part of the building had collapsed. George held up his hands. "We're with the Custodians."

I felt cold tingles not far away, intermingled with another new sensation. Templars in black nightingale armor shimmered into visibility all around us. A hulk of a man stepped forward and nodded. "Hello, George."

"Good day, Templar Borathen." George looked around. "I take it you were attacked?"

Templar Borathen? This man wasn't Thomas, but he did bear a slight resemblance to him.

"We're on lockdown." The big man made a gesture and the other Templars marched away to resume their secretive activities. "Unless you have an important matter, it's best if you leave."

"We're here on official Custodian business." George's forehead pinched. "Why do I get the feeling you don't trust us?"

The big man stared at us without expression for a moment. "Why are you here?"

"This is Emily Glass. Perhaps you've heard of her."

He blinked. "The Great Banisher?"

It was my turn to blink. "The great what? Am I a circus act now?"

"I'm Michael Borathen." He held out his hand. I tentatively offered him mine and he gripped it in a firm shake. Michael turned to Tyler. "Tyler Rock?"

"Yep." Tyler shook his hand. "I guess you're Thomas's kid?"

Michael didn't crack a smile. "That's right." He turned toward the barn. "Let's go below."

"You don't trust us, but you trust Miss Glass?" George looked a little hurt. "Is this about the Custodians' decision to remain neutral in matters of state between Commander Borathen and the Synod?"

Michael grunted, but didn't answer. We entered the horse barn where a ramp in the middle of the floor led underground. We'd ridden in the car the last time here and I wished we'd taken it again, because it was quite a walk to the bottom, and an even longer walk across a vast garage to a lift. Michael took us down without saying another word.

I, for one, was rather curious to find out how I'd earned a nickname.

"Your handling of the Demonicus Incident was impressive."

Michael's words startled me from my reverie. "Thank you. Is that how my new name came about?"

"It's what the demons call you," he replied. "Many fear and hate you." Michael led us to a waiting room with several couches and a coffee machine on a table in the corner. "You should watch your back."

"That's the very reason we're here," George said. "I have to say, I don't appreciate this second-class treatment."

Michael glanced at him and left.

George looked at Mr. Sticks and nodded. "I agree."

When he didn't elaborate, I butted in. "Mind telling us what you agree with?"

"There must have been an attack on the Templar compound." George went to the coffee machine and poured himself a cup. "I would bet the Synod had something to do with it."

I felt the new sensation from earlier. It was a chill not unlike what I felt from Templars, but it felt less unsettling, almost pleasant. Whereas the white sphere within George tingled with cold heat, this felt cool and calming. I stared at the doorway, anxious to see the source. A female Templar walked past briskly a moment later, and the sensation faded with distance.

"What's up, Em?" Tyler's jade eyes watched me curiously.

"Some Templar auras are different than the ones I've glimpsed before." I closed my eyes and tried to sense more, but they were too distant to grasp.

Moments later, a man with the normal Templar aura came to collect us. He escorted us to a small conference room where Thomas Borathen stood in front of a holographic map. He turned it off and nodded at us. "I'm afraid time is limited, so this must be quick."

"Miss Glass is under threat of assassination from agents of Domathus," George said. "I request a blessing from the Clarion so she'll be better equipped to protect herself."

Thomas pursed his lips. "How did you know about the Clarion?"

"Commander, why do I get the feeling we aren't welcome here?" George clasped his hands behind his back. "We are a neutral third party in this dispute between you and the Synod."

"The Synod assassinated two commanders last week during our first ceremony with the Clarion. They would have killed all of us if not for the quick actions of Justin Slade."

George, for once, seemed at a loss for words. "What about the damage to the church?"

"A suicide bomber." Thomas's icy blue eyes met mine and seemed to peer into my soul.

I sensed a great burden lurking behind those eyes. "That's awful. Your forces helped us win the battle against Domathus, Commander. For that, you have my full support."

"I was unaware of these incidents." George glanced at Sticks. "We don't condone the Synod's actions, but as Custodians we can't simply declare allegiance to factions. It is our sworn duty to protect the Overworld from noms at all costs. We would severely hamper our operations if we breach our neutrality."

"I understand," Thomas said. "Your dedication is the only reason you're here speaking with me, Mr. Walker." He tapped a badge on his collar. "Nightliss, are you free to see someone right now?"

A tired female voice with a strange accent answered. "Of course. Shall I come to you?"

"I can send her to you, if that's acceptable."

"Yes, please," she replied. "I'm in my quarters."

Thomas nodded at me. "Just you, Miss Glass." He motioned to the Templar who'd escorted us in. "Take her to the Clarion's quarters, Jenkins."

The Templar pressed a hand over his chest. "Yes, Commander."

My stomach fluttered. All of this had happened so suddenly, and I had no idea what to expect. Did one bow to the Clarion? Was she an angel like Daelissa, or something else?

My eye twitched. *Oh, dear. Should I pray first?*

I squeezed Tyler's hand for reassurance. He kissed my forehead and offered his standard grin.

"It'll be okay, Em."

I nodded and gathered my wits. *Don't act like a fool in front of everyone!* "Yes, of course. I'll see you soon." I followed the Templar into the hall-way, a corridor smoothly carved from granite. There was nothing of decoration on the walls or strategically placed tables with tasteful vases. It was about as utilitarian as everything else Templar.

My stomach twisted again, nerves mingling with fear. Surely this would be pleasant. I hoped it didn't involve a trial by fire or intense pain. I almost asked the Templar what to expect but didn't want him to see the fear in my eyes. I steeled myself and moved onward to whatever destiny lay ahead.

He stopped outside a door and knocked.

"Come in, please."

She has the voice of an angel at least.

The Templar put his back to the wall and stood there. Realizing the next move was up to me, I opened the door, stepped into the room, and prayed for a miracle.

CHAPTER 4

A hint of lavender hung in the air, and an assortment of lovely flowers sat in a vase atop a table on the side. A small bed occupied the back corner. A petite woman with olive skin and dark hair sat in a chair in the middle of the room. She was beautiful, but not in a threatening way. Her green eyes looked wise and kind. Her cheeks looked sunken, as if she hadn't eaten much lately.

I swallowed the panic rising in my throat and closed the door behind me. "I'm afraid I'm not acquainted with protocol, mighty Clarion. Should I kneel, or curtsey?"

Musical laughter danced from the Clarion's throat. "No. Most Templars bow or salute, but I think it is silly."

"Very well, then." I stood awkwardly. "What do I need to do, Clarion? Will it hurt much?"

She laughed again. "Please call me Nightliss."

"That's an interesting name." I grimaced at voicing my thoughts out loud. "But in a good way."

"What is your name?"

I stepped forward and held out a hand, certain she wouldn't bite, or if she did, it wouldn't hurt much. "Emily Glass."

Nightliss splayed her fingers without touching mine and motioned to a chair next to her. "Please sit."

I did and remained quiet, waiting for her to do whatever she needed to do to me.

"Are you a Templar?"

I shook my head. "I'm a Custodian—well, part time anyway. Sometimes they ask me along on missions due to my special skill set."

Her eyebrows rose. "Oh, and what can you do?"

As my nerves calmed, my sixth sense began to tingle. An aura of cool calm radiated from this woman, and I realized it was similar to what I'd sensed from the other Templar but much stronger. *It must be the blessing I sense.* I wondered how it would feel to have that same energy radiating inside me. But there was also something else inside, her—and it reminded me of a vampire aura.

But it wasn't an aura so much as a parasite attached to Nightliss's aura. I tried to reach for it, to probe the toxic force, but white tendrils spread deep into the ultraviolet aura. It was firmly rooted and spreading like cancer.

"Emily?" Nightliss leaned toward me. "Are you okay?"

I gasped. "There's something wrong with your aura. Are you sick?"

Nightliss seemed taken aback. "How did you know?"

"I can glimpse things about people—see their powers." I shivered. "Yours looks as if it's being taken over by something else."

Nightliss looked down. "I fought Daelissa and she did this to me. So I am doing what I can in secret until I am too weak to help."

"You need help. Doing what you're doing now is probably just weakening you faster."

"Perhaps." She shrugged. "Commander Borathen has assigned Meghan Andretti, the most skilled healer he has, to help me. Meghan is working on potions to fight the curse."

"It's rooted in your aura." I shook my head. "I can try pulling it out, but I don't know if it would work."

Nightliss leaned toward me. "Tell me more about your powers."

I tapped a finger on my chin. "Well, I sense auras. For example, most Templars I've met emit a cold burning tingle. Others are cold but calm. Vampires are squirmy and cold, like a worm."

"Eww." Nightliss wrinkled her nose. "That must be..." she trailed off as if searching for a word. Her green eyes flared. "Gross."

"Well, it's not gross unless I reach into them and grasp their vampirism." I shuddered at the memory of the last time. "I can pull it out and turn them back to normal humans."

"Really? Can you remove the blessing from Templars?"

I pursed my lips. "I never really tried."

"Anything else?" she asked.

I nodded. "I sense demons. If I touch a person possessed by a demon, I can see the pattern and name of the spirit. Then I can command it back to Hell."

"Do you mean Haedaemos?"

I shrugged. "I see them as one and the same."

"You have very powerful gifts, Emily. What do you call your kind?"

I shrugged again. "I have absolutely no idea. What sort of supernatural being are you?"

Nightliss put a dainty hand to her chest. "I am Seraphim. Some people here call us angels."

Even though I'd expected such an answer, I gasped. "Goodness!" I fanned my warm face with a hand and blurted a foolish question. "Do you know God?"

Nightliss burst into laughter. "No. I'm afraid I know no such being."

"Well, you seem like a very nice angel." I nearly reached over and patted her hand. "I'm glad Thomas chose you, because I heard some rather nasty things about your predecessor."

"All true." Nightliss's face turned downcast. "Do you think you can remove the curse from my aura?"

"Maybe." I leaned closer to her. "Want me to try?"

"That would be wonderful. What must I do?"

"I'll just need to touch you." I put a hand on her chest and closed my eyes. Calm coolness washed over me. I glimpsed the ultraviolet sphere and the squirming mass of dirty white latched onto it. I reached out and grasped the tumor, gently pulled on it.

Nightliss sucked in a ragged breath.

I continued to pull, trying to uproot the mass, but the ultraviolet sphere flickered and Nightliss began to moan in pain. I released it and backed away. "I don't dare try to remove it. I'm afraid I'll damage your aura or even kill you."

The angel sagged wearily. "I thank you for trying." She managed a smile. "I hope you can use your abilities to help us. A war comes and it will consume all of Eden unless we win."

I still thought of Eden as a garden, but those in the Overworld called Earth by the same name. Despite my Overworld initiation, I still had trouble grasping the breadth of this unseen universe. "I'm willing to pitch in and do my part." I took a breath. "What do I need to do?"

"I will touch you and imbue you with the blessing." She reached a hand toward me.

"Are you sure you're up to it after what I just did to you?"

"I am fine." Nightliss put a hand on my sternum and closed her eyes. A cold so deep I could barely fathom it sank into my skin and right down to my bones. It seeped into my core, infusing with my very soul. Images danced before my eyes. Great cities of crystal. Angels with wings of blazing white battled angels with wings of black fire. Raw energy blazed from their hands and blood rained from orange skies.

And then I was back in the room with Nightliss.

I blinked, shocked by the savagery of my vision. "I saw a battle. Light and dark angels fighting."

"I saw it too." Nightliss shuddered. "I have not regained all my memories, but I sense this is something from my past." Her brow furrowed in concentration. "It is so hard pushing the blessing into your spirit. I have never encountered this before."

Ultraviolet energy shimmered beneath my skin. Goosebumps traveled from my head to my toes. I felt something swelling inside me. Pressure built in my chest and abruptly exploded outward. A translucent shockwave reverberated from the center of my being and the shadow dissipated like fog in the sun.

Nightliss withdrew her hand with a gasp.

I studied my hands. Squeezed my fists to see if I felt any stronger. I didn't. "Am I blessed now?"

Nightliss shook her head. "No. Your spirit rejected it." She touched my sternum and closed her eyes. "Something ancient and powerful slumbers inside you, Emily."

I gulped. "I'm possessed?"

"No. It is part of you. I sense you have only scratched the surface of what you can do."

"But I could really use some physical strength right now. I'm weak as a normal human." My hands trembled at the thought of what Domathus had in store for me. "Do you think Justin Slade could help me?"

"I'm afraid he is at the very center of the coming storm." Nightliss's brow pinched with worry. She took my hands and squeezed them. "I pray I can recover and help him. Until then, perhaps you could remain here under Templar protection."

"With all that's happening to the Templars, I'm not sure this place is safer than anywhere else." I sagged. "Maybe there are no safe places when a demon overlord wants you dead." I didn't know why I told her, but I did. "My Aunt Lydia had a vision that I'd be dead by October sixth. Seems like I'm well on schedule."

"I truly wish I could help you. As I said, you can stay here if you wish, and we'll do everything we can to protect you." Nightliss stood and pulled me to my feet. Then she gave me one of the best hugs I'd ever had.

She was shorter and smaller than me, but that woman knew how to hug. I melted in her embrace and felt some of my worries slipping away. "You could make a business of this, you know. Not everyone can hug like this."

Nightliss laughed and pulled away. "I like hugs. They are one of the few joys left to me these days."

I held her hands for a moment. "Thank you. I hope the Templars can heal you."

A tear pooled in her eye. "I feel so powerless to help you. I wish I could do more."

"Even angels have limits, dear." I kissed her cheek. Backed away.

"Goodbye for now." I left the room and found Jenkins outside. "Please take me to the others."

He led the way without comment.

Tyler's trademark grin faded when I entered the room. "What's wrong, Em?"

I swallowed and did my best to keep my voice from cracking. "It didn't work."

Thomas frowned. "What do you mean it didn't work?" Despite the even tone of his voice, he sounded surprised.

"She said my body rejected it." I shrugged. "I don't know what else to say."

George looked at Mr. Sticks and over to Thomas. "How many Templars has the Clarion blessed?"

"Twenty, all successfully." Thomas folded his arms over his chest. "They're every bit as strong as those blessed by Daelissa, and their regenerative abilities are even better."

I shook my head. "She shouldn't be doing that until she's cured of her curse."

Thomas frowned. "She told you about that?"

"I glimpsed it." I held out my hands helplessly. "I tried to remove it, but it's beyond me."

George raised an eyebrow. "She's sick?"

Thomas ignored the question. "Did Nightliss say why the blessing didn't work?"

"She thinks it has something to do with my abilities." I didn't want to mention what else she'd said for fear it might sound preposterous. How could I possibly have ancient powers if I was still as weak as any other human?

Tyler snapped his fingers. "You banish demons and can take away a vampire's powers. Maybe your abilities naturally rejected the blessing."

Thomas pursed his lips and walked over to me. "Can you remove my blessing?"

I gulped. "I really don't want to."

"Can you sense if it's possible?"

I took a breath and nodded. Placing my hand on his chest, I closed my eyes. A white sphere appeared in my mind's eye. Unlike others I'd seen, this one burned stronger and brighter. It felt older. My senses pushed through the physical shell and gripped the miniature sun. The sensation was that of cold fire, burning and freezing at the same time. I tugged ever so slightly.

Thomas grunted. I released the blessing at once and heard gasps rise up around me.

"Emily, keep doing what you're doing, but open your eyes," Tyler said.

Concentrating on Thomas's aura, I did what he said. What I saw shocked me. My hands extended in front of me as they had when I touched Thomas's chest. But they didn't stop there. Shimmering like ghosts, phantom arms reached out, grasping at the air.

I shrieked and jumped back. The ghost arms vanished.

"So that's how you grab their auras." Tyler made jazz hands. "You've got spirit hands."

"Remarkable." George stared at me. "I've never seen anything like it."

Even Mr. Sticks didn't hide the surprise in his eyes.

"I believe the answer is yes." Thomas put a hand over his heart, as if making sure he was still in one piece. "Miss Glass can remove a blessing." He picked up a glass of water and took a drink. "It's one of the most unsettling feelings I've experienced."

George's eyebrows rose. "Coming from you that's quite a statement."

Tyler circled a finger in the air. "Yeah, so back to our original predicament. How's Emily supposed to protect herself without a blessing? She can't use her powers if she's mobbed by the possessed."

"She can stay here under our protection," Thomas said. "Though I must warn you that recent events mean this compound might come under attack."

"Yeah, no." Tyler shook his head. "Damn. I'll just do it myself."

Thomas nodded. "Perhaps you can hire a security force that can protect her."

"Demon assassins versus normal humans?" I scoffed. "Doesn't sound very effective." I felt weak and hopeless. I had no blessing, no supernatural strength. I certainly couldn't banish an entire mob of demons at once. Without Templar help, Tyler and I wouldn't survive long.

George regarded Thomas for a moment. "Miss Glass has proven herself a valuable asset. Her unique skillset could be the difference between victory and defeat, should a war come to pass. It would be in the best interests of the Templars to protect her, perhaps in a safer location."

"We're stretched to the breaking point, Mr. Walker." Thomas folded his arms over his chest. "I can't spare anyone right now."

Mr. Sticks pressed his lips into a thin line like he usually did when he heard something he didn't like but accepted it as truth. I'd been on enough missions with him and George to at least know that.

George sighed. Nodded. "I truly hate to see division in the Templars, especially in light of other troubling events. We will do our best to keep Miss Glass safe, even though our own resources are rather strained."

"Be careful who you trust, Mr. Walker." Thomas's gaze seemed to soften ever so slightly. "There are less honorable people who will not accept your neutrality."

Mr. Sticks nodded.

George raised an eyebrow and looked up at him. "Then I will exercise due diligence."

"Thank you for trying to help me, Commander Borathen." I twisted my engagement ring and grimaced at the sting of raw skin. "I hope everything works out."

He nodded at me. "For you as well, Miss Glass."

As Mr. Sticks guided the flying car up and away from the Templar compound, I felt as if I'd left behind my last shreds of hope. A blessing from Nightliss might have allowed me to protect myself. *What's wrong with me? Why can't my body accept a blessing?* Apparently, the only thing my body was good at accepting were more inches when I indulged in sweets.

If there truly was a war coming, I feared for the future. Nightliss was dying from a curse, and the Templars were at war with each other. The Overworld seemed ripe for plucking, especially if Domathus decided to take another go at it. I gripped Tyler's hand and held onto it. He was the one person I could count on no matter what.

George turned around in the passenger seat. "There are supernatural mercenaries who might be of help. They accept most nom currencies."

I caught a scowl from Sticks in the rear-view mirror.

I stared back at him. "You don't approve?"

"Mercenaries often cause trouble, especially for Custodians." George faced forward again. "They tend to take jobs protecting nom celebrities and display a bit more strength or fang than they should."

"I don't care," Tyler said. "Do you know anyone I can contact?"

"What about Joe?" I said. "He knows a lot of military types." Tyler's bodyguard-slash-chauffeur might be a nom, but he certainly wasn't a pushover.

Tyler shook his head. "I need someone with a lot more brute force and the ability to sniff out a demon."

"Agreed." George looked over his shoulder. "Shall we drop you at your condo, Mr. Rock?"

"That'd be great, but not the one you know." He pointed to a gray tower on the horizon. "I got a place that's off the books."

"An excellent idea, Mr. Rock." George took out his arcphone and tapped on the screen. "I sent you contact information for several vetted mercenaries who have proven less troublesome over the years than others. I suggest you and Miss Glass lay low for the time being. That means letting others run your companies."

"I know what it means." Tyler frowned. "But we can't hide forever. We need to get to the root of the problem."

"Agreed." George looked over his shoulder. "The penthouse, I presume?"

"Yeah, the entire top floor." Tyler leaned forward, a grin returning to his face. "It's got a helicopter pad, a garden, and even a swimming pool."

Mr. Stick shook his head disapprovingly.

Tyler's grin broadened. "Did you bring your swimming trunks?"

"I'm afraid not, Mr. Rock." George put away his arcphone as the car landed on the helicopter pad. "Please give us regular updates on the situation, and let me know how the mercenaries work out."

I would normally be excited over a new flat, but my stomach twisted in knots thinking about secreting myself away, hiding from the world. I'd be a prisoner in my own home, living in fear. It was the sort of torture Domathus most likely had in mind when he put the price on my head. I barely said anything as I slid out of the seat and walked to the edge of the helicopter pad.

The car was nothing but a blur on the outside, its camouflage magic hiding it from nom eyes. The smudge in my vision rose into the air and quickly vanished into the sky.

Despite my predicament, Tyler seemed giddy with excitement. "Don't you love this place, Em?"

Twisting the ring on my chafed finger, I surveyed this new wonderland of his. The helipad was an elevated platform in the corner of a lush paradise. The red leaves of a Japanese oak swayed in the wind. Ornately manicured shrubberies lined stone paths, leading to a grassy area where I supposed one might take pets to relieve themselves.

A waterfall ran down a stone fountain, splashing into the blue waters of a swimming pool that extended beneath the wall and into the flat. A bamboo hut stood next to the pool, its glass shelves fully stocked with top-shelf alcohol.

I tried to appreciate the moment but found it hard to see this place as anything except a luxurious prison. "It's marvelous, Tyler."

He sighed. "It'll be okay, babe. I promise. We'll get to the bottom of this and you'll be free to roam the streets in no time."

A man in a gray business suit rose from behind the bar. I jumped back a foot and made a little squeak. The man's skin didn't look quite right. In fact, it looked almost gray. "Who is that?"

"Holy shit!" Tyler jumped in front of me. "Who in the hell are you?"

The man leapt lithely over the bar and walked toward us, face completely emotionless. He slowly reached into his jacket pocket, and I felt with certainty that the assassins had already found us again.

CHAPTER 5

Tyler dashed forward so fast he was nearly a blur. He gripped the man's wrists and twisted. A white envelope fluttered into the air and landed face down on the surface of the pool. Tiny ripples disturbed the placid surface. The gray man didn't react to Tyler's rough ministrations and tried to bend down to pick up the fallen envelope.

Tyler let go of the man and backed away, almost comical confusion on his face. "What's going on? Who are you?"

The gray man plucked the envelope from the water and held it out to Tyler. Tyler tried to take it, but the other man didn't release it. He pointed to me. I cautiously reached around Tyler and took it. Though damp, the thick, high-quality paper maintained its integrity. A gray wax seal on the back bore a fancy cursive "G". I stared at it in confusion. "How curious is this?"

"More creepy than curious." Tyler walked in a circle around the silent gray man. "Do you talk?"

The man shook his head, his gray eyes never leaving me.

I broke the seal and opened the envelope. Inside was a card adorned with gold foil. It said: *You are cordially invited to brunch with Fjorn Gray. Tuesday October 2nd at 10 A.M.* Below that were two checkmarks for yes or no. In fine print at the very bottom was something far more chilling. *Domathus is not your only problem.*

"Who is Fjorn Gray?" I asked.

Tyler looked away from the gray man and blinked. "That's from Fjorn Gray? He's one of the richest men in the world."

I showed Tyler the fine print. "He's not simply a man. Or if he is, he knows about the supernatural."

Tyler turned back to the silent gray man. "What does Fjorn want with Emily? How does he know about Domathus?"

No answer.

Tyler tentatively touched the other man. "His skin is warm, but it feels strange."

I walked over and touched a hand. It felt a bit slick, but normal. "Everything is off about this man. I've never seen anyone living with such a sickly complexion." Now that I'd recovered my wits, I also sensed a strange emptiness about the man. I had never applied my powers to sensing normal people, but now that I stood in the presence of this person, I realized he was different.

Strange energy emanated from him instead of the normal quietness of most humans. I had to speak with Fjorn if for no other reason than to find out what was wrong with this fellow.

I looked at Tyler. "Do you have a pen?"

He shook his head. "You told me to stop carrying pens and to start using these fancy computer phones."

"Yes, because you're the leader of a technology company." I sighed.

The gray man reached inside his jacket and withdrew a gray pen.

"You're consistent, I'll give you that." I took the pen and unscrewed the top. I had my reservations, but none overcame my curiosity, so I checked yes and handed him the card and pen. The gray man took both and pocketed them then gave me a card with an address and instructions. Without even so much as a goodbye, he ran and leapt over the side of the building.

I stifled a scream of alarm and ran to the railing. Tyler beat me to it and burst into laughter. "You've got to be kidding me!"

A look over the edge identified the source of amusement. The gray man stood on a rug—a flying one at that! I'd heard of flying carpets and brooms, but I'd never seen one in action. Having arrived here in a flying car, I shouldn't have been surprised. The gray man rippled into camouflage and vanished.

"Guess that answers that." Tyler chuckled. "Wow. Fjorn Gray is a super. I never would have guessed it."

"Do you know him?" I asked.

"Not personally." Tyler went to the bar and started mixing a drink. "Want anything?"

My nerves were still aflutter, and my heart pounded in my chest from having seen the man jump off the building. "Absolutely." I watched him for a moment. "Aren't you going to question my decision?"

"About seeing Fjorn?" He shook his head. "I think it's the right call."

I stared out at the cityscape and hoped it was.

Tyler mixed a skinny margarita for me, and a dark and stormy for himself. The latter cocktail seemed a metaphor for my future. Then he gave me the grand tour of the new flat. The penthouse, a square contemporary structure, occupied one half of the roof. It started on the story below the roof and rose two stories above it. The pool curved inside, encased in glass so anyone on the floor below could watch swimmers.

The first floor was wide open like a loft, with the kitchen, den, and dining areas all visible to each other with the pool wending through the middle like a blue river. The top floor held a large master bedroom and two guest rooms. A place like this would have astounded me not so long ago, but even the strong margarita did little to melt my apprehension.

"Joe hired a crew to quietly move some of our things over here, so we'll have clothes."

"Yes, a change of clothes would be nice." I licked a bit of salt off the rim of my glass and took another sip of the margarita. "I could certainly use a change of undergarments after everything today. In fact, I'd love a shower."

"That can be arranged." Tyler winked and led me through the master bedroom and into the master bath. Two large showerheads hung side-by-side from a wall of white pebble tile. Nozzles protruded from the walls on both sides, promising a luxurious experience.

I set down the margarita and began to disrobe, eager to wash away the tribulations of the day. "Oh, yes, that will do."

I was also eager to end the day so I could meet Fjorn Gray and find out what he wanted.

After the shower, Tyler helped take my mind off things by enticing me into the bedroom with his gentle kisses and his electric touch. He was particularly gifted in tiring me out in the most wonderful of ways. By the time he was done with me, I drifted peacefully to sleep in his arms.

I awoke shivering in the dark of night.

I tried to curl up next to Tyler, but his side of the bed was empty and cold. "Tyler?" I fumbled for the light, but nothing happened when I turned the switch. I couldn't find my phone on the nightstand, so I got out of bed and groped for the wall, trembling from cold. "W-what's wrong with the thermostat?" My teeth chattered. Goosebumps rose on my arms. I found the wall and slid my hand along it until I located the light switch. It clicked on, but nothing happened.

Not even the city lights shined through the windows. *Maybe the power is out?* If so, it was particularly widespread. And that still didn't explain why my phone didn't work.

Fear sharpened my senses and adrenalin washed away my fatigue. *Something is wrong.* I'd learned from my experiences as a Custodian that not everything had a normal explanation. Tyler must have realized the same thing and gone to investigate. The cold grew so intense I couldn't stop shivering.

A spot of warmth drew my attention to the left. It wasn't dry and toxic like the aura of a caustic demon, but comforting. I walked towards it, the sensation growing stronger until I stood in the middle of the warmth. A humanoid form flickered into existence, white noise in a sea of black. A face appeared for only an instant, but I recognized it immediately.

"Mum?" Tears wet my cheeks. "Mum, is that you?"

The ghostly figure flickered again, whispering words I could barely make out. The face appeared again, smiling gently at me and repeated the words. Another image flashed, that of the blond woman who looked like me.

Mum appeared again and spoke. "Another." Her faint whispers barely reached my ears.

I reached out to her, praying this was real. The warmth vanished. Intense cold swept up my limbs, covering me in frost and freezing me in place.

"Mum!" I jerked upright in bed. "Mum!"

Tyler turned on a lamp. "Em? What's wrong?"

I looked around the room in confusion. The city was back outside the window. The lights worked. The room was no longer freezing.

"Babe, why are you crying?" Tyler wiped my cheeks with his thumbs. "Did you have a nightmare?"

"Yes—no." A lump formed in my throat. "I don't know. It felt so real."

He kissed my forehead. "What was it about?"

"I thought I saw my mother." More tears trickled down my cheeks. "She had a message for me."

Tyler nodded as if it were entirely plausible. "What did she tell you?"

"Never stop moving forward."

He chuckled. "That sounds like Victoria. She didn't stop for anything."

I felt a small smile stretch my lips. "No, she didn't. She lived strong and she died strong."

"I think you should take her advice."

"You don't think it was a dream?"

Tyler squeezed my hands. "With you? Not a chance."

My eyes filled with tears. My mother's mortal shell had died, but her strong soul may have reached me across the abyss between life and death itself. *It wasn't a dream.* That was what I chose to believe.

"She also seemed to be trying to tell me something about the blond woman." That part of the vision wasn't quite as clear. "I think she said, 'Another.'"

"Probably means we're going to see that imposter again." Tyler blew out a breath. "This time I'll be there to help."

"I know, baby." I closed my eyes and tried to reach out with my mind, tried to find my mum. Even with Tyler snuggled up behind me, I sensed that calming warmth I'd found in the freezing cold.

It wasn't physically here in the room, but it was out there somewhere.

And it was real.

I felt refreshed and happy the next morning, all thoughts of my imminent death pushed to the back of my mind. Tyler called Joe and instructed him to drive the BMW to his office the next morning, pretending to chauffeur Tyler as normal, so any demons watching the place wouldn't know we were in hiding.

Tyler chose a baby blue Camry with tinted windows as the chariot to convey us to Fjorn's address. I'd expected a mansion but wasn't terribly surprised when we arrived at a corporate address in Buckhead. We pulled into the private parking garage around the back as instructed by the address card.

The same man from yesterday waited outside the private entrance, a smile on his face. I blinked a few times, realizing that his skin now had a healthy pink hue to it instead of the sickly gray.

"Good day, Miss Glass." He walked over and extended a hand. "I'm Lornicus. Very pleased to meet you."

I tentatively shook his hand. It wasn't as slick as it had been yesterday. Instead of a low hum, his aura thrummed with power. I glimpsed a white sun colliding with a black star, their juxtaposition a mass of gray. It oddly reminded me of Nightliss's aura even though hers didn't alternate like this one.

"Mr. Rock." Lornicus shook Tyler's hand as well.

I couldn't stop myself from blurting, "What in the bloody hell is going on? Why didn't you speak a word to us yesterday and now you're all smiles and warmth?"

Lornicus chuckled. "Ah, yes. Quite simply, that was not me." He put a hand on the biometric reader on the side of the door and it clicked open. "That was a golem."

"Whoa." Tyler's jaw dropped open. "Like a magical robot?"

"From fairy tales?" Once again, I was more surprised than I should have been. "I thought they were made of wood or stone."

Lornicus closed the door behind us and led us down a hall. "These golems are far more advanced than anything you've seen."

"Yours was the first," I said. "I've never seen one before."

"Oh, then you're in for a treat." Lornicus stopped at a door and opened it. A light flickered on inside.

I nearly shouted in alarm. Dozens of men in gray business suits stared blankly back at us from a large room. It was the creepiest thing I'd seen aside from the time I'd chased a vampire into a mannequin factory.

"Freaking insane." Tyler stepped inside and touched one. "You can mass produce these things?"

"My master can." Lornicus turned to me. "I didn't mean to surprise you, Miss Glass."

"Oh, I think you did." I fanned my face, but it did little to cool the embarrassment. "Shall we get on with it?"

Lornicus smiled. "Of course."

We stepped into a private lift and rode it to the top floor. The doors opened to a large office overlooking the city. I hadn't remembered this building being so tall. In fact, I knew it wasn't. I went to the window and looked down. We were nearly fifty stories above even the tallest buildings! *How is this possible?*

Someone cleared their throat. I turned to see Lornicus's twin watching me from behind an ornate desk. My face warmed with embarrassment once more. I hadn't even seen him when I rushed inside. *Now you've made a fool of yourself again.* I walked over to the man. "I'm so sorry, Mr. Gray."

"Good morning, Miss Glass." He didn't even crack a smile. "The world knows me as Fjorn Gray, but you may call me Fjoeruss."

He didn't offer a hand to shake, so I nodded. "And you may call me Emily."

Fjoeruss nodded at Tyler. "Good morning, Mr. Rock."

"Good day, Fjoeruss." Tyler didn't extend a hand. "This is quite an office you have here."

Fjoeruss answered in a matter-of-fact tone. "Yes, it is."

Since he was all business, I decided to get straight to the point. "How did you know where to find me and what do you know about Domathus?"

"We can discuss this over brunch." Fjoeruss looked at Lornicus. "We're ready."

The other man nodded. "Yes, master."

I flinched. "Why do you call him master? He isn't a king."

"He created me." Lornicus held out his hands helplessly. "I am but a golem."

"You're a golem too?" Tyler actually walked up and prodded him as if he were testing a plush toy. "That's amazing."

Lornicus didn't flinch, but something in his eyes betrayed discomfort or maybe even indignation at Tyler's touch.

I looked back at Fjoeruss. "Why don't you make them all look realistic then?"

"It takes great effort to create even one as lifelike as Lornicus. The others are far less complex." Fjoeruss motioned to the door. "Now, if you please, Lornicus."

"Yes, master." Lornicus walked to double doors and opened them to a balcony with a small circular table. He pulled out a chair for me. "Please make yourselves comfortable. Your food will arrive shortly."

I walked to the railing and looked over the side. The height was as dizzying as it was mesmerizing. The sounds of the city were so far below us I could barely make them out. I leaned further out and examined the outside of the building, but it didn't seem to be camouflaged.

"Marvelous, isn't it?" Lornicus stood next to me. "For safety reasons, this building doesn't employ camouflage. Instead, it uses perception magic to make it look shorter from the ground. If it were camouflaged, the sidewalks would be littered with dead birds." He shrugged. "Avoidance wards guard it against airplanes."

"Sounds groovy." Tyler put a hand on my back. "We could use some avoidance wards for the house." He stiffened abruptly. "Speaking of which, how did you know about our new penthouse?"

"I own the building." Fjoeruss sat at the table, his stony face betraying no emotion. "I took interest in Miss Glass during the Demonicus Incident. That is why I invited you here."

I took the seat next to Fjoeruss and tried to get a read on him. I glimpsed a crystal sphere crackling with lightning. It was so strange I didn't realize he was still talking to me.

"Em?" Tyler put a hand on my shoulder.

"Oh, sorry." I did my best not to look at Lornicus while comparing his aura to that of Fjoeruss. His seemed even strong than that of his master. Or perhaps Fjoeruss was masking his true aura from me. I cleared my throat. "What is it you want from me, Fjoeruss?"

He settled into his chair. "Though I followed the Demonicus incident, I still don't quite understand your abilities. I'd like you to explain them to me."

"How about you tell us what you think you know." Tyler sat down across from him, leaving me the seat between them.

A woman in a French maid outfit came onto the balcony with pitchers of orange juice and water. She stood about my height, but that was where the similarities ended. Luxurious black hair flowed down her back. A pert nose perched above plump rosebud lips. She was pear shaped, with wide hips and an ample bosom. In short, she was nearly perfect.

She also wasn't real.

I sensed the same low hum from her as the golem from the day before. And that was when I came to another realization. We were speaking to the wrong person.

This meeting was a sham.

CHAPTER 6

I stood up.

"Where are you going?" Fjoeruss asked.

I ignored him and turned to Lornicus. "I don't like being toyed with. Unless you tell me exactly who you are and why you invited us here, we're leaving."

Tyler's eyes darted back and forth between me and Lornicus. "Em, what's going on?"

Lornicus's smile faded and he waved a hand at Fjoeruss. The other man stood and left without a word. "How did you do that, Miss Glass?"

"What in the world—oh!" Tyler snapped his fingers. "Fjoeruss was a golem and Lornicus is the real deal."

"Exactly." I arched my eyebrows. "Kindly answer my questions, sir, or you'll get nothing else from me."

Lornicus—the real Fjoeruss—waved a hand to the table. "Please sit and I'll tell you."

I looked at the maid. "I take it you make lifelike sex toys as well?"

He shook his head. "No, but I do experiment with form." Lornicus—Fjoeruss sat and looked up at me.

Discomfort showed in his gray eyes. He didn't enjoy being in a less powerful position, so I let him wallow for a moment before taking the seat next to him.

I looked at our host. "Now, about yourself?"

"I am Fjoeruss, one of the first Seraphim to come to Eden." He smiled, though not in the way he had in the guise of Lornicus. This seemed more reassuring than anything. "A great danger lurks on the horizon, and I need help ensuring it doesn't threaten this world."

"Are you talking about Daelissa?" I took a sip of orange juice. "I don't understand how I can help against her."

He shook his head. "Daelissa is one grave threat, but efforts are already underway to counter her." Fjoeruss leaned his elbows on the table. "Domathus is one of the most powerful overlords in Haedaemos. Though he failed to manifest in Eden, he proved it was possible to do so even when lacking enough willing souls. He proved it's possible to use thralls as conduits to reap the souls of the unwilling."

"Yes. And he bound souls into a corporeal form for demon lords." I grimaced. "You think he might try again?"

Tyler shook his head. "The logistics of creating another daemonculus are staggering. They'd have to find willing sacrifices and kidnap dozens of people to make it happen."

"Agreed." Fjoeruss leaned back and steepled his fingers. "But I have heard whispers from the underworld that someone is working on another way to allow demon lords to roam the physical world without a shell of souls. That, in fact, there may be a way to forcibly possess a person."

I shuddered at the imagery flashing through my head. Karak and other demon lords had bound themselves in bodies of souls torn from unwilling hosts through the power of a demonicus. It pained my heart to think of how many died before we were able to stop them. "Why don't the demon lords simply possess a human?" I asked.

Fjoeruss shook his head. "They can't access their full power in a human body. They need something more powerful."

Three men dressed in butler livery delivered silver platters loaded with poached eggs and toast. Another set a teapot and a cup in front of me. I lifted the lid and let the odor of Earl Grey tickle my nose. "This is quite acceptable."

"I'm glad you approve." Fjoeruss gave me a moment to prepare my tea with a spot of milk before speaking again. "I utilize variations of lifelike golems in my operations. Though they are capable of carrying out duties and following orders, they are not completely autonomous."

Tyler munched on toast. "So you remotely control them?"

"Yes." Fjoeruss shrugged. "I can make golems that look and feel human, but I cannot create true life."

Tyler nodded at the French maid golem. "Em was right. You could make a killing if you sold those things as sex dolls."

"I have no interest in such things." Fjoeruss cut a piece of bacon with a knife and ate it with a fork. "Several of my golems have gone missing over the past few months without my knowledge. I constantly track and monitor the whereabouts of each one, making such a theft nearly impossible."

"You can't possibly know everything about every golem all the time," I said. "How would you have any spare time?"

Fjoeruss tapped his wristwatch. "This tells me if a golem goes offline, or if it goes somewhere it shouldn't be."

Tyler grunted. "If I snatched one of your golems off the street and drove him across town, that watch would tell you?"

"Not only that, but each golem possesses supernatural strength. Even a vampire or lycan would be hard pressed to overcome their self-defense mechanisms."

Tyler whistled. "I don't know a thing about your golems, but it sounds like someone would need to hit the off switch before trying anything."

"Do they even have an off switch?" I asked.

"I can deactivate them remotely, but they don't have a switch on their body."

I sipped my tea and gathered my thoughts. "What do missing golems have to do with demons?"

Fjoeruss seemed to consider his next words. "I believe someone wishes to use them as demon vessels."

Tyler laughed and stopped. "Oh, you're serious." He shook his head. "Demons can't possess golems, can they? Don't they need a soul?"

"I don't believe it's possible. But I was also given information that key personnel at many of my companies were possessed against their wills."

"Who gave you this information?" I asked.

"A former knight of Lord Karak. Astra."

I flinched at the name. "Vallaena Slade banished her to Haedaemos and told me she wouldn't be able to return for some time. How did she manage to speak with you?"

"Intermediaries." Fjoeruss didn't elaborate. "Domathus lost considerable power after you banished him and his lords. Karak dismissed Astra for her failure. She is now considered ronin—a demon knight with no lord."

I frowned. "Astra has no lord?"

"Correct. As a former knight, she has valuable information. Normally, Karak would have devoured or weakened her so she would be unable to survive on her own. But his banishment at the hands of Miss Glass weakened him severely as well." Fjoeruss pursed his lips as if impressed. "I have been able to restore Astra's power and keep her safe."

I had no animus for Astra. As a ruby demon, she had been far more honorable and reasonable than the disgusting caustics I'd met. "Does she know who's behind the golem thefts and possessions?"

"No, but with war threatening, several demon overlords are eyeing the mortal realm as conquest. They believe Domathus acted prematurely." Fjoeruss's gaze seemed to study my responses each time he mentioned Domathus. "If Daelissa launches a full-scale attack, you can be certain another overlord will make an attempt to breach the physical realm."

"Do you think they're using these possessed individuals to steal your golems?"

He shook his head. "They are noms with no knowledge of my true nature. It seems to be a two-pronged attack."

"Hm." I frowned. "I still don't understand why you asked me here. Is it to help track down your golems?"

"I know about the price Domathus placed on your head. Astra told me how you instantly knew her true name." Fjoeruss leaned forward again. "Even today you knew Lornicus was me. You can track down possessed individuals quickly so I can track them. I am not as concerned about the missing golems. There is no way I know of that a demon can possess a soulless artificial construct. They would need flesh and soul."

"Yes, I could probably do that for you." I poked an egg with my fork. "But I do have a price on my head. I can't show my face on the streets without risk of having my throat cut."

Fjoeruss nodded. "That is how can I help you, Miss Glass. Quite simply, you have to die."

I gripped the fork as I might wield a knife and stared him down. "Explain yourself, sir."

Tyler rose from his chair. "Did you just threaten her?"

Fjoeruss held up his hands. "No. What I mean is the demons must believe Miss Glass is dead. I have the power to make that happen."

Tyler stared rigidly at the other man for a moment before relaxing. "You want to make a golem lookalike."

"Precisely." Fjoeruss tapped on his watch. "If I can fashion a mold, it will hasten the process."

For the first time since Aunt Lydia predicted my death, I dared feel hope. "In exchange for this, we'll help you track down possessed employees?"

Fjoeruss nodded. "Once we've faked your death, you will be free to investigate."

Tyler eased back into his chair. "Except once we start looking, the demons will realize she's still alive."

"Not if she changes her appearance. You'd be surprised what a change of hair color and style can do. I can also provide enchanted jewelry that employs illusion to make minor facial changes." Fjoeruss stood. "If you agree, then we should start right away. It will take at least a day to produce the golem."

"Only a day?" Tyler stuffed an egg into his mouth. "That's not long."

"Twenty-four hours of meticulous design and creation is no easy task, Mr. Rock." He indicated the French maid. "That one required a week of intense work. I have since improved my method."

"How exactly do you take the mold?" I tried and failed to imagine what the process might be like.

"It is somewhat unpleasant, but quick."

"But is it dangerous?" Tyler said. "Are there any risks to Emily?"

"She will be in no danger at all." The French maid opened the door and Fjoeruss stepped inside, leaving me and Tyler alone on the balcony.

I looked at Tyler and nodded. "I'm doing it."

"Why don't we just use illusion disguises or something to hide you?" Tyler finished his last piece of bacon. "There's no reason to go through all this."

"But if we convince the demons I'm dead, then I'll be much safer." I took his arm and pulled him to his feet. "Plus it might be the answer to my aunt's vision. She saw me lying in a coffin, but what if it was really my golem?"

Tyler's mouth dropped open. "Oh. I didn't even think of that." His eyes lit with excitement. "So she was right, but wrong at the same time!" He clapped his hands. "Yes!"

"Let's not celebrate too early." I hooked my arm in his. "But I think this might be the answer to my dying problem."

Fjoeruss waited by the lift inside the office. "Have you decided?"

"I'll do it." I walked over to him. "But you realize that unless I remain in hiding for the rest of my life, this is only a temporary solution?"

"True. Domathus will simply renew his bounty for your head if he discovers you're alive." Fjoeruss held out his hands helplessly. "Even I have no way to prevent that. But whoever is behind these forced possessions may be another threat to contend with."

I wondered if Domathus might be making another play on Eden, or if another overlord might have similar aspirations.

The lift doors opened and Fjoeruss motioned us in. The gray man punched a digital keypad and we began a descent that seemed to stretch on forever. My nerves coiled around my stomach as I thought about what came next. Soon there would be a perfect copy of me walking this world.

I perked up as an unpleasant thought hit me. "Do you promise to never make another copy of me without my consent?"

Fjoeruss raised an eyebrow. Nodded. "Why would I have reason?"

"I don't know, but it's better to be safe."

"Maybe we need to get everything in writing," Tyler said.

"And what judge will review that contract?" I scoffed. "We simply have to hope his word is good."

The lift slowed to a halt. "It is." Fjoeruss seemed to think that was enough to assuage my doubts and stepped into a large corridor carved from stone.

"How surprising." I ran a finger along the smooth stone. "An underground lair."

Fjoeruss walked silently ahead, a golem twin pacing behind us. We passed nearly a dozen doors before stopping in front of one that looked no different from the rest. Fjoeruss opened it and stepped inside. My mind ran wild with expectations, though I truly had no idea what lay in store for me. Did he mean to create a plaster mold of me, or did he utilize magical means?

A long gray pad bisected an otherwise empty room. I couldn't help but feel a bit disappointed. "What's that?"

"I'll need you to disrobe." Fjoeruss looked at Tyler. "It's necessary to take accurate measurements."

I stiffened and was about to make a rude remark but caught myself. *Surely, it's no different than a visit to the doctor.* This man had probably seen thousands of naked bodies to create his French maids and other human dolls. "Very well."

Tyler blinked. "That was easy."

I'd worn flats, jeans, and a t-shirt in case running for our lives had become a necessity. I'd had enough of running in high heels, thank you very much. I took off my shoes and socks. Peeled off the jeans to reveal my unicorn panties. My face warmed. I hadn't expected anyone but Tyler to see those.

As if it might preserve my modesty a bit longer, I took off my blouse and bra next. Doing my best not to seem uncertain, I dropped my panties and stood naked and vulnerable in front of our Seraphim host. Hand on hips, I gave him a look. "What now?"

Fjoeruss looked up from a tablet computer. "Please stand on the red dot in the middle and remain absolutely still. This will take several minutes." He looked back down without batting an eyelash.

"Is this the unpleasant part?" The room was decently warm, but goose-bumps already crept along my arms and legs.

He shook his head. "Not unless standing still is unpleasant for you."

"Oh, it is." Tyler flashed a grin.

I rolled my eyes. "I bore easily."

Fjoeruss ignored our banter and tapped on the tablet. "Ready when you are."

I stepped onto the red dot. "Do I need to stand a certain way?" It was a struggle not to cover my breasts in front of the other man.

This was certainly not what I'd signed up for, but if it saved me from demon assassins, then it was worth it.

CHAPTER 7

"**A**rms to the sides, please." Fjoeruss tapped on the table. Machinery hummed and a silver ring arcing with blue electricity dropped from the ceiling and clanged on the floor around me.

I flinched and caught a disapproving look from Fjoeruss. Gathering my dignity, I stiffened into a pose and waited. Without any visible means of support, the ring slowly rose into the air. Static electricity danced along my skin, making it hard to remain still. *I hope this thing can't electrocute me!* The process took the promised several minutes, but I was so fascinated that boredom remained a distant thing.

The ring vanished into a slot in the ceiling. Fjoeruss tapped on the tablet computer for a moment then, looked up. "Walk to one end of the pad. When I tell you to, walk as you normally would to the other end, turn around, and walk back."

"Should I expect another ring to drop from the ceiling?"

He shook his head. "You will feel a tingle."

Tyler chuckled. "You're making me tingle, Em."

"Good lord, Tyler." I rolled my eyes. "Not in front of the angel, please."

Fjoeruss didn't seem remotely amused and waited until I reached my position. Then he tapped the tablet. "Please start walking."

A pleasant tingle did indeed work its way up my toes, along my skin and all the way to the top of my head. I felt resistance at the first step I took, like pushing through water. It wasn't enough to stop me, but it was certainly enough to slow me down. I walked back and forth several times. Then he had me jog, and then run. I desperately wished for a sports bra with every unpleasant bounce of my breasts.

I performed like a circus bear for the next half hour, going through a range of motions, squatting, punching, kicking, and even spinning in a circle. By the time I was done, I'd worked up a nice sheen of sweat and was too tired to care about my nudity.

"Almost done." Fjoeruss walked toward me. "This will be cold and unpleasant, but necessary."

I resisted the urge to complain. After all, this entire exercise might save my life. "Ready when you are."

Fjoeruss wove his hands through a pattern. Fine threads of ultraviolet energy drifted across my skin, chilling me to the core. They clung to me, slowly covering every inch. A violent shiver worked up my body. I clenched my teeth to keep them from chattering, but it proved impossible. He might as well have slowly dipped me in ice water. The threads covered my torso, my arms, and then climbed up my neck.

"Take a breath and hold it," Fjoeruss said.

My breaths became quicker. "How long do I—" There was no time to finish the sentence. Threads covered my mouth. Heart pounding, I sucked in a desperate breath through my nose. I tried to move. Tried to claw away the threads, but I couldn't move, couldn't breathe, couldn't scream.

Panic raced through my veins. I heard muffled shouting. Felt a burn in my lungs as my racing heart rapidly depleted the stored oxygen. This felt like the end. *He copied me so he can kill me!*

Light stung my eyes. Muffled words became clear. I gasped for breath and staggered forward. Strong arms wrapped around me. Tyler's unnaturally warm body embraced me in a cocoon of protection.

"What the fuck, Fjoeruss!" Tyler stroked my hair. "You could have warned her sooner."

"She was in no danger."

I blinked the blurriness from my eyes. Without thinking, I leapt up and punched Fjoeruss in the stomach. It felt like I'd struck a brick wall. "You bastard!"

The Seraphim looked down at me like one might consider an ant. "Apologies for the inconvenience, but I now have everything I need. I'll be unavailable for the next twenty-four hours." He checked his watch. "Please return here tomorrow at ten A.M."

I was still furious and didn't even know why. I pressed my hands on his chest and grasped at the twin suns burning at his core.

Fjoeruss gasped and froze in place, wide gray eyes looking down at me. "More powerful than I thought," he hissed through clenched teeth. "You will be the unknown savior if you survive."

I tugged ever so gently on his essence and elicited another gasp from him. Then I released him and backed away. "I'm sorry if that was unpleasant for you."

Fjoeruss smiled for the first time since dropping his act as Lornicus. "A part of you is even more ancient than me, Miss Glass. I suggest you get to know it. Daelissa may be powerful, but even she would be no match for the overlords of Hell, should they find a way to physically manifest."

Tyler whistled. "I knew she was a keeper."

I elbowed him in the ribs. "Quiet, or I'll make you gasp too."

"Please do." A wolfish grin covered his face. "By the way, you're still naked."

I huffed and walked over to my clothes. Despite having sweated during the first part of the ordeal, I felt cleaner than I'd ever been after the freezing cold of Fjoeruss's magic. "What did you do to me, Mr. Gray?"

"I wove Murk, the force of creation into a shell around you." Fjoeruss summoned an orb of ultraviolet flame in one hand. "I created a mold of you. Everything else was to record how you move so the golem will behave realistically."

"Pretty cool." Tyler pinched my butt before I pulled up my jeans.

I yelped and jolted upright. "Watch yourself, mister."

He grinned. "I'm so happy, Em. You're going to live!"

I certainly hoped he was right.

A golem led us back to the lift. During our ascent, I touched the golem to see if I could touch its aura. I might as well have jammed a fork into an electrical outlet. With a cry of surprise, I yanked back my hand from the painful jolt. The golem didn't move a bit.

Tyler flinched. "Did you try to touch its aura?"

I examined my fingers, but there wasn't a mark on them. "Yes. It felt like raw electricity."

"Or the magical equivalent." Tyler tapped a finger on his chin. "And yet it didn't hurt to touch the aura of a powerful angel?"

"That is rather odd." The lift slowed to a halt and I stepped past the golem and into a parking deck. The lift door slid shut behind Tyler, leaving us alone.

"Well, that was an adventure." Tyler took my hand and led me to the blue Camry. "I guess we'll just go to the penthouse and hole up for the next twenty-four hours."

"I'd like to tell my father what's going on and talk to Isabel." I sighed. "Is there some way we can do that without giving away our location?"

"Absolutely." Tyler opened the passenger door for me, then went around and hopped in. "There's always a way." He pulled out of the parking deck and drove slowly down the street until something caught his eye. He pulled to the curb in a no-parking zone. "Be right back."

Before I could ask him anything, he vanished inside. I looked around nervously, praying a police officer or parking attendant didn't notice the car. Tyler returned perhaps two minutes later, but it felt like an eternity. He slid into his seat and put a plastic bag on my lap, then pulled the car back into traffic.

I found a prepaid phone inside the bag. "My very own burner phone. How wonderful." I leaned over and kissed him on the cheek. "Might I see your phone? I don't actually remember Isabel's or my father's numbers."

He dug into his pocket and produced his smartphone. "There you go."

I entered my father's number first and called it. As usual, there was no answer, so I left him a message about the current situation. Isabel didn't answer when I called either, presumably because she didn't recognize the number. "I suppose I could have just used your phone," I said.

Tyler shook his head. "Not now. In fact, I should probably get rid of it just in case it can be tracked."

"How would demons track your phone?"

"They might possess someone at the wireless company and look me up." He veered into a strip mall parking lot. "Jack told me they can track smartphones."

"Yes, I suppose that's possible." In fact, it sounded quite probable. I opened the menu on his smartphone. Tyler had perhaps three contacts in the phone and had barely used it for anything since buying it, so I reset and wiped it to factory settings. "Let's put this in a trash can."

Tyler grinned. "I have a better idea." He pulled closer to the sidewalk in front of a store and dropped the phone into a public mailbox. "That ought to keep them wondering."

"What if Isabel calls your phone?" I said.

He shook his head. "She won't once she gets your message."

"What if the mail person takes your phone home?"

Tyler frowned. "Knowing the mail service, the phone will be broken long before anyone finds it."

"I certainly hope so." I didn't want caustic demons assaulting someone innocent.

Isabel phoned me while we rode the lift up to the new penthouse. Reception was spotty, so I heard only dead air when I answered. I impatiently waited for us to reach the top and called her back while Tyler negotiated the biometric locks guarding the penthouse.

"Em, are you okay?" Isabel sounded worried.

"I'm fine for now, but it's been wild couple of days." I filled in the details for her and told her Fjoeruss's plan to clone me.

"What? You met two angels?" Shock resonated in her voice. "You didn't even ease me into this one, Em."

I laughed. "I'm sorry. I suppose I've become a bit desensitized to what's crazy and what's not."

"So this Nightliss angel couldn't give you the blessing, or whatever you called it?"

"No. Whatever gives me my abilities also rejected it."

Isabel blew out a breath. "But this other angel dude thinks cloning you will work?"

"I certainly hope so. Otherwise, it's a life on the run for me."

"Nothing new." Isabel sighed. "God, Em, when will you just get to live without someone trying to take over the world or kill you?"

"That is an excellent question." I shook my head. "I need you to be extra careful. The demons might not know about you, but I don't know for sure."

"Well, I haven't been back to our condo since that other demon murdered our neighbors and dumped them in the bathtub." Isabel made a disgusted noise. "Jack said I can stay with him as long as I want."

"Do that, but still be careful. I love you, sis."

Isabel choked up. "I love you too, sis. I want to see you soon. I can't stand knowing that you're supposed to be dead in a few days."

"Perhaps my clone will solve the problem." I told her goodbye and ended the call before I burst into tears of my own.

"I can't take this either." Tyler stared out the window at a cloudy sky. He turned to face me. "Em, I want to get married right away."

I faltered back a step. "As in right now?"

He shook his head. "If you'll have me."

"Of course I will, but getting married won't solve anything. And if I die, you'll just be a widower."

"That's a grim way to put it." His shoulders slumped. "I just want to be with you forever."

"Is that all?" I gripped him in a tight hug and pressed my cheek to his chest. "And I want to be with you for the rest of my life. But I won't let a murderous demon overlord dictate how and when I get married." I wished I could wrap my hands around Domathus's spirit and crush it. Unfortunately, that didn't seem to be in my skillset.

The next twenty-four hours were brutal. Tyler and I passed some time with a nice romp in the bedroom, by eating, watching television, and staring out at the glorious sunset from the helipad. Despite my rising anxiety, I managed to enjoy all the alone time with my love. When we went to bed, my active mind refused to let me sleep. Tyler, as usual, seemed to doze off moments after his head hit the pillow.

Restless, I got up and walked around the large house. I went downstairs and walked aimlessly through the wide space, talking to myself like a madwoman. I nearly walked into a wall of boxes stacked neatly in the dining area. White labels generically described the contents as clothes, toiletries, or electronics. I went to the kitchen and located a knife suitable for slicing packaging tape.

The first box held several pairs of my shoes. The next contained dresses and jeans neatly folded and stacked. "Joe must have hired women," I muttered to myself. Men would have simply thrown the clothes into the box.

A dented box a darker shade of brown than the others caught my attention. It was larger than even the clothing box in front of me. I tugged and slid it across the hardwoods, no easy feat since it seemed to be weighed down with bricks. A white label on the side caught my eye. The perfect handwriting looked familiar. It was my mother's. Heart racing, I cut the tape around the seams and opened it. There was only one thing inside—a gray metal container with more sides than I could count.

"No bloody wonder it was so heavy." It was much too heavy to lift out, so I used the knife to carve open the cardboard box. Soon, I had the packaging spread out flat around the strange object. I knocked on the metal. It rang hollow, but the dense material only vibrated for a second before going quiet. It rested atop a small wooden pallet, held in place by metal straps.

Digging around in the packaging materials did me little good. Mother hadn't packed a letter or even a note with a description of this bizarre object. I examined the shipping label and was surprised to find it had come all the way across the pond from England to Tyler's other condo. I didn't recognize the address. It wasn't my Aunt Lydia's house in London, but from Salisbury.

What was this thing and how had Mum shipped it after her death?

CHAPTER 8

"**M**um, what were you up to?" I looked at the back of the label just in case she'd decided to be clever and hide something there, but it was blank. A smaller box of similar material sat atop a pile of other boxes. I set it next to the mystery object. When I opened this one, I found a perfectly ordinary object inside.

It was grayed with age, the fabric rotting around the edges, but this had to be the wicker basket my grandparents discovered on their doorstep so many years ago. Aunt Lydia had told me she still had it, but after Mum's funeral, she'd been unable to find it. A letter nestled in the fabric told me why.

Hey Sweetheart,

Your mother always wanted you to have a normal life. She didn't want you brought into the Overworld like she was. I guess life had different plans, because you were dragged in just like Victoria. I know you'd planned to dig into your mother's origins and find out why you, her, and Lydia have a sixth sense unlike anything I've ever seen. I took the baby basket from Lydia after the funeral, and Victoria had been keeping that weird thirteen-sided polyhedron (I think it's called tridecagon) in storage.

We had it tested by Templar experts, but no one could figure out what it was or if it opened or did anything special. Victoria's adoptive parents found it next to the basket and stuck it in their basement until Victoria and Lydia found it by accident.

I knew you'd want to have all this, so I went to Salisbury, got the tridecagon and shipped it to you. I also decided to join the Borathen Templar faction. I probably should have told you in person, but I haven't been myself since Victoria died. I promise I'll touch base soon.

Love, Dad

I wiped tears from my cheeks and read the letter once more. I hadn't told my father about Lydia's vision. He had no idea my funeral was only days away. I hadn't wanted him worrying about me, spending every minute trying to stop the inevitable from happening. It still felt like the right decision.

The tridecagon looked seamless. The joints felt perfectly smooth to my fingers. There were no signs of welding or flaws. Every side looked identical to the last even when I wrestled it off the pallet and rolled it around on the area rug. If Templar experts had been unable to discern the nature of this thing, I certainly had no chance of success.

That didn't stop me from trying. I tapped on each side with my knuckles, listening for any change that might indicate a hollow or a moveable panel. So involved was I with it, that I shrieked when a shadowy figure stepped into the room.

Tyler grinned. "Didn't mean to spook you." His eyes lit on the tridecagon. "Whoa. What's that?"

I took deep breaths to calm my racing heart. "You nearly gave me a coronary, Tyler."

He caressed me and planted a kiss on my forehead. "Does that make it better?"

I giggled. "Yes. A little." I left the comfort of his arms and retrieved the letter for his inspection.

His eyes wandered back and forth across the paper. A grunt. "Challenge accepted."

"What challenge?"

"That thing." Tyler handed me the letter and began running his hands around the tridecagon.

I watched, somewhat amused at the intense expression on his face as he peered closely at every angle and side. "You realize the Templars couldn't even figure out what that thing is?"

"Yep. Doesn't mean I can't, though."

"Your confidence is adorable."

Tyler chuckled. "Exactly what I was aiming for."

I went to the wicker basket and turned it around in my hands. It was made from thin reeds laced with slightly thicker twigs. At one time it might have been fairly flexible, but old age and poor storage left it brittle and dusty. It bore no stickers or brand symbols. It might have been hand crafted, or perhaps the identifying marks had simply worn off with the passage of time.

The rotting fabric inside was crocheted and almost certainly not store bought. It could have originated anywhere.

Why were Victoria and Lydia left where they were?

My grandparents were very kind, welcoming people, but I'd known them only from the perspective of a child and not as much as an adult. For that reason, I hadn't had many deep conversations with them about life, the universe, and everything. I only knew that they were always happy when we visited and produced more food than was possible to eat for any occasion.

By the time I had been old enough to start caring about what made my grandparents who they were and what they cared about, we'd moved to the States and had barely seen them since. I'd adjusted to my new life and had done a poor job keeping in touch with my grandparents. In fact, I hadn't even known my mother and aunt were adopted until my mother told me.

That made me think my grandparents had intentionally kept secrets from me, perhaps at my mother's request. It might be prime time I had a talk with them and found out more about my mother's origin.

"Gah." Tyler rolled the tridecagon across the carpet away from him. "Might as well use that thing as a giant paperweight, because there's nothing more to it."

I patted his arm. "In that case, you should take it to the office and put it on your desk."

He laughed. "Maybe I will."

I checked the time on my phone. With the five-hour time difference, it was nearly six in the morning in London. I decided to wait until later to call since my grandparents likely wouldn't be up at this hour. Making that decision somewhat calmed my emotional turmoil.

"Let's try to get some sleep." Tyler took my hand and led me back to the bedroom. He tired me out in his wickedly delicious way, and sleep finally took me in its warm embrace.

Loud clangs tore me from slumber. It was as if someone had thrown pots and pans down the wooden staircase. Tyler sprang from bed in a blur. "Wait here." Teeth bared, he stalked out of the room.

I should have followed his instructions. Instead, I skulked after him, padding lightly on the hardwoods behind him. He stopped at the end of the hall and peered out. He flinched and looked back at me, a confused look on his face.

The clanging continued unabated for several seconds and then change in volume and pitch, as if the pots and pans weren't moving quite as fast as before.

Tyler looked back out and then back at me. He rubbed his eyes. "Am I dreaming?"

"What's out there?" I poked my head out of the hallway and saw the tridecagon rolling along the middle landing of the stairs. It reached the next flight and rolled up them with an incredible racket. I felt my jaw drop open. "What in the bloody hell is going on?"

The object reached the top and rolled toward us. I shrieked and ran down the hall to the bedroom. Tyler backed away a few steps, braced himself, and planted both hands on the tridecagon. It stopped in place. He let go with one hand and held it with the other.

"It's not hard to stop."

I had already climbed on the bed. "How is it moving on its own?"

"I don't know." He let go and hopped back. After a moment, the tridecagon thumped after him. Tyler got out of the way and watched as the object continued toward me.

"What are you doing?" I shouted.

Tyler grinned and stopped the tridecagon with a single finger a few feet shy of the bed. "This is so weird. It's drawn to you like a magnet."

"But why?" Even though I'd touched it earlier without consequence, what if something had changed? "What if it explodes when I touch it?"

Tyler frowned. "It didn't explode earlier. What makes you think it'd do that now?"

"I don't think my father would have failed to mention this thing rolling around of its own accord." I stood at the far edge of the bed. "It's almost as if I activated it somehow."

"And that means it wants to hurt you?"

"Quite possibly. What if it's demonic?"

Tyler shook his head. "I have a sense for that and it's not tingling right now."

I looked down at the tridecagon and inched across the bed toward it. Curiosity, it seemed, was stronger than my survival instinct. *Don't be a ninny!* I took a deep breath to steel myself and stepped down off the bed. "Release it."

Tyler hesitated, then let it go. The tridecagon rolled toward me and stopped a foot shy from my toes. I stepped around it and backed up down the hallway. A moment later, it rolled after me and stopped a foot away.

Tyler grinned. "Looks like it just wants to be loved."

I groaned. "What in the world is going on? I can't have this bloody thing following me all over creation."

Tyler put a hand on his chin. "Yeah, I suppose that would be inconvenient." He scooped up the metallic enigma and took it downstairs.

"What are you doing with it?" I followed on his heels.

"Crating it like a dog." He put it on the shipping pallet and strapped it down. "Walk a few feet away."

I did so and waited. The tridecagon remained in place. "Thank goodness it doesn't take much force to hold it."

"I wonder if it can home in on you at any distance." Tyler gazed through the windows. "Is it limited to a few hundred feet? A mile or more?"

"Questions that are best answered another time." I watched the strange object, a sense of foreboding snaking through my chest. Mum and I had planned to investigate our mysterious lineage, but she'd been killed in the battle against Domathus. I blinked back tears. "Let's go to sleep."

I was simply too tired to worry about anything at that point. Curled in Tyler's arms, I quickly drifted into unconsciousness.

I got out of bed and shivered violently. Freezing cold penetrated my skin all the way to the bone. My breath frosted the air. I turned around and gasped at what I saw. My body was curled up in bed, sound asleep. "Is this a dream?" My words echoed as if I stood in a vast space. I turned in a circle and found darkness on all sides. Except for the bed and myself, nothing was visible. Goosebumps rose on my neck. I turned and saw a pale face in the darkness.

This time I shrieked. "Who are you?"

The face drifted closer. Dread rose in my chest and it took everything not to run away. But running into the dark void seemed like an even worse decision. The face stopped at the edge of the light illuminating the bed. Dark mist swirled into the light and coalesced into human form. The blurry face resolved into someone familiar.

"Mum?" I stayed on the opposite side of the bed. "Am I dreaming or is that you again?"

She began to speak, but I caught only bits and phrases from her muffled words. "Another child...great care for she...infernal blade."

The last words caught my attention. "Infernal blade?" I ran around the bed and tried to touch her, but my hand passed through the figure, leaving swirls of smoky vapors in its wake.

Mom's forehead furrowed and she spoke faster, desperately trying to tell me something, but it was like trying to listen to a bad phone connection. Her lips began to make the same pattern, and I heard what she was trying to say.

"Danger. Danger. Danger."

"From what?" I tried to touch her again, but a dark form rushed into the light, hands outstretched and shoved me. I flew backward and landed atop my slumbering form. I jerked upright in bed. "Mum!"

Tyler leapt from the bed and landed in a fighting stance. He blinked and shook his head. "Did you have another dream about your mom?"

My teeth chattered as if I'd just come out of the freezing cold. "Yes. It was so strange." I described it to him.

Tyler whistled. "Wow. Almost sounds like an out of body experience. I wonder if you astral projected or something."

I couldn't stop shivering. "I don't know what I did. But I wish I knew what Mum meant by infernal blade and danger."

"Sounds like she's talking about the demon assassins after you." He climbed back in bed and wrapped his warm arms around me. "I wonder if it really is your mom trying to reach you from the afterlife."

"It felt so real. It just has to be her." Tears pooled in my eyes. "I miss her so much. I wish I could really talk to her."

"I know, baby. I know." Tyler stroked my hair and before I knew it, I fell back asleep.

I woke to pleasant breakfast odors drifting from the kitchen. My tummy rumbled for a slice of bacon, but I was too eager to speak with my grandparents to eat. I grabbed my burner phone and dialed the number from memory.

"Jon Winters." Grandfather answered in his usual formal way.

"Grandpa, it's Emily. How are you?"

His formal tone vanished. "Little Em! How nice to hear from you, dear." There was a clunk as if something covered the microphone, and his voice grew muffled. "Abigail, it's little Em."

Another clunk, a handset lifting from another phone, and Grandma spoke. "Darling, how are you?"

"I'm quite well, thank you." I couldn't stop a childish grin from spreading across my face. It was good to hear their cheery voices again. "I hope I'm not intruding on lunch."

"Absolutely not." Grandpa grunted. "Just enjoying our tea before we go to town."

I wasn't sure how to elegantly segue into questions about my mother's past, so I simply did it the way most Brits would and apologized in advance. "I'm sorry to bother you, but I received some peculiar packages from my father and hoped you might have insight to share."

"Oh, dear. He must have sent you Tilden."

I blinked. "Tilden?"

Grandpa chuckled. "That's what we named the metal ball that accompanied Lydia and Victoria."

"Why Tilden?" I asked.

"It was just the first name that sprang to mind," Grandma said. "Before that we called it the bumpy metal ball."

"A mouthful." Grandpa snorted. "I banged and pried away on that thing for months. Couldn't even mark it with a torch welder, though. So we tucked it away and forgot about it."

"Until my mother found it," I said.

"Yes, but we still didn't know what it was." Grandma sighed. "Truth be told, we didn't really care. We couldn't have children of our own, so finding those babies and Tilden on our doorstep was a blessing from God. Some mysteries aren't meant to be solved. You just accept them on faith."

"Mum and I planned to investigate her origins." I swallowed hard. "Before she passed."

"She certainly did her best to find out from the moment we told her she wasn't ours." Grandpa sounded a little sad and a little proud all at the same time. "Victoria was quite headstrong."

"It worried us," Grandma said. "We moved to another town since there would be too many questions where we lived. We uprooted our lives just to have children."

"So you didn't even try to find out where they came from?" I said.

There was a moment of silence that stretched to the point of awkwardness. Grandma ended it. "We didn't want to, and I'm not the least bit ashamed of it. Maybe I should be, but I loved those little girls like they were my own flesh and blood."

I softened my tone. "I'm not judging you, Grandma. I just need to know."

"Why is it so important, dear?"

"Because it was important to Mum."

"I'm sorry, dear." Shame tinged Grandpa's reply. But Abigail Winters wore the pants in that family, so he probably hadn't argued too hard when she wanted to keep the children left at their doorstep.

But it did give a clue as to the motive of the mysterious benefactor. "Whoever left the children must have known that you'd do whatever it took to keep them. You were the perfect couple to raise them, no questions asked."

"Why do you say that?" Grandpa asked.

"Hmm." Grandma seemed to latch onto my line of reasoning. "They knew I couldn't have children."

"Did many people know that?" I asked.

"No." She replied in a subdued voice. "After trying for two years, we went to London for testing so we could keep it secret. I had abnormalities of the uterus that made me infertile."

"So only the doctor who saw you would know that?"

"I assume so." Regret crept into her words. "It was one of the most painful days of my life, second only to losing Victoria." She sniffed.

"There, there, darling." Grandpa's voice sounded distant. He must have put down his handset and gone to comfort his wife. "You raised a good woman."

"She was the best." I choked up. Tears burned my eyes. I took a deep breath and carried on. Mother would not want sentiment to stand in the way of the truth. "Did my mother track down the doctor?"

Grandma cleared her throat. "No. We never even thought my infertility might be the reason someone gave us Victoria and Lydia."

Hope swelled in my heart. "Do you know the doctor's name?"

"I'll never forget it," Grandma said. "Doctor Bernard Wolf."

"That's not a very British name."

"That's because he wasn't," Grandma said. "He was German."

"Age?" I asked.

"He was young. Perhaps in his thirties," Grandpa said.

"We were younger than him at the time," Grandma said.

"How long after that did Victoria and Lydia arrive at your doorstep?" I asked.

"Oh, let me see." Grandpa clucked his tongue a few times. "Would've been about four years and maybe two months later."

"December sixth," Grandma said. "Four years, three months after the day Dr. Wolf told me I would never have children of my own." She sounded almost triumphant. As if fate had proven the doctor wrong.

"Did you ever think of adopting?" The question wasn't really relevant, but four years seemed an awfully long time to wait.

"We tried," Grandpa said. "But it was expensive, and we were turned down twice."

"Who in the bloody hell would turn you down?" I said, aghast.

"We wanted babies," Grandma said. "If we'd asked for older children, it would have been no problem. But I didn't want that. I wanted a child no older than a year." She paused. "And yes, it was very selfish on my part. But I couldn't help myself."

I couldn't blame her. The poor woman had been devastated and fixated on the one thing she thought would make her happy. Mum had been thirty-seven when Martin Drang's cruel spell mortally injured her. I pushed back the pain and did some quick calculations. Dr. Wolf would be in his mid to late seventies by now, provided Grandpa's age estimate was correct.

What if he'd felt terrible for my grandmother? What if a pair of twins had been orphaned, the parents killed in a tragic accident? The likelihood was small, but it was the only lead I had.

Dr. Wolf might know who my mother's real parents were.

CHAPTER 9

I prayed the link to my mother's past still lived. "At which hospital was Dr. Wolf?" I asked.

"Queen's Cross," Grandma said. "It was the only one that agreed to see us on short notice."

I opened the nightstand drawer and found a pen and paper since Tyler preferred antiquity to modern contraptions. I jotted down notes. "Were there any nurses present?"

"None that I recall," Grandma said. "It was a rather small hospital. Almost a clinic, if I'm to be honest."

"I'm sorry to pelt you with so many questions."

Grandma laughed. "I understand, dear. Your mother interrogated us more times than I remember. It almost makes me feel like I'm talking to her again."

I swallowed a lump in my throat. "Do you remember any other people at all?"

"After the diagnosis, I'm afraid everything else became a blur."

I certainly understood. Shock and trauma seemed to either crystallize a moment or obliterate it. Since there seemed little else to discover about the hospital, I circled back to the enigmatic tridecagon dubbed Tilden. "Did Tilden ever exhibit peculiar behavior?"

A long pause followed.

"What do you mean?" Grandpa asked. "It was peculiar in every way."

"But did it do anything?" I asked.

"It sat in place and looked odd." There was a rustle of fabric. A shrug from Grandpa, perhaps. "It didn't glow or make sounds."

I said, "So it never rolled around of its own accord?"

He said, "Rolled around?"

Grandma interjected. "What are you saying, Emily?"

"Oh, nothing." I didn't think my grandparents knew about the Overworld, and I certainly didn't want to bring them into it. "I'm just making sure it wasn't mechanized or something."

"Ah, I see." The mundane explanation seemed to make sense to Grandpa. "I never could tell if it had inner workings."

It didn't follow my mother or aunt, but it follows me. What had changed? "Did the wicker basket they arrived in have any markings that might indicate where it came from?"

"It did," Grandma said. "I believe there was a tag from Hastings still attached to it."

Hastings was a fairly common convenience store chain in England. But it might not have been quite as common thirty-eight years ago. I wrote that down. "Where did you live when the babies arrived?"

"Gloucester Road, Bedford." Grandpa sighed. "It wasn't a lovely house, but it was a house."

"A duplex," Grandma said. "But the neighbors were quiet."

"Must have been hard keeping the babies a secret from them," I said.

"Not really. They were often away on holiday." Grandpa tutted. "But the neighbors across the street were unbearable."

"Oh, the McConnells." Disgust filled Grandma's voice. "They took in more foster children than they could handle, and then left them to fend for themselves when they went on holiday."

"But you moved rather abruptly after finding the babies," I said.

"Surprisingly, we found a buyer for the house within a day of listing it, even though Bedford wasn't the sort of place many would move, given a choice." Grandpa grunted. "Your grandmother was insistent we sell it with the furniture and take as little with us as possible."

"It was the right decision," Grandma said.

"I suppose it was." Grandpa chuckled. "Not that I had any choice in the matter. You know how strong-willed your grandmother is."

"Where do you think my mother got it from?" If Mum got her head-strong tendencies from Grandma, Lydia must have gotten her meekness from Grandpa.

"Sweet Victoria." Grandma sniffled. "She was a true gem."

Something about the sale of the house stuck in my mind. "Did you get what you asked for the house?"

"To the pence," Grandpa said. "They even paid closing costs because they wanted to move in right away."

"You didn't find that odd?" I asked.

He said, "At the time I was under too much pressure from your Grand-mother to care. I took the money and gave thanks."

"Who purchased the house?" I asked.

"Oh, I don't remember their names." Grandpa paused. "Might have been the Browns."

"Yes, I think so," Grandma said. "I only remember seeing Mr. Brown, but I'm certain he said he had a wife and child."

"Did he say why he so urgently needed to move to Bedford?"

"I don't recall ever asking." There was rustling again. Another shrug from Grandpa, perhaps.

We continued talking for a time, but there was little else to uncover. As a teenager, Mum had tracked down the neighbors in Bedford and interrogated them about the night she and Aunt Lydia had appeared. Even though it had been so long ago by then, someone might have remembered a shadowy figure dropping off a basket at a doorstep, ringing the bell, and vanishing into the night.

It all seemed a rather cliché, but effective way to rid one's self of unwanted children.

I thanked my grandparents and promised to visit soon.

I stared at my sparse notes and drew an arcing line to connect *Queen's Cross Hospital* with *The Browns*. Could they possibly be connected? My imagination ran wild with conspiracy theories. Perhaps Mr. Brown worked at the hospital and learned of Abigail Winter's infertility. Some years later, perhaps he and his wife unexpectedly conceived twins and decided to foist the responsibility on someone who wanted children.

I scoffed. "Emily, that's the worst hypothesis ever."

"Hey, babe." Tyler stood in the doorway, shirtless, a pair of boxers low on his waist. "Your grandparents have anything interesting to say?"

I licked my lips almost reflexively at the sight of him. "Indeed. Though I feel as though I've clutched at straws and am trying to weave them into a basket."

"Talk about it over breakfast?"

My tummy rumbled. "I believe that's a yes."

He wrapped me in his arms and kissed me until we had to come up for air. "Today's the day."

I put a hand on his muscular chest and recovered my breath. "Goodness. A woman needs to breathe."

"And keep on breathing." He carried me down the stairs effortlessly and set me down next to a granite-topped table. "I hope good old Fjoeruss comes through."

A flutter of nerves disrupted my appetite, but the succulent odor of bacon quickly revived it. I sat down and plucked a piece of bacon from a platter piled high with it. "Yes, I hope so too."

Tyler stacked six pancakes on a plate and dumped syrup over them. "Tell me about your grandparents."

I took a bite of bacon and savored it while eyeing Tyler's stack of pancakes. His supernatural metabolism made me sick with envy. I told him what I'd discovered and hoped he had some insights I didn't. "My grandparents desperately wanted children but had no luck conceiving. To protect their privacy in a small town, they went to a hospital in London. A Dr. Bernard Wolf diagnosed my grandmother with infertility. Four years later, two babies showed up on their doorstep."

I nibbled at the bacon and continued. "My grandmother wanted to keep the babies, no questions asked. But because keeping secrets in a small town is impossible, they decided to sell their house and move elsewhere."

"Did anyone else in town know she couldn't have kids?" Tyler asked.

I shook my head. "No, they kept it to themselves."

"I guess showing up with two babies after not being pregnant would raise a few eyebrows." Tyler cut the pancakes with the edge of his fork. "But selling a house in a small town on short notice isn't that easy either."

"Oh, but it was." I told him about the eager Mr. Brown and his generosity.

Tyler finished chewing his food and looked at me expectantly. "Anything else?"

"They named the tridecagon Tilden and said it never moved of its own accord."

He worked his jaw back and forth. "So Tilden following you around like a puppy is a new thing."

"Precisely." I took a sip of orange juice. "My grandfather tried cutting it open with a torch and didn't make a mark on it."

"And it left the Templars clueless too." Tyler shook his head. "Em, you are something else."

I raised my eyebrows. "What's that supposed to mean?"

He chuckled. "Not even a lifeless hunk of metal can resist you."

I rolled my eyes. "Cheesy, but I like it."

Tyler laughed and stuffed his face with more pancakes. He didn't chew for long before pausing and looking at me. A look of understanding dawned on him. He swallowed hard and chased it down with orange juice. "What if that Mr. Brown had something to do with leaving the babies? Why else would he swoop in and buy the house so fast?"

"I don't know." I offered nothing else to see what else might occur to him.

Tyler frowned. Shook his head. "He must have been desperate to get rid of those babies, though. Maybe he and his wife couldn't support twins but didn't want to separate them either."

"It sounds logical, right?"

He scoffed. "You've got to be awfully desperate to go through all that trouble. And why pick your grandparents of all people? I mean..." He trailed off and I could practically see him connecting another dot. "Unless they knew how desperate your grandparents were to have kids."

At this point in his reasoning I realized I'd overlooked something. Dr. Bernard Wolf wasn't the only person who'd known about Abigail Winters's infertility. My grandparents had tried to adopt and been turned down twice. Surely the adoption agencies had asked why they wanted children. Supposing they'd told the truth, there might be paperwork at those agencies.

I jumped up from the table and picked up my burner phone. A short redial later, Grandpa answered again.

"Jon Winters."

"Grandpa, it's Emily again. I'm so sorry to bother you, but I thought of another question."

"Of course, dear."

Another clunk of a handset and Grandma said, "What is it, Emily?"

"You were turned down twice by adoption agencies. Did you tell them about the infertility?"

A long pause. Grandma said, "The first was an agency in London. We didn't tell them about my infertility. The second was an orphanage. I didn't tell them either, but the woman there winnowed it out."

"She was a strange one," Grandpa said. "Gave me the shivers just looking at her."

Grandma said, "They offered to let us foster children, but said they had no babies for adoption."

"It was rubbish." Grandpa cleared his throat. "On the way out, I distinctly heard a baby crying."

"So there's no chance the adoption agency knew about your infertility?" I asked again to be sure.

"No. They didn't even question us on the matter." Grandma sighed. "The entire process was heartbreaking."

"When did you go to the agency and the orphanage?" I asked.

"We went to the agency a year after my diagnosis," Grandma said. "It took another two years before I recovered from the disappointment and tried the orphanage."

"How long after did Victoria and Lydia appear?" I asked.

"A little over a year after the orphanage."

"What was the name of the place?" I asked.

Grandpa answered. "Little Angel Orphanage."

"Felicity Goodleigh was the evil bitch who denied me children." Venom dripped from Grandma's words.

I flinched at the seething anger in her voice. "She was that unpleasant?"

"Oh, yes."

"How old was she?" I asked.

"Mid-thirties at the most," Grandpa said. "I still have the advert stuffed away in a file somewhere."

"An advert?" I leaned forward. "Is that how you found them?"

"Yes. I could find it and telefax it to you."

I smiled. "Or you could take a picture and email it."

"I'll take it to the shop in town and ask them to do it." Grandpa huffed. "I don't much care for computers."

"A man after my own heart," Tyler murmured.

I gave him my email address, made him repeat the spelling twice, and then ended the call.

"We going to England?" Tyler asked.

"Yes, but not right away." I chomped on the bacon and tore off a chunk. "First, we have to fake my death."

I hoped and prayed Fjoeruss had good news for us.

CHAPTER 10

I waited anxiously for two things. One, for Fjoeruss to tell us my clone was ready, and two, for Grandpa to email me the advert for Little Angel Orphanage.

Tyler took his phone and made arrangements for him to take an extended leave of absence. Although executives already handled the day-to-day business of his various holdings, dropping off the face of the Earth wasn't an option for the CEO. Stocks would tank if Tyler vanished without warning. Since we might very well have to go into hiding for a time, it seemed prudent to prepare for the worst.

I took my MacBook to the lovely miniature park on the roof and sat at a glass top table. Pale, golden light peeked above the cityscape to the east. I lit the gas fire pit and wrapped a blanket around me to ward off the morning chill.

Using Google Maps, I examined the street where my grandparents used to live. I viewed the house from street view and clicked the arrows to move up and down the street. Most of the homes were duplexes. Most looked virtually identical, even several streets over. It was as if a single architect baked them all in the same cookie mold.

I wondered if the Browns still lived at the old address on Gloucester Street. I wondered if they'd ever actually lived there or sold it shortly after my grandparents left. What was Mr. Brown's connection? Had he worked at the orphanage or was it merely coincidence?

I didn't get a single hit when I searched for Little Angel Orphanage with three different internet search engines. Either the place didn't exist anymore, or they kept a very low profile. Even in this day and age it wasn't inconceivable that someone or something could keep themselves hidden from big data firms. But it certainly couldn't be easy.

My email dinged a few minutes before noon. The sender was from a shipping store and an image was attached. I had never clicked on something so fast. The picture was clear and crisp. The subject of the picture, not so much. A young man and woman played with a group of children. Joyful smiles lit their faces. The yellowed newspaper bore faded print, still legible.

Make the world a better place one child at a time.

Visit Little Angel Orphanage and find out how you can become a foster parent.

Below that was an address and a phone number. It seemed an odd advert to run in a newspaper. I didn't know much about fostering children, but certainly it couldn't be as easy as going to an orphanage and picking them up, could it? Perhaps nearly forty years ago it had been that simple.

I noticed italic words beneath the pictures of the young couple in the advert. I zoomed in and was barely able to make sense of the faded ink. *Felicity and Marcus Goodleigh, wards.*

They looked much younger than the ages Grandpa described. More like mid-twenties than mid-thirties. They would at least be in their sixties by now, provided they still lived. I stared at the kind faces for a moment, trying to imagine these people being as cruel as Grandma described. I supposed it was all a matter of perspective. Felicity had denied my grandmother the one thing she most desired in life.

A lump rose in my throat. Tears welled in my eyes. I allowed myself a moment to empathize with my grandmother. To imagine how it must feel to be deprived of motherhood. To be unable to create life of my own.

Grandma might not have given birth to my mother, but she had given her a life and a purpose. She was the strong woman my mother modeled her own existence on. My mother and I rarely got along when I was little. I'd always felt closer to my father, Patrick, because Mum pushed me so hard and expected so much. Only as an adult and only recently had I realized what a gem my mother had been.

And now she was dead, a pale ghost I saw in my dreams.

I wiped tears from my cheeks. "Get a hold of yourself, woman!" Mum would be displeased to see me wallowing in pity like this. I cleared my eyes and typed the address for the orphanage into Google Maps.

Street view displayed a wrought iron gate flanked by gray-stoned walls. Through the narrow gap in the black iron bars, I saw a long drive leading to a large estate. The house was shaped like a V, or perhaps more like an L, but it was difficult to discern through the bars. Moving the view up and down the street only blocked the view with the great stone wall.

Overhead satellite view displayed a lonely estate in the middle of farm and pastureland. Zooming in close, I decided the house was shaped like an L, one wing longer than the other. Behind it were several outbuildings—barns, stockyards, and a dark swatch that might be a pigpen. Cottony spots in a green pasture were likely sheep. Brown dots in another might be cows.

I had little doubt the orphans spent their days helping on the farm. It seemed a rather idyllic place for orphans to live—much better than dingy old buildings in the middle of the city. On the other hand, it might not even be an orphanage anymore. Perhaps someone purchased the land years ago and turned it into a farm.

Provided I survived faking my death, visiting the orphanage took first place on my list. I would track down Mr. Brown or his relatives and find out why he helped my grandparents. I considered that I might be on the wrong track, but this just felt right.

Somewhere between this orphanage and Mr. Brown, I would find a connection leading back to my biological grandparents and possibly the origin of my abilities. But if the orphanage was no more, it would make the trail to the past far more difficult to follow.

Tyler was still busy in his home office, so I made myself a sandwich for lunch and three more for him. He gave me a grateful grin and polished them off while discussing a multimillion-dollar deal on the phone. I went downstairs and outside to the roof garden with a bottle of white wine. After half an hour of trying to track down Mr. Brown via the internet, I gave up. The name was too common, and cross-referencing him with Bedford, the orphanage, and other nearby towns proved useless.

Unable to come up with further leads, I decided to call Isabel and give her another update. The phone rang four times and went to voicemail. I left her a brief message. "Hey, it's Emily again. Call me back when you get a chance."

The phone rang an instant later. "Em, are you okay?"

"Just waiting on the grace of an angel." I brought her up to date.

"When can I see you? I really want to give my sis a hug."

I sighed. "I don't know. After we fake my death, I'm headed to England to track down my real grandparents."

"It's so mysterious." She made a thoughtful sound. "Do you think they'll know what this Tilden object is?"

"I hope so, because I'm a bit tired of mysteries." I took gulp of wine. "I could really use a spa day right about now."

"You and me both." Isabel sighed. "So this angel guy"—she laughed as if she couldn't believe she'd just said that—"is going to clone you like in Star Trek or something so you can fake your death?"

"Um, yeah, pretty much." I snorted at how preposterous it sounded. "You know, the normal way to avoid demonic assassination."

We broke into giggles.

Isabel ended the laughter with another sigh. "Well, I know this pales in comparison to what you're going through, but I'm looking for another job."

"Huh?" I let go of my own worries for a moment. "I thought senator what's-her-name really loved you."

"Elizabeth Abrams." Isabel made a frustrated noise. "We beat her opponent by almost twenty points last November. Her approval rating is over sixty percent, and now she's the chairman of the Senate Arms Committee. That woman is living the dream."

I didn't much care for politics, but Isabel lived and breathed them. She'd gotten an internship with a state senator right out of college and finally moved up to the federal level last year. Even so, she didn't talk about work very often because politics wasn't exactly the best icebreaker unless you wanted to start a street fight. "So what happened?"

"I don't know." Isabel groaned. "She started bringing in new staff and asked us to train them. Then she brought me, Jim, Angela, and Mark into her office last week and let us go."

"That's awful!" I didn't know who those people were, but that didn't matter. The whole thing sounded cruel and unusual. "What reason did she give?"

"She said it was time for change." Isabel sniffled. "I asked about positions with other senators, but I don't think it's going to happen. I think I'm all the way back to the beginning again and it sucks."

"Wow, I can't even." Politicians were such assholes. "How can she just dump you for no reason? It sounds like everything was going so well."

"Angela thinks it's because we pushed back on her new policy plans. She wanted to allow private contractors to operate as sanctioned military forces on U.S. soil." Isabel blew a raspberry. "We don't even know where she got the idea from, but her voter base would have abandoned her in a heartbeat if she voted for something like that."

"You mean she wanted to allow private armies to do their own thing?" I shuddered. "That sounds like the worst idea ever."

"The war hawk senators liked the idea, but they were still two votes shy of passing it on to the Senate." Isabel blew out a breath. "The other members are way too liberal to let it pass."

"I'm so sorry, Izzy." I felt so bad for her. It was as if the senator single-handedly flushed her career down the toilet. "I just can't believe she'd fire you because you didn't like one of her policy suggestions."

"I should've known," Isabel said. "She used to laugh and joke with us all the time. She even took us out to lunch once a week. Then about two weeks ago it was like she became a different person. She didn't joke around, or even really talk to anyone very much. Anytime we went to her office she acted like all she wanted was for us to leave her alone."

"Do you think something bad happened to her?" I said. "Maybe someone close to her died, or one of her children disappointed her?"

"She's divorced and her kids are all grown and doing fine as far as I know." Isabel made a thoughtful noise. "She would've told us if something personal was getting her down."

"I would think so, considering how close you were." I bit the inside of my lip. "Why don't I ask Tyler if he knows anyone? I'm sure he'd love to help with his connections."

"Do you think so?" Hope lit her voice. "I don't care how I get back in. I worked so damned hard to break through the first time that I deserve a little friendly nepotism."

I laughed. "Isn't that the very definition of politics?"

"More or less." I heard Isabel clap her hands. "Oh, Em, thanks so much! I don't know why I didn't think of asking Tyler in the first place."

"He's got a security software company with all sorts of Washington contacts," I said. "I'll tell him right away."

"Thanks, babe." Isabel made a smooching noise. "You're the best."

"Well, I do try."

Isabel laughed, but abruptly sobered. "So I guess all this demon business has put your wedding on hold."

"Looks like we'll need to postpone."

She sighed. "There's always someone or something more powerful than us that wants to ruin our lives, right?"

I let that sink in a moment. "It does seem that way. Maybe it's time we told the powers that be to bugger off."

"Yeah, that's the spirit!"

"I'll talk with Tyler." I made a smooching sound. "Love you, sis. I'll get back to you soon, okay?"

"Love you too." Isabel ended the call.

I closed my laptop, refilled my wineglass, and marched back inside the house. Tyler was finally off the phone and pecking away hopelessly at his laptop keyboard. "Got a moment?"

He rose and came for me in a blur. Pressed me against the wall and kissed me so hard I thought I might lose consciousness. "I would break the universe to make time for you, Em."

I nearly swooned. "Tyler, how do you turn such an ordinary question into something so magnificent?"

A wolfish grin stretched across his face. "Because you light my fire."

I felt a bit weak in the knees but gathered my strength. "Before you ravish me, I have a request."

Tyler nibbled my earlobe. "Request away." His hot breath tickled my skin.

I told him about Isabel's plight.

Tyler nodded. "I have lobbyists with strong connections to the Senate." He nipped my neck and sat back down at his desk. "I'll ask them to find Isabel another position."

Without him so close, I suddenly felt quite cold. I walked up behind him and hugged his back. "That would be wonderful." Tyler began pecking at the laptop keyboard. I giggled and pulled the laptop to me. "Perhaps I should do this."

With his help, I found the lobbyists in his contacts and emailed them a request. I turned toward him and gently bit his lower lip. "Now about that earlier kiss."

There was a knock—the sound of knuckles on glass. I turned to look towards the roof garden. A gray golem stood outside.

It seemed Fjoeruss was ready.

CHAPTER 11

"**L**ooks like we'll have to revisit that kiss later." Tyler patted my bottom. "Now let's go see if it's possible to copy perfection."

I rolled my eyes. "You are too much, Mr. Rock."

Tyler slid open the glass door. "Same address?"

The golem stood on a wide gray carpet, perhaps five feet long and four feet wide. He—or it—pointed at us and then down at the carpet.

"Oh, this'll be fun!" Tyler clapped his hands like an excited schoolboy. "A magic carpet ride!"

I felt far less enthused trusting my life to a thin piece of fabric with nothing but empty air beneath me for hundreds of feet. "I'd prefer to take the car."

"No way. This'll be so much faster." Tyler put an arm around my waist and hustled me onto the carpet.

"Tyler Rock!" I struggled, but it was too late. The carpet rose from the roof and dove out over the edge of the building. It happened so fast, I shrieked out of sheer reflex. The carpet accelerated much faster than my upright body could handle. It should have been much like someone jerking the rug from beneath my feet. Instead, my feet remained firmly attached to the carpet, and an invisible force steadied my body.

I held up a hand and waved it around freely. But when the carpet took an unexpected turn, the invisible restraint once again held me upright.

"Oh my. This is so strange." I felt a bit queasy as the carpet wove between skyscrapers. Those people I could see inside didn't so much as glance out at us.

Tyler poked his head out over the edge of the carpet and whooped. Wind blew his hair around until he pulled it back. "There's a camouflage bubble around us. It's like an invisible windshield too."

The golem stared blankly ahead, not moving in the slightest.

"Do you suppose it's driving?" I asked.

Tyler shrugged. "All I know is that I want one of these. We need to go back to the Grotto sometime and snag us some arcphones and flying carpets."

"I'd prefer normal means of transportation."

An amused grin tugged on the corners of his lips. "Define normal." He pointed down. "This is totally normal for the Overworld."

He was right, but I didn't want to admit it. The carpet climbed at a steep angle, drawing another shriek from my throat. Looking behind me was nearly the same as looking down. The tallest building in Atlanta was below us, the downtown street grid covered with toy cars and people the size of ants. I clung to Tyler, unashamed at my fright.

The carpet leveled out and continued onward. My eyes wanted to look in any direction but straight ahead. I felt the subconscious urge to steer the carpet elsewhere. To avoid whatever lay before us. I remembered the aversion charms Fjoeruss told us about and forced myself to look. A veil seemed to lift from my eyes, revealing the impossibly tall building. The carpet slid inside an open bay. Dark sedans, gray motorcycles, and other curious contraptions lined the floor. I assumed all the vehicles inside flew unless they took a stupidly long lift ride up from the parking garage over a hundred stories below.

This monstrous construct dwarfed even the Burj Khalifa in Dubai. It continued to rise until it nearly kissed the cirrus clouds overhead. How did such a building maintain integrity?

Magic, of course.

We stepped off the carpet, and the golem led us to a lift. We ascended. The doors slid open with a whoosh, revealing the same office as yesterday. Fjoeruss sat behind his desk. His face was pale, cheeks sunken. He looked as if he'd caught the flu.

"Goodness, are you all right?" I asked.

Fjoeruss nodded. "Twenty-four hours was perhaps a bit optimistic. It took far more effort than I thought." He rose from the chair. "But I'm pleased with the results."

Double doors to our right opened and a petite figure stepped inside. She wore a black hat with a veil and a silky black dress. A widow dressed for a funeral. She turned and shut the doors behind her then walked towards me, hand extended. "You must be Emily. Pleased to meet you."

The voice sounded slightly different than it did inside my own head, but it was definitely mine. I backed up a step. "Take off the veil, if you please."

She removed the hat and tossed it casually on a gray chair. Dark brown hair framed a fair face, the nose speckled ever so faintly with freckles. Her neck was thin, shoulders and arms small, her hips wide and legs and posterior thick. I looked down at myself, surprised that I was so pear shaped. Amusement danced in her brown eyes, but she said nothing.

"Wow." Tyler walked around her and held out a finger as if to poke her arm. He paused and looked at Fjoeruss. "Can I touch her?"

Fjoeruss sat back down. "Do with her as you will. She is fully functional in almost every way."

Tyler's trademark amused grin lit his green eyes. He looked at me and waggled his eyebrows. "Threesome?"

My face grew hot. "Tyler Rock, don't you even think about it!"

He burst into laughter.

My copy laughed with him. "Oh, Tyler, you're so funny."

This clone wouldn't survive to fake my death, because I was going to kill her myself.

Fjoeruss nodded as if satisfied. "Personality off."

Golem Emily's face went slack. The slight lean in her stance straightened. Her eyes stared blankly ahead, just like the gray golems I'd seen. Now she was nothing but a doll.

Tyler whistled. "Very impressive."

Fjoeruss tapped on his watch. A gray man stepped inside and walked over to the Emily golem. It unzipped the black dress and slid it off, leaving her nude. I was oddly thankful that her nethers were neatly groomed, but also embarrassed for her nudity. It was an unsettling feeling.

Tyler walked around her, a man inspecting a prized horse. He grunted and nodded. "Pretty impressive. He pointed to the top of her thigh. "But you're missing my favorite mole here, and Em's got a super cute freckle just above her left cheek." He pointed to an area above her buttock. "Em also has a faint scar on her shoulder blade that the golem doesn't have."

I went from wanting to slap Tyler to leaping into his arms and kissing him. I hadn't realized he knew every inch of my body so well. Then again, I'd nearly memorized every delicious curve of his physique right down to the freckle just above his—

"Right, Em?"

I blinked and realized I was staring at Tyler's crotch. I met his laughing eyes and my face grew hotter. "Yes—I think?"

He chuckled and turned to Fjoeruss. The Seraphim didn't seem the least bit amused by my discomfort.

"What now?" Tyler asked.

"Though the golem resembles Miss Glass in nearly every way, it does have shortcomings." Fjoeruss leaned back slightly in his chair. "It can bleed realistically, and it has the internal workings of a human to a certain degree, but if she were disemboweled, it would be apparent that vital organs are missing. There are no kidneys, no ovaries, and no intestines."

"But you said it was fully functional." Tyler looked a bit disappointed.

"Everything is boiled down to essentials," Fjoeruss said. "Even I am not skilled enough to duplicate every working complexity of the human body. I gave some thought to using the organs from a cadaver but discarded the idea."

"My clone has a vagina, but no stomach?" I said.

He nodded. "They are made to mimic humans as closely as possible on the surface, but if they eat, the food simply goes to an internal pouch."

"Do they poop it out?" Tyler said.

Fjoeruss raised an eyebrow. "They squeeze out undigested food from their anus. The pouch is charmed to keep the food from rotting."

The lesson on clone anatomy was disturbing, to say the least. "What's the bottom line, Fjoeruss?" I looked the clone up and down. "She needs to die, but not in a way that exposes her inner workings?"

The angel nodded. "We must ensure that the demon doesn't get too carried away. A stab to the chest or a bullet in the head is sufficient. But caustic demons are well known for excess."

Tyler shuddered. "I've seen caustic possessed rip open a man's chest and eat his heart."

I grimaced. "I didn't need to hear that, Tyler."

"There is another consideration," Fjoeruss said. "The golem has no soul."

"Shouldn't matter," Tyler said. "Most caustics aren't aware enough to sense souls, especially while they're sharing space in a body with another soul."

"Domathus would surely send some of his knights after Miss Glass," Fjoeruss said. "They can certainly sense souls in close proximity."

"You know a lot about demons," I said.

"I have had a long time to learn about them, Miss Glass."

Tyler pursed his lips. "So we have to make sure there aren't any knights present." He looked at me. "You can sense the difference in demon spirits. Maybe we can use that to our advantage."

Fjoeruss tapped on the top of his desk and a holographic overhead map of Midtown Atlanta appeared in the air. Two familiar locations were marked red—OnTech, and Tyler's condo at the Gregorian. "For obvious reasons, I believe possessed are surveilling these locations." He zoomed in on the condo. "It would be best if you and Miss Glass discreetly confirm this to be true. We must know if only caustic possessed are present. A knight could easily derail the plan."

I nodded. "And then what?"

"Your copy will expose herself at the best location and get into a car. At this point, there are two possibilities. Either the possessed will chase her or they will track her." He traced a red dotted line on the map. "In either scenario, the vehicle will proceed north along the interstate and arrive at this house." Fjoeruss drew an X on a house surrounded by trees. "Mr. Rock will need to be present to defend the golem and spirit away the body so the possessed cannot take it."

Tyler bit his lower lip. "What if we blew up the car and burned the golem? Would it leave behind a convincing corpse?"

Fjoeruss shook his head. "I'm afraid not. We must make certain the possessed do not take the corpse after the deed is done. Besides, according to Lydia's vision, we must have an intact corpse for the funeral."

"You're asking Tyler to put his life on the line for a golem?" I gripped Tyler's arm. "This is madness. Can't we use other golems to retrieve the body or hire security?"

"Bringing normal humans into the equation is out of the question," Fjoeruss said. "And if we use golems, we risk revealing outside help to the possessed. If they destroy a golem and realize what it is, they might suspect their target was also a fake."

"I'm not fighting for this thing." Tyler waved a hand at my copy. "I'm putting on a show to save your life, Em." Tyler's jaw set in determination. "I'll make it work."

I couldn't bear the thought of losing Tyler while he defended something that wasn't even alive. But this was one ledge I couldn't talk him down from. I frowned. "What am I supposed to do the entire time? Hide?"

"Once you identify the best location for the decoy, you will remain behind. Mr. Rock and the decoy will get into a car and lure the possessed to the target location." Fjoeruss circled the house with a finger. "If the plan fails, I will have grays on standby to assist Mr. Rock."

"By grays, you mean these golems?" Tyler nodded at the silent golem.

"Precisely." Fjoeruss tapped a small gray pendant on his suit jacket. "You will each have one of these for communications."

I felt somewhat relieved to hear this backup plan. "In that case, let's get this bloody awful thing done."

Fjoeruss checked his watch. "Rush hour traffic has already started. It's best if we wait until ten tomorrow morning so a traffic jam doesn't derail the plan immediately."

The gray man who'd escorted us here reached into its suit pocket and withdrew two gray, star-shaped pendants identical to the one Fjoeruss wore. I took mine and rolled the sharp points against my fingers, wondering if the star shape were symbolic of something. For some reason, it reminded me of the mysterious tridecagon waiting at home.

"Before we leave, I have a mystery you might be able to help us with." I described the thirteen-sided object and told Fjoeruss how it followed me.

The angel's brow furrowed. "You say it's perfectly seamless and impervious to harm?"

"It is."

Fjoeruss stared at me without speaking for so long, it seemed he might not say another word. But then he said, "I think there is significance to the number of sides, thirteen to be exact."

Tyler frowned. "You think it's demonic?"

"How does that make it demonic?" I asked.

"Thirteen sides—thirteen levels of Hell." Tyler shrugged. "If there's a connection, I don't know what it is."

Fjoeruss pursed his lips. "Given its affinity for Miss Glass, we can assume her soul powers have awakened it. Perhaps those very powers will also unlock it."

"So you have no idea what it is?" I said.

He shook his head. "No. But it's best if you keep it locked away. It might not be benevolent." Fjoeruss held up a hand as if to ward off further discussion. "Provided tomorrow's events go as planned, we will have a great deal to discuss, the first of which is your assistance to me."

I nodded. "Rooting out demonic agents at your companies."

"Yes." Fjoeruss closed his eyes for a moment. "I might also be able to find out more about this object and we can discuss trading information."

"Is everything a bargain with you?" I said. "Are you sure you're not Satan himself?"

The hint of a smirk touched his lips. "I have already given you far more for free than anyone in recent memory."

"My abilities are the key to cleaning your house of demons." I put a hand on my chest. "Don't you think helping me discover my lineage might aid me in those efforts?"

Fjoeruss shrugged. "You already sense and banish demons. There is little else I require of you."

"And here I thought we were becoming besties." Tyler sighed. "I guess that means you won't come to my birthday party?"

A sudden thought occurred to me. "How many people are in your employ, Fjoeruss?"

Something glinted in his eyes and the hint of a smirk returned. "Thousands worldwide."

That was when the weight of the task struck me. "Good lord. It'll take me weeks to examine everyone, won't it?"

Fjoeruss tilted his head slightly. "No, Miss Glass. It will take months."

CHAPTER 12

I very nearly called the man a bastard but bit my tongue. "In exchange for my life, you've made me your servant."

"You son of a bitch." Tyler shook his head slowly. "I should've known it was too good to be true."

Fjoeruss drew a deep breath and released a long sigh. "Is your life not worth a few months of work, Miss Glass?" He turned to Tyler. "Would you prefer she die, Mr. Rock?"

Tyler and I looked at each other then back to him and shook our heads.

"If anything, my price is too low." Fjoeruss massaged his forehead as if warding off a headache. "But I'm certain we can reach an agreement to uncover Miss Glass's past once this unpleasantness is behind us."

I swallowed my anger. Fjoeruss's price *was* rather low compared to the alternative. "Very well, sir. We will see you tomorrow."

He seemed relieved to watch us go.

The gray walked to the lift and pressed the button. The doors slid open without hesitation. Tyler and I followed it inside.

Tyler leaned against the wall during the descent. "Maybe Tilden is demonic somehow. I wish I had someone to ask."

The lift stopped, the doors opened, and we stepped into the landing bay. "Maybe it's anti-demon." I stared with trepidation at the flying carpet but stepped onboard without too much hesitation. "After all, I do banish demons."

Tyler got on next to me. "You might be right."

The golem stepped onto the carpet and we took off without further ado. Once safely deposited back at the new condo, I marched inside and up to the restrained tridecagon. "Tell me what you are."

It vibrated slightly in its restraints, lured by my presence, but did nothing else to indicate it understood me.

"Do you have any secrets to tell me?"

Nothing.

Tyler went into the kitchen and began cooking. I opened his laptop and ran a search on tridecagon and other related terms. The search engine assumed I misspelled the word and searched for something entirely different. I supposed that was as good as saying it had nothing for me. I tried cross-referencing it with "tridecagon" and "demon" but that returned too many results.

"Maybe we're using the wrong search engine," Tyler said. "Maybe we need a magic version."

"That's a great idea." I pinched his firm bum. "You're a looker *and* a thinker."

He laughed. "A man's gotta be talented to keep a woman these days."

"Yes, he does." I stood on tiptoe and kissed his nose. "Now make me a sandwich."

I dreaded the morning. I feared what might happen to Tyler. Caustic demons could be unpredictable unless whipped into submission by a greater power. And what if the human authorities intervened?

THE GRAY ARRIVED at nine the next morning and waited while we finished breakfast. We didn't go to Fjoeruss, but instead flew to OnTech. From the safety of the camouflaged bubble around the carpet and a height of about twenty feet, I watched ordinary humans walking down the sidewalk, riding bikes, and departing buses on their way to work.

"Sense anything?" Tyler said.

The sickly warmth of caustic demons grated my senses. "Oh, yes." I closed my eyes and felt six blips on my supernatural radar. A fifth blip burned brighter and hotter than the rest. If I concentrated hard, I saw flashes of red.

"Several caustics and at least one ruby." From this distance it wasn't easy discerning who were the possessed among the noms.

Tyler pointed out two men leaning against a car. "They're watching everyone like hawks. I'd bet their possessed." His finger found another suspicious individual, a dark-haired woman with yoga pants and a tight top. A newspaper hid most of her face, but her eyes peered over it. "She's not even reading her newspaper."

I closed my eyes and glimpsed a flash of red. "She's a ruby."

THE HIGH-PITCHED WHIR of small blades came from above. I looked up and spotted two black quadcopter drones circling the outside of the building at the same level where OnTech resided. Tyler noticed them too.

He whistled. "Damn, they've gone high tech."

Once, Jack had taken his expensive drone to the park and shown us how he could record aerial footage with his phone. His controller wasn't large, but still easy to spot. I looked below and saw no one holding wireless remotes or other means of controlling the drones.

Tyler pointed to a windowless black van parked at the curb. Two tall antennas sprouted from the roof. He whistled again. "Damn, they went with a surveillance van and everything. I'll bet the drones are being controlled from inside there."

"I agree."

Tyler turned to the gray golem. "There are way too many possessed here. Let's go to the Gregorian."

It didn't respond.

I tapped the pendant Fjoeruss gave us and told him what I'd told Tyler.

The gray came to life. It turned towards us and spoke. "Perhaps dropping the lure at the Gregorian is better."

My forehead pinched. "Fjoeruss, are you speaking through the golem?"

It nodded. "I am using its eyes and ears as well."

"Neat trick," Tyler said. "What's the point of the pendants if you can use the golem?"

Fjoeruss didn't respond. The flying carpet rose and swooshed above the buildings until we reached the Gregorian. We hovered about twenty feet over the crowd on the sidewalk below.

The ground below swarmed with demonic heat. I closed my eyes and glimpsed so many auras, it took me a moment to count them all. "Houston, we have a problem."

Tyler's eyebrows rose. "What is it?"

I grimaced. "I sense at least a dozen caustics and two rubies here."

Tyler pointed out three drones circling not far above. His finger lowered to street level and identified another black van at the curb. He shook his head. "I can't believe Domathus is going through so much trouble to kill you. He's got all the time in the world, but he sent no less than three knights after you. Why is he in such a hurry?"

The golem spoke. "It is odd." Fjoeruss sounded bemused as well. "Perhaps it's not merely revenge. Perhaps Domathus has plans Miss Glass might foil."

I concentrated on the sidewalk around the Gregorian and managed to pick out candidates for the ruby possessed. Some caustics stood out merely because of their haggard appearance and mannerisms.

My blond lookalike stepped out of the sliding door from the black van and looked around. "Look, that's her!"

Tyler growled. "That must be an illusion disguise. Domathus wants to mind-fuck you hard before finishing you off."

I focused on her and closed my eyes. "I think she's a ruby."

TYLER SHOOK HIS HEAD. "What does this mean for the plan?"

"It means we improvise," Fjoeruss said. "We drop the lure at OnTech. I dispatched two grays to monitor the operation. If possible, they will separate the ruby from the caustics."

"What if they can't?" I said.

"Then we kill the possessed. The ruby will return to Haedaemos none the wiser."

Tyler nodded grimly. "Then let's do it."

One of the drones began to beep as it drifted closer. It spun on its axis, the lens of a small camera fixed straight on our position. Fuzzy gray light beams emanated from a small bulb beneath the camera.

The gray peered at it. "That's no ordinary drone." Its limbs jerked spasmodically. "Something from the drone is disrupting the aether." The golem went stiff, but its mouth still moved. "You must control the carpet. There's—"

"How?" Tyler said.

The gray didn't respond. I tapped the pendant, but whatever broke Fjoeruss's connection to the golem affected it as well. The carpet began to spin, and the golem toppled over the side. Our ride veered drunkenly towards the Gregorian, an aircraft without a pilot. Without the magical inertial dampeners, we struggled to maintain our balance.

"How in the hell do you control this thing?" Tyler gripped the sides of the carpet, but it didn't respond. The carpet spiraled out of control, lurching up several feet then diving towards the ground. The only question was whether we'd hit the building before we crashed into the ground.

The slow spin made me dizzy. I grasped Tyler for support. He growled and swept me into his arms. "Hang on, babe."

I looped my arms around his neck. The carpet clipped one of the saplings lining the semicircular drive in front of the Gregorian. The clockwise spin abruptly stopped. If not for the magic holding us firm to the carpet, we would have flown off. The carpet tilted forward and accelerated towards the granite balustrade around the second-floor terrace.

A stretch Hummer steered into the driveway. Tyler glanced at the building, then down at the vehicle and seemed to make up his mind. With a grunt, he leapt, clearing twenty feet of open air. His feet slammed onto the roof of the Hummer, but the sideways momentum proved too much. He fell sideways. I flew from his arms and rolled across the roof, down the windscreen, and came to a stop on the hood.

The wide eyes of a chubby limousine driver looked back at me. I pushed up to my knees and slid off the hood, past the grill and onto the driveway. Despite my spill, I was still intact. Tyler leapt to the ground next to me.

"We've got to go!" He said.

But a jubilant shout and the whirring of drones drew my attention to the demonic crowd on the sidewalk only fifty feet away. Mad howls and lascivious grins met my view.

"It's the bitch!" One shouted.

"Tear her apart!"

My lookalike locked eyes with me, a feral smirk on her face. "There you are, dear Emily!"

And the chase was on.

Startled noms stumbled out of their ordinary routines and watched in shock as a dozen people dashed from their midst and rushed me.

"Fuck!" Tyler tried the door to the stretched Hummer, but it was locked. He swept me up and threw me over a shoulder, dashing madly away. He abruptly turned, but I couldn't see why, because my head bounced against his back. I braced my hands on his hips and looked behind us.

Insanity gleamed in the eyes of our pursuers. A man and the blond woman in tight athletic gear followed not far behind. Their calm, calculating demeanors identified them as the ruby possessed. They were there to confirm my death. Caustics, as a general rule, could not be trusted.

The concrete sidewalk gave way to the asphalt drive leading to the guest car park behind the building. Tyler set me down roughly on my feet. Someone cursed and grunted. I staggered dizzily.

"Asshole!" The sound of a fist and another grunt.

I leaned against a car to steady myself and saw a man in a black leather jacket lying on the ground. A matching helmet lay inches from his outstretched fingers. Tyler climbed on a black motorcycle, twisted a key, and pressed a button. The engine roared to life. He gave me an impatient look. "Get on!"

All the jostling against his back must have addled my wits, but I somehow had the presence of mind to sweep my leg across the seat and wrap both arms around his waist. The engine throbbed deep and loud. Tyler planted a leg on the ground. Rubber screeched against asphalt, spinning the bike one hundred eighty degrees in the parking space.

Tyler's leg came off the ground and the bike leapt forward. He veered left toward the car park exit. Unfortunately, there was nowhere to go. A fence surrounded the car park, and the driveway led into a garage beneath the Gregorian. Our pursuers seemed to realize this. Half of them spread out to block our path back to the garage. The others reversed course and ran towards cars parked at the curb in front of the building.

Two snarling caustics produced machetes from beneath their coats. They were the least of our worries, I realized, as several others drew pistols. One held a short-barrel rifle with a scope.

"Shit." Tyler leaned hard right. Shots popped like firecrackers. Bullets dinged against cars. People screamed and shouted in the distance. "Fjoeruss, we need some help!"

The pendant crackled and the angel's voice came through with static. "The drones have anti-magic arcnology. Golems will not function near them."

The three drones hovered overhead, cameras tracking us. A dozen armed possessed stood between us and the only means of escape. The iron fence around the car park was too tall and too substantial to drive through.

It seemed I would be the one in the coffin after all.

CHAPTER 13

Tyler drove to the far end of the car park and stopped behind a white pickup truck. Bullets whizzed through the air. Windows shattered and metal pinged. He grinned and looked at me over his shoulder. "Enough excitement?"

"Too much!" I buried my face in his back. "I love you, Tyler. I'm sorry it's going to end this way."

His grin widened. "They were idiots to arm those caustics. They'll run out of bullets before they even get to us." Tyler cocked his ear. "I hear sirens. The police are on the way."

"They won't be here soon enough," I said.

Tyler peered around the corner of the truck. "Doesn't matter. Hold on."

"For what?" Shots rang out, some distant, others seemingly feet away.

I poked my head up and peered through the broken windows on the pickup truck. The car park was three rows wide and perhaps fifty yards long. The possessed formed a cordon across the only way out and walked briskly down the outer aisle. Some fired random shots into the cars, cackling with glee. The ruby possessed followed a short distance behind them.

My blond lookalike laughed with glee. She cupped hands around her mouth and shouted, "It's over, Emily. Come on out and let us end this quickly."

"Never!" I shouted back.

"Not even to meet your dear cousin?"

I wanted to punch her so badly my hands curled into fists. "I don't have any cousins, you demonic bitch!"

"Oh, but you do." She laughed as if it were the funniest thing in the world. "Your Aunt Lydia never told you, did she? Never told you how she got rid of me when I was a babe."

I resisted the urge to stick out my head and stare her in the eyes. "It's a trick," I said to Tyler. "They're stalling us."

"Tricky bastards." Tyler revved the motorcycle engine. "Then we'll have to trick them right back."

The other group of possessed guarding the parking garage began working their way towards the main group. Only one of them held a weapon—a black pistol. Isabel and I had frequented a gun range with our redneck college friends, but I'd never taken the time to thoroughly educate myself about pistols or become proficient shooting them. But there was one thing I remembered. The slide on the top of the pistol was back, exposing part of the barrel. That meant it was out of ammunition.

I pointed it out to Tyler. "At least they can't shoot us."

"Good eye, babe." Tyler bit his lower lip. "Hang on. Here we go."

The motorcycle shot from behind the pickup toward the entrance to the parking garage. Shots rang out behind us. The possessed with the empty pistol aimed it and pulled the trigger several times to no effect. He threw himself in front of the bike, pistol upraised like a blunt weapon. His companions angled toward us, but they were too slow. Tyler dodged the diving caustic at the last instant, and we sped past them.

"Are we going to the condo?" I asked.

"No way. For all we know, they booby-trapped it." Tyler angled right, but all I saw ahead was a concrete wall and the entrance to the garage.

"Then where are we going?"

Tyler steered into the garage and drove down the ramp. He screeched to a stop at the elevator and punched the button a dozen times in rapid-fire succession.

"I thought we weren't going to the condo!"

"We're not." He hit the button again.

Shouts echoed. Footsteps pounded against concrete. Silhouettes appeared at the garage entrance a few hundred feet away. Shots exploded. Bullets zinged off concrete. One took a divot out of the wall next to the lift. A bell dinged, and the doors slid open.

"Get the bitch!" someone shouted.

My fake cousin's voice rang out behind them. "Cover the front of the building."

The engine revved and the bike lurched into the lift. The front wheel hit the back wall, but we fit, barely. Tyler pounded the lobby button. Bullets rained around us. I expected to feel the burn of lead penetrate my flesh at any moment. The doors slid shut and the shots became muffled. Seconds later, the doors opened into the lobby.

A man with yellowed teeth waited just down the hall from us. He leered and lunged. Tyler revved the bike and accelerated out of the lift. The rear wheel slid sideways on the slick marble floor. Tyler lifted a leg and kicked the man square in the chest. With a terrible shriek, the caustic flew back and slammed into the wall.

The concierge lay slumped over his desk, blood pooling on the floor.

"Damn it!" Tyler pounded the handlebars. "They killed Kenny."

"Those bastards!" I'd only spoken to the man a few times, but he'd been very kind.

The engine thrummed. Rubber found traction on the marble and we flew toward the exit. I expected Tyler to ram through the double doors, but instead, he slowed and gently nosed them open with the front wheel.

Sickly heat pinged against my senses. The sliding door on the surveillance van gaped open. Two caustic possessed knelt on the side-walk, rifles at the ready. We had nowhere to go.

"Police! Put down your weapons!" Dark uniforms swarmed between parked cars near the van.

The possessed open fire at us. We ducked. The cops responded with a hail of bullets and the gunmen went down. Tyler patted his chest, as if checking for bullet holes, then revved the throttle and angled for the road.

"Police! Halt!"

Tyler ignored their commands.

A black pickup roared down the driveway from the guest car park on our left. Tyler veered onto the road. The truck rumbled in pursuit, a silver sedan and a red coupe close behind it. I saw the determined face of my blond lookalike behind the wheel of the pickup. The road was practically empty, and the sidewalks clear of all but a few pedestrians. Word of a shooting had probably put the entire area on lockdown.

I looked back and up. We outdistanced the drones easily, but the pickup and two cars were another matter. Tyler took turns seemingly at random. The communication pendant crackled on, and I struggled to hear Fjoeruss over the rush of wind.

"You're going the wrong way."

Tyler shouted back. "How do I get to the interstate?"

A moment passed. "Change of plans," Fjoeruss said. "Continue south and turn right on Fourteenth Street."

"How do you know where we are?" I said.

"The pendants of course."

I should have known.

Midtown traffic grew heavier, but not enough to slow our progress. Unfortunately, the pickup and two cars pursuing us had plenty of room to maneuver around vehicles. We flew up an incline and caught air for an instant. Tyler accelerated through a red light, dodging between cars. The pickup clipped the tail of a compact car and sent it spinning. Engine roaring, it surged after us. The red coupe slipped around the pickup and quickly gained ground. I saw flashing lights and heard sirens, but the police were too far away to be of any help.

Tyler leaned hard right at the next intersection. A pedestrian shouted and jumped out of the crosswalk. Horns blared. Tires screeched behind us. I looked back and saw the red coupe only a few car lengths back. A man in the passenger seat leered back at me. I only sensed one caustic close enough to be in the car, so one of the people in that car wasn't possessed.

The pickup's tires chirped as it tried to take the corner, but it wasn't up to the task. It slowed and lost ground. The blue sedan dodged around it, nearly hit another car, and veered back into the lane.

"We're on Fourteenth," Tyler shouted. "Where to now?"

"Right at the dead end, and the next left on Huff," Fjoeruss said.

The man in the passenger seat of the red car leaned out and brandished a pistol. Tyler looked in the rear-view mirror. "Shit!" He swerved around an SUV and pulled directly in front of it. There was nothing else ahead for a hundred yards. A shot rang out.

The driver of the SUV went wide-eyed and yanked his steering wheel right. The vehicle spun out of control. White smoke boiled from the tires. I expected Tyler to speed up. Instead, he jammed on the brakes. The SUV spun past us. The acrid stink of melted rubber burned my nose.

The driver of the red coupe was too busy dodging the SUV to notice us. Surprise registered in the passenger's eyes as we dropped back even with him. Tyler chopped his left hand down on the other man's wrist and in one smooth motion grabbed the pistol. But he had it by the barrel, not the handle.

"Ow, it's hot!" He thrust it around his side. "Take it, Em!"

I released my death grip on his waist with my left hand and gripped the handle. I wasn't left-handed, but we were so close, I didn't need to be. I swung the pistol towards the passenger and fired. The driver cried out in pain and the car swerved toward us.

Tyler hit the brakes again and the red coupe spun out in front of us. The roar of another engine sounded from behind. I looked back just as the blue car tried to ram us. The motorcycle leaned left, and the bumper of the blue car narrowly missed the back tire. My arm swung automatically back around Tyler. I took my finger off the trigger so I didn't accidentally shoot him.

Our lost momentum gave the pickup time to catch up. Tyler made a U-turn. The blue car and pickup skidded around after us. But the motorcycle was far nimbler. Tyler barked a laugh and turned us back around again, aiming right between them.

"Shoot them!"

I barely had the presence of mind to know what he meant. I leaned left, aimed at the pickup and fired three shots. Bullets pierced the windscreen. The two possessed ducked. I aimed at the blue car and fired a shot but missed. We dodged between our pursuers and accelerated. The red coupe sat sideways in the roadside ditch, wheels spinning in mud.

My ears rang and my arm ached from the weight of the gun and the kickback. The wind drew tears from my eyes. I rested my left hand on Tyler's leg and wiped my face on his shirt.

We reached the next intersection and followed Fjoeruss's directions. The pickup and blue car followed behind, but we had a hundred yards on them. Another left, a right, and a sharp left took us on a rutted asphalt road that soon gave way to gravel. A chain-link gate hung open next to an empty guard booth. Thick forest to one side and tall weeds on the other closed in around the gravel road, blocking my view.

Fjoeruss's voice came over Tyler's pendant, but I couldn't make out what he said over the roar of the motorcycle.

A black sedan pulled out of the weeds and blocked the road.

My heart rose in my throat. "Watch out!"

Tyler skidded to a stop. "Get off, Em!"

He unslung my right leg with a gentle push. I wobbled unevenly. Something pushed past me. Someone else grabbed me and yanked me into darkness. A car door slammed, and we lurched backward. The motorcycle engine roared and Tyler sped past in front of us, my twin holding onto his waist.

The front of the car shimmered into invisibility. An instant later, the pickup and blue sedan sped past. A gray sat to my left. Another occupied the driver's seat. The one to my left gave me a pair of glasses. I blinked in confusion before realizing I was supposed to put them on.

When I did, I my perspective shifted as if looking through virtual reality glasses. I looked down from a vantage point perhaps twenty feet above and to the side of the motorcycle. Forest stretched ahead of me, the cityscape of Atlanta rising in the distance. I turned my head and the view rotated. A great field of grass and weeds led to more trees and something else I couldn't quite make out. I heard wind rushing past and roaring engines in the near distance.

"You're looking from the perspective of an all-seeing eye," Fjoeruss said, presumably through the gray to my left.

The ASE paced the motorcycle as it raced along the road toward a great mound of dirt straight ahead. The road twisted left, but a chain link fence blocked it. Tendrils of cold fear snaked around my heart. "Where are they going?"

Fjoeruss didn't answer.

It was then that I identified the strange geological formation ahead. Trees grew on a cliff some distance away from the mound. The viewpoint rose higher and more cliffs came into view. The image resolved into a complete picture—a vast pit with sparkling blue water hundreds of feet below.

"It's a bloody quarry!" And Tyler showed no signs of slowing the motorcycle. "Fjoeruss, what's he doing?"

The angel spoke through the gray next to me. "Under the circumstances, the only thing we can do."

The motorcycle leapt the mound and flew into empty space. I screamed and reached out as if I could cradle Tyler in my hands and save him. But all I could do was watch helplessly as he tumbled over the cliff. The motorcycle slammed onto the rocky shore below, throwing my shrieking clone head over heels through the air. She slammed into a boulder. Blood splattered from her head.

I couldn't stop screaming.

CHAPTER 14

"Please calm yourself, Miss Glass." The gray gripped my hand. "Mr. Rock is unharmed."

The viewpoint dropped lower. Tyler hopped nimbly off a flying carpet not far from the wreckage and flopped onto the ground, crying out in pain. My ragged cries died in my throat. I wiped tears from my eyes.

I looked past the visuals in the glasses and glared at the gray. "Why didn't you tell me a flying carpet was waiting?"

Fjoeruss spoke through the gray. "I did. You should have heard the instructions through the pendant."

I probably hadn't heard them over the rush of wind and engine noise while on the motorcycle, but that made me no less furious. I put the glasses back on and watched. The viewpoint rose back to the cliff where the pickup and blue car skidded to a halt. The possessed gathered at the edge and looked down.

The caustics from the red car howled with laughter and glee. "She's dead!"

"Splat!" The other smacked his hands together.

The blond woman's face twitched between a smile and a frown, as if she couldn't find the right emotion to express.

Tyler's tortured shouts echoed from the quarry. "You fucking killed her!" I looked down at him. He struggled to his feet, favoring a leg as if it were broken. "I'll have your souls for this, you goddamned bastards!"

That only made the caustics laugh harder.

The blonde held a pair of binoculars to her eyes and looked down. Her jaw tightened and her face once again flicked through a series of emotions. She handed the binoculars to the male. He gazed down for a moment. Nodded. I couldn't hear what they said to each other, but it seemed as though they agreed I was dead.

The male pointed towards the pickup and the chain link fence. He punched a fist into his other hand, perhaps talking about ramming down the fence.

One of the caustics shouted, "I want to eat her!"

The other yelled, "I want to fuck her and eat her and kill and fuck the other one!"

The blonde backhanded a caustic so hard he slammed into the red car. She climbed into the driver's seat of the pickup. The male slid into the other side. They seemed to argue for a moment before reaching a decision. The pickup angled for the fence. The tires spun in the gravel and it picked up speed. The front end rammed into the fence.

Apparently, it was no ordinary chain link, because it stopped the pickup cold in its tracks. They slammed into it again. The hood buckled. Steam shot from beneath the hood. The caustics burst into laughter, pointing and shouting obscenities at the others.

The pickup shuddered and the engine died. The blonde and her male companion got out of the pickup and stalked towards the caustics. With a savage twist, the woman broke the neck of one caustic. The male kneed the other caustic in the stomach, picked him up, and threw him over the cliff. His howls ended abruptly.

I looked down at Tyler. He stared at the dead caustic fifty feet from the motorcycle wreckage, then started cursing the pair atop the cliff. They watched him for a moment, then the blonde said, "Sucks that she's dead, but I can definitely take over if you want."

"Fuck you!" Tyler shouted.

The blonde grinned. "That's the idea, hot stuff."

She and the male possessed turned and got into the blue sedan. The car backed up and turned around, then drove away. I took off the glasses and waited. A moment later, the blue car sped past us. Not long after, Fjoeruss's voice emanated from the gray. "The possessed have left the area. Stand by for retrieval."

The car lifted off, the camouflage around the hood shimmering as it adapted to the change in scenery. We flew over the quarry and landed near the wreckage.

"Do you sense any demon presence?" the gray asked.

I concentrated but felt nothing except the sensual heat coming from Tyler. "It's clear."

The gray got out and picked up my dead clone, then deposited it into the boot. Tyler slid into the back seat next to me, a wolfish grin on his face. I wanted to slap it right off.

"Why are you so fucking amused?" I said. "I thought you'd killed yourself!"

Alarm flashed in his eyes. "You didn't hear what Fjoeruss told me to do?"

"No." I couldn't decide if I should be crying with relief or burning with anger. "I had no idea what was going on."

"I'm sorry, baby." His grin faded and he gripped me in a tight embrace. "But we did it." He wiped tears from his eyes. "You're safe."

His tears unleashed a flood of emotions from me. I was so happy. So relieved. So glad it was over for now. Even if I belonged to Fjoeruss for the next few months, it was worth it. I buried my face in his chest and took deep breaths to keep the sobs at bay.

A mountain of stress slid off my back. I gasped with relief. Having a price on my head had been more frightening than I'd wanted to admit, especially when it involved an army of infernal spirits.

Fjoeruss spoke through the gray again. "We aren't quite done yet, Miss Glass. Now you must plan the funeral."

Another burden settled on my shoulders. "Must I really?"

"Yes, you must." The gray's unblinking eyes stayed on me. "I suggest you have it in England. That way you can minimize who attends and it will spare you having to lie to local friends."

I gave it some thought. "So I don't need to tell Isabel?"

"It's best to keep those involved to a minimum. Domathus will certainly send a minion to watch the proceedings. A smaller crowd will make an outsider easier to identify."

I nodded. "We'll tell my father about the ruse. He'll be able to plan the funeral better than I can."

Tyler blew out a breath. "Man, I feel so much better. It's like I've been carrying a lead weight in my stomach."

The gray reached into its suit jacket pocket and withdrew a black lace choker with a gray gem on the front. "Wear this if you must go into public and press the gem to activate the charm. An illusion will disguise your features. It must be deactivated for thirty minutes to recharge, so do not use it for more than three hours at a time."

I took the offering and coiled it in my palm. "When do I start my work for you?"

"I estimate it will take a week to execute the funeral. Report to me two weeks from tomorrow. That should be sufficient." The gray looked away from me and leaned back in the seat.

I suspected Fjoeruss had disconnected from it.

"Man, must be a power trip having an army of superhuman puppets." Tyler prodded the gray with a finger. "I'll bet Fjoeruss has spies everywhere."

"They aren't particularly lifelike." I studied the pale gray skin. Humans would certainly notice the strange hue, though it might not even occur to them that the golem wasn't a person. "But the copy of me could have replaced me outright." I looked at the gray, almost expecting Fjoeruss to chime in, but he didn't.

Tyler shrugged. "It looks like you, but it couldn't act like you in the long term."

The car reached the new condo and landed on the helipad. Tyler and I hopped out. With the door closed, only a slight ripple betrayed the car's position as it glided silently away.

"I don't know about you, but I'm hungry." Tyler took my hand and led me inside to the kitchen. "Dumping this stress really restored my appetite."

I had to admit I was ravenous too. "I believe I could eat anything right now." I walked to a mirror and slipped the choker around my neck. I barely felt the material against my skin. A light touch against the gem made my face ripple. I gasped. An older woman stared back. Her hair was as long as mine but streaked with gray. Her eyes a dull brown, her nose slightly crooked. Fine wrinkles lined her face and creased her brow. She wasn't homely, but no man would give her a second look.

"Holy shit." Tyler stared at me from across the room. "Fjoeruss hit you with the age stick a few times, babe."

I smiled and the woman smiled back with passably white, but crooked teeth. I winked and she winked. It was quite surreal. I turned toward my love and said, "Does this mean you don't want to have sex?"

He chortled. "Babe, I will never turn down sex with you, no matter how you look."

I giggled a little. "Maybe we should put that to the test after we eat."

Tyler's wolfish grin appeared. "Oh, we definitely will."

And we did.

After our celebratory romp, I went outside to the roof with white wine and a book to enjoy the hot tub in the garden. Tyler came out moments later, gloriously naked despite the cold wind blowing across the roof. His demon spirit made him abnormally warm most of the time, while I sprouted goosebumps from even the slightest of chills.

He slid into the water next to me and kissed me on the cheek. "Not to spoil the mood, but maybe we should contact your father and let him start on funeral preparations."

"I already sent him a text from the burner phone." I closed my book and set it on the marble ledge. "Hopefully he'll reply soon." I picked up the phone and looked at the screen, but there were no new notifications. I shrugged. "He usually takes his time to answer."

"It's not like we can't plan things ourselves." Tyler leaned back and traced a finger up my thigh. His eyes grew serious. "Who would you want at your funeral?"

"At my real funeral? You, Izzy, Dad, Aunt Lydia, Jack." I tapped a finger on my lips. "Anyone else is optional."

"Well, since Isabel and Jack aren't going to know about it, sounds like we only need to plan for a couple of people." Tyler frowned. "Seems awfully sparse."

"Yes, it does." I smiled. "Perhaps we need some filler people, so my fake funeral doesn't appear abysmal."

"Maybe we should tell Lydia," Tyler said. "I'll bet she could drum up a few extras."

I nodded. "That might be wise. I'll ask my father whenever he calls." My mind turned to packing for an overseas trip. Tyler had chartered an airplane for our last vacation so it was less of a hassle. Thinking of England returned my thoughts to the mystery of my mother and aunt's origins. The two weeks Fjoeruss allotted me might grant me time to do a little digging.

"Deep thoughts?" Tyler nudged me with his shoulder.

I blinked from my trance and nodded. "I'd like to get to England as soon as possible. I want to see if there are any records of my mother and Lydia at Little Angel Orphanage."

"What makes you think that orphanage would have them?" Tyler asked.

"My grandmother couldn't have children, but only a doctor in London and this orphanage knew." I shrugged. "It's no random coincidence two baby girls were left at my grandparent's house. I think whoever did it knew they couldn't have children."

Tyler nodded. "Solid deduction, Em. Sherlock Holmes would be proud."

I chuckled. "It's elementary, my dear Watson."

"Then let's go tomorrow." Tyler grinned. "We don't even have to fly. We can drive."

I frowned. "How do you propose we drive across the Atlantic?"

"The Obsidian Arch, of course." He shivered with excitement. "We'll drive down to the Grotto and head on through. From what I understand, you can go straight to London."

I felt a bit daft for not thinking of magical methods of travel. "That's a lovely idea. But I wonder if you can even drive your car over there without the proper license plate."

He snapped his fingers. "Damn, I didn't think of that."

But his enthusiasm infected me. "Perhaps Fjoeruss can help. I need to tell him where to send the body anyway." I felt a little morbid discussing my deceased copy even though it was literally an animated doll and nothing more.

"Yeah!" Tyler jumped out of the bubbling water and headed toward the condo. "I'll get a comm pendant and ask him right now."

He returned moments later, more excited than a kid on Christmas morning. "We are all set, babe." Tyler hopped in the hot tub, splashing water everywhere. "Tomorrow morning, we're headed to England."

CHAPTER 15

A gray delivered one of Fjoeruss's magical sedans for the journey the next morning, landing on the helipad. It handed Tyler a parchment of instructions for changing the configuration to fit whichever country we happened to be in. A few taps on a magical computer tablet moved the steering wheel to the right side of the car and changed the license plates to British.

"Wonder if it can shoot oil slicks and drop caltrops too." Tyler tapped away on the tablet like an overexcited boy, heedless of what havoc he might cause if he activated the wrong function.

His fooling around caused the boot lid to pop open. I walked around to close it and shrieked in fright. A battered body wrapped in clear plastic stared at me with dead eyes. I soon realized it wasn't a hooker, but my clone. "Good lord. If the police pull us over how will we explain this?"

Tyler walked around and laughed. "Why in the world didn't he use a body bag? It's like something out of a horror movie."

"Indeed." I shuddered. "Shall we pack the car and get going?"

Tyler nodded. "Yep. I'll be right back." He rushed inside and returned a moment later with all our suitcases. The large boot held everything easily even with the dead clone inside. Tyler covered her with a blanket and said, "Creepy as hell."

"It's horrid." Fake or not, I didn't relish traveling with a corpse in the boot.

He went back inside and returned with Tilden the tridecagon, which he strapped next to the suitcases. "Just in case we find someone who knows what this is."

"One can always hope." I climbed into the passenger seat. The gray that had piloted the car sat on a bench near our back door and went still. I supposed it would wait there, rain or shine, until our return.

Tyler examined the controls. "Looks pretty similar to George's." He tapped a button to turn on the illusion cloak and the hood shimmered into near invisibility. The pull of a lever levitated the car. The accelerator thrust us forward, and the steering wheel turned left or right. Within moments we traversed Midtown and landed at the truck loading zone behind Phipps Plaza in Buckhead.

The loading zone was empty, so Tyler uncloaked the car and drove it into the parking garage. He drove into a dead end and proceeded through an illusionary wall. A winding ramp took us at least a mile belowground to a massive car park. All manner of vehicles sat in the slots, from Toyotas to Bentleys to a purple Tesla with green polka-dots.

Innocuous double doors to the left of the car park led inside the Grotto, a pocket city filled with all manner of wonders we had yet to fully explore. Several long queues wrapped around a maze of cordons, travelers waiting their turn to enter the Obsidian Arch. The arch itself towered to the right, nearly reaching the ceiling of the massive cavern.

The arch was tall and wide enough to easily accommodate several city buses side-by-side, so it would be no problem driving the sedan through. Tyler parked next to a pink Ferrari. I activated my disguise and we joined the queue at the ticket booth. Unlike the travel queue, it was fairly short. I wondered if most regular travelers had a daily pass they used instead of purchasing a ticket every day.

My senses tingled from every direction. I felt the cold emanations of vampires, hot copper-scented auras that might be lycans. Images of flaming blue orbs flashed through my mind's eye. I knew from my orientation classes they were from magicians—or Arcanes, as they preferred to be called. The swarming sensations nearly overwhelmed me, so I blocked out as much as I could.

"What in the world are those?" Tyler pointed to a frightening sight. A creature that resembled a gelatinous brain with long tentacles drifted the border of the parking lot. I risked opening my senses to see if I could identify it, but it was too far away.

"Minders," a young man behind us said. "They're using them like guard dogs now." He grimaced. "Don't know why."

"What the hell do you mean, no discounts!" A man in a cowboy hat ahead of us glared at the man inside the ticket booth. The young man next to him frowned and ran a hand through thick black hair. He looked oddly familiar, but I couldn't quite place him.

"Conclave ruled it was unfair the Arcanes got discounts while others paid full price." The ticket master grunted. "Take it up with them if you don't like it."

"Four hundred tinsel is a rip-off!" The other man's face flushed bright red.

The ticket master shrugged and began fiddling with a computer tablet.

The young man looked uneasily at his cowboy friend. "Uh, how much is that in dollars?"

"The exchange rate sucks right now." The man in the cowboy hat clenched and unclenched his fists. "One tinsel is worth two bucks."

Tyler blew out an impatient sigh and rolled his eyes. He seemed ready to say something when the young man jerked his friend away from the ticket booth and pulled him to the side. I couldn't stop looking at him, trying to figure out why he looked so familiar. He resembled someone I'd met before.

I risked a peek at his aura and sensed demonic heat. He wasn't possessed. He was a demon spawn—a Daemos. His friend was an Arcane.

What an odd pair.

I almost asked him who he was, but the young man stiffened with fright. I followed his gaze and saw a cute blond girl skipping out of the doors that led into the Grotto. He yanked his older companion out of sight behind the ticket booth.

What in the bloody hell was that about?

Tyler stepped in front of me with a pair of silver tickets. "We're good to go."

"How much?" I asked.

"I sprung a couple thousand tinsel for fast-pass tickets so we don't have to wait in line." He took my hand. "What were you looking at?"

I nodded toward the blond girl. "That young man in front of us seemed awfully frightened of her."

Tyler's forehead scrunched. "Man, there are some real weirdos around here."

"I'm inclined to agree." We went back to the car and got inside. "What's really odd is the young man was a Daemos and his friend was Arcane."

"I thought most people didn't like Daemos." Tyler settled into his seat. "I wish I could become one."

I rubbed his hand. "Perhaps we could contact David Slade and ask if he's heard from Kassallandra."

"Yeah. I just hate to bug him."

David Slade had helped us fight Domathus and his minions in our final battle with them. I didn't know why people disliked Daemos. All the ones I'd met had been quite pleasant. David's sister Vallaena was perhaps the most impressive person I'd ever met. And that was when it hit me. I snapped my fingers. "That young man looked a lot like David Slade."

Tyler's eyes widened. "Yeah, you're right. Maybe they're related."

Tyler drove to a separate area for fast passes where we caught poisonous glares from the people waiting in the normal queues. The words *Queens Gate* flashed in the air above the travel queues. "That's us," Tyler said. "Queens Gate was five destinations away until I got the fast pass."

"They really need to optimize their queue system," I said. "This looks like an awful mess for daily commuters."

"That's for sure." Tyler pulled up to a line and stopped the car.

Dozens of other cars pulled in behind us. A young boy guided mules and other beasts from a manger and paired them up with travelers in the lines. I couldn't imagine how anyone kept it all straight in their head. It was enough to drive anyone suffering from OCD quite mad.

A klaxon wailed. A low hum grew louder and louder until it vibrated down to my very core. White and purple lightning flashed all around the giant black arch. One last brilliant flash, and the air tore open into a gateway.

An Arcane in black and yellow-striped robes waved Tyler forward like a traffic cop.

Tyler snorted. "That robe is ridiculous. Makes him look like a bee."

I spotted others wearing the same robes. "Must be the required uniform here."

The other cars didn't follow us straightaway. I looked back and saw the others driving forward once we'd nearly reached the arch. Apparently, the fast pass was quite the VIP experience. As we crossed the gateway threshold, the world seemed to narrow to a tunnel and snap back an instant later. My insides lurched as if I'd just ridden the shortest roller coaster in the world.

In a flash, we were in another arch waystation very similar to the one we'd just left. But this one was thousands of miles away in England. I should have been in awe, but it felt as if we'd barely gone a hundred yards. Tyler drove past a queue of cars waiting to go in the opposite direction and parked in the first slot he found.

He slapped the steering wheel. "Damn, that was awesome!" He gripped my hands. "Can you believe that's all there is to traveling anywhere in the world? I'm never flying again!"

I squeezed his hands. "I'm so happy, darling. Now, can we get on with business?"

Tyler grinned. "You're not impressed."

"It's very impressive, yes, but there's not much to it." I shrugged. "Perhaps it'll hit me when we go to London above."

"Yeah, but first we've got other business." He pointed to ornate double doors. "I want to go into town and get myself a new phone."

"Town?"

He nodded. "Yeah. Queens Gate."

I used the timer app on my burner phone to let me know when I needed to deactivate my disguise charm. "I didn't think you cared for technology."

Tyler caressed the tablet screen in the car. "Yeah, but arcnology is awesome."

I groaned.

On the other side of the parking lot a rope cordon held in a large mob of protesters. People thrust signs into the air and shouted, "Queens Gate is for everyone!" A woman with a pale face waved a sign that said,

Vampires are people too! A pack of bearded men howled in haunting unison. It was quite a spectacle.

"What in the hell is going on here?" Tyler took my hand and we made our way toward a group of soldiers in red uniforms. The tall bearskin hats of the Queen's guard perched atop their heads. The line to enter the doors wasn't very long and we soon reached a man in a dark suit.

"What's your business in Queens Gate?" he asked.

"I want to buy an Orange phone," Tyler replied.

The man nodded. "Very well." He waved a wand at Tyler and said something that sounded very much like *Scooby Doo*. Glowing words appeared in the air.

Demon, Null, AP-N/A

I frowned. "What does AP mean?"

The man ignored me and wore a frown of his own as he studied the words. "Interesting," he muttered. "You're clear to pass."

I stepped forward and he waved the wand over me, repeating his magic words. "Are you really saying Scooby Doo?" I asked.

He ignored me once again and studied the results of his magical scan. This time the words said, *UKNOWN, UNKNOWN, AP-ERROR.* He shook his wand and examined it as if something might be wrong. "What in the bloody hell?"

It was refreshing to be surrounded by British accents again, but the results of my scan were a bit worrying. "Shouldn't it say human?" I said.

"Are you a nom?" the man asked. "If so, it should read nom, nom, AP zero."

"Well, try again." I straightened and put my hands to the side as if entering a scanning machine at the airport.

He repeated his performance and received the same results. He said another magic word and ran the wand up and down my body. "You're wearing a disguise illusion."

I stiffened. "Yes, I am. Is that a problem?"

He gave me a suspicious glare. "Deactivate it."

I tapped on the gem.

"What's the problem?" Tyler said.

"Why would you make yourself look older?" The man's forehead scrunched as if he thought I was crazy. He shook his head and ran his scan again. The results remained the same. He threw up his hands. "I don't know what's going on." He waved us on. "You're not vampires, so that's all that really matters."

"I take it vampires are not welcome here?" I said.

"Not since they attacked Arcane schools." The man glared at the protesters, his lips curling into a snarl. "They're filthy animals."

Tyler took my hand. "Um, we'll just be going then."

I reactivated my disguise. The Queen's guard opened the doors and revealed a marvelous sight. Sunlight danced on green hills. Mountains rose in the distance. My jaw dropped open. "That's bloody amazing!"

Tyler barked a laugh. "Now I know how to impress you."

We'd arrived in Queens Gate and it was magnificent.

CHAPTER 16

A wide yellow-brick road wound its way down through a valley and to a distant city. Cliffs towered above us in all directions, forming a giant box of stone. The doors we'd just come through were set in the rocky cliff behind us. We stood on a crest, giving us a perfect view of nearly everything the valley had to offer. The roofs of buildings were also visible atop the cliffs to the left and right.

The city of Queens Gate stretched from one side of the valley to the other. It resembled Victorian-era London, complete with Tudor houses at the outskirts and tightly-packed row houses further in. A massive clock tower rose between two domed buildings in the center of town.

A trail of fire and smoke hung in the air to the right. I spotted a silver rocket ship ascending toward the cliff on the right. A bright red cable car made its way up to the cliff on the left. A dozen people waited around a slab of black stone where the cable car presumably stopped. No one waited on the rocket ship pad.

A quaint cottage sat to the left side of the yellow brick road. I assumed it was a ticket booth of some sort since it seemed too small for anyone to live in, but none of the windows were open, and a knock on the only door didn't rouse any residents. Tyler tugged my sleeve and pointed down the road. "Look at that."

An ornate wooden carriage rolled up the hill toward us. Though it had a seat at the top, there was no driver directing it and no horses pulling it. "A horseless carriage that's not a car." I exchanged a look with Tyler. "Will the wonders never cease?"

He chuckled. "Probably not."

The carriage pulled in front of the cottage. The wheels turned ninety-degrees and the vehicle rotated until it faced back toward town. The door clicked open, so we climbed inside and took a seat. When it didn't automatically depart for town, I wondered if perhaps we had to do something more to direct it.

Two young women in dark blue robes climbed inside the coach and sat opposite us. "Twenty-three Dorset, please," the shorter woman said.

The other made as if to speak but simply stared at Tyler, mouth agape. A foolish grin dimpled the cheeks of her dark-haired friend.

"Oh, bother." I rolled my eyes. "Good day to you both."

"Hi." The dark-haired girl sighed longingly. Not even the coach lurching into motion jolted either of them from their hormonal haze.

Tyler sniggered like a little boy, apparently unable to control his mirth. I relaxed my guard and glimpsed the two females. Both harbored the same glowing power I associated with Arcanes, though theirs seemed dimmer than some I'd seen. I wondered if that indicated their relative power, or their inexperience.

"You're Arcanes?" I asked.

The shorter of the pair blinked and seemed to see me for the first time. "Good day, Miss."

I waited for an answer, but she apparently hadn't heard me. "You're Arcanes?" I asked slowly and enunciated clearly in case she was daft.

"Oh, yes." She gripped the dark-haired girl's arm. "I'm Lisa, and this is Phoebe. We're third-year students at Arcane University."

"Very nice to meet you." I didn't exchange names, just in case.

Lisa seemed to lose herself once again in Tyler's green eyes, then snapped out of it. "I'm sorry. I can't help myself."

"Me either." Phoebe seemed to force herself to look at me. "I'm very sorry."

"Well, he's a demon." I flashed a grin.

They both shrank away in terror. "A Daemos?"

Tyler frowned. "No, I'm a jade spirit trapped in a man's body."

"Trapped." I rolled my eyes again. "How tragically romantic."

He burst into laughter.

The girls seemed to forget their fright at the sound of his mirth.

"Where is a good place to purchase an Orange smartphone?" I asked.

Lisa's forehead wrinkled. "You mean arcphone?"

I nodded.

"I prefer to go to their headquarters in the Grotto, but there's a small store near the Copper Goose." Lisa tapped on the door panel and a holographic map sprang into the air between us. She zoomed into a spot and flipped the view to street level. There was indeed a giant copper goose sitting in the middle of the street. Lisa swiped from right to left and the view moved to a group of row houses converted into shops. The first bore a sign that said *Arcnology Addicts*.

"They're just a dealer so they charge more," Lisa said. "You can save some tinsel by going to the Grotto."

"Make sure you get the Orange Peel Twenty-Nine S Max Plus." Phoebe held up a small rectangular device with a partially peeled orange logo on the back. "It's got the latest hardware."

I peered at the model information on the back. "This is the twenty-ninth model?"

Phoebe nodded. "Yeah, they don't come out with new ones very often." She tucked the phone back into her purse.

I wondered how long the magical world had phones like this available if there were twenty-nine iterations.

"They don't like us having arcphones at the university, but I couldn't live without mine," Lisa said.

"We're a bit new to all this," I explained. "This is our first time to Queens Gate."

She smiled. "It was definitely overwhelming my first time here."

The carriage slowed to a stop before some brownstones and the girls climbed out. Lisa turned and looked at me. "Just tell the carriage where you want to go, and it'll take you."

I'd gathered as much from watching her do it earlier but smiled. "Thank you."

"You're welcome."

"Is he really a demon?" Phoebe asked.

Tyler peered around me and shouted, "Boo!"

The girls shrieked and jumped.

"I'm so sorry." I closed the door and burst into laughter. I managed to give the carriage our destination when I caught my breath. "Copper Goose, please."

The carriage moved out.

We arrived a few moments later and walked next door to the arcphone dealer. The inside of the shop was wide and spacious despite the narrow exterior of the row house. The walls, floor, and ceiling were white. A glossy white table supported a large Orange logo and an assortment of devices. A logo shaped like a sparkling magic wand stood on a black table a few feet away with more devices.

A young man with a thick beard grinned and walked over to greet us. "Looking for an arcphone or arctablet?"

"We'd each like an Orange Peel Twenty-Nine, please," I said.

"Absolutely." He picked up a palm-sized device from the Orange table and handed it to me. "They really hit it out of the park with the flex size. It's a lot better than the PCD method MagicSoft used with their Wand Twelve."

Tyler raised an eyebrow. "PCD?"

"Yeah, partially collapsed dimension." The man shrugged. "Sure, it made the phone seem smaller, but sometimes the code glitched and phones just vanished." He laughed. "Turns out all the phones were slipping into the pocket dimension. Some students at Science Academy sent a probe into the pocket and found a pile of arcphones twenty feet high." He snorted. "Oh, those were the days."

I held up the Orange arcphone. "I assume this won't vanish into a pocket dimension?"

"Yeah, no way." He took it back and tugged on the corners. The phone stretched out to tablet size. He pinched the corners and it shrank back to fit into my palm. "I don't know how they did it, but Orange came up with flexible organic displays." He shook his head in wonder. "It's the coolest thing yet."

"We'll take two," Tyler said. "Do you take US dollars?"

"We take anything." The man pulled an arcphone from his back pocket and tapped on it. "That'll be two thousand, forty-three dollars."

Tyler removed a wad of hundred-dollar bills from his wallet and counted them out. Moments later, we left the store with our new arcphones.

"Don't forget to watch the tutorials," the salesman called out from behind us. "A lot changed from the Twenty-Eight."

Since the entire arcphone experience was new to us, I planned to watch every minute of tutorials I could find.

Tyler stretched and collapsed his phone with glee and went straight to tapping on the screen without bothering to read any instructions at all. I half-expected him to vanish into a pocket dimension if he hit the wrong icon, but the controls proved very intuitive, even for a Luddite like him.

Tyler stared at the screen. "Where's the internet search?"

A robotic male voice answered. "Moogle or Tangerine?"

Tyler nearly dropped the phone. "What's the difference?"

"Moogle is provided by MagicSoft, while Tangerine is provided by Orange," the phone answered.

Tyler giggled like a boy. "This is so freaking cool!"

I couldn't help but smile. "Yes, well perhaps we should call a carriage and get to London. I'd like to get that body out of the trunk."

"Would you like to learn more about disposing of bodies?" my arcphone said in a voice identical to Tyler's phone.

"Dude, yes!" Tyler giggled.

"No!" I gave my arcphone a stern look. "We would not like to learn more."

Tyler laughed until he went red in the face. He held the phone to his mouth as if it were a walkie-talkie. "Hey phone, can you get us a carriage?"

"I have summoned a carriage," the phone replied. "Did you know you can personalize my name and other items in options?"

"Like what?" Tyler said.

"Here, let me show you." A holographic list appeared.

Tyler spent the next few minutes naming his phone, setting a regular phone number in case a nom number tried to call him, and more. I decided to do the same with mine. I gave it a British female voice, named it Penny, and assigned it a nom phone number.

Tyler gave his phone a German accent and named it Klaus, which seemed to amuse him to no end. "Klaus, say 'get to the choppa, Billy!'"

"Get to the choppa, Billy!"

Tyler burst into laughter.

"Well, at least I know how to keep you entertained."

A carriage arrived and delivered us back to the exit. We left the lush valley and stepped through the doors and into the Queens Gate waystation. A klaxon blared. People huddled far from the black-striped yellow border around the arch, many of them recording something with their arcphones. It soon became clear what caught their attention.

The man with the cowboy hat and the young man from the Grotto were being sucked inside a great gray rift in the air. The young man held the older tucked beneath an arm as if he weighed nothing. He lost his footing and his chin slammed onto the slick black stone. Gasps rose from the crowd as the pair slid across the floor towards the rift.

"It's a Gloom rift!" someone nearby said. "They're doomed if they get sucked inside."

The young man shouted, and a glowing web shot from his hands and wrapped around the base of the giant arch. The web tethered him in place long enough for the man tucked under his arm to wave a wand. A gelatinous glob formed and drifted into the rift, patching it like a burst tire. The young man raced out of the danger zone so fast, he was nothing but a blur.

"Holy cow, that kid is fast." Tyler looked around. "Where did he go?"

"I have no idea, but what in the world is a Gloom rift?"

Tyler asked his phone.

"The Gloom is a shadow dimension of our own," Klaus replied. "Not much is known about it, except that only specialized rescue teams have been able to extract people successfully before they are lost forever."

I shuddered. "That's terrifying!"

"And cool." Tyler wrapped an arm around me. "Let's get out of here. I think I've had enough magic stuff for one day."

I completely agreed.

Tyler configured the car for England, and we climbed inside. "Where to first?" he asked.

I texted my father from my new phone and updated him on our status. He still hadn't replied to the burner phone, and I didn't know if he ever would. Since I wasn't sure if we should contact Aunt Lydia, it seemed we had time to continue the investigation about my heritage.

I located Little Angel Orphanage on the map. "Let's go fishing."

"Fun time!" Tyler rubbed his hands together and mocked a British accent. "The game is afoot, Watson."

I wasn't sure if the knotting in my stomach was from anticipation or anxiety, but I certainly wouldn't consider travelling to an orphanage fun. "I'm sure it will be wonderful."

Tyler drove the car up a long winding ramp until we eventually emerged from behind a wall illusion and into a parking deck. He steered out of it and onto the streets of London. We drove through town, stuck in the ebb and flow of traffic. He slapped the steering wheel. "God, it's worse than Atlanta traffic!"

"I'm not sure about that," I replied.

Tyler slapped a palm to his face. "What am I thinking? This is a magic car!"

It hadn't even occurred to me that we had other means at our disposal. "Well, let's fly then."

He pulled onto a side street and found a narrow alley where he activated the camouflage. We lifted off and flew above the city. Tyler whooped. "I'm gonna be so spoiled by the time we get back to Atlanta. Maybe Fjoeruss will sell me one of these beauties."

"Contrary to what George says, perhaps there are magical car dealers in town."

His eyes brightened. "Man, I hope you're right."

We soon left the city behind and followed the mapped route far out into the country. Tyler landed on a narrow country lane not far from the destination and deactivated the camouflage.

Tyler gave me a strange look. "Your face is flickering."

"Oh no." I'd completely forgotten to turn off the charm illusion. "I need to recharge the charm. Perhaps we should come back later."

Tyler stared at me with a blank expression. Shook his head. "What are the odds we'll find agents of Domathus in an orphanage? It's probably safe to turn it off."

I pressed the charm to deactivate it. "I certainly hope so."

"Talk about the middle of nowhere." Tyler looked at the map on his arcphone. We're right across the road from Wales."

"It's almost as if they don't want to be found," I said.

The road terminated at thick iron gates. I regarded the creepy building looming against the dusky sky and hoped it held the answers I needed.

CHAPTER 17

A tall, beefy man in dark coveralls approached the gate before we got out to ring the bell. Everything about him was thick and muscular, even his bushy hair. He stared at us from the other side of the gate and spoke in an oddly high voice that belied his meaty frame. "You lost?"

I stepped out of the car. "No, I'm here to inquire about fostering children."

The man scratched his head. "Answering the adverts on the net?"

I assumed he meant the internet. "Yes. Is that okay?"

"I suppose." The massive iron gate swung open easily with one pull of his thick arm. He pointed to the circular drive. "Pull up and ring the bell."

I nodded. "Thank you."

His nostrils flared as if he smelled something, and his eyes settled on Tyler. I'd been so nervous, I hadn't noticed the signals emanating from the man at first, but the hot coppery sensation gave away his nature at once.

He's a lycan!

With his enhanced senses, I wondered if the gatekeeper smelled Tyler's demonic nature. I didn't dare say anything unless he did, but he seemed content to let us pass. Tyler seemed to remain unaware of the situation, since he had no special sense for detecting supers. I had no way to warn him without the lycan noticing. Tyler drove the car up the circular drive and parked in front of the house.

"That man is a lycan," I whispered, hoping the gatekeeper couldn't hear us at this distance. "I think he smelled your demon scent."

Tyler's eyes widened. "A werewolf at an orphanage? Man, that's not a good sign at all."

I grimaced. "Good lord. I hope he doesn't eat children."

He shuddered. "I hope the whole place isn't full of werewolves."

"Only one way to find out." Steeling myself, I walked up to the front door and rang the bell. Several uncomfortable moments ticked past. The gatekeeper walked up the drive toward the house, his predatory gaze fixed on us.

Tyler watched him with a frown. "I don't know if I can take on a lycan."

"Let's hope it doesn't come to that."

The door swung open just as I finished my sentence. A fair-skinned woman with dark eyes and equally dark hair regarded us for a moment before saying anything. "Good day. How may I help you?" She spoke in a posh accent. It seemed oddly out of place in this part of England.

"I'm Emily and this is Tyler." The woman didn't seem keen on shaking hands, so I continued. "We saw an advert on the net about fostering and would like to know more."

Her lips pursed, eyes taking me in. Just when I thought she'd turn us away, her lips spread into a smile. "I'm Felicity Goodleigh, the mother of Little Angel Orphanage. Please come in."

That was when it struck me. *This is the woman from the newspaper advert over four decades ago!* She bore hardly a wrinkle or sign of aging and could pass for someone in their early thirties. Once again, I'd let anxiety block my sixth sense. When I opened myself, I expected to detect another lycan before me. Instead, I glimpsed something quite different.

An inky, bubbling mass flashed into my mind's eye. An Arcane aura burned at its core, but it was tainted and stained. It was so unnerving, I gasped. I flashed a smile. "Sorry, I'm excited."

"As are many who come here," Felicity said. Her black dress rustled as she stepped back and opened the door. "My husband is away on business, so you must forgive me if I cannot spare much time."

"Absolutely," I said.

We walked across foyer floors made of dark-stained wood. Carved wooden trim covered the walls and thick wooden beams angled up to form a vaulted ceiling far overhead. A grand staircase led upstairs. The echoes of our footsteps were the only sounds I heard as we followed the woman into an office.

"Beautiful architecture," Tyler said.

Felicity looked at him with a raised eyebrow as she settled into a red leather chair on the other side of an ornate wooden desk. "You're American?"

"Yep." Tyler settled into a leather chair on our side of the desk.

"Whereabouts are you from?" Felicity asked.

I couldn't easily lie since one glance at our drivers' licenses would betray us, so I told the truth. "Atlanta in the United States."

Felicity nodded as if it were quite normal. "Are there any particulars about the child you'd like to foster?"

I wasn't sure how to answer since that wasn't why we were here. She seemed like the sort of person who'd kick us out the moment we revealed our lie. Considering the darkness around her aura and the lycan patrolling the grounds, I didn't trust this woman at all. Something nefarious was going on at this orphanage.

Tyler reached across and squeezed my hand. "A boy and a girl would be nice."

"Well, there are plenty of those to choose from." Felicity leaned back in her chair and steepled her hands. "But first let us cut through the subterfuge."

I blinked. "What do you mean?"

"You arrived here in an Arc Corp car." She looked at Tyler. "You are a Daemos." Her eyes found me. "And you are something of an enigma."

"Please, let me explain—"

Felicity offered a condescending smile. "I completely understand your desire to maintain anonymity, but that is why the backchannels must be adhered to. The safeguards must be honored if we're to keep the Templars ignorant of our activities."

I was so confused I didn't even know what to say. Thankfully, Tyler stepped in.

"A man in my position can never be too careful." He leaned forward and put on an award-winning smile. It didn't seem to affect Felicity in the slightest. "I hope you understand."

"Daemos are already profoundly disliked in the Overworld. Even so, you're right to be cautious." She laid her hands flat on the desk. "Please go through the proper channels and then we can talk."

"Can we at least have a look?" Tyler said. "We did come quite a distance."

Felicity sighed. "Very well. But we will keep it brief." She walked to the door and ushered us into the hallway. "The children are eating." She led us down the hall and around the corner. Hushed tones emanated from the far end.

I tried to think of some way to ask her the questions I really want answered. Had twin girls passed through here four decades ago? Where had they come from? I wished I'd been forthright about our visit from the beginning even if it meant she'd turned us away.

We reached a dining hall no less ornate than the foyer. Dozens of children sat at rectangular tables, shoveling brown mush into their mouths. I grimaced at the sight of the awful food. An older woman, perhaps in her late sixties, walked between tables, apparently ensuring orderliness. She rounded a table and came towards us. When she looked up, she stopped cold in her tracks, eyes wide.

She was looking straight at me.

Felicity cleared her throat. "Is there a problem, Nancy?"

Nancy shook her head. "No, madam. I was not expecting guests."

Sensations tingled across my sixth sense. I glimpsed budding arcane auras from the children, and what seemed to be small but growing seeds of power inside the younger ones. Nearly every child in here was an Arcane. There was nothing ordinary about this orphanage, and certainly nothing good. Something sinister, something insidious happened within these walls and it made me sick to think about what might happen to these children.

But Nancy and the other adults I saw had no auras at all. *Are they all noms?* I wondered.

"Many of them show great promise," Felicity murmured in my ear. "Doctor Cumberbatch says we have a very promising flock this year."

"Indeed." My throat felt dry as dust.

"You don't have many on staff," Tyler said. "Have they been here long?"

"Most have been here at least twenty years," Felicity said. "It's best to find a few but loyal employees."

"Twenty isn't bad." Tyler looked toward the kitchen where a middle-aged man dished brown slop into bowls for waiting children. A young woman emerged from the kitchen and placed clean bowls on the counter.

I didn't know why he expressed such keen interest in the staff, or if it was just a way to make small talk.

Felicity turned and led us out into the hallway. I knew with great certainty if I told her my real reason for coming here, we would probably not escape with our lives. Between her and the lycan, escape would be difficult.

Tyler showed no such concern for our well-being. "Do you get many identical twins through here?"

"Very few." Felicity looked over her shoulder at him as she walked. "They command a premium."

"I would imagine. Do many twins see their full potential?"

"There was a pair twenty years ago who turned out rather well, but only three sets of identical twins have passed through here in the last century."

I stifled a gasp. *How long has this place existed?*

"Wow, that's not many." Tyler grunted. "Were they boys or girls?"

"One set was female, and the other two male." Felicity stopped and faced him. "If your interest lies solely in identical twins, I'm afraid we have nothing to offer at this time."

Tyler waved his hands. "Nah, I just think it would be cool, you know?"

"Cool." Felicity drew out the word with disdain. "You Yanks and your slang." She began walking again.

Tyler's forehead wrinkled and his lips quirked. I could tell he was trying to think of another question to ask.

That was when something occurred to me. "Truth be told, I'm the one who would love twins. Do you keep records of how the children turn out? I'd be quite curious to see information on twin sets."

Felicity didn't even look back at me. "As I said, we have nothing to offer."

"The more information the better," I said. "It will determine if we go through the trouble of the back channels."

Her shoulders stiffened and she turned, an imperious tilt to her nose. "No such information will be given out unless and until you have gone through proper channels." She regarded me for such a long time, I wondered if she planned to call the lycan to dispose of us. Instead, Felicity turned around and walked to the exit. She opened the door wide and motioned us out.

We stepped outside.

Tyler put a hand on the door to keep it from closing. "We're staying just down the road in Presteigne if you change your mind." He said it loud enough to wake the dead.

I did my best not to give him a strange look even though I was definitely confused by his outburst.

"That will not happen." Felicity shut the door.

I turned around and nearly shrieked. The lycan man stood next to our car, a grim set to his huge jaw.

Tyler cleared his throat uneasily and walked towards him.

"Always wondered if Daemos are as strong as I've heard," the lycan said in his curiously high voice.

"Have you ever seen one spawn into demon form?" Tyler said. "That might answer your question."

"Maybe you'd like to show me."

Tyler touched the lapel of his jacket. "And ruin a thousand-dollar suit?

No, thanks." He opened the door for me and blinked in confusion when he saw the steering wheel. "Oh yeah, it's all reversed here."

The lycan laughed and walked away. "Bloody Yanks."

I opened the passenger door myself and got in. Tyler closed his door and activated the camouflage. Perhaps ten minutes later, he set down on the country road and we drove normally into the small village of Presteigne.

"Are we really staying here?" I asked. "We could easily make it to London before it's too late."

"Yep." Tyler grinned. "Because I have a plan." He looked at his phone. "Klaus, where's the nearest bed and breakfast?"

"Radnor House is the closest," his phone replied in its ridiculous German accent.

"Map it out." Tyler followed the directions and parked in front of a lovely house moments later.

I crossed my arms and looked at him. "I'd like to hear this plan before we go another step."

Tyler showed me a picture of four cars in a car park outside the orphanage. "Did you notice these cars?"

I shook my head. "No, why?"

"Did you notice the nervous Nancy in the dining hall?"

I nodded. "Yes. What do parked cars and the lunchroom lady have to do with anything?"

"Clues, my dear Watson." Tyler cupped his hand as if gripping a pipe and spoke in a passable British accent. "I believe a mystery is afoot."

I groaned. "I'm afraid I wasn't as observant as I should have been, Holmes."

He barked a laugh. "The cars most likely belong to people who work at the orphanage. That means they go home every night." He zoomed in on the license plates. "Klaus identified the area codes on the plates. They're registered in this town."

"Doesn't mean they live here," I said.

"No, but that's why I shouted where we were staying before we left."

I pursed my lips. "So someone in particular would hear it. Someone named Nancy."

"Exactly." Tyler smiled knowingly. "She nearly lost it when she saw you. It was like she saw a ghost."

My brow pinched. "But that would mean she's seen me before."

"Not you. Your mother."

I shook my head. "My mother?"

"Do you really think whoever gave your grandparents those babies would never check in on them?" He raised an eyebrow. "I'll bet they looked in on them regularly."

"And Nancy saw my mother in me?"

"I'm betting on it." Tyler tapped on the map. "I say we saunter down to a local bar in a little while and ask a few questions."

I scoffed. "I'm sure the locals will be more than happy to tell a couple of strangers where Nancy lives."

Tyler grinned. "That's where my demon pheromones come in."

"Be careful you don't cause the local men to murder us because you've seduced their women," I said dryly. "That would be most unfortunate."

"I think the locals are the least of our worries." Tyler's gaze grew distant. "Felicity thought I was a Daemos. I think that's the only reason she indulged us as long as she did."

"That woman and her pet lycan are dangerous." I scowled. "I imagine her husband is no less so."

He frowned. "If she hadn't mistaken me for Daemos, we might not have gotten out of there so easily."

"Considering the darkness tainting that woman's aura, I believe you're right." I shuddered to think of the children in her care. "I certainly hope we don't cross paths with her again."

It seemed digging into my heritage was considerably more dangerous than I'd bargained.

CHAPTER 18

Tyler hadn't brought British currency with him, but Radnor House took credit cards just fine. "Beautiful country out here." Tyler smiled at the old man who'd answered the door. "You been here all your life?"

The old man frowned grumpily. "No. I moved out here after retirement. It was my wife's bloody idea to run a bed and breakfast." He took us upstairs and showed us our room. "Supper is served at six sharp. Breakfast is from seven to nine. It's tea and biscuits, not an entire larder of food like your American breakfasts."

I feigned shock. "Not even an Irish breakfast?"

He shook his head. "No. If you fancy something like that, there's a place across the road."

"I'm sure it'll be fine." Tyler stretched. "I have to thank our friend Nancy for recommending this place."

The old man turned around and started for the stairs.

"Do you know Nancy?" Tyler said. "She works down at the orphanage."

The man spoke without looking back or breaking stride. "I know a dozen Nancys and not a one who works at an orphanage." And then he was gone.

Tyler grunted and stared at the small room. "Looks cozy."

"Yes, quite." I walked in and sat on the edge of the bed. I'd tried not to think too much about my funeral, but my father still hadn't returned my texts and I really wanted to make arrangements before someone discovered the body in our trunk. Tyler's spur of the moment decision to stay here certainly wasn't helping matters. "I should call Aunt Lydia. Let her know about my fake death. I don't even know where to begin planning the funeral."

"Probably for the best." Tyler sat down next to me and traced a finger up my leg. "I'll go down and get the suitcases. Then maybe we can break in this bed."

I bounced on the squeaky mattress. "I'm certain we'll alert the entire inn."

He flashed a wicked grin. "Good for them." Tyler nipped my neck with his teeth then vanished through the door.

My phone rang. I bolted to my feet, dug through my purse, and answered. "Dad?"

"Hello, Miss Glass. This is George." His face appeared on the screen.

My jaw dropped open. "How in the bloody hell—"

"As you might recall, there was quite an incident in Atlanta yesterday." George didn't pause to let me respond. "During cleanup, we were rather surprised to find footage identifying you and Mr. Rock. It would seem you solved your demon problem, though not in the most elegant manner."

I tried to wedge in a question. "Yes, but—"

George continued. "We found you through our ASE network and sent an agent to follow your trail in Queens Gate. We requested your arcphone information from the shop where you purchased them. That is how I know your symbols."

"You mean numbers?"

George chuckled. "We use symbols to call people in the Overworld. The noms use numbers."

I took a deep breath to collect myself. "Why did you wait until now to contact me?"

"We needed to make sure no one else was tracking you," George said. "So far, your adversaries think you're dead."

"So I'm safe?"

He nodded. "For now." George cleared his throat like a father about to scold a child. "While I'm glad you found a way to fake your death, I am concerned about how you did it. Since the ASE footage shows you loading a body into a car, I can only deduce that you didn't use illusion to fool the demon agents."

"We had help from someone powerful," I said. "He probably wouldn't appreciate me telling you who he is."

"It's Fjorn Gray," George replied. "He's the only person we know of who can make such lifelike golems."

My mouth hung open again. "Why even bother calling me if you know everything?"

"We don't know everything, but this confirms my suspicions."

"Are you telling me we've done something illegal?" I asked.

"Not at all, Miss Glass. Just be careful who you accept favors from. There are some very dangerous people, and you are still new to the Overworld."

My anxiety levels rose even higher. "So I've discovered. I don't suppose you can help me plan a fake funeral, can you?"

"We can. Simply provide me with a list of invitees and I will meet with you in two days."

I breathed a sigh of relief. "That would be wonderful, George."

"It's the least I can do for the Great Banisher." He ended the call before I could ask him not to call me that ridiculous name.

Tyler came through the door a moment later and set down our bags. He rubbed his hands together eagerly. "Ready to do some detective work, Watson?"

With the load of my funeral off my back, I found myself quite eager. "Yes, Holmes. Let's get to it, shall we?"

Tyler pulled me in for a hot kiss. "Damn, I love it when you get all Watson on me."

I snorted with laughter. "Watson was a man."

"Not in this case, babe." I told him about George's call. He seemed nearly as relieved as me to have the funeral taken care of by Custodians.

When we left the room, supper was being served downstairs. The beef stew didn't look appetizing but was actually quite delicious and filling. Then we set off for the Dukes Arms pub at a recommendation from the young woman who served our meal.

It was only a few blocks away, so we walked and enjoyed the chilly evening air. Notes from a trumpet reached my ears when we were nearly there. A clarinet and fiddle completed the ensemble when we opened the door and the music washed over us. The pub was crowded and lively.

A thin, bearded man danced in circles as he stroked his fiddle, while two middle-aged women bounced in place with their trumpet and clarinet.

The low roar of conversation battled the music for dominance in the tiny space.

We managed to find two seats at the bar. Tyler ordered us each a pint and we sat back and surveyed the room. Many a gaze lingered on us, two strangers in an establishment frequented by the locals. Tyler tried to start a conversation with the man sitting near us, but the portly gentleman shook his head and tapped his ear.

"Can't hear you," he shouted a couple of times.

Tyler gave him a thumbs-up and nodded. He turned to me. "God, I hope they stop playing. This music is awful!"

God was apparently listening, because the music ended just when Tyler said how awful it was. Several unfriendly gazes locked onto us.

Tyler burst into laughter, not even remotely embarrassed. He held up his beer. "Barkeep, the next round is on me! Cheers!"

Angry looks dissolved into astonished delight and applause. And suddenly, everyone was his best friend.

Our neighbor at the bar had no trouble hearing that his next pint was free, and with the musicians busy getting their own drinks, Tyler took the opportunity to ask a few questions. I barely had time to listen in before Tyler began moving around the room, prying information from people with his considerable charisma. I loved watching him work. Loved how smoothly he operated, all while gracing me with his sexy grin. It was enough to make me tingle in all the right places.

Besides, interrogating strangers was not my idea of a good time. I remained in place, content to drink my white wine. I was well into my second when Tyler returned, a confident grin on his face.

He nuzzled my ear with his nose and whispered, "Bingo. Nancy is in the hizzouse."

"She's here?" I looked around.

Tyler chuckled. "No, but I have an address and it's not far."

"You're sure it's the right one?" I said.

"Fingers crossed." He took my hand. "Let's go find out, shall we?"

Tyler paid his tab with a credit card.

"What if demon agents are tracking your credit cards?" I said.

"Why would they?" Tyler said. "You're dead."

"Oh, I suppose you're right." I touched the illusion choker and checked the time. We hadn't been here more than a couple of hours, but I would probably need to deactivate the charm to recharge it soon.

Tyler used his arcphone to find Nancy's address on Kings Court. It was nearly a mile away, but we decided to walk.

Traffic was scarce in the quaint town. A few pedestrians roamed the sidewalks, their anonymity maintained by the dim street lamps. We reached an intersection and turned right.

Tyler checked the directions on the phone and motioned towards the East Radnor Leisure Center. "Let's cut across the athletic fields. It'll be faster."

Though I'd worn flats, my feet were tired. "Anything to make the walk shorter."

We circled around the side of the building and discovered a tall fence. Tyler grunted. "Climb onto my back."

"So you can scale the bloody fence?" I shook my head. "We'd look ridiculous!"

He looked around. "I don't see anybody."

I sighed.

"Come on. It'll be a lot shorter this way." He bent over slightly.

Begrudgingly, I climbed onto his back like a child. "I'm ready for my piggy-back ride, sir."

He snorted. "Where's your sense of adventure, Em?"

"You have enough for the both of us, dear."

Tyler leapt halfway up the tall fence. I squealed in fright at the sudden lurch. Another lurch and he swung over the fence to the other side and dropped. He made a choking sound and pried my frantic grip from his throat. "Need air."

I released him and stood on wobbly legs. "Goodness. I don't know if that was worth it."

He laughed like a schoolboy. "Your reaction was totally worth it." Tyler took my hand and we started across the field. He stopped a moment later, his grin fading. He tilted his head slightly to the left.

I sensed what he heard a second later. A faint ping on my supernatural radar approached from behind. That single blip multiplied into four. I closed my eyes and concentrated, but they were too far away for me to glimpse. Even so, I could tell they weren't demons. The unidentified entities sped towards us at inhuman speed. They must have crossed the threshold of my outer limit because raw, savage heat pressed against my senses.

"Four lycans," I said in a hushed voice.

Tyler bared his teeth. "Shit. I was hoping it was just one. They must be from the orphanage."

"What do we do?"

"I don't think we can outrun them." Tyler grabbed my arm and slung me onto his back. "But we can try."

I clung to him as tightly as I could without choking him and Tyler raced across the open field. The pinpricks of heat grew closer and closer. I didn't see how we'd make it halfway across the field, much less all the way across. And once we did, then what?

A bone-chilling howl pierced the night air, soon joined by three others. The creatures were in wolf form.

"Son of a bitch," Tyler growled. "It's just not fair. If I was a Daemos I could just turn around and beat the shit out of them."

"They seem awfully confident." It was hard to speak, bouncing up and down on his back, but I persisted. "Maybe a single Daemos can't beat four lycans."

He didn't answer.

I reached back, stretching my senses to their outer limits. *If only I were stronger!* I didn't know how my powers would work on lycans. I could remove the parasitic aura from a vampire, and could apparently remove the blessing from a Templar, but lycans were something different. And even if I could affect whatever made them wolf shifters, I still had to touch them. By then, it would be too late.

In fact, it was already too late.

Two great gray wolves raced past us. A massive mottled wolf nipped at our heels. One of the gray wolves leapt in front of us and bared its teeth. Tyler ground to a halt and the wolves surrounded us. He let me down off his back and managed one of his confident grins. "Is there a problem?"

The mottled wolf shifted. Bones cracked and popped as if someone repeatedly broke a bundle of twigs across their knee and then the meaty gatekeeper from the orphanage stood in its place. A fur loincloth covered his privates, but the rest of his muscular frame was bare. He showed a mouthful of wolfish teeth. "Mrs. Goodleigh didn't like your questions. When she checked your aura on her security charms, it turns out you're not a Daemos after all."

The incongruity between his fierce exterior and high-pitched voice made me both want to laugh and cry at the same time.

Tyler shrugged. "What's your point?"

"You're a demon." He cracked his knuckles. "Balthazar sent no word, which means you're not one of his."

"Guilty as charged." Tyler held up his hands. "I'm not a minion of Overlord Balthazar."

"Well, that's unfortunate for your host and this old lady."

Another lycan shifted into a young man. "What's the word, Brickle?" He licked his lips and looked me up and down.

The big man bared his teeth in a feral grin. "Fun is the word, Timmy."

"A hunt?" Timmy's eyes glowed with excitement.

The other two wolves yipped.

Brickle laughed. "A hunt, indeed."

CHAPTER 19

I wondered how confused the authorities would be when they found my mauled body in this field and the mangled clone in the trunk of our car. It would be quite a mystery. Then again, perhaps the Custodians would clean up the mess before anyone became the wiser.

"Surely we can come to an agreement," Tyler said. "My master will pay handsomely."

"We only deal with Balthazar," Brickle said. "Mrs. Goodleigh wouldn't dare break a demon accord."

Tyler raised an eyebrow. "Not even if the son of Baal himself asked?"

Brickle bared his teeth again. "Mrs. Goodleigh says even Baal abides by accords. The word of a demon has to mean something, eh?"

"So you can't deal with any other demons at all?" Tyler said. "Not even if there's a ridiculous sum of money involved?"

"Not even." Brickle cracked his knuckles. "The only other question is, how much of a head start should we give you?"

"Let's drop 'em in the forest." Timmy pointed a thumb over his shoulder. "Be more fun hunting in the forest than the pastures."

"Aye." Brickle nodded. "It would be."

It didn't seem Tyler's wits would save us, so I decided to step in. I held up a hand. "You will do no such thing, or the Templars will hunt you down."

Brickle barked a laugh. "They won't ever know."

"Oh, but they will." I tried to make myself bigger and walked straight up to the brute. "I'm a Custodian."

A shade of uncertainty passed through his eyes. "You don't smell like a bleeding Templar. You don't smell like anything but a nom."

"She don't smell as old as she looks, either," Timmy added. "Might be some extra fun in it for us."

I showed Brickle my teeth. "I'm investigating an old case. Twins who passed through the orphanage nearly forty years ago."

He blinked, off guard for the first time during our encounter, but a hard gaze quickly covered it. "Are the Templars investigating us?" He stepped right up to me and grabbed my arm. "What do they know?"

Not enough, I thought. With skin-to-skin contact, I glimpsed a blood-red moon in my mind's eye and felt his savage heat burning against my senses. It was so primal, so alluring, I nearly lost my train of thought. I nearly demanded that he release me on sheer reflex, but instead looked up at him with a cold stare. "I am only interested in the twins, where they came from, and what became of them."

"She ain't no Templar," Timmy said. "Probably a private investigator."

"Tell me what I need to know, and things don't have to become unpleasant." I showed him as many teeth as I could muster. I felt that ghostly part of myself seeping into the lycan's skin. Felt it wrap around the hot blood moon at the center of his power.

"Custodians don't deal with demons." Brickle's grip tightened painfully around my bicep. "The only unpleasantness will be on your end."

"Let me have her." Timmy grabbed my other arm. "Let me give her a taste of heaven."

Tyler growled, but I gave him a warning look and shook my head.

"I like that idea, Timmy." Brickle released me and shoved Tyler hard. He laughed. "Right here. Right in front of the demon."

Outrage nearly boiled my blood. Almost on instinct, my spirit plunged its hands into Timmy, gripped his lycan aura, and ripped it from him.

Timmy made an awful sucking noise, as if I'd just drained his life through a straw. But instead of releasing the aura, my spirit absorbed it. I felt a hot surge in my veins. Felt a primal rage burning at the core of my very soul. I lifted Timmy as easily as I would a stuffed doll and flung him into Brickle. Timmy screamed. I bared my teeth and snarled.

"What in the bloody hell?" Brickle caught Timmy and stared at him. "He smells wrong! What did you do to him?"

The bones in my hands cracked. Dark claws speared from beneath my fingernails. My muscles bunched and thickened. I wanted nothing more than to tear out Brickle's throat and assume dominance over his pack.

"Jesus, she's a lycan!" Another man stood where a grey wolf once had.

The other wolf shifted into an older man. As with Brickle, some sort of furry loincloth covered their privates, but they looked every bit as muscular.

"I'm so weak. So cold." Timmy's fur loincloth was gone, leading me to believe it must have been part of his shifter magic. "She did something to me, Brickle."

It was only then that I realized exactly what I'd done. I'd taken his aura for myself. I was no longer a frail human, but a supernatural being of claw, fur, and fang. I tested a low growl in my throat and was pleased by how fierce I sounded.

"Holy shit," Tyler said. "Fuck them up, baby."

I took a step toward Brickle. Though I was still every bit as short as before, he took a step back.

"Do you want to be like Timmy, Brickle?" I reached down and picked up the hapless little prick by a leg and let him dangle. I could hardly believe how strong I was. I felt as if I could take on the entire world. I traced a claw down the man's leg and drew blood. "I can turn you all into help-less little boys. And then I'll castrate you because you fucking deserve it."

Brickle tried to run. I was just a shade faster. I snagged the big man's arm and yanked him towards me. My spirit sense gripped his aura. The other two lycans blurred away at top speed, leaving their pack leader at my tender mercies. Brickle resisted, but a slight tug on his aura brought him to his knees.

Tears pooled in his eyes. "Please, no!"

"Don't try to run, or you'll become just like Timmy." The laugh that emerged from my throat was almost maniacal. "You think you can just murder us, you little prick? I'll turn you back into a nom and tear out your throat." I could almost taste his blood on my tongue. Almost feel the heat coursing down my skin as I imagined ripping the meat from his bones.

"Em, are you okay?" Tyler stepped into view, a concerned look in his eyes.

Seeing him snapped me back into focus. The lycan instincts were so strong, I'd nearly lost myself for a moment. My conscious mind warred for dominance against bloodlust and the thrill of the hunt. I concentrated on Tyler and kept myself from slipping over the edge.

"You stole what he is from him." Brickle trembled. "What are you?"

"Your worst nightmare."

Tyler grimaced. "Ouch. Kind of cliché, babe."

His joke brought me back from the primal edge. I almost laughed and shook my head. Then I looked back down at Brickle. "Tell me about the twins and I'll spare you."

I'd never heard a man talk so fast in his life. "I nicked the twins you're talking about. The parents were powerful Arcanes, so when they had children, we knew they'd be worth something. I went to Iceland and took them. They were too young to measure, so we put them in the infant ward. They vanished a week later. Mr. and Mrs. Goodleigh interrogated all the ward staff and found the bloody laundry woman, Mildred, did the deed. But the old hag wouldn't tell us where she took the babies and we never found them."

I feared the answer to my next question. "What became of Mildred?"

"Mrs. Goodleigh dusted her." Brickle didn't seem the least bit regretful about it. "Mildred signed her own death warrant."

"Why did she do it?" I asked.

Brickle shook his head. "I don't bleeding know. She was an idiot."

And now, the most important question. "I want the names and address of the couple you stole the twins from."

"I don't remember." I tugged on his aura and Brickle's eyes flared with fright. "Please, I really don't."

"Then say goodbye to your wolf." I tugged slowly, unthreading his aura a little at a time from his body.

Tears poured down his cheek. "Oh, god, no! Please stop. I don't remember."

"Then you didn't live up to your end of the bargain, did you?"

He shuddered. "Wait! I think the last name was Anaga. Anagonye." He held up his hands. "Anagnos! It was definitely Anagnos."

"That's a strange last name for Iceland," Tyler said.

I stopped pulling on his aura and narrowed my eyes. "If you're lying to me, I'll be back. I leaned down into his face. "I will rip out your aura and neuter you like a dog."

"We know where you live," Tyler added. "So tell us right now if this is just a lie to get out of it."

"I swear its' the truth." Brickle still held up his hands in surrender. "They were on the southern coast near a black sand beach."

"How did you get there?" Tyler said.

"I took the Queens Gate arch to Selfoss with a car. It was less than an hour from there."

"Do you have records?" I said.

He shook his head. "We purge records all the time just in case."

"You people are evil, filthy scum." I hated to let the man go, but he apparently didn't have much more to tell me. I shoved him away. "Get out of my sight."

He was literally gone in a flash, leaving poor Timmy rolling around naked in the grass. Much as I wanted to slash the man's throat, I just kicked him in the ribs and left him groaning in agony.

"Where are we going?" Tyler said.

I nodded towards our original destination. "Let's make sure Nancy doesn't have additional information."

Tyler gripped my hand. "You've really got to explain what happened back there."

I felt a bit giddy, and a bit frightened by the experience. More than anything I felt exhilarated. I wanted to drop to all four legs and race into the night. I wanted to hunt, kill, and eat. All my senses felt so sharp I could barely stand it. The sensuous brimstone lurking beneath Tyler's human scent lured me like a fish to a worm.

"Babe?"

I shook my head. "Oh, God, Tyler. I don't know if I'm cut out to be a werewolf."

"Hot damn. Just when I think you can't get any more amazing." He laughed. "How in the hell did you do that?"

"I have no idea. It just happened."

He took a breath. "You've never felt anything except human emotions all your life. Dealing with a wolf's instincts won't be easy at all. It'll take time."

I groaned. "It takes all my concentration not to run off and kill a bloody deer."

Tyler wrapped an arm around my shoulders. "Hang in there. We'll figure this out."

When we reached the tall fence at the back end of the athletic fields, I ran at it with the intent to jump halfway up and climb it as Tyler had earlier. Instead, I cleared it by a fair margin and crashed into a tree. Fortunately, it didn't hurt more than my ego. I dropped to the ground and growled. "That was unexpected."

Tyler couldn't stop laughing. He pointed down at my shoes where dark claws pierced the fabric. "Someone needs a pedicure, stat."

I wanted to cry. "This is awful, Tyler." I inspected my clawed hands. "I can't walk around like this."

He hugged me and rubbed my back. "Just calm down, baby. Focus on your body returning to normal. It might make the claws go away."

It was hard to think about anything but murdering the sheep I heard bleating in the distance, but Tyler's comforting embrace seemed to bring the inner wolf back under control. My claws receded, and soon I was back to my normal self. I kissed his cheek. "Thank you, darling."

Tyler grinned. "I like the new you. Maybe we can go hunting later."

"Oh, hush." I stuck out my tongue.

Nancy's house was a red brick affair that looked nearly identical to all the other red brick affairs in the neighborhood. I deactivated the illusion charm as we approached. Nancy answered after two knocks. Her mouth fell open and a cup of tea smashed onto the brick threshold.

"Hello, Nancy." I tried to offer her a reassuring smile. "We need to talk."

The woman seemed almost too frightened to answer, but she backed inside, and we followed. The odor of cats assaulted my newfound sense of smell and I regretted it profoundly. I tried to block the odor but found it impossible. "How many cats do you have?"

A chorus of hisses and feline growls met me when we stepped inside. Nearly a dozen cats scattered to the winds and out of sight. Only a single black one remained. It stretched and looked up at us with a devil-may-care attitude.

Nancy couldn't stop staring at me. "You look so much like them. Like Lydia and Victoria."

I nodded. "I'm Victoria's daughter. I'm trying to find out who her parents were."

"Oh, my." Nancy fanned herself with a hand. "I just knew it the moment I saw you." She sank into a chair at a small wooden table.

My nose acclimated to the cat odor, so I sat next to her and patted her hand in what I hoped was a comforting way. "Do you know anything about my mother's real parents? Do you know where she came from?"

Nancy took a shuddering breath and nodded. "When I first started working at Little Angel, I became best friends with one of the ward nurses. Her name was Mildred." Nancy shook her head and looked down at her hands. "Mildred despised the Goodleighs, but she wanted to help the children as best she could."

I wondered how much Nancy knew about the true nature of Little Angel, but I didn't interrupt with questions.

Nancy continued. "There's such a low adoption rate among younger children from there, Mildred suspected that the Goodleighs intentionally didn't let anyone adopt children under age fourteen. One day she told me of a pair of beautiful twins had just arrived. She didn't want them to live their childhood years in the orphanage, so she found them a home on her own."

"How so?" I asked.

"She later told me it was a couple who desperately wanted to adopt because the woman was barren." Nancy looked up at me. "So she took the babies and left them on their doorstep, just like in a fairy tale. I told her she was mental, but Mildred was certain it was for the best." She stood and made herself another cup of tea. "She told me who the family was and asked that I help check in on the children every once in a while, just in case the Goodleighs found out what she'd done and fired her."

Tyler grimaced. "So what happened to Mildred?"

"The Goodleighs interviewed all the ward staff. They fired Mildred and sent her home that day." Nancy sighed. "Mildred lives in Kinsham, so it took me a few days to get over to see her. She didn't have a phone, so I had no way to call her. By the time I got there, her house was completely packed up and empty. I never heard from her again."

It seemed the Goodleighs knew how to commit a perfect murder.

CHAPTER 20

I didn't want to burden Nancy with the truth about poor Mildred, so I offered her a platitude instead. "No good deed goes unpunished." I sighed. "I assume you checked in on the children?"

"At least twice a year until they were maybe ten. Then I stopped for a while and didn't get back until they were in their late teens. The last time I saw them was when they were in their early twenties." She looked at me. "You look just like those lovelies."

I was glad I hadn't used the disguise illusion during our visit to the orphanage, or Nancy would have never known. "Any idea who their birth parents were?"

She shook her head. "Mildred tried to look into their records, but the only thing she found was that they were in Vik, Iceland."

At least it confirmed what Brickle told us. I remembered another important detail and wished I'd remembered to ask Brickle about it. "Was there a strange object that Mildred took with the children as well?"

Nancy shook her head. "Strange object? I don't recall her mentioning anything like that."

"About this big, metal, and with thirteen sides." Tyler held out his hands to approximate the size.

"I think Mildred would've mentioned something like that," Nancy said. "There's a large gray barn where they keep any personal belongings that might come with a child, but Mildred wouldn't have had access."

We spoke with Nancy for a while longer, but she didn't have much more to say. So I hugged her and thanked her for looking in on my mother and aunt, and for keeping the secret. "You should find another job," I told her. "Little Angel Orphanage is not a good place."

Nancy nodded. "I know, but the children have no choice."

I swallowed the lump in my throat and resolved to get the Templars involved right away. "You're a saint." Another hug, and we left.

We walked around the athletic fields on our way back. I cursed myself for not remembering to ask Brickle about the tridecagon. Mildred must have discovered it and sent it along with the twins, because no one else at the orphanage would have done it. Despite my new lycan powers, traipsing to the front door of that place would only make me an easy target for the Goodleighs.

Tyler squeezed my bum. "It's a lovely night out. Maybe we could sneak one in under the stars."

"And get filthy?" I couldn't resist my sexy man. "How romantic."

We didn't return to the bed and breakfast until nearly midnight. I immediately took a shower in the shared water closet. Once I was nestled in bed, I texted George what I knew about the villainous overseers of Little Angel Orphanage and requested an immediate Templar investigation.

His reply didn't come until the next morning while Tyler was in the shower. *I forwarded your request to the Queens Gate Templars. Do you have the particulars for your funeral?*

I leaned up against my pillow and thought about who I could invite.

Only my father and Aunt Lydia came to mind, so I sent him the very short list. He replied a moment later.

I will improvise to make it look more realistic. Will send the details soon.

With that off my mind, I longed for tea and biscuits. I stood up. My body seemed to weigh more. The incredible lightness and strength I'd experienced last night was gone. I tried to lift a corner of the bed and barely moved it.

"It's gone." I felt terribly ordinary all of a sudden. I closed my eyes and tried not to cry. In that instant of darkness, I glimpsed a burning ember far away. Keeping my eyes shut, I focused on it. It seemed to come closer, or perhaps I was moving toward it. In an instant, I was close enough to recognize the blood moon—the image my mind associated with the lycan aura.

I reached for it and felt the carnal lust surging through my veins again. I released it and let it sink into the dark depths once again. I opened my eyes and gasped. The aura wasn't gone. It simply wasn't active. Some-how, I had made it a part of me and then separated it from my normal self.

"Does that mean I can activate it anytime I choose?" I paced in a circle for a moment and stopped. "Why don't I have Stephen's vampire aura?" I thought back to the awful incident. His aura had dissipated while I held it and turned it to goo. Either I couldn't integrate a vampire aura, or I simply hadn't known how to at the time. Then again, I didn't know how I'd done it this time.

"Do I even want a vampire aura?" I asked myself. A part of me longed to experiment. Another feared for my sanity. I wondered if a vampire aura would be as difficult to control. But I couldn't simply pluck the aura from an unsuspecting vampire. I had to find one who deserved it. For the first time, I hoped to run into another asshole like Stephen.

Tyler entered the room, his hair still damp, a towel wrapped around his delicious waist. I looked at him and licked my lips. "Don't you just look yummy?"

"I could use food." His stomach growled. "A lot of it."

I decided to give him sexual respite for now and began to dress. "Let's get breakfast."

George texted me instructions for the funeral. I would be buried next to Mum at the same small graveyard north of London. George had invited Lydia and my father, but not my grandparents. There was no need to unnecessarily traumatize them with my fake death. But we needed at least a couple of family members to make it realistic.

The flying car brought us to a small funeral home within an hour.

George recognized me despite the illusion charm. "Good morning, Miss Glass." He nodded at Tyler. "Mr. Rock."

"Hey, George!" Tyler flashed a grin. "Can you get the body out of our trunk?"

George led us down the hall to a viewing room where an open casket sat on a pedestal. There were ten rows of five chairs facing the front of the room. "This funeral home is owned by a nom who has been through Overworld orientation. It should be ideal for staging the funeral."

"Who will give the sermon?" I asked. "I'd like a proper sendoff."

George smiled. "I arranged everything." His smile faded. "I must admit that I'm rather bewildered about your arrangement with Fjorn Gray. He is a very powerful Arcane who keeps to himself."

"He's concerned that demons have infiltrated his companies and asked me to look into the matter." I shrugged. "It seems I'll be in his employ for a few months."

George nodded. "His business enterprise is extensive. Even we don't know the full extent of it. But as far as we know, he hasn't broken any

Overworld laws, and there's nothing preventing him from doing business with noms, so long as overt magic isn't involved."

I wondered if George knew Fjorn the Arcane was actually Fjoeruss the Seraphim. It might be important for George to know, but I had mixed feelings about exposing a being who was so private. On the other hand, I had news George would definitely find interesting. "We've been digging into my ancestry," I said.

George quirked an eyebrow. "Have you discovered anything?"

"A little." I told him about our adventure last night, drawing an uncharacteristically surprised look from George.

"Can you repeat that, Miss Glass?" George wiggled a finger in his ear as if clearing it out. "Did you say you removed and absorbed a lycan's abilities?"

I nodded. "It's dormant right now, but if I concentrate, I can tap into it again."

"That's fascinating." George folded his arms across his chest and looked at my belly as if I stored the lycan aura there. "It didn't work that way with the vampire aura."

"Probably because my abilities were still maturing back then," I said. "It's possible I could do it with vampires too."

"I wonder if another aura would replace the other, or if you can just keep piling them in," Tyler said.

"I've never thought of abilities, whether gifted or innate, to be transferrable," George said. "It flies in the face of everything we understand about how supernaturals work. Lycans and felycans are born and made. Vampires are only made. Arcanes and Daemos are only born that way."

Disappointment flashed across Tyler's face, but he didn't say anything.

"The original Daemos were made," I said.

Tyler gave me an appreciative look.

George didn't address my contention and continued to make his point. "To transfer the abilities from a lycan would be like removing blocks of their supernatural DNA and making it a part of your own." He pursed his lips. "We need to test your new ability with a vampire."

"Aren't Templars made?" Tyler said.

"The blessing sometimes transfers to children of Templars," George said, "but only rarely."

Tyler snapped his fingers. "What about demons?"

George's left eyebrow rose. "Demons are spiritual beings, not abilities. Miss Glass can glimpse their true names and patterns just as she glimpses the true nature of other supers."

"Why don't I see anything about noms?" I said. "Surely, I'd see something about them even if it's mundane."

"Perhaps you always have." George shrugged. "But you've experienced it all your life. So much so, that you filter it out without even realizing it."

I shook my head. "I've tried glimpsing noms, but nothing happens even when I concentrate."

"Perhaps there is simply nothing to see," George said.

I wondered if I could steal Seraphim abilities. The thought was so tempting, I felt guilty. "After the funeral, we plan to visit Iceland and track down my Mum's origins."

George nodded. "I'm hopeful you find answers, because I have never heard of anyone with abilities such as yours, Miss Glass. It's apparent even your nickname isn't quite enough to describe you."

I scoffed. "Perhaps the Great Banisher is simply the Great Ability Thief."

George chuckled. "No. You are far more than you think."

I felt certain he was right. And it frightened and excited me all at the same time.

My funeral took place the next day at two in the afternoon. I watched from the back of the room, a stranger, while Tyler put on quite a performance as the grieving widower. My father, Patrick, was there, tall and stoic. He'd shown up at the last minute. Apparently, he'd lost his phone during a mission and had only found out about the funeral because George tracked him down.

Dad sat across the aisle from Lydia, unwilling or unable to be near the woman identical to his dead wife. Grief and anger etched his face. His hands clenched and unclenched, as if choking an invisible person. I hated that he had to endure this ruse unknowingly, but George wanted his reactions to look genuine.

Lydia cried silent tears for me, but she looked oddly comforted. Perhaps seeing her vision of my funeral come true gave her a sense of order to the universe. I tried to glimpse her but detected nothing out of the ordinary about her. She and Mum had visions about the future, but neither of them could control it. Perhaps her abilities were too weak for me to detect.

Of the thirty people present, most were Custodians or random locals drawn in with the promise of free food and alcohol. George thought it important to inflate the numbers so any demonic agents would feel more comfortable appearing. But try as I might, I detected no demons in anyone present except for Tyler. Numerous Templar auras hummed in the background of my sixth sense, but that was it.

The locals consisted of a few middle-aged couples and a group of people my age who probably came on a lark. Most of them stared at their smartphones the entire time. I wanted to go slap them for disrespecting my funeral, or at the very least glare at them. But their backs were to me, sparing them the brunt of my wrath. The priest kept the eulogy short and sweet, and neither of my relatives elected to speak.

When the service was over, Dad went to the casket and gently kissed my forehead. A small frown flashed across his lips and he stared at the body for a long moment before moving away. He gave George a murderous look but said nothing.

He knows that's not me.

It made me happy.

I rode with George in the funeral procession to the graveyard. Once there, I stood at the far back of the small crowd while they prepared to lower my body into the grave. Lydia tried to stand near Dad. He stiffened and did his best not to look at her. It was painful, even for me, to look at that face and not see Mum. But Lydia was the complete opposite of her sister, meek and submissive where Mum had been the strongest woman I'd ever known.

Lydia stared blankly at the casket for a long time. I couldn't stop staring at her. She flinched and her eyes flared. She wasn't looking at me, but at something across the grave. I saw the group of people my age—four men and two women. None of them were particularly remarkable except a woman who wore a knowing smirk on her face.

It was my possessed lookalike. Except this time, she wasn't possessed. I focused on her, but there was nothing to glimpse. She was just as ordinary as the other noms—no demon lurking inside this time.

Who are you? The urge to shout the question was almost irresistible. I wanted to slap the woman, if only to confirm she used an illusion charm to look like me.

My lookalike crossed her arms and winked at Lydia. My aunt's face blanched. She obviously saw the resemblance to me. Perhaps she even thought it was me in disguise and was shocked to see me among the living.

She had no idea it was the woman who'd killed me.

CHAPTER 21

My father stared at my casket, seemingly unaware of the silent drama unfolding right next to him. Lydia bit her lower lip and didn't look away from the girl. I dearly wanted to find out what this was about but didn't dare risk blowing my cover.

I tapped the com pendant George had given me and whispered into it. "George, look across from my Aunt Lydia. That's my blond lookalike!"

He didn't respond, but his gaze shifted to the individual in question. His eyes flared slightly as he also saw the resemblance. I desperately wanted to capture the woman, but if she was here to confirm I was dead and in the casket, we had to let her be.

At long last, the priest concluded the service and the crowd began to disperse. The blonde sauntered over to Lydia and spoke with her. Dad stared at her with narrowed eyes. He said something, but I couldn't hear it from this distance.

I pushed my way through the crowd. I finally got close enough to hear what they were saying. The girl spoke in low tones to Dad and Lydia. Judging from their reactions, it wasn't something they wanted to hear.

Before I got close enough, someone gripped my shoulders and pulled me to the side.

"The car is parked over here, Karen." I tried to wriggle free, but George held me firmly and gave me a warning look. "Your disguise is flickering."

"Bloody hell." I let him lead me to a black sedan and slid into the back seat. George got in next to me and took an arcphone out of his pocket. I deactivated my disguise to let it recharge.

"You really don't have to eavesdrop, Miss Glass." He turned on a video. "Everything here is being recorded by ASEs."

"Is that woman wearing a disguise to look like me?" I said.

"I don't know." He started the video. "Let's find out what they're saying."

"Hello, Mother." My lookalike gave her a knowing smile. "I hoped you might be here."

"It can't—can't be." Lydia put a hand to her heart. "They said you died. I tried to find you again."

"Oh, really? Had second thoughts after giving me up for adoption?" The girl wore her smirk like a shield. "I survived. Had a very rough go of it, but here I am."

My heart skipped a beat. "Holy shit. She's actually related to me?"

George frowned. "It would seem Lydia confirmed it."

"Lydia." Dad looked back and forth between them. "You and Mick had a child?"

She seemed unable to speak for a moment. "Yes."

Dad turned to the girl. "What's your name?"

"Olivia." She held out a hand. "And you're my Uncle Patrick."

Dad shook her hand. "Pleased to meet you, Olivia."

"That bitch! She's the one who killed me!" I wanted to claw her eyes out.

"Your father doesn't know that," George said. "If she's here for Domathus, we have to let her be."

He was right, and it infuriated me.

Lydia looked back and forth between the blonde and my father, her complexion so pale as to be green.

"There's something more to this, it would seem." George raised an eyebrow. "I'm sorry family drama has eclipsed your special day."

I saw Tyler in the background, shaking hands and accepting condolences. His gaze found the trio of family members and his lips peeled back in a snarl.

"I hope Tyler backhands Olivia straight into my grave!"

"I told him the same thing I told you," George said. "Tyler won't harm her."

Tyler stalked over to Olivia and glared at her. "You're not welcome here."

"Oh, is that all you've got to say?" Olivia fluttered her eyelashes. "Sweet Emily is gone. You can have me now, you luscious little tart."

Tyler's fists clenched. "If this wasn't a funeral, I'd end you right here and now."

"What's the meaning of this?" Lydia said.

Tears rolled down Tyler's cheeks. "She killed Emily!"

I couldn't help but smile. "He deserves an Oscar for this performance."

"He is rather convincing," George said.

"Killed Emily?" Dad bared his teeth. "I think we'd better go somewhere else to discuss this."

Olivia shook her head and mocked a sad frown. "I'm afraid I have pressing business elsewhere, but I'm certain we'll meet again."

Tyler put a hand on her shoulder as if to restrain her. "Going to bow down to your master?"

Olivia licked her lips. "You're such a sweet jade, aren't you?" She patted his hand. "Perhaps when you're done mourning, we could have a little fun."

"You killed Emily?" Lydia seemed to have recovered from her shock.

Olivia laughed. "Not directly, I'm afraid. Tyler drove her off a cliff."

Tyler reared back his fist as if he wanted to hit her.

Olivia laughed again. "I see you like it rough." She winked. "I can dish it out all you like." She backed away and motioned to her young friends. They crowded around her and walked away.

"Can you at least follow her?" I said. "After she reports in to Domathus, I'd dearly love to catch her."

"Already on it," George said.

I leaned back. "I can't believe it. I actually have a cousin who consorts with demons."

"You said she was possessed the last time you saw her."

I nodded. "She was, by a ruby spirit. But this time she wasn't. That means she willingly and openly deals with Domathus and his minions."

"She referred to Tyler as a jade," George said. "It would seem she knows what sort of spirit he is."

"I need to talk to Lydia and Dad right now."

George nodded. "Let the situation die down a bit, and I'll arrange it."

He flicked his arcphone screen to an overhead view of Olivia walking with her friends. They walked down the sidewalk a distance and stopped at a black SUV. Olivia shook her head slowly. She turned and looked up. Then she stuck out her tongue and made a swatting motion with her hand. The screen went black.

George blinked as if unable to believe what he'd just seen. His gaze met mine. "She just disabled the ASE that was following her."

"How did she even know it was there?"

He shook his head. "I don't know." George spoke into his com badge and the crowd around my grave dispersed in minutes. Undercover agents directed the attending locals to the memorial reception. Mr. Sticks opened the front door and climbed into the driver's seat.

"Mr. Sticks, I didn't know you were here." I almost patted his shoulder but stopped myself.

He looked back at me and simply nodded. It was quite a sign of respect from someone of his nature. Without even a glance at George, Mr. Sticks pulled onto the road and drove us a short distance to a brick duplex. We went through the front door and into a small foyer with a tea room to the right and a family room to the left. The leather furniture had seen better days, but those days were perhaps thirty years past.

It looked as though children, cats, and possibly even a dog had left their mark on the wide divan, and the easy chair in the corner was so cracked, worn, and filthy, it seemed someone might have died in it and remained there for some time until discovery. An old-fashioned box television sat against the wall, and a blackened fireplace occupied the wall to its right.

"What a marvelous home, George." I wrinkled my nose. "How many people have been murdered here?"

He shrugged. "I'm afraid it's the best we could do on short notice. One of our demonic agents lives here."

My bottom jaw dropped. "The Custodians employ demons?"

"Not directly. He's more of a consultant and informant. In return, we don't force him from his host."

My opinion of the Custodians plummeted. "That's evil, George. You allow a hapless host to be used just for your benefit?"

Mr. Sticks watched me with a neutral expression, which meant he might approve of my commentary.

George held up his hands defensively. "Miss Glass, it's not like that at all."

I sensed a dry heat growing closer. The source was somewhere outside, and I knew it wasn't Tyler. Tyler's jade presence felt calm and reassuring. This one radiated power but lacked the nauseating aura of a caustic. The door clicked open and a stocky man stepped inside. His head was shaved bald, and his skin looked a bit too pink, but he didn't bear the usual signs of demonic decay.

"You're a ruby demon," I said.

He looked at me and blinked. "Emily Glass? The Great Banisher?" His eyes lit up. "Bloody hell, what an honor!" He held out his hand.

That wasn't quite the reaction I'd expected. Then again, the demon possessing him was obviously quite tricky. I didn't extend my hand. "I can't believe the Custodians let you inhabit this man's body against his will."

The tone and timbre of the voice changed noticeably. "It's not like that, ma'am. I love having Chlor around. I'm stronger, smarter, and the ladies like me more." He patted his belly. "And he sure keeps the weight off."

The voice changed back to a rich Oxford tone. "It's a rather symbiotic relationship, you see." He smiled. "I saved Raymond's life once and we've been inseparable ever since."

"Absolutely," Raymond added.

It was bizarre listening to two different entities speak through the same mouth. I looked from Raymond to George and back again. "Raymond, how do you know Chlor isn't simply tricking you into this arrangement?"

Raymond walked to a table next to the rotting divan. A framed picture lay face down on the table next to it. He picked it up and turned it toward me. Raymond stood next to a petite woman with curly brown hair. He was nearly as round as he was tall, and his complexion was pitted with acne scars. I looked from the picture to the man.

"I look so much better already, and it only took a few months to make me the man you see today." He held out his hands as if presenting himself. "It's wonderful."

I looked around at his decrepit house. "Why does it look as if caustic demons live here?"

"I'm too busy living life to worry about my house," Raymond said.

Chlor spoke. "I haven't convinced him that we should tidy up. This is how it looked when we first met."

I shook my head and looked at George. "Well, I suppose if Raymond is willing, then you aren't as morally bankrupt as I first thought."

George looked hurt. "I thought you knew me better than that, Miss Glass."

I rolled my eyes. "I suppose I should have known better."

The door opened again. Tyler, Lydia, and Dad filed inside. Dad grinned when he saw me and crushed me in a bear hug.

"Daddy!" I buried myself in his chest. "I'm so sorry we had to deceive you."

He backed off and scoffed. "That wasn't even you in the casket, though she could've passed for your twin."

"Speaking of twins." Tyler watched Lydia's face. "Someone's got some 'splaining to do."

Lydia ignored him and caressed my cheek with a hand. "Well, it seems my vision was both right and wrong." She kissed my cheek. "I'm happy to see you alive, dear."

Tyler grunted. "You didn't look too happy to see Olivia alive though."

"We have serious matters to discuss." George motioned to the couch. "Let's sit and talk."

Tyler's lips peeled back in disgust. "I'm not sitting on that thing." He sniffed the air and looked at Raymond. "That man is possessed."

"Pleased to meet you. I'm Chlor." He nodded slightly. "It's an honor to be in the presence of the Great Banisher's mate."

I rolled my eyes. "Why would a demon be honored to meet me?"

"Because you destroyed the balance of power in the netherworld." He released a delighted sigh. "Domathus lost considerable power. Many of the demon lords fell from power, casting others of us free. It is because of you I had the freedom to at last leave the service of Domathus and seek my own freedom. It is why I am now with Raymond."

His reply shocked me. I'd never actually thought about making demon's lives better. I thought of them mostly as vile and evil, a hypocritical stance considering the love of my life was one of them. It certainly gave me pause. "I'm glad you found happiness." I tried to mean it but couldn't quite muster the enthusiasm.

"Don't we all just want to be happy?" the demon replied.

"Some of us at the expense of others." I looked away from him and down at the divan. "I think we'd be much happier with cleaner accommodations."

"The kitchen isn't bad," Chlor said. He showed us down a narrow hall past the staircase to a room that looked as if it hadn't been used in a while. A wooden table with six chairs sat in the middle of the room. Amazingly, the sink wasn't piled with dirty dishes.

"My ex-wife took all the silverware and dishes when she left me," Raymond said. "I eat takeout most of the time—or at least I did before Chlor found me."

"It'll do." Tyler pulled out a chair for me and then sat on the end next to me.

Dad sat on my other side. George took the other end of the table. Lydia sat alone opposite of me, her shoulders hunched as if bearing a burden nearly too great to bear. Whenever our eyes made contact, she looked away.

George got straight to the point. "Olivia is no ordinary person. She disabled an ASE without touching it, and according to Emily, seems to allow demons to possess her while maintaining control."

Lydia trembled. "She allows demons to possess her?"

"She definitely had a ruby demon inside her the last few times I saw her." I shook my head. "She seemed to be completely in control of her body, but with demonic strength."

"My god." Lydia pressed a hand to her face and closed her eyes. "I thought she was dead."

"When did you have her?" Dad seemed just as stunned. "I don't remember you being pregnant."

"She's only a little older than Emily." Lydia wouldn't look at either of us. "I tried to find her years later. Apparently, she was shuffled around the foster system. The last family lived in a wretched apartment complex in Peckham, London. They claimed she died."

"They lied." Dad narrowed his eyes. "Did Victoria know about Olivia?"

"Victoria never kept a secret from you, Patrick." Lydia's eyes lifted from the table and met his. Pain etched her forehead. But something else flashed through her eyes. It was more than pain. It was longing.

I had a feeling she held a secret more terrible than I could imagine.

CHAPTER 22

Lydia rarely came around when I was a child. In fact, she'd rarely come around at all that I remembered. It wasn't until I was older that she began visiting me. I remembered seeing that longing look in her eyes when we'd gone out alone for lunch on occasion. It was as if she saw something she desperately desired.

And that was how she looked at my father. "Aunt Lydia!" I said it in the same tone one uses to scold a child. I grabbed her other hand and stared at her with open-mouthed horror. "Don't keep secrets from us anymore. It's too important."

"But you'll never forgive me." Lydia's voice choked with pain. "You'll hate me."

"No, never." I rubbed the top of her hand. "Please tell us."

"I—I had the child a day before Victoria gave birth to you, Emily." Tears pooled and trickled down her face. "I couldn't keep her, so I put her up for adoption."

She went silent, but I knew there was more to it. "Who is the father?"

"You didn't meet Mick until well after Emily was born." Dad's eyes tightened. "I don't remember you seeing anyone else at the time."

The look of longing flashed through her eyes again when she met his gaze, but it quickly turned to shame. "I met you first, Patrick. Long before Victoria even knew you existed." Lydia lifted her chin as if trying to show confidence. "We met and you talked to me for hours. You told me I was pretty, but that I needed more confidence. You said you liked me but that I was too quiet." She wiped tears from her eyes. "I never wanted you to meet Victoria, but you did. She was everything I wasn't. Everything you wanted me to be."

Dad's forehead wrinkled with confusion. "We were friends, Lydia. You never once expressed romantic interest in me."

"Because you told me to be someone I'm not!" Lydia pounded a fist on the table.

It was the first time I'd ever seen her do such a thing. Even at her angriest, the most Lydia usually did was walk away.

She wasn't done speaking. "My sister got you and it tore me apart inside. So when you wanted to have children, I didn't want her to be first. That one night when we all got drunk playing board games, it wasn't Victoria you bedded. It was me!"

"Jesus!" Dad stumbled up and back, toppling his chair over.

I gasped and reeled back. Tyler steadied my chair before I fell over backwards. He gripped my hand, an anchor in a world that suddenly went mad.

Dad shook his head. "It can't be true. You passed out. You wore a green dress, and Victoria had on red."

Lydia continued her story. "I drugged my sister's drink. When you stepped next door with the neighbor, Victoria passed out and I changed into her clothes." Lydia deflated a bit. "Your neighbor helped me distract you, but he thought it was because we were planning a surprise for you."

Dad's face blanched just as Lydia's had at the funeral. "You're saying Olivia is my daughter."

Lydia nodded. "She is. Until today, I hadn't seen her since I signed the papers to give her up for adoption." She looked down at her hands. "I never thought I'd see her again, and I certainly don't know how she found out about me, since they promised to seal the records."

"Lydia, this is monstrous!" I couldn't control my anger any longer. "You betrayed my parents for some sort of petty revenge?"

"Having a child goes far beyond petty revenge," Chlor said. "That was masterful."

I didn't appreciate his opinion.

George held up a hand. "I know this is very painful to discuss, but we should focus on the bigger picture. Olivia might have powers similar to Emily's. It also seems she knows more about you than you know about her."

"We should find her and ask what she wants," Tyler said.

"How?" I said. "She destroyed the ASE following her just by flicking her fingers."

"Perhaps, but we got the license plate of her vehicle," George said. "I've requested agents to look into it. We should have an address soon."

Shoulders slumped, back bent, Lydia no longer looked anything like Mum, despite her identical face. Mum had never looked so broken in her entire life, not even when she died. In a single act of defiance, Lydia had tried to take what she wanted, but instead ended up with a terrible burden. I didn't know whether to feel anger or pity.

It was infuriating and horrifying to realize the demon assassin after me was my half-sister. I wanted to go straight to Hell and choke the life from Domathus.

George grunted. "I've got her records." He took out his arcphone and projected the information in a hologram.

What I read over the next few minutes made my physically ill. Olivia had been adopted by a couple in London. But the adoptive father was arrested for sexual abuse, and drug dealing. Olivia had gone from foster to foster over the next few years and ended up in Peckham, London by age twelve. At fifteen, she'd vanished during a fight between drug gangs and the police at her apartment complex. She was still listed as missing.

She had a police record for drug use, prostitution, and assault with a deadly weapon.

"My god!" Tears poured down Lydia's face. "What have I done?"

Dad's jaw clenched tight with anger. He seemed ready to unload on Lydia, but somehow held his tongue.

Part of me wanted to comfort Lydia. The other part wanted to slap the shit out of her. She'd doomed her own flesh and blood to a horrible life. It was no wonder Olivia consorted with demons. They were probably nicer than the humans in her life.

"I know this is very sensitive," George said, "but objectively speaking, it appears that Olivia is extremely dangerous and very angry. I would guess she killed Miss Glass out of a sense of jealousy."

"Fake killed her." Tyler shook his head sadly. "And now she wants me as her prize."

"She must have only recently found out about her real family," Dad said. "Otherwise, we probably would have heard from her before now."

"Agreed," George said. "Lydia and Mr. Rock might still be in danger. She also doesn't appear to know that you are her real father."

It was petty of me to notice, but apparently George called people by their first names only if he didn't know their last.

"Maybe she should know." Dad clenched his fists and cracked his knuckles. "Maybe it's not too late to turn her around."

"Yeah, except she killed me!" I took a breath to calm down. "She's probably killed before."

"Perhaps." George turned off the arcphone projection. "Olivia might also have valuable information about the underworld. Domathus went through a great deal of trouble to kill Miss Glass quickly with minimal torture. This is quite unlike most demonic assassinations."

Tyler nodded solemnly. "An overlord like Domathus would stretch out the torture for years if possible. I think he's got another plot brewing, and Emily is the only one who could stop him."

"I also suspect Olivia and Domathus only recently crossed paths," George said. "Otherwise, she might have made an appearance in the Demonicus Incident."

"Either that, or he didn't think he'd need her," Tyler said. "So in addition to this war that's brewing, we might have to worry about another major demonic incursion."

I slapped the table. "You really think Domathus is planning round two?"

Tyler cupped his hand as if holding a pipe and spoke in a British accent. "When you have eliminated the impossible, whatever remains, however improbable, must be the truth."

"Thanks, Sherlock." It was just like him to make light of the situation. "If that's the case, then we need to capture Olivia immediately. The loss of life the last time was horrific because we didn't stop Domathus quickly. Let's not make the same mistake this time."

Dad gave me a strange look, as if he'd just seen a ghost. He patted my hand and nodded. "Spoken like your mother."

Lydia flinched and looked down at the table. "You didn't detect a demon in her this time?"

I shook my head. "No. I didn't detect anything from her this time. She seemed normal. I never glimpsed anything with you or Mum either, so maybe your abilities are just invisible to me."

Lydia seemed to consider her next words. "My visions gave me insight into Victoria's life, but no one has ever told me exactly what it all meant. I don't know what it is you do, or who these people are."

George raised an eyebrow. "It appears we've completely broken protocol. In our haste to discover more about Olivia, we have forcibly brought a nom into the fold."

Lydia looked down at her hands. "I know there are supernatural forces at work. I know there are demons, because I have seen Victoria deal with them in my visions. But I have never heard the whole story."

Dad stood. "I need some time alone to process everything." He picked up the chair and shoved it under the table. "Emily, let's get together and talk later, okay?"

I patted his hand. "Okay, Dad."

He nodded at the rest of us and left.

Lydia's lips trembled. Tears trickled down her face, but she didn't make a sound. She glanced at me and just as quickly looked away.

A part of me wanted to console her. Another part wanted to slap her. But she was the closest thing I still had to Mum in this world even if she was only the palest of shadows compared to her. I moved to the other side of the table and put a hand on her shoulder. "I forgive you, Aunt Lydia."

She managed a smile. "I know you don't really, but thank you, dear."

"Mum would probably be proud of you in her own twisted way." I wiped away tears of my own. "She believed in taking what she wanted."

"I don't think Patrick will ever forgive me." Lydia wiped her cheeks.

"Just give him time." But Dad would need plenty of that. Betrayal was not something he forgave lightly.

George regarded Lydia. "We'll debrief you, Ms. Winters."

Apparently, he'd found her maiden name in Olivia's records.

"That would be nice." She wiped her face again.

George turned to me. "Until we arrest Olivia, it's imperative she not discover that you're alive."

"Agreed," I said.

George nodded. "What are your plans now, Miss Glass?"

I looked at Tyler. "I've got another week before I have to report for duty with Fjorn. Until then, I think we'll be in Iceland."

"To track down your origins?" George said.

"And it's a good place to avoid notice." I scooted my chair sideways so I could see Lydia better. "I found out where you and Mum came from."

Lydia's eyes flared. "How is that possible when even Victoria failed to find our origin?"

"Mum wasn't perfect. She overlooked a couple of small clues." I told her how I'd narrowed it down to the orphanage and the information Nancy told us. I left out the part about the lycans and the discovery of my new ability. "Right now, the trail leads to Iceland."

"It would be useful to know about your origins," George said. "I think the sooner you depart London, the better. We don't want Olivia to accidentally stumble on you."

I shrugged. "I doubt that's likely."

"We'll keep in touch." George pocketed his phone. "As soon as I have information on your sister, I'll let you know."

I grimaced. "She's not my sister. She's a bloody murderer who needs to be locked away forever."

Mr. Sticks offered a slight nod from his corner of the room, as if he completely agreed. My eyes lingered on him and I allowed my mind's eye to peer at his aura. As with George, I saw a glowing white orb at the core of his aura. But I also sensed something else. Something even closer to the center of his being. It felt like digging my feet into freshly churned earth. Like planting myself in the ground.

I flinched at the alien sensation. Mr. Sticks gave me a knowing look, as if he knew what I'd seen and felt. He sometimes spoke telepathically with George, but even in this moment where it seemed he might finally utter a word, he remained maddeningly silent.

There was no reason to pry into his privacy, so I let the moment pass and got up from my chair. "Since time is of the essence, I'd like to leave for Iceland immediately. I hear there's an arch in Selfoss."

George nodded. "I'll have you cleared for priority travel."

"Please send Templars to investigate that awful orphanage as well. It's unconscionable that those children be left under those conditions."

"I already notified the Queens Gate Templar division, but with civil war brewing, I don't know when they'll have time to investigate."

I gave Lydia a firm hug. "Give my father time. I think he'll forgive you."

"But he'll never love me as I love him." Fresh tears trickled down Lydia's face. "I loved him from the start but have never been worthy of him."

"There's someone right for you out there," I said. "You're still young, Aunt Lydia. Let Dad go and find someone else."

"Like Mick?" She scoffed. "When you truly connect with someone, there are no others who can compare."

Tyler's eyes seemed to glow as he looked at me and nodded. "Amen to that."

My face heated. I took his hand and walked for the front door. "We're going."

He touched my neck. "Don't forget your charm, Em."

"It probably needs more time to charge." I activated it anyway, figuring it could charge in the car.

It was a good thing I turned it on. Because the first thing I saw when we stepped outside was Olivia perched on a brick wall across the street.

CHAPTER 23

Olivia flashed a smile and leapt off the wall. She walked straight up to Tyler and ignored me. "You know what's strange?"

"You are," I said. I had to repress what I really wanted to say since I wasn't Emily, but Karen, an older woman with no apparent connection to Tyler.

She continued to ignore me. "I get that Emily was a Custodian and that they'd want to show their condolences. But this felt a lot more like an operation than a funeral." Olivia looked at the house. "You've got a demon and two Custodians in there with my mother." Her eyes went back to Tyler. "So what's the deal?"

I did my best to hide my surprise. *How does she know who's in there? How did she find us?*

Tyler snarled. "What in the hell are you doing here?"

Olivia grinned back and tutted. "Oh, Grim, you're such a sexy beast."

He flinched. "How do you know my demon name?"

"Oh, baby, finding demon names is child's play." Her eyes wandered up and down Tyler. "How about I show you what else I'm good at?"

Tyler growled.

Olivia's eyebrow quirked. "Too soon?"

"I should kill you where you stand." Tyler advanced threateningly.

"You really think you can hurt me?" Olivia smirked. "Maybe if you were an overlord."

Tyler backed away. "You have powers like Emily's don't you?"

"The Great Banisher?" She laughed. "What she did was nothing. My cousin couldn't do shit compared to me."

It took all my willpower not to defend myself. *You're not Emily, you're Karen.* And Karen was a nosy bitch who called the cops on people. So I butted in. "You're a rude little bitch, aren't you?"

Olivia blew out a long sigh and finally looked at me. "Look, grandma, if you want to keep breathing, shut your mouth hole."

My temper boiled to a hundred degrees, but I had no idea if she could back up her boast or if they were just empty words.

She turned back to Tyler. "So what's with the big production here? Were you trying to trap little old me?"

"I don't know what you're talking about," Tyler said. "It was a fucking funeral for the woman I loved." His lips curled into a snarl. "So show a little respect."

"I'd prefer to show you something else." Olivia tilted her head sideways, as if trying to glimpse Tyler. Her brow furrowed. "Damn, I guess I can't compel you. I was really hoping to make this easy."

Tyler scoffed. "Compel me? What are you, a vampire?"

The group of people who'd accompanied Olivia to the funeral piled out of a black SUV parked just down the road and walked toward us.

"Why don't you take your little pals and go home?" Tyler backed up a step. "Don't make me kick your asses."

Olivia slashed a pattern in the air with her hand. A small glowing rift formed and sickly yellow mist poured from it and into her companions. Their bodies contorted, muscles bulging grotesquely. In seconds, they looked like subhuman creatures from the dawn of man. They smiled, showing rows of razor-sharp teeth. Olivia smiled. "Now, come along or you'll be the one getting your ass kicked."

"Holy fuck!" Tyler jumped back.

I tapped my com badge and said, "George, we need you outside right now!"

Olivia backhanded the shit out of my cheek. I spun around and face-planted on the grass. I heard her muttering in her guttural voice again. I turned over as she traced another pattern in the air. Another rift opened and red mist poured out of it and into her. Unlike her friends, the changes to her physique were subtle. Her muscles firmed and her eyes glowed red.

"I'm going to break you like a twig, you stupid bitch." Olivia lunged toward me.

Tyler slammed into her with his shoulder. It would have knocked a nom across the road, but Olivia remained upright, her feet skidding through the dirt. George and Mr. Sticks flashed outside. Mr. Sticks produced his namesake weapon and identified the misshapen humanoids as the immediate threat.

George's gaze flashed to me, to Tyler, and then to Olivia and her companions. Despite the confusion on his face, he joined Mr. Sticks in the defense.

Olivia lunged for me again, but Tyler put his martial arts training to good use. He gripped her arm and used her own momentum to flip her onto her back. I gathered my wits and crawled away on hands and knees. I was so weak. So useless. I was still dazed from the blow to my head, unable to even stand up. I couldn't fathom what Olivia had done. Had she somehow drawn demons into the bodies of herself and her companions? Had she intentionally possessed them?

It didn't make any sense. You needed patterns, rituals, and blood to summon demons.

Tyler maintained a standoff with Olivia. George and Mr. Sticks held back the possessed hosts, but the enemy threw themselves relentlessly at them. Across the road, a small crowd gathered, watching the spectacle. Olivia flashed another grin and slashed another pattern. More demon spirits snaked out, yellow tentacles seeking their prey. They found the onlookers.

Shouts and screams cut off abruptly as the onlookers twisted into the subhuman creatures like the others. Suddenly, the fight was decidedly lopsided. I had to help. But how?

It occurred to me that I was a fool for not having thought of it earlier. I closed my eyes and found the lycan aura. I drew it from that empty pocket of darkness and back into me. Strength rushed through my veins. My mouth salivated with bloodlust. I would tear these creatures to shreds.

I lunged at Olivia so fast the world became a blur. Unlike Tyler's first blow, she felt this one. Her body hurled backward and slammed into the brick wall. Cracks ran across the masonry and dust rained down in her hair.

Claws grew from my hands and I felt an instinctual change trying to force its way onto me. A howl erupted from my throat.

"A bloody lycan!" Olivia brushed away the dust and laughed. She flicked her wrists. Orange flames gathered around her hands. "Do you really think a dog can beat me?" The flames sharpened to points, twin blades of pure energy. Oily black smoke trailed from their tips. The air reeked of brimstone.

"Try me," I growled. "I will taste your blood, demon." *What am I saying?* It was becoming more difficult to control the savage instincts.

Olivia licked the tip of a fiery sword and smiled. "I am the right hand of the Netherlord. I am power incarnate." Her voice turned guttural and demonic. She threw her hands out to the sides and her body turned into a pyre, a living sword of fire. "I am the infernal blade, you insignificant speck." And then she rushed me.

Frightening as she looked, she still wasn't as fast as a lycan. I blurred to the side. Lashed out to hit her. I might as well have plunged my hand into the sun. Before my hand even got close to her, intense heat drew a yelp of pain.

"It's hellfire," George shouted. "Don't get near it."

"How in the bloody hell am I supposed to fight her?" I said.

"I don't think we can." George slammed another possessed to the ground, but then he and Sticks backed away from the mob.

Chlor was nowhere to be seen, hopefully far from here by now.

Tyler and I backed up to them, forming a tight core. "What do we do?" I asked.

"Can you banish the demons from these people?" Tyler said.

George shook his head. "No. I think retreat is the only option here."

Tyler frowned. "Run away?"

George nodded. "I'm afraid so."

Olivia threw back her head and laughed, demonic voices mingling with her own. "You can run all you want, Custodians, but you can't hide from the Netherlord."

"I'm afraid that's a new name to me," George said. "Care to explain who the Netherlord is?"

"If you're lucky, you'll live to meet him." Olivia clashed her fire blades together. "But I don't think you'll be lucky."

In the moment her blades made contact, I glimpsed something. My mind's eye seemed to travel into the hellfire and down through a blazing tunnel to a pit of orange flame. Screams echoed all around me. Ghostly shades flitted through the air, a great flock of crows circling the lake of fire. Their wails echoed into eternity.

I gasped and the vision blinked away. Olivia and her fiends stalked toward us. The only way to go was back. I stared at her and tried to glimpse her again. I didn't see the lake of fire again, but I noticed something else. The flames around her were dimming ever so slightly. I probably wouldn't have noticed if not for enhanced lycan sight. The corners around her eyes looked strained.

Summoning this much power must be demanding. But her collapse didn't appear imminent. Tiring though the hellfire might be, she seemed to have plenty of stamina to finish us off. I didn't want to run back through Chlor's house. That would only bring these hellions with us. Since we couldn't even touch her in her current state, I couldn't barge past her. That left only one real escape route.

"Hold on, Tyler. This might hurt."

He blinked and gave me a surprised look. "Say what?"

I grabbed him around the waist and slung him over a shoulder. Then I took a great running leap at the fiends. I still wasn't used to lycan strength. Not only did I soar over Olivia's minions, but I launched us clear over the brick wall.

"Get my prize!" Olivia screeched.

I dropped Tyler to his feet. "Time for you to get on my back, babe."

"But—"

"Just do it!"

He climbed onto my diminutive frame, but he felt no heavier than a backpack. When Olivia and her gang rounded the corner, I flipped them off and ran. Parked cars blurred past. My heightened senses almost helped me, but not quite. The moment I ran out of street, I didn't stop nearly in time and plowed into a car at the stop sign. Tires screeched and the vehicle skidded into the intersection.

Tyler sounded as if he'd been punched in the gut and nearly lost his grip. I looked back, but the fiends weren't even halfway to us. Apparently, speed wasn't their forte. The driver of the car got out and shook his fist at us. A shout died on his lips when he saw the much taller Tyler riding piggyback on little me.

"Terribly sorry," I said. "Cheers." And I ran again. This time I took it much slower. We went a few blocks, much to the awe of nearby pedestrians. Jaws dropped and a few women cheered me on. I finally stopped and let Tyler off, much to his masculine relief.

"Do you eat a lot of kale?" a nearby woman asked. "You're incredibly fit for your age."

"She literally bathes in liquefied kale," Tyler told her.

"Will you hush?" I slapped his arm and looked at the woman. "For God's sake, stay away from kale. It's disgusting and vile."

"Kale baths," Tyler reiterated.

The woman looked uncertain, so I dragged Tyler away by his hand and around the next corner so we could make sure no one was following us.

"I don't know if I should feel emasculated or really turned on right now," Tyler said. He nipped my neck as I looked around the corner. "I think I'm turned on."

I rolled my eyes. "You're impossible, do you know that?"

"No, I'm totally possible, right now if you want me." He pinched my butt and chuckled. "Damn, you really knocked the hell out of Olivia before she did her infernal blade thing."

"I wonder where George and Mr. Sticks are." I tapped my com badge. "George?"

His voice crackled through the link. "Are you safe? Olivia and her minions went after you, so we took your car and ours and are driving to a safe location."

"Yes, we're good." I breathed a sigh of relief. "How did she find us?"

"I'm afraid she simply followed us from the funeral." George sounded ashamed. "I let my guard down. I nearly cost us our lives."

"Will Chlor be okay now that Olivia knows where he lives?"

"I don't think she cares about him. She seems to be fixated on Tyler."

"Can't blame her," Tyler said. "I'm devilishly handsome."

I ignored him. "We need to talk about what just happened. Where can we meet?"

"Best if we find you since we have your car."

I looked for an intersection and gave them the street names. "Be careful. I don't know if she's still looking for me."

"Understood," George said. He drove our car into the alley moments later and got out. "I deployed several ASEs over the area. No sign of Olivia or her companions." Mr. Sticks parked the Custodian sedan on the curb.

Tyler got into the driver's seat. I stood at the passenger door. "What now, George?"

"Follow us to Queens Gate. I think we'll be safe there for the time being."

"I certainly hope so."

My murderous half-sister was far more dangerous than we'd realized.

CHAPTER 24

We made it to the Queens Gate waystation without incident and joined George and Sticks in their car to talk. I had so many questions, I didn't know what to ask first. Unfortunately, George seemed just as confused.

"Netherlord? Infernal blade? Hellfire?" I held up my hands helplessly. "Where do I begin?"

George nodded solemnly. "This is only the second time I've ever seen hellfire. You can recognize it by the brimstone odor."

"I've never seen hellfire," Tyler said. "And I sure as hell have never seen possessed people transform into monsters."

"She turned innocent bystanders into those creatures." The thought made my heart weak with fear. "Shouldn't that be impossible?"

"Almost none of it makes sense to me," George said. "I didn't think it was possible to force demons into people, and I didn't think any physical being could handle hellfire." He shook his head. "From what little I know, hellfire comes from the very core of Hell. By Hell, I don't mean

Haedaemos, I mean the deepest layer of Haedaemos just before the Abyss."

I shook my head. "But everyone told me that Hell and Haedaemos are the same thing."

"There are theories that Hell is a distinct part of Haedaemos, or maybe it's the other way around." George shrugged. "I'm no specialist."

"I glimpsed something about Olivia." I told them about the burning lake and the cyclone of dark spirits flying around it. "I think that's the source of her power."

George produced his arcphone and dialed symbols. "I think we need an expert consultation."

"That would be lovely," I agreed.

A young man in gray robes appeared on screen. "Hello, George."

"Hello, Zuba. I'm here with Emily Glass, Tyler Rock, and Mr. Sticks."

Zuba nodded. "A pleasure speaking with you again. How can I help?"

"We have something of an enigma wrapped in a mystery," George said.

"A caper is afoot," Tyler said in his Holmes voice. "We must deduce a devilish plot."

I groaned. "Ignore him, please. This is extremely serious."

Zuba grinned. "I do love a good caper. Please continue."

George and I told him everything. The professor nodded and took notes but said nothing until we reached the end of our tale.

"This is fascinating." His eyes lit with delight. "It would seem Emily has glimpsed the mythical lake of fire, also called the infernal pit, or the infernal fount. I have interviewed a number of powerful demons and not a one would directly speak of it. I believe the pit is the center of demonic magic, something of a well that supplies them with power."

"Like an aether well?" George said.

Zuba nodded. "Except this is their source. There are rumors that at the other end of the spectrum is another origin of power called the primal fount, but information on it is nearly as scarce as that on the pit."

"So my half-sister can draw directly from this infernal well?" I said.

"It would seem so." Zuba pursed his lips. "According to demon lore, the black shades circling the pit are the souls of the devoured, sentenced to burn forever." He shook his head sadly. "A demonologist I consulted on a particularly gruesome case told me that when a demon devours a soul, it leaves behind a dark shade, a shadow soul. Those are probably what you saw."

"How awful." I shuddered to think of the agony. "Are they still conscious?"

"They are souls without light," Zuba said. "You said you heard them wailing. This leads me to believe they are still conscious, even if far removed from what they once were."

"Why didn't Domathus or his demon lords use hellfire during their invasion?" I asked. "They might have beaten us soundly if they used that sort of magic."

"I don't know if demons can actually use such magic in the physical world," Zuba said. "To think that a human is capable of such a thing is astounding and frightening beyond belief."

"That's not reassuring," Tyler said.

"Haedaemos is a layered realm with the lesser demons and spawn existing around the top few layers. Only the most powerful demons can even venture into the deeper levels." Zuba seemed to be looking at something off-screen. "The problem is, it's nearly impossible to find the exact names of powerful demons, and harder still to get direct answers from them without compelling rewards."

"Would a demon lord know anything?" I said.

"Almost certainly. Even a demon knight might know about the infernal fount." Zuba turned his gaze back to us. "The only references I have to the Netherlord are from ancient Cyrinthian writings. He was some sort of godlike figure in Hell. Oddly enough there were no mentions of Haedaemos in those writings."

"What about infernal blade?" George asked.

"I searched all my records but found nothing." Zuba shrugged. "Perhaps Olivia just made up the name."

I shook my head. "It's not made up. My mother told me the name in a dream."

That raised a few eyebrows, but the others seemed to accept it and move on.

Tyler sighed. "I hate to admit it, but it's kind of a cool name."

"It is rather catchy." Zuba cleared his throat. "Despite Domathus being soundly defeated by Miss Glass, it sounds as if he might be making another play for the mortal plane."

George frowned. "Any signs of this in the demonologist community?"

"Nothing other than the usual plots." Zuba paused and frowned. "Although one of my colleagues has heard the term 'infernus' bandied around a bit lately. He asked us if we'd ever heard it. Another colleague had, but she didn't know what it meant either."

"Infernus?" Tyler's forehead furrowed. "I heard that term in my father's court not long before I had my first adventure possessing a mortal on earth."

Zuba's eyebrows perked up. "Oh? What does it mean?"

"Two demon lords were discussing it. It had something to do with..." His voice trailed off and he looked at me. "Bloody hell, Watson. I've discovered a clue."

I rolled. "What is it, Holmes?"

He grinned. "An infernus was supposed to be a golem possessed by a demon."

I sucked in a breath. "That would connect to Fjorn's missing golems."

"Indeed, Watson!" Tyler smoked his imaginary pipe. "The demons are plotting something. I can smell it."

"Demon golems are impossible, as far as I know." Zuba shook his head. "They need a soul to latch onto."

"But this body doesn't have a soul anymore," Tyler said. "It's just me in here."

"You inhabited that body right when the soul left it," Zuba said. "In effect, your demon spirit is now the soul. If the previous owner died before you entered it, it wouldn't have worked. Otherwise, demons would take over dead bodies all the time."

"So it's a dead end?" George said.

"I believe so," Zuba replied. "But if Olivia can force-possess people with multiple demons at once, it seems that this Netherlord could have an instant army at any time."

"She might have limits as to how many she can force-possess at once," George said. "Otherwise we would have seen a large-scale invasion by now."

"But why now?" My forehead pinched. "Why would my sister come out of the woodwork to murder me now? Why wasn't she around for the Demonicus Incident?"

"You weren't even on Domathus's radar before then," Tyler said. "There was no Great Banisher. But the moment you sent Domathus screaming back to Haedaemos, you became the number one danger to all demon plots."

"Now, they think you're gone." George tapped a finger on his chin. "And someone with similar powers is on their side."

"I suspect another demonic incursion is imminent." Zuba looked at something off-screen and began typing. "I'll put my colleagues on high alert. I'll let you know if I hear anything."

George pressed his lips together. "This couldn't come at a worse time. The Templars are in disarray, and the Custodians are stretched thin. It's imperative Miss Glass find out as much as possible about her powers." He turned to me. "I hope Iceland holds the answers you need, Miss Glass."

"No pressure, right?" My shoulders sagged with stress again.

"Live on pay per view, the Great Banisher versus the Great Possessor." Tyler patted my hand. "My money's on you, babe."

A fight with Olivia was one I'd certainly lose. "Why don't I just tell Olivia I'm alive? Perhaps that will put a pause on a demon invasion."

"Then Domathus will renew the price on your head, and we'll just be hunted again." Tyler shook his head. "We need to find out what you can do and surprise the hell out of Olivia and pals next time we fight them."

"Agreed," George said. "In the meantime, I'll coordinate with Zuba to find out more about Olivia's abilities. Perhaps there's another way to stop her."

I scoffed. "I can certainly say holy water won't work."

Mr. Sticks made a sour face.

"Well, let's go then." Tyler opened his door.

"You're on a high-priority list now for Obsidian Arch use, Mr. Rock." George gave him a stern look. "Don't abuse it, please."

Tyler flashed a grin. "Wouldn't dream of it."

We got back into our car, and Tyler spoke with one of the worker-bee Arcanes managing the arch queue. The Arcane grimaced but relayed the destination. Including us, there were exactly five people travelling to

Iceland. The other three travelers rode flying brooms toward the gateway when it opened.

Tyler saw them in the rearview mirror. "I want a flying broom too."

I scoffed. "Not satisfied with a flying car?"

"Oh, I love it. But a broom would be like having a flying motorcycle."

We drove through the gateway and emerged in a smaller waystation with not even a third of the crowd. It seemed nearly everyone was queued up to exit Iceland through the gateway we'd just used. We left the waystation behind by driving up a long winding ramp and emerged in a dimly lit tunnel. Sunlight filtered through cascading water ahead.

"Wow, that's a waterfall!" Tyler whistled. "Pretty cool."

The water diverted to the sides at the last minute, leaving the car dry, and just as quickly concealed the tunnel exit when we were out. A black gravel road led us through a winding mountain pass. We followed it and emerged behind a small farm. Ponies grazed nearby. A few grungy sheep were scattered among them.

"They eat ponies here," Tyler said. "We should get a horse steak before we leave."

I grimaced. "How could you eat a cute little pony?"

"With horseradish, of course." He barked a laugh, but I didn't find it the least bit amusing.

I checked the map on my arcphone. "There's hardly anything around here."

"Hardly anything except some of the most beautiful scenery on Earth." Tyler motioned at the flat plains of volcanic rock and the mountains rising seemingly out of nowhere. "Man, it's so primordial, so raw."

I gazed at the scenery, at the snow-capped peaks in the far distance. "I expected snow everywhere."

"Me too. But I'm glad there isn't any yet." He mapped the route to Vik. It took us twenty minutes of driving to reach the two-lane highway. Then we stopped and changed the driving mode for Iceland which moved the steering wheel back to the left.

Tyler drove on the wrong side of the road until I corrected him. Even then, it took him a little while to adjust back to driving on the right side of the road.

I smiled. "Confused yet?"

He shook his head like a wet dog. "Completely. Instantaneous travel has a few downsides, I guess."

Tyler turned on the camouflage and took to the skies. The landscape was breathtaking. Cliffs towered above black sand beaches. Monolithic rock formations jutted from the ocean, battered relentlessly by powerful waves. Even the algae-covered plains of volcanic boulders were beautiful. It was like being on a newly formed planet.

We landed outside of town and drove to the closest restaurant since Tyler was famished. "I hope it's safe to use a credit card," he said. "Do you think Olivia can track them?"

I shrugged. "I suppose anything is possible, but unless you have local currency, we don't have much of a choice."

"Yeah, I should've gone to the exchange at Queens Gate." He patted his rumbling belly. "Guess we'll take the chance."

There was no horse on the menu, so Tyler had lamb and beef. Our meal cost a small fortune. Even the chicken I ordered was nearly forty dollars. The waitress spoke perfect English, so I used the opportunity to ask a few questions.

"Are you familiar with the Anagnos family? We met them abroad and they told us they live here in Vik."

The waitress watched Tyler with dreamy eyes. "Do you need more water, sir?"

I wanted to reach out and thump her on the nose. This was the down-side to Tyler's charisma. But there wasn't much he could do to cover up his demonic pheromones.

Tyler smiled at the waitress. "Can you tell me where to find the Anagnos family?"

She blushed with delight. "They used to live here but moved a few years ago. You could ask the seashell ladies who live down the road. I know they were good friends with them." She licked her lips. "I can take you there if you'd like."

I suppressed a groan. *Where is your Viking fortitude, woman?*

After our meal we followed the directions supplied by the waitress and ended up on a gravel road a few miles down the highway. It wound down to a farmhouse with the black sand beach as its backdrop. A herd of ponies and goats crowded the pasture to the left. The field to the left bore the stems and leavings from the previous year's crop. I couldn't imagine what grew in such harsh conditions.

A small blue car sat at the end of the drive. An oasis of greenery surrounded a small yellow cottage. Colorful flowers and bright green grass and shrubberies contrasted the desolate environs just a hundred yards away.

"Must be some hot springs nearby," Tyler said. "I read that they grow a lot of stuff in greenhouses over hot springs."

"Sounds like a wonderful way to keep a home toasty in the winter." I regarded the house for a moment. "I wonder why the waitress calls these people the seashell ladies."

"Probably a couple of crazy old women who sell crap they find on the beach." Tyler chuckled and got out of the car.

I went ahead of him and gave the door three quick raps.

Something tingled against my senses, muted but not distant. It was as if a translucent membrane concealed something and left only a vague silhouette. I actively concentrated on it and glimpsed a great storm-tossed sea of sapphire and jade hues, swirling into one another like liquid gems.

The door opened and a little old lady stood on the other side. She looked perhaps seventy, but I sensed something even more ancient lurking behind her eyes. She certainly wasn't an ordinary seashell lady. The woman spoke in Icelandic.

I shook my head. "I'm sorry, we speak English."

The woman smiled. "Are you here to buy seashells?"

"You sell seashells by the seashore?" Tyler asked.

I elbowed him in the stomach.

"Not directly to tourists," the woman replied. "The shops in town carry all my wares."

"That's not really why we're here." I took a deep breath and got straight to it. "We're looking for a family who had twin girls stolen from them about four decades ago. Their last name was Anagnos."

The woman's eyes flared with surprise. "Who are you and how did you come by this information?"

I put a hand on my chest. "I'm the daughter of one of the twins." I sensed another muted presence growing closer. A woman who looked the same age as the first stepped into view.

"Let them in, Vita." She spoke with a strange accent that almost sounded Italian.

Vita frowned but stepped out of the way. "Please come in."

"I am Lumia," the other woman said.

"I'm Emily, and this is Tyler."

Lumia didn't offer to shake our hands. "Would you care for tea?"

"That would be wonderful." I concentrated on the barrier muting her aura. Golden sunlight warmed my skin, and a fresh spring breeze brushed through my hair. I must have moaned with contentment because when I opened my eyes, the two women regarded me with concern.

"You have seen us," Lumia said. "Only a formidable power could penetrate our veils."

"Your veils?" It took a moment for me to make the connection. "You mean the barrier hiding your auras?"

"Wait, they're not noms?" Tyler said.

"She really must be the child of the twins." Vita's wrinkled skin shimmered away, leaving behind a woman who looked no older than thirty. Aquamarine hair flowed about her shoulders as if she floated underwater.

Lumia underwent a similar transformation, but her frame shrank, leaving behind a woman so small she might pass for a child. She held her arms open in greeting. "Child of the twins, you are welcome in our home."

The entire house underwent a transformation. The inside filled with lush vegetation, the floor became a bed of seashells and pearls. Living wood formed furniture, and flowers sprouted from the walls.

"Holy shit!" Tyler nearly fell over backward.

Lumia's eyes narrowed. "There is something different about this male."

"He's a jade spirit." I prepared to launch into an explanation, but the woman cooed as if I'd just handed them a baby.

"Oh, my, a jade." Vita peered into his eyes as if inspecting a horse. "What a rare prize. Is he pure spirit, or Daemos?"

"Pure," I said quite proudly. "He's rare specimen, indeed."

"Jades are so rare because very little divine magic still exists these days."

Lumia shook her head sadly. "Much of it was lost in the Sundering, and the old gods have shown no sign of returning."

I had no idea what they were talking about. A million questions sprang to mind. Unfortunately, I was here for something more mundane. "Do you know the Anagnoses? Are they my grandparents?"

Lumia shook her head. "No, child. They are not."

CHAPTER 25

Tyler groaned. "Seriously? Who else could they be?"

It took a moment to find my voice. "Then who are they? Who are you?"

Vita spoke first. "I am Vitania, once a Siren, now a simple woman."

"And I am Lumia of the Fae," the other woman said.

I gasped. "You're a fairy?"

Lumia's nose wrinkled. "I do not care for that mortal term."

Tyler stared at Vitania. "When you say Siren, do you mean the mermaids who lured sailors to their deaths on the rocks?"

The Siren grimaced. "There were some troublemakers in the early days of man, but our kind has largely retreated to our home realm, Aquilis. I prefer Eden and this simple life."

"Whoa." Tyler seemed unable to speak, a rare occurrence indeed.

Despite this flabbergasting discovery, I still felt a sense of crushing defeat. "Do you know who my grandparents were? Do you know where my mother and her sister came from?"

Lumia and Vitania looked at each other for a moment. The Fae nodded at her companion before looking back at me. "Your grandfather may still live, but he is unknown to us. Your grandmother still lives but is likely not in this realm."

"Not in this realm?" I frowned. "Where else would she be?"

Tyler tapped a finger on his chin. "Is she a Siren or a Fae?"

Lumia shook her head. "She is neither, for she is more ancient than either of our species."

"Dude, that's really old." Tyler gave them a sheepish grin. "I mean, but you both still look really young for your age."

The reference to her age didn't seem to faze Lumia in the least. "The goddess came to us while great with child. She asked us to find mortal care for her unborn daughters since they would be happier among people than with her in solitude."

"A goddess?" Tyler's mouth dropped open. "As in a real divine goddess?"

Lumia smiled, apparently amused. "She is a goddess, yes, but her divine nature is subject to debate."

I grimaced. "That doesn't sound promising."

"How did she get pregnant in the first place?" Tyler asked.

"She has lain with mortals from time to time, as she is wont to do when boredom becomes too much. Her attempts to live among them proved quite maddening since most humans are childlike." Lumia sighed. "Even the best of them are tiring to the soul."

"And yet she banged one?" Tyler shook his head. "That doesn't compute."

"The goddess is not what one might expect." Vitania held out her hands helplessly. "She simply does what she wills with little or no explanation."

"This goddess is my grandmother?" I had trouble speaking. "If my mother was the daughter of a goddess, how could she die?"

"Your mother is dead?" Lumia's eyes tightened with worry. "I am saddened to hear that."

I didn't quite believe her. "How were my mother and her sister kidnapped with a Siren and Fae watching over them?"

"We did not watch over them," Vitania replied. "We did as the goddess asked and located mortal parents for them."

"We found them a good home with Aiken and Parna Anagnos." Lumia's brow pinched. "When the babies were kidnapped, we thought the goddess had reclaimed them or was displeased with our choice of wards."

"It was no longer our concern," Vitania added.

Something unspoken seemed to pass between them. I felt as if they were hiding something. Maybe they were ashamed for losing the babies so soon after finding them mortal parents. I was a bit shocked by how little they seemed to care. Then again, they'd dealt with the whims of a goddess. Perhaps they really felt they'd done everything she'd asked for.

Since they didn't seem to know or care what had happened to the babies, I filled in the blanks. "They were stolen by a lycan who works for an orphanage in England. The people there steal children from powerful Arcanes. Fortunately, one of the caretakers spirited my mother and her sister from that evil place and left them on the doorstep of my grandparents."

"It is good they found another home," Vitania said. She and Lumia shared another look, but I couldn't decipher what it meant.

Lumia clasped her hands. "Did the girls have a good childhood?"

I nodded. "The best." They didn't really seem to care that much so I circled back to my earlier question. "I still don't understand how my mother died if she's the daughter of a goddess. Shouldn't she be immortal, or at least tougher than usual?"

Vitania went silent for a moment before continuing. "The goddess culled the children of immortality and powers so they would not be different from other mortal children."

My heart turned to stone. "She stripped them of immortality?" I wanted to scream. "What sort of horrific goddess is she?"

The women silently contemplated each other, as if deciding who'd explain such things to this silly girl.

Vitania answered with a non-answer. "Eve is complicated."

"Eve?" Tyler's forehead pinched. "As in Adam and Eve? The biblical first woman?"

"She was that woman," Lumia said. "But also much more."

"And quite a bit less," Vitania said in a disapproving voice. "Eve does what Eve wills, no matter the consequences."

For the umpteenth time, I began to question everything I'd ever believed. "So Adam was a god too?"

Lumia and Vitania bubbled with laughter.

"Oh, goodness, no." Lumia spoke between bouts of laughter. "Eve gave birth to Adam, the first mortal man, and when he had grown, she lay with him to make the next humans. From what I've been told it was a highly controversial move, and generally regarded as a bad idea."

"One of Eve's worst decisions," Vitania said.

"To make men or other humans?" Tyler asked.

"Both," Vitania replied.

Lumia nodded.

"You're not wrong." Tyler grimaced. "Mankind has made a mess of things."

"Certainly, though they still haven't wreaked the same havoc as the Apocryphan or come even close to rivalling the wars between Sirens and Seraphim." Vitania sighed. "Most species have committed atrocities in their long histories."

"Even the Fae." Lumia shook her head. "You cannot fairly judge Eve without judging yourself."

Tears burned my eyes. *Mum should have been immortal.*

Lumia put a hand on my shoulder. "Do not weep, child. Though your mother's mortal coil is gone, her immortal soul persists."

Vitania walked out of the room and returned a moment later with a curved shell that resembled a teapot. She produced four seashell cups and filled each with light blue liquid. "This is my special brew. I think you'll enjoy it."

I regarded the colored liquid with suspicion. "This is tea?"

"From my home realm, yes." She nodded. "Try it."

I took a sip and was pleasantly surprised at the bitter taste. "It's good. Perhaps nearly as good as Earl Grey."

Vitania smiled. "High praise from a Brit."

Tyler took a sip and nodded. "Better than coffee."

Lumia moved her hand over the floor between us. A sapling grew from the floor, branches weaving to form a tabletop. Flat-topped mushrooms sprouted beneath our backsides. I did my best to contain my surprise and took a seat. The mushroom top was quite soft and conforming to my bottom.

For the first time since our arrival, Lumia and Vitania seemed to relax. There was definitely something about the kidnapping they didn't want to discuss, but I left it alone. There was so much I could learn about my past from them, and I didn't want to wear out our welcome.

"This is so cool." Tyler inspected the table. "Could you two come redecorate our condo? I'd love an ocean theme like this."

"This is the most interesting thing to happen to us in quite some time." Lumia patted my hand. "I would love to divine what you've inherited from your grandmother."

"I'm certainly no stronger or more resilient than a mortal," I said. "If anything, I was quite normal up until a few months ago."

Vitania nodded eagerly and took another sip of tea. "Tell us everything."

"If I do, do you think you can help me understand my abilities?"

"Perhaps, child." Lumia's mushroom chair rose higher than ours due to her diminutive frame. She adjusted herself like a child awaiting a delightful bedtime story. "We will help you however we can."

"Agreed," Vitania said.

I took a long drink of the tea and then told them the history of Emily Glass. I told them how I met Tyler, about my parents, the Exorcists, and the Demonicus Incident. Then I brought them up to date on my faked death and my monstrous long-lost sibling.

The Siren and Fae looked positively delighted at my misfortunes and astonished at my abilities.

"It would seem you have no natural inclination to immortality, strength, or resilience," Lumia said. "But you do have godlike powers."

"Only a god could strip the powers from another being or divine the true names of demons from a simple touch." Vitania shivered with delight. "It would seem Eve unwittingly unleashed chaos."

"But I'm not chaotic," I protested.

"Not you, dear. Your sister, Olivia." Lumia set down her tiny teacup and refilled it. "One of you is the banisher, and the other, the summoner."

"So Olivia and I are polar opposites?"

"Perhaps," Lumia said. "Or perhaps you simply developed different abilities based on your experiences."

"I wonder if Emily could wrest our powers from us," Vitania said. "I would test her."

I shook my head. "I don't want to take your powers. I only did it to the vampire and lycan because they deserved it."

"I would have you try it anyway," Vitania said. She reached a hand across the table. "Test your might, child."

My hand trembled beneath hers. Vampires and lycans seemed like nothing compared to either a Siren or a Fae.

She squeezed my hand. "Don't be afraid. Do it."

I gathered my wits and closed my eyes. The crash of distant waves reached my ears, but it came from within the Siren, not from the ocean near the house. Once again, the vision of swirling green and blue waters filled my mind's eye. I reached out, grasped the Siren aura and gently tugged.

Vitania gasped. Someone grabbed my hands and shoved them away from the aura. I opened my eyes and grabbed the table to keep from falling over. But my physical body was in no danger of toppling. I caught a glimpse of my spirit hands and arms collapsing back into me.

"Powerful indeed." Vitania put a hand to her chest and shivered. "Had I been younger, I might not have known how to free myself from your grasp."

"I'm so sorry." I fumbled with my teacup and nearly spilled it. "I told you I didn't want to do it."

"You are a babe with powers you do not understand." Vitania looked at

Lumia. "I believe she could remove powers from anyone without the will to resist."

"How did you push me out?" I said. "That's never happened before."

"Child, I am quite old. I know how to shield myself right down to my very soul." She offered me a kind smile. "Perhaps if you were more experienced you might overwhelm me, but it's not likely."

"How fascinating and frightening." Lumia reached out a hand. "I would like to go next."

I regarded her tiny hand as I might regard a snake. "Are you certain?" I didn't want to be shoved again. It wasn't painful, but it was certainly unpleasant having my spirit form pushed around.

"Absolutely." Lumia gave me a come-hither gesture with her fingers. "I must know how it feels."

Once again, I closed my eyes and found the Fae aura. Vibrant flowers and wonderful scents tickled my nose. The aura was so calming, I nearly forgot to reach out and pull it. Lumia shrieked with delight when I gave a gentle tug. But she didn't reject me as Vitania had.

"I am tempted to let her take it," Lumia said. "I would feel the pull of mortality on my bones and know the peace of eternal slumber."

Vitania's eyes flared. "You would not dare."

I blinked open my eyes and withdrew from Lumia. "I would never take it from you."

Tyler sat on his mushroom watching with his typical amused grin. I could tell he wanted to interject a cute joke or opinion, but he seemed to know it wouldn't impress these women.

"Can I improve my control?" I said. "Are there are abilities I haven't discovered?"

"Only Eve could say for sure," Lumia said. "But I wouldn't dare let her know."

Her words planted dread deep in my stomach. "Why is that?"

"She would immediately strip you of your powers. Eve does not like to admit her mistakes, but she corrects them when she can." Lumia patted my hand. "Just pray she never discovers you exist."

"Not just her," Vitania said. "If any god learned of a mortal with godlike powers, they would quickly kill you."

CHAPTER 26

It was frightening to know my grandmother was a goddess who would strip me of my powers, but even more terrifying to know that the other gods would kill me because of them.

"You would be wise to keep your abilities to yourself," Vitania said. "If you must use them, do so discreetly."

Tyler's amused grin flat-lined. "How likely is it a god would find out about her?"

"Considering we have heard nothing from them in eons, I would say very unlikely," Lumia said. "But it's likely the old gods left behind minions who could report to them if they discovered something important."

"Where did they go?" Tyler said. "What do they do in their free time if they're not messing with mortals?"

"Creating other worlds, or perhaps exploring the universe." Lumia spread her hands wide. "I have never met an omniscient or all-powerful god. Even they were created from stardust and know little about the origins of the universe."

"That's somewhat reassuring." Tyler reached over and squeezed my hand. "So we'll just keep your powers on the down-low."

I nodded. "Yes. I'll speak with George about it." I turned back to Lumia and Vitania. "Olivia seems far more powerful than me. I'm afraid she's more likely to alert an old god than I am. Is there any way you could help me stop her?"

"We cannot," Vitania said. "If we tried to stop every evil in the world, then we would have no peace."

"But she's not just another evil," I said. "She could raise a demon army by herself."

Lumia held up a hand. "Peace, child. You can say nothing to sway us. We tired of conflict and politics long ago. Vitania and I come from two different worlds, but we found love and peace. There is something to be said of this quiet life, and we will not abandon it."

"Strong words from you, love." Vitania raised an eyebrow. "Especially when you spoke of shedding the yoke of immortality so you might die."

"There is a great burden to eternal life in this world." A tear glinted in Lumia's eye. "But also great joy to be had. I fear boredom sometimes drives me insane."

"I'll bet." Tyler grimaced. "I'm not very old, but I felt the same way trapped in Haedaemos."

"It is refreshing to have such intriguing visitors." Lumia wiped her eyes. "It keeps life interesting."

I wasn't surprised they turned down my request for help. They'd isolated themselves for a reason, and there wasn't much I could do to change their minds. But I could ask them for advice and knowledge. "Since you won't actively help, is there anything you can tell me? I really need to stop my sister from helping this Netherlord character."

Lumia chuckled. "What an archaic term. I have not heard it used in millennia."

"Long before the Sundering," Vitania said. "Before Haedaemos, when there was only Hell."

"Wait, there was a time when Hell existed?" Tyler said.

"Eve gave mankind part of her everlasting soul, so they could live on after departing their mortal coil." Vitania shook her head. "Hades saw the power in controlling these souls and created the underworld that he might draw them there and accumulate power."

"But Eve created a hidden world above the clouds where the souls of the departed would find peace in the afterlife." Lumia smiled fondly. "She placed another god in charge that he might battle Hades for every soul."

"Uh, would that be God with a capital G?" Tyler asked.

"Elohim took on many names. But after the Sundering, Hades vanished, and Elohim decided there was nothing more to do." Vitania took a sip of tea. "He was among the last to leave."

"Who could be the Netherlord now?" I asked.

"Perhaps there is a power struggle in Haedaemos," Lumia said. "The overlords war from time to time. It would not surprise me if one crowned himself Netherlord."

"The true Netherlord, Hades, is long gone," Vitania added. "If he returned, we would certainly know."

Lumia quirked her lips. "There was a time, after Hades left, when Xanos called herself Netherlord."

"Xanos and her games." Vitania scowled.

"So you think Xanos is this Netherlord?" I said.

Vitania shook her head. "Xanos, like the other Apocryphan, is trapped within the Abyss. I made sure not even Baal himself could pierce the veil."

"So you had something to do with trapping the Apocryphan there?" I said.

Vitania waved a hand dismissively. "Yes, but it was long ago, and the Apocryphan can no longer trouble the realms."

Tyler looked troubled. "If Baal, the grand overlord of Haedaemos can't penetrate the veil between his realm and the Abyss, then how can Daemos banish souls to the Abyss?"

"They cannot." Vitania frowned. "There is no way to bring forth or send any soul into the Abyss. It is an eternal prison with no door."

"I'm afraid that's not entirely true," I said. "I've seen a Daemos banish someone to the Abyss, and I've even seen an Abyssal demon before."

Vitania shook her head. "You are mistaken. The Apocryphan and the souls of their minions were sealed inside the prison by the eternal flame."

Tyler tilted his head. "Do you mean the infernal fount?"

"Yes. Were it not for the aid of Eve, it would never have been possible." Vitania seemed a bit perturbed by our questioning. "Let us speak of other things. Whoever uses the Netherlord title is simply someone who wishes to stir up old fears. If Baal discovers the troublemaker, he will be sure to quench their flame."

"I don't think the Netherlord can do much if we stop my sister," I said. "The problem is, I don't know how I'm supposed to stop someone who can possess someone against their will."

"She has soul powers like your own," Lumia said. "She forces the demons into bodies much differently than a normal possession. That probably causes the body to manifest physical attributes of the demons."

"What kind of damage does that do to a person?" Tyler said. "It can't be good."

"I imagine it's traumatic both physically and mentally," Lumia said. "I cannot say whether it causes permanent damage."

"So how do I stop Olivia?" I asked.

"From what you described, she can affect people without even touching them," Vitania said. "You must be able to do the same if you are to banish the demons she brings forth."

Tyler grunted. "I think she draws a demon summoning pattern in the air. Then she somehow pulls through a swarm of spirits. It shouldn't be possible."

Vitania shook her head. "As far as I know, a demon summoning pattern requires solid lines and can only admit the specific demon it names. But even with my vast experience, there is much I do not know."

"I am not as familiar with demonic summoning as Vitania," Lumia said, "so I cannot say if it is possible or not."

"As you probably don't know, the Sirens built the Obsidian and Alabaster Arches." The pride in Vitania's tone was hard to miss. "We built them to reconnect the realms after the Sundering, since not even the Apocryphan had the power to bridge the gulf between worlds. The archways were the most complicated feats of magical engineering we undertook, not because they needed to be, but because we could not risk the Apocryphan discovering there were easier ways to travel the realms."

Easier ways to travel? I felt like a tiny speck in the grand scheme compared to everything these women had witnessed.

Tyler clapped his hands. "You created complicated enchantments and archways as a red herring for the Apocryphan?" Tyler laughed. "Now that's funny."

Vitania looked quite pleased with herself. I didn't understand how Tyler took all of this in without feeling a bit mad. Everything I'd been taught as a child about religion was completely wrong. Then again, it shouldn't have been so surprising, considering most religious texts were written after centuries of being passed down as stories.

Vitania continued her tale. "The Apocryphan were far too full of themselves to do the dirty work and learn what caused the Sundering and how to create gateways. The details are quite simple. Imagine each realm as a bubble. Some are small, others are large. Some are perfectly round, and others oblong or irregular. That is because the Sundering split the physical world into pocket dimensions all within the same relative space."

Tyler wrinkled his nose. "I'm sorry, but this Sundering thing is totally new to me."

"The Apocryphan warred with each other. The conflict focused on the ancient city of Juranthemon, unleashing such incredible powers, that the Earth was split or sundered into multiple realms, casting many species apart from the others." Vitania waggled a hand. "That is more or less what happened."

Tyler still wore a frown, but he nodded slowly. "Gotcha. Big fight, big bang."

"While the realms were first forming, they occupied the same physical space, but in different dimensions. Then they began to drift apart. The only thing holding them together were quantum tunnels." Vitania motioned to Lumia. "Can you illustrate?"

"Of course, dear." Lumia rubbed her fingers together. Golden light gathered in her palm. She flicked her fingertips and dust sparkled in the air, coalescing into the blue and green marble we called Earth. An explosion rippled through the planet and strange, ghostly shapes drifted in and out of the globe. Another wiggle of her fingers turned the image translucent, revealing the outlines of hundreds of objects all separate but within the same space as the planet.

My mouth dropped open. "My god, that's amazing."

Lumia smiled at me. "I will speed up time." She did her magic again, and the shapes changed form, some approximating Earth's size and shape, others shrinking, and still others warping into bizarre shapes. They all began to drift outward, like a debris cloud slowly clearing an explosion.

Vitania nodded and Lumia froze the image. "This is where we noticed the problem." She pointed to the intricate threads connecting the realms. "Once they drifted too far, the quantum tunnels would snap." She pointed to a vibrant green sphere that had drifted out farther than the others. "The realm with most of the world's unicorns drifted too far. All of its quantum tunnels snapped."

The breath caught in my throat. "What happened to it?"

Vitania snapped her fingers and the green realm poofed away. "It collapsed in upon itself. Any creatures in that realm were snuffed from existence."

"Jesus." Tyler shivered. "No wonder all the unicorns are gone."

"Not all," Lumia said. "Many still live in my home realm."

Vitania ignored the side banter. "That was when we realized we had to stabilize the outward velocity of the realms."

"Sounds more like science than magic," Tyler replied.

"It was a great deal of both." Vitania paused for another sip of tea. "We turned the most stable realm into a center of gravity and tethered the realms to it with quantum strands. I cannot begin to describe the thousands of hours of work it took to stabilize the realms, or how difficult it was to engineer such a feat without the Apocryphan understanding why it had to be done. But once we finished, we realized how easy it was to travel the realms, provided one could access the quantum tunnels."

"So you made it look a lot harder than it is," Tyler said.

"Exactly." Vitania looked to me. "Perhaps Olivia has tapped into the magic behind the quantum tunnels. That must be how she can draw forth demons without a pattern."

"Does it mean she can travel anywhere?" I said.

"I don't know." Vitania tapped a finger to her chin. "I think she has probably fumbled through discovering her powers just as you have. It's likely she can only open rifts between Eden and Haedaemos."

"Can you teach me how to access the quantum tunnels?" I asked.

Vitania raised an eyebrow and looked at Lumia. Silent agreement seemed to pass between them, because the Siren nodded at me. "Yes, I think I can."

"Hey, there's another thing you might be able to tell us." Tyler got up. "Be right back."

I frowned, surprised as he dashed out the front door. He returned a moment later with Tilden—the tridecagon had been in the boot—and put it on the floor. "What is this thing and why was it with Emily's mom and aunt?"

Vitania frowned. "I have never seen it before."

"Neither have I," Lumia said.

"Then where did it come from?" I said.

"Watch this." Tyler put it on the floor. Tilden clanked and rolled until it reached my feet.

Vitania pursed her lips. "I cannot sense anything about it, but if you wish, I can study it further."

"That would be wonderful," I said.

"Where do you want it?" Tyler asked.

Vitania picked it up under one arm. "I will store it in a chest for the time being." She went into another room and returned a moment later.

I looked at them expectantly. "So with that out of the way, what do I do next to learn about quantum tunnels?"

"Next, I explain the science and magic behind the tunnels. To do a thing, you must first understand it." Vitania turned to Tyler. "You may amuse yourself however you wish. There is food in the cupboard, and a nom television in the other room."

Tyler's green eyes saddened. "I can't go learn with her?"

"It would be a waste of time. You do not possess the ability." Vitania walked over to a table and picked up a small seashell. "You may also go for a swim. The song of the sea will allow you to breathe and keep warm underwater." She pressed it to his neck and it stuck there. "Does that appeal to you?"

Tyler's eyes widened with delight. "I can swim and breathe underwater? Can I talk with fish?"

"I'm afraid they have little to say." A smile touched the Siren's lips. "There is large clamshell in the other room. Open it and you will find access to the ocean. Just don't wander too far, please."

Tyler gave me a hug and a kiss. "This is going to be way more fun than what you've got to do." He winked. "Love ya, babe."

I smiled at his boyish enthusiasm and watched him vanish into the other room. "I just hope he doesn't try to build an army of dolphins to scare the tourists."

Vitania led me into a room where the top of a tree sprouted through the floor. Lumia brushed the bark with a hand and a spiral staircase of tree branches formed, leading down. I followed the pair down a few feet and gasped. Golden sunlight warmed a large flat disc of land. A small forest spread out beneath us, bisected by an icy blue river. The tree we stood on towered far above the rest. Green seas bordered the land on all sides. Beyond the water was nothing but an ocean of stars.

"What is this place?" I tried not to look down since there was nothing between me and the ground but evenly spaced tree branches. "Is that a flat Earth?"

"This tree protrudes through a quantum tunnel. We are now in the tiny realm of Avin." Vitania sighed with contentment. "I have spent my years researching all the realms. I have catalogued over a hundred."

"How many are there?" I said.

"Hundreds, but I do not know an exact number," she replied.

"This is how we amuse ourselves," Lumia said. "This is why we have not gone mad with boredom."

"It's absolutely beautiful." I stepped carefully down to the next branch. "But the height is terrifying."

"There is no need to fear heights here." Lumia took my hand and Vitania took the other. Then they leapt off the tree.

I screamed as gravity yanked us down. Wind rushed against my face. I looked down and prepared to splat. Our momentum slowed and we gently touched down in a clearing.

Cold sweat trickled down my back and my legs felt like jelly. "You frightened me nearly to death."

"Delightful." Lumia sighed. "If only I could feel such raw emotions again. It would be wonderful to forget everything and start anew."

Vitania wrinkled her nose. "You've become mentally fragile in your old age. There is plenty in this universe to experience for the first time."

I touched Lumia's dainty hand. "There is nothing new under the sun, but there is still plenty you haven't seen."

The Fae smiled. "Yes, I know. It is why I abandoned my kingdom. Otherwise, I might have gone completely mad."

The dense forest parted into a wide clearing. Crimson waters lapped at shores covered in blue ferns. Golden flamingos waded in the shallows, plucking tiny white fish in their large bills. Moss-green monkeys danced in the treetops, and a troupe of furry rodents drank at the water's edge.

"Why is the water red?" I asked.

"The red clay leeches into the waters," Vitania said. She lifted a hand. The water rippled. Birds took to the air and land animals scattered. A huge domed shell rose from the water. Fish slid down its smooth surface and plopped back into the water.

Lumia shook her head. "So unnecessary."

Vitania didn't respond. A small portal opened in the shell and she stepped through. I followed her and nearly stumbled over my own feet when I saw the inside. It was filled with stars.

A wave of the hand banished the stars and left behind walls lined with hundreds of shells. "Welcome to my library." Vitania plucked a white shell and held it up. "Prepare yourself child, for today your education begins."

CHAPTER 27

I wasn't mentally prepared for my first lesson. Vitania spoke at length about the science behind the quantum tunnels and how they connected not only the realms, but other dimensions as well. Lumia excused herself and left the library. I clenched my teeth and did my best to stay awake for the lecture.

The white shell projected an illustration of the realms and quantum tunnels similar to what Lumia had shown me earlier.

"Well?" Vitania looked at me expectantly. "What is your answer?"

I blinked out of my stupor. "I'm sorry. I didn't hear the question."

Vitania traced a finger along the glowing rim of a small amoeba-shaped realm. "What is this?"

I tried to recall the last thing she'd said, but my memory was blank. "The realm border?"

She frowned. "I will have to sharpen your wits." What she did next was unexpected. Her mouth opened unusually wide and eerie notes drifted into my ears. It seemed impossible for one throat to produce such a chorus of notes and foreign words all at the same time. The fast pace energized my mind. My focus sharpened and all my senses came alive. The song seemed to fill not only my ears, but my entire perception of reality.

The song trailed to silence. Vitania gave me an appraising look and grunted. "Let me explain again."

"Wait, what did you do to me?" I stared at my hand and marveled at how every pore, every wrinkle seemed so sharp and vivid.

"Sirens work magic through song. All of life is a chorus, a beat, a melody." She brushed a lock of flowing hair from her face. "I sang the song of learning to enhance your mind."

"It was the most amazing thing I've ever heard." Even now, I noticed small details I'd filtered out before.

"Let us continue." She began her lecture again.

The next time she asked the question, I knew the answer. My mind felt so sharp and alert, I felt as if I could answer all the questions in the world. "The glowing border is the quantum layer," I said. "It permeates the realm at a subatomic level and connects the quantum tunnels. Does this mean you can open a rift to a tunnel from anywhere?"

"Precisely." Vitania looked pleased. "There is more you must understand." She launched into another lecture which I followed without so much as a yawn. By the end, I felt as if I had a basic understanding of the cosmic web of quantum fields that connected everything right down to the smallest atoms. It was a huge step for someone who struggled at maths and science.

"Very few beings are powerful enough to bend the universe to their will," Vitania said. "This is what separates the old gods from the Apocryphan."

"The Apocryphan can't make worlds?" I asked.

"The Apocryphan are destroyers and usurpers." The Siren shook her head sadly. "They are not true gods."

"Is Eve one of the first gods?" I asked.

"She might be the oldest, or somewhere in between, but Eve is sensitive about her age." Vitania shrugged. "She is obviously powerful enough to make beings with souls."

"Aren't all women?" I said. "Humans have souls, and all humans come from women."

The Siren laughed. "Quite true, child. Eve granted this gift to all women. Bringing a new soul into this existence is perhaps the greatest magic of all." She abruptly changed the subject. "You have absorbed all you can today. You will need rest. The song of learning exacts a toll on the mind."

I looked at my arcphone and was surprised to see we'd been at it for nearly five hours. "It doesn't feel like we've been in here that long."

"Your mind has handled the strain far better than any normal mortal's would have." Vitania took my hand. "Perhaps you have more of Eve within you than we realized."

We left the shell library and walked back to the great redwood tree. Lumia fluttered above on gossamer wings, motes of sparkling dust dancing in the sky around her.

"She's so beautiful," I breathed. "Are all Fae so lovely?"

Vitania sighed, as if marveling anew at the sight of her companion. "The Fae are magnificent beings. Lumia hides her true beauty, as it is too much for mortal minds to bear." A blush crept into Vitania's cheeks. "Sometimes I wonder why she chose me."

"Because you have a beautiful mind." I sighed with wonder. "And you are the only one who keeps her sane and rooted in this existence."

"Wise words, child." Vitania lifted her chin and sang a brief but happy melody.

Lumia flitted down, sunlight framing her fairy form like a halo. She hovered just above Vitania and pecked a kiss on her nose. "This place brings me peace. I am glad I came with you."

Vitania smiled. "You are usually glad when you take my advice."

"Too true, love." Lumia landed, and her wings vanished against her back.

When we neared the giant redwood, I wondered if we'd actually walk the spiral staircase of branches up into the sky. I knew to expect the unexpected and was not disappointed when a gust of wind hurled us straight upward at breathtaking speed. This time, I simply let it carry me. I looked down and watched the small realm recede.

I couldn't repress a whoop of delight. It seemed Tyler's boyish enthusiasm was rubbing off on me.

The wind gusted to the side and we landed neatly near the top of the tree where it vanished into the sky.

"Very good, child." Vitania pinched my cheek gently. "You did not scream once."

I smiled. "I didn't think you'd kill me after spending so much time teaching me." I paused to pass my hand through a cloud as we climbed the branches where they vanished through a hole in the sky.

We emerged in the room in Eden. Tyler sat in the kitchen eating oysters. Face flushed with excitement, he ran over and gave me a hug, then proceeded to tell me about his undersea adventure.

"The whales are so cool, you wouldn't believe!" He held his hand apart as if trying to express their size. "I felt like I could almost understand them, you know?" He pulled out a chair and offered me a plate with a steaming pink fish on it. "I guess Sirens don't have anything against eating seafood."

"Food is food," Vitania said. "Though I prefer not to eat land animals."

Lumia grimaced. "I would never eat the flesh of land animals. Only that of fish."

I hadn't realized just how ravenous I was. By the time I finished eating, I'd consumed a Tyler-sized portion of fish, scallops, and some strange sea vegetables.

Vitania showed us to a room with a seashell bed. "Sleep well, for we will test your abilities tomorrow."

I lay in the soft sheets and cuddled against Tyler.

"So, what did you learn?" Tyler asked.

I started to speak, but my words slurred together, and my eyelids grew heavy. Try as I might to speak, my body refused to respond, and my eyes closed. When I opened them again, my arcphone told me it was morning, and Tyler was asleep next to me.

I felt rested, but a mild headache nagged me. I went into the kitchen area. Vitania and Lumia sat at the living tree table, drinking tea and talking.

"Eat well, child, for today will be strenuous." Vitania motioned me to a mushroom seat.

I was even hungrier this morning than I'd been last night and stuffed my face with pastries and lightly salted fish. I wondered what Isabel would think if she saw me eating like a pig. *She'd make fun of me and then join in.* I wondered how she was doing and how the others at OnTech fared without Tyler around.

We hadn't been gone that long, but it felt like forever since the day the demons tried to kill me on the streets of Atlanta. Now, I was nearly a world away. It was so strange how life could drastically change in a matter of minutes.

Tyler joined us for breakfast just as we were finishing. I gave him a kiss and told him to have fun with the whales again.

"I was hoping for some other kind of fun before you left." Tyler's shoulders slumped. "Maybe when you get back."

"I'd love to, hot stuff." I nibbled his ear. Traced my lips across his cheek and gently bit his lower lip. "We'll finish this later." Then I turned and followed Vitania.

"That's so wrong," Tyler called after me. "How am I supposed to go swimming with this huge boner?"

I giggled and blew him a kiss over my shoulder.

When we reached the library, Lumia left us again. I followed Vitania inside and asked, "Will you sing me the song of learning again?"

She pursed her lips. "Your mind does not seem overly strained from yesterday, so it is probably safe."

Once again, she filled my mind with eerily beautiful music that left me more alert than a kid on a sugar rush. Vitania wasted no time getting to the meat of the lesson.

"The universe, like anything, runs on rules." An image of the world filled the center of the library. "These rules dictate how magic and science work. They dictate how we interact with the world around us. Most beings can manipulate these rules on a small scale, while a rare few can use them to create worlds." Streams of tiny symbols crept across the world, replacing it with dense lines. I squinted my eyes but, even so, I couldn't read them.

"What are those?" I asked.

"Symbols and equations we use to interpret the rules of the universe." She zoomed in on one stream and paused it. "This represents the travel of photons through physical objects."

The code was too dense for me to understand, but bits and pieces looked familiar. "I think I've seen some of that before."

"This?" Vitania zoomed in further. "These are Cyrinthian symbols, the language of the old gods."

"But that looks like something I remember from physics in high school." I hadn't done well at all in physics, but I did recall some symbols.

"Yes, even nom science utilizes Cyrinthian without even realizing it." She swiped away the image. "I believe Olivia utilized Cyrinthian code to unlock a portal to Haedaemos. I will not show you that. Instead, I will show you the code to open a portal to Aquanis."

My forehead pinched. "I thought you said the Siren home realm is Aquilis."

"Yes, that's right." Vitania began tracing her finger in the air, leaving a trail of blue symbols. "Aquanis is another aquatic realm I discovered. The only islands there are perched on the backs of massive sea turtles."

"Massive turtles?" I tried to envision what she meant and failed. "What happens if they go underwater?"

"Everything would get wet, I imagine." Vitania stepped back and inspected her handiwork.

I counted nine symbols, some of which I'd have trouble reproducing without a lot of practice. Even so, it seemed opening a portal required far fewer symbols than I'd feared. "So I just draw these in the air and a portal will open to Aquanis?"

"Obviously not, or one would have opened when I drew them." Vitania took my hands and held my gaze with hers. "A being of great power could open a rift by simply imagining the symbols. Despite your ancestry, I believe your powers are heavily diluted by your mortal blood. That means it will be more strenuous."

I nodded. "I'm ready to try."

She nodded at the symbols. "Reproduce everything I've written. Keep at it until it's perfect. Speed is of the essence for beings of lesser power. If the symbols are not strung together in a precise rhythm, they will not coalesce properly, and your willpower will falter."

"And that's the trick to opening the portal?"

Vitania shook her head. "It's only a small part. Willpower is even more vital. It infuses the symbols with the energy to tear a hole in the quantum layer." She released my hands. "Now, go to it."

Despite my clear mind, it took over a hundred tries and two hours for me to perfectly replicate the symbols. The air in the middle of the room resembled a classroom chalkboard where a naughty student expressed remorse at bad behavior.

I will not curse in class. I will not curse in class.

My fingers ached, and I'd cursed more times than I could count during the exercise.

"Beautiful." Vitania looked up from a seashell book she'd read while I practiced. "Now, you must be able to do that within twenty seconds."

I groaned and circled the two most complex symbols. "It takes me a minute to do each of these."

"Then you must do better." She swiped a hand in the air and all but the original line of symbols vanished. "Continue."

"Why twenty seconds?" I said. "Why not thirty-one or seventy-seven?"

"Every symbol must be tightly controlled by your will until you complete the final pattern." She tapped a finger to my forehead. "The strain of such an undertaking increases exponentially with every passing second. You will understand when we reach that lesson."

I had no idea what she meant, but I got back to it. I lost track of how long I practiced drawing the symbols. By the time Vitania called a halt, I'd shaved my time down to forty-five seconds. I wasn't anywhere close to where I needed to be. My arms and fingers ached, and I was exhausted.

What she wanted me to do seemed impossible. I simply wasn't a match for Olivia.

CHAPTER 28

I barely remembered eating or cuddling up to Tyler and then it was morning again. I didn't feel nearly as alert as the morning before, and my head throbbed.

Lumia's eyes flared when she saw me at breakfast. She gave Vitania a concerned look. "You're pushing her too hard."

"I could simply let her remain weak and ignorant." The Siren sipped her blue tea. "One cannot hope to learn everything within the space of two days."

"You should give up this quest, child." Lumia pressed her hands to my temples. Soothing energy drained the aches. "Go home and enjoy your life."

Vitania sighed. "You know this is for the best, love. Do not discourage her."

"Positive mental attitude?" Tyler walked into the kitchen and slung a leg over a mushroom chair. His brow furrowed when he looked at me. "Dark circles under the eyes. Lack of focus. Babe, you need a vacation."

I shook my head. "No, I feel much better, thanks to Lumia."

The Fae continued treating my headache. "I am no healer, but if you give me two hours, I can siphon off most of the stress chemicals."

"The child needs every hour she can get." Vitania put a hand over mine. "Perhaps today you will hit the timing, and we can open a gateway."

"Yes, I'd like that." I only had a few days before my work for Fjoeruss began. I had to prepare myself in case Olivia showed up again.

"Then finish eating and let us go." Vitania regarded Lumia with a displeased side-glare.

Lumia walked behind me and put her fingers back on my head while I ate. When we left, the headache was gone, and I felt much better.

"I will remain here today," Lumia said. "Perhaps I will adventure with Tyler."

"Really?" Tyler looked almost comically relieved and happy. "Swimming with the fishes is fun, but they aren't great company."

"Yes, enjoy your day." Vitania took my hand. "Let us go, child."

Vitania sang me the song of learning as we descended the great tree. The moment we reached the library, I went back to practicing. But try as I might, I simply didn't have the precision and dexterity to hit the required mark. By the time lunch rolled around, I was ready to give up.

"It's too much for my feeble hands." I sighed and felt like collapsing in on myself. "I just don't understand how Olivia did it so fast."

Vitania frowned. "Your movements are quick and precise. You have mastered the symbols, but perhaps your human limits hamper you." She put a hand on my chest. "Summon the lycan aura and try again."

I slapped a palm to my face. "Why didn't I think of that yesterday?"

"Your lycan aura comes at a cost. I believe the primal urges may prove detrimental to your concentration, but you can try."

I also hadn't considered that. It certainly made me appreciate why dogs couldn't resist the lure of squirrels. The instincts of the lycan aura were overwhelming to someone who hadn't learned to control it with years of practice.

The moment I summoned it, strength surged through my body. My vision sharpened and my nose detected the faintest of scents even though the library was an almost sterile environment. Vitania smelled like cold ocean water. But another scent lurked beneath that—something a little sour. Lycan instinct recognized it as fear.

She's afraid I can't do this. I can't let her down!

The primal urges felt muted and distant—much different than the other times. I knew it wasn't because I'd learned better control. "How strange. I don't feel the urge to kill an animal and eat it raw."

Vitania smiled. "The song of learning strengthens your conscious mind. Perhaps a side-effect is suppressing basic instincts."

"If the lycan aura was always like this, I'd use it every day." I shuddered with excitement. "I really think I can do this now." And I did. Not right away, of course. At top speed, my hand blurred, making scribbles from the patterns instead of neat lines. Even my enhanced dexterity couldn't compensate. I had to slow down and focus.

At long last, I finished the Cyrinthian code in nineteen seconds. I knew I could do better if I kept practicing with the lycan powers enabled. The fear in Vitania's scent vanished. She smiled wide with elation.

"The first step is complete, child. Now for the true test." Her fear scent increased once again. "Now you must learn to bind each symbol to your will."

I didn't like sensing her fear, because it made me doubt my abilities, nesting a pit of anxiety deep in my stomach. I nodded. "I'm ready."

Vitania drew the first symbol with her finger. It flashed white and dimmed to a dull glow. "The symbol is bound to my will. It will draw energy from me until the circuit is closed."

"Circuit?"

"Each symbol is a piece of the completed code. When you complete the string, you must close the circuit with a circle." She demonstrated by drawing all but the last symbol. Hand open, she swooped it in a precise circle. The air seemed to smolder with heat, but nothing else happened.

I put a hand next to the glowing symbols and felt heat emanating from them. "If you had drawn the last symbol, would a rift have opened?"

She nodded. "I would have imagined the size and shape of the rift and where I wanted it to open." Vitania made a swiping motion at the symbols, and they poofed away.

"Are the symbols usually visible, or is that just because we're using this holographic chalkboard?"

"You can make them visible by willing them to be, but all that is important is you keep them fixed in your mind." She demonstrated by drawing a couple in thin air and left them hanging for a moment before wiping them. "Now you try."

I concentrated my will on the first symbol and drew it. It flashed, fizzled, and vanished. "I-I did it! I made it flash!" I clapped my hands and giggled. "Does that mean I'm magical?"

Vitania frowned, as if confused by my elation. "That was hardly even a start, child. You must maintain the symbol until the code is complete."

"Yes, but I made it flash!"

The Siren tried on a smile but couldn't make it work. "Try again."

I did, but this time I concentrated harder on the first symbol. It sparked, fizzled, flickered, and vanished. My elation evaporated. "I don't understand. I tried really hard that time."

Vitania nodded. "You must maintain your will on each symbol. You cannot release it when you draw the next one."

"But I was trying to hold onto just that one."

"In your effort to concentrate, you lost focus." She drew the symbol. It flashed and dimmed as before. "I am holding this symbol by willing it to remain and clearly focusing on its exact dimensions. Will, clarity, and focus work in unison."

I didn't understand what she meant, but I tried again. It took another twenty tries before something finally clicked and the symbol flashed and dimmed. I felt as if I had to burn the image into my mind to keep it properly focused. But the moment I tried to draw the next symbol, the first vanished. "No!" I pressed my hands to my cheeks. "Where did it go?"

"You must learn to maintain the previous symbols when you draw the next." Vitania mimicked drawing the first. "Once you have completed the first, you must continue to will it to exist, and so forth and so on, until the code is complete."

I soon learned that drawing the symbols was child's play compared to what came next.

By the end of the day, I finally got the second symbol to coexist with the first. The strain felt as if a steel vice squeezed my brain. I released the symbols and squeezed my eyes shut. "My god. No wonder you said it has to be done quickly. It's like eating ice cream too fast and getting brain freeze."

"It grows easier with time, child." Vitania offered a comforting pat on the shoulder. "I must warn you that completing the final circuit is far more draining because that is when you must supply it with the magical energy it needs to open."

I blinked. "How do I do that?"

"If you have truly inherited Eve's abilities, it may come naturally. You are not an Arcane who must draw in aether and charge like a battery, nor are you a Seraphim who channels aether like a conduit." The Siren pursed her lips. "Gods draw power as naturally as living creatures breathe air. Until you complete the pattern, I cannot say if you have the ability."

The reality felt like a blow to the stomach. I'd assumed I could do it because Olivia could. But what if I hadn't inherited everything she had? "Isn't there a simpler way to test my powers before going through all this trouble?"

"You have already proven your powers, child." Vitania took my hand. "The strength of a lycan flows through you because of your soul powers. If that came naturally to you, then logic dictates that your focused abilities must be even greater."

I felt somewhat relieved by her optimism but passing this first test seemed like an insurmountable hurdle. "Do the symbols even mean anything?" I drew them on the holographic chalkboard. "Or are they just random?"

"There is nothing random about them." Vitania sighed. "You must scribe them in the proper order."

"But what do they mean?" It was like staring at written Mandarin or Japanese—gibberish to me.

Vitania released another sigh but relented. She underlined the first five symbols. "This is Cyrinthian for Aquanis." She circled the next three symbols, two wavy lines like lightning bolts, an eye with a line through it, and a pear with a flame on top. "*Xhi budi tuan*—I will to be." The next symbol was a series of concentric circles, each one with a small section missing. It had been the hardest for me to draw.

The Siren underlined it. "*Zot*. Rift."

My forehead scrunched. "You're telling me these complex symbols actually mean Aquanis, I will to be rift?" It sounded stupid in English.

Vitania said it in Cyrinthian. "Aquanis, xhi budi tuan zot." She transliterated it into the Latin alphabet beneath the symbols. "That is precisely what it says. They are words of power."

I repeated it in Cyrinthian, over and over again, imagining the symbols as words. "Why does Aquanis take so many symbols when the others are just one each?"

"It is a proper name which gives it location in space and time. Some words are combinations of symbols. Some symbols are entire words."

I pointed to the curled lines at the end of some symbols. "What are these?"

Vitania's jaw tightened, but she explained. "The *sholot*—terminus—indicates where a word ends."

I could tell Vitania thought this was a waste of time, but it had already helped me immensely. German language classes in college had been extremely challenging to me at first until my teacher diagnosed my problem.

Whenever I read or spoke German, I translated the words in my head, so I knew what to say. As a result, my word order was often wrong, and it took me minutes to get out a single sentence. He'd told me to think in the language, not translate it. At first, I hadn't understood what he meant, but it finally clicked. I never became fluent in German, but my speaking and reading improved by leaps and bounds.

Cyrinthian was another beast altogether. It had a different alphabet and complex rules that made learning Chinese sound simple. But I knew if I could start thinking in the language, it would probably make holding the words with my willpower easier somehow.

Vitania watched me expectantly. "Any more questions?"

I shook my head. "I think I have enough information. I just need to talk this out for a while."

The Siren nodded and walked toward her seashell books. "Do what you must."

Despite her words, the lycan aura sensed impatience and frustration. I didn't know how it figured that out just from smell and visual cues, but I just accepted it and moved on to more important tasks.

I regarded each symbol and practiced saying them. "Xhi." I put a hand on my chest. "Xhi budi tuan." *I will to be.* Closing my eyes, I imagined burning each symbol into the air as I spoke it. "Xhi budi tuan zot." I did it over and over again, thinking in the language instead of translating. A sudden gasp snapped me from my trance.

Translucent symbols floated before me, flickering as if on fire. I was so startled, I lost my concentration and the words vanished.

CHAPTER 29

"**D**o it again, child." Vitania stood next to a table. "You nearly had it."

"How did I do that?" I touched the air where the symbols had been an instant before.

"You drew them with your mind." A faint smile illuminated her face. "Keep trying."

I resisted the urge to ask her how I'd drawn it with my mind. Obviously I'd done it by imagining the symbols and thinking in the language. I hadn't focused on the first part of the sentence, namely the five characters that spelled Aquanis. So I worked on those next, repeating and drawing them in my mind over and over.

Countless attempts later, I finally manifested the symbols for Aquanis in the air before me. Piecing them together with the final four was easier than I'd expected. I completed the string and drew a circle around them in my mind.

"Imagine a gateway opening before you," Vitania said.

I'd only seen the gateways in Obsidian Arches, so I imagined a great rift tearing open. Wind roared around me. Salt water splashed in my face. Vitania cried out.

I opened my eyes and shrieked. The rift towered fifty feet high and nearly as wide. But that wasn't what frightened me. A massive blue wave on the other side of the gateway rolled straight for us. "Go away!" I waved a hand at the rift, but nothing happened. "Stop!" The wave crashed through. Somehow, I wasn't swept away and smashed to a bloody pulp. Cold water pooled around my feet, but the wave itself hovered only inches away. I tentatively poked it with a finger, and it jiggled like gelatin. Then I heard the eerie song emanating all around me.

Vitania walked through the water, still singing as if she didn't need air for her lungs. The water receded slowly, withdrawing through the portal and back into the ocean on the other side. Dark clouds filled the sky. Lightning flashed, and wind gusted.

The Siren touched my hand. "Wipe the circle, child."

I'd lost sight of the symbols and saw them hovering a few inches away. I imagined the circle around them being rubbed away. The symbols flickered and vanished. The rift wavered and collapsed in upon itself. All that was left was a puddle on the library floor.

"You are more powerful than I could have imagined." Vitania kissed my forehead, my cheeks, my lips. "You will soon be my goddess."

It was an odd thing for her to say, but Vitania was full of surprises. I put a hand to my chest. My knees felt like jelly and my heart pounded. I felt more frightened than jubilant. "I thought I was going to die."

"Your rift was incredibly large." Vitania laughed. "Child, you must temper your power. Open a gateway more fit for your size, not that of a tartha."

"A what?"

"A giant beast from the deeps of Seraphina and Aquilis." She clasped my hands. "I think you will master this in no time."

My next rift came easier, though it was barely large enough to fit my hand through. I imagined one a little taller and wider than me, and it formed. Apparently, imagining the rift was the easy part. Each time, I opened a window onto the storm-tossed seas of Aquanis. That brought about another question.

"Is there a way to control where on Aquanis the portal opens?"

Vitania nodded. "Yes, but it is more difficult with a world where there are few static landmarks. To open a rift to a certain place, one must have an image of that location fixed firmly in their mind."

"And there's no way to do that in a realm of mostly water."

She waggled a hand. "The surface bears few landmarks, but the deeps are another matter."

I scoffed. "Except I'm not a mermaid."

The Siren smiled. "Not yet."

I frowned. "You want me to steal a Siren aura?"

"It would be an interesting experiment." She pursed her lips. "But there are no Sirens here in Eden. We would have to find one on Aquanis."

I waved my hands. "I'm not stealing the aura from an innocent Siren. You'd have to find someone really evil for me to even think about it."

Vitania blinked. "Yes, of course, child. I think it best we continue your studies as long as possible. You must be prepared for your half-sister if she finds you once you leave this place."

"Thank you, Vitania." I touched her shoulder. "I can't tell you how much it means that you'd take all this time to teach me."

Something like surprise flashed across her face. "It is no trouble, child."

I disagreed. This ancient being was going far out of her way to help me.

I suspected it was because of her strong bond with Eve. I just hoped I didn't let her down.

When we returned to the house, I found Tyler already setting out food for supper. Bubbling over with excitement, I told him about my great success.

"That's great, babe." He planted a hot kiss on my lips. "Wanna celebrate?"

My stomach rumbled. "After dinner. I'm starving." I barely made it through half of my fish before growing so tired, I nearly passed out. I tried to apologize to Tyler, but it was all I could do to keep my eyes open. I felt Tyler's arms around me. Felt the bed beneath my bare skin.

And then darkness came.

Waking the next morning was painful. My head throbbed and my body ached. My gorge rose and I barely made it to the seashell toilet before throwing up.

"Damn, Em." Tyler scooped me up off the floor and rinsed my face with some water. "Are you okay?"

I groaned and leaned my face against his bare chest. "I don't know what's wrong with me."

He carried me into the kitchen and set me gently on a mushroom stool next to Lumia. "She's sick as a dog. Do you know what's wrong with her?"

The Fae touched my temples and frowned.

"Magic poisoning," Vitania said from the doorway. "I should have given her something to mitigate the effects."

"The girl needs a day of rest," Lumia said. "Her body is not accustomed to such power."

"No, I've got to learn." I tried to rise, but my knees denied me.

"Surely you can help her," Vitania said. "She has little time left."

"Please." I clasped Lumia's hands. "I have to leave in a few days. I promised Fjoeruss."

"The old trickster." The Fae frowned. "You should be more careful making deals with ancient Seraphim."

"Please." I put her hand to my forehead.

She looked from Tyler to me and back at him. "Go into my studio and fetch the vial with the light green liquid."

He nodded and dashed away, returning with the requested item. Lumia uncorked it and pressed the vial to my lips. "Drink it all, girl."

It tasted sweet, but with a slimy texture that only made me want to throw up again. I forced myself to hold it down and hoped it worked fast. "What does it do?"

"It will clean your body of toxins." Lumia smiled apologetically. "It will not be entirely pleasant."

She wasn't kidding. Moments later, I felt a strong urge to use the bathroom. *Legs don't fail me now!* I found the strength to go back to the bedroom and dropped onto the seashell toilet. By the time I was done, I felt as if I'd shed ten pounds. The odor and color were absolutely unearthly and disgusting. Thankfully, the magical toilet made it all vanish within seconds.

While I didn't feel one hundred percent, I certainly felt better. The nausea and headache were gone, and my knees felt stronger. I went back into the kitchen to find Lumia, Tyler, and Vitania speaking in heated tones.

"She cannot take days more of this," Lumia said. "It is unhealthy to clean her system every time. Her training should be spread out over months, not compressed to days."

"But she has so little time." Vitania shook her head. "She has the blood of a goddess. She will adapt quickly."

"Are you certain?" Tyler leaned on the table. "I think you're pushing her body to the breaking point. She's not immortal, and she's not invulnerable like Eve. You need to give her a break. We can always come back."

"When?" Vitania frowned. "Fjoeruss will press her into service and never release her."

"He said it'd only be months," Tyler said.

"She signed a contract with him. He will bend it to his advantage."

"That is probably true," Lumia said. "He is the first Seraphim, just as we are the firsts of our species."

"He's the first?" My mouth dropped open. "You're the first?" I knew they were old, but they were positively ancient. "Does that mean you existed before mankind?"

"Not by much," Vitania said. "The other gods wished to create beings in their own images. Eve thought their creations too strong. Her contribution was mankind."

"She didn't make you?" I asked.

"Eve gave birth to many of us, but we were put in her womb by other gods." Lumia touched the side of her face as if hardly believing she was real. "At least that is what they told us. You must remember, we were children, always asking questions."

"Receiving very few answers." Vitania scowled. "Then they left us to figure it all out ourselves."

"If mankind came from Eve, then what makes me different?" I shook my head. "I mean, if her blood flows in all mankind, then why don't they have her powers?"

"Some do have powers," Vitania said. "Arcanes and lycans are manifestations of Eve's powers, or so I believe."

"Did earlier people have more powers?" I asked.

The Siren shook her head. "No. Adam was culled of powers at conception, as were their children, Cain and Abel."

"Yeah. That didn't turn out so well," Tyler said.

"Cain did not murder Abel, but that is a story for another time," Vitania said.

"Eve culled Adam's powers, and those of their children, and most humans don't have powers." I frowned. "But she also culled Mum's powers, but I have them. How is that possible?"

"Eve came to us extremely weakened after giving birth," Lumia said. "Perhaps she did not remove her powers from the children as thoroughly as she thought."

"Eve is not perfect." Vitania shook her head. "Perhaps she simply made a mistake."

Lumia nodded in quiet assent.

"Eat, child. I think you are well enough for more lessons." Vitania set down some vegetables in front of me. "These will be easier to digest."

"I think I'm well enough to eat fish." I tried sea bass and didn't have the urge to throw up, so I filled my rumbling belly.

Tyler watched me with a concerned look the entire time I ate. Before I left with Vitania, he took me aside.

"Em, I'm really concerned about you. You and Vitania are obsessed with packing all your education into a week." He squeezed my shoulders. "It's not good for you."

"I'll be fine, Tyler." I took his hand and kissed it. "Just a few more days and then I'll have tons of time to rest."

"Days?" His jade green eyes bore deep into mine. "Please, Em. Just take one day off. I'm begging you."

"I told you—"

"It's just one day."

"No." I backed away from him. "I'm doing this, and that's final."

"I'm only saying this because I care, Em." He held out a hand. "Let's go explore, just for a day."

A surge of anger heated my face. "Tyler, don't make this harder than it needs to be. I have to become strong like Olivia, or I'll be on the run for the rest of my life." The lycan aura flushed through me with primal rage. I bared my teeth and snarled, "So let me do what I need to!" It took all my effort not to shout. A part of me knew it was the lycan savagery coursing through my veins, but the other part of me didn't care. I had to do everything it took to become stronger than Olivia.

Everything.

Tyler looked at me with a dazed expression.

I turned on my heel and left before his sad green eyes changed my heart and mind. When we returned that evening, he was gone. A note told me he'd gone exploring Iceland and would return at the end of the week.

I nearly teared up. I felt awful for ignoring him and would dearly miss him lying in bed next to me. We'd hardly spent a night apart in months.

"This is good," Vitania said. "He is a distraction."

"Yes, a mere distraction." Lumia glared at Vitania and stormed out of the room.

Apparently, both our significant others were angry with us.

I couldn't blame them. But time was running out before I had to work for Fjoeruss. This couldn't be helped, right?

The Siren began preparing supper. "Emotion has its purposes, child, but it clouds the mind." She tapped a finger to her temple. "We cannot afford that right now."

Already, I felt the effects of the song of learning fading. Felt exhaustion creeping into my mind and body. "Should I drink more of Lumia's concoction tomorrow?"

"I will put some near your bedside," Vitania said. "I suspect your magic poisoning will not be as severe tomorrow, provided you are more goddess than mortal."

I didn't know how to take her words, so I simply nodded and ate my fish before I passed out. Tyler wasn't here to take care of me, and that made me incredibly sad. *It's your own damned fault, you ninny.* I held back my tears until I reached the privacy of the bedroom. Before I had time to miss Tyler's warmth and his gentle kisses, I fell asleep.

Morning brought a fresh round of nausea every bit as terrible as the previous morning. Lumia's mystery drink purged me of toxins, and once again I felt reasonably well enough to go learn.

When we reached Vitania's library, I prepared myself for more rift practice. Instead, she rubbed her hand across the top of a giant clamshell. It opened, revealing a staircase down into darkness.

"What's this?" I asked.

"Something new." She led me down a tunnel of gently glowing coral. At the bottom was a cave of brightly colored coral. Glowing algae lit a large crystal-blue lake in the center.

"My god." I looked up and around with awe. "It's so beautiful." The lake looked shallow enough to wade in, but it stretched for hundreds of yards before ending at the far wall. Giant conch shells rose from the shallow depths at irregular intervals. I hoped they didn't contain equally large sea creatures.

"Beautiful though it is, this place holds great evil." Vitania took my hands in hers. "You must tell no one of this place, not even Lumia. There are many here who should have died for their crimes. But I saw fit to grant them mercy."

It took a moment for her words to register. "This is a prison?"

"Of sorts." She sang a brief melody and the nearest shell unfurled, revealing a slimy white worm nearly six feet tall.

I gasped and gagged at the awful sight. My hand clapped over my mouth and I backed away. "What is that thing?"

The top of the worm peeled away to reveal that it wasn't a worm at all, but some kind of cocoon. The creature inside looked like an ape. The single eye in the middle of its forehead was closed. A long horn protruding from its crown. Its fur was mottled dark green and brown, almost like camouflage.

"This is Bort, a creature responsible for nearly wiping out the Fae during the early days of their creation. The other gods were content to let him wreak havoc. When Bort turned his eye on the Sirens, I knew I must do something."

"What species is he?" I asked.

"He is one of a kind." Vitania looked at the slumbering creature dispassionately. "I would like you to remove his aura."

CHAPTER 30

"Take that monster's aura?" I grimaced. "I don't want whatever that thing is offering."

Vitania smiled. "You do not have to take it. Simply remove it from him and let it dissipate into the ether. Then I can free him from this eternal prison, and he can live out his days."

"I guess that would be a mercy." I stepped closer to water's edge, about five feet from the shell. "This is the oddest bloke I've ever seen."

"He is quite ordinary compared to some in here." Vitania nodded toward him. "See if you can remove his aura."

It required me to get wet, but I supposed that wasn't the worst thing ever. The water came just above my knees. It was pleasantly warm and tingled against my skin, as if slightly electric. The cocoon holding Bort peeled down a little more so I could touch the tall creature's chest.

His fur felt coarse and slightly sticky. He growled and jerked. I shrieked and jumped back, nearly falling. But the beast must have been having a nightmare, because his eye never opened. I stepped up to him again and put a hand on his chest. I closed my eyes and let my senses wander.

I glimpsed a world bathed in crimson. The bitter taste of copper filled my mouth, as if blood poured in. The violence in this creature was unimaginable. It was as if he lived only to slaughter. Lycan bloodlust paled in comparison. All I wanted was to get this creature out of my head as quickly as possible.

My spirit grasped the aura. I gave a gentle tug, but it was like uprooting a boulder from mud. I pulled harder and harder. Bort growled and trembled. His limbs jerked, but the cocoon held them in place. I sensed another presence, something fighting me.

I realized with a start it was Bort—or at least his subconscious. I concentrated harder, focusing my will on removing the blood-soaked aura. I felt claws raking my arms. Sensed unfathomable rage and fury. It wasn't my physical body being attacked, but my spirit form.

This inhuman creature was stronger than I'd thought, backed by intelligence that only made me fear and despise him more. He wasn't a mindless beast, but a cunning, evil monster. *You don't deserve to live!* His resistance made me furious. I focused all my will on the stubborn aura. My spirit seemed to swell with strength. I wrapped my arms around the bubbling crimson and ripped it from the creature.

My physical form stumbled back. My bottom splashed into the water. A massive heart-shaped chunk of meat squirmed in my hands. A mouth formed in the top, sharp teeth chomped on empty air. I screamed and nearly threw it away. It fought me, trying to squirm back into its host. I held it up, blood dripping into the water, trickling down my arms.

"Yes, child, yes!" Vitania cheered me from the shore. "Kill it!"

I didn't know how to kill an aura. So I just held onto it until its motions slowed. It went slack and dissolved into mushy liquid that dribbled into the lake and coated my arms. That was what had happened to Stephen's vampire aura. I wondered if back then I could have absorbed his aura like I did Timmy's, or if that was part of my recent growth.

I dropped what was left of Bort's aura into the water and watched the crimson stain spread across the blue. Then I thoroughly rinsed my arms of the disgusting goo. It would eventually fade to nothing, but I wanted to bathe in rubbing alcohol to get the scent off me.

Tears trickled down Vitania's cheeks. She waded into the water next to me. "Child, you will save us all." Gone was her scientific detachment, replaced by conviction and desire.

Save us all? What did she mean by that?

The cocoon unfurled and Bort fell face-first into the water. He spit and sputtered, rising slowly to his knees and looking around in bewilderment. Then he saw Vitania. He spoke in a rasping, guttural voice, a language I didn't understand.

Vitania laughed and spit in his face.

He roared and jumped, clearing maybe a foot before splashing back into the water. Bort stopped and stared at his hands, his legs, as if they weren't his own. Vitania waded over and grasped him by the neck. She lifted him from the water, snarling in the strange language.

Bort wriggled and tried to free himself, but it was no use. Whatever powers he'd had before were gone. Then he seemed to see me for the first time. His eyes flared wide.

"Eve!" He shouted the name with a strong accent. Then he spoke more gibberish.

"What's he saying?" I asked. "I don't understand."

"He asked why you did this to him. He thinks you're Eve." Tears poured down Vitania's cheeks even as she smiled with glee. "For you see, this monster is one of Eve's children." She said something else, then threw Bort back into his cocoon. Before he could utter another syllable, it sealed up and the monster was back in its cage.

I was still trying to comprehend what Vitania said. "Eve created Bort?"

"She birthed him and set him free to destroy all sentient creatures of the world." Vitania shuddered. "For you see, Eve wished to wipe the world clean and start anew."

I shook my head. "No, that can't be true. That's horrible!"

"Eve failed to realize the might of species united." Vitania stared at the cocoon. "We imprisoned Bort, but he is a lesser god, and as such, difficult to keep imprisoned."

"A—a god?" My heart skipped a beat. "You didn't tell me he was a god!"

"A lesser god, but a god nonetheless." Vitania smiled through her tears. "And you tore his godhood from him as if he were nothing." She abruptly smothered me with a hug and kisses. "The strain of maintaining this prison weighs heavily on my people. Every month, four Sirens come and sing the songs of silence, sleep, and dreams to keep the waters charged. It takes them seven days and nights and leaves them weak and exhausted."

"I can understand how exhausting it would be to sing for that long." I replayed the end of Bort's aura and the way it disintegrated into goo. "I hope now that Bort is powerless, they can stop singing."

She shook her head. "There is another in this prison who must be made powerless. Then and only then will the world be safe. You are the only one who can do this."

I trembled with nerves. "Who is it?"

"First, I will tell you why you must do this." She led me to the shore and sat down, patting the ground next to her.

I sat. "I mean if this person is as evil as Bort, it's fine. I'll do it."

"Do you know the origin of the Apocryphan?" she said.

I shook my head. "No. I thought they were the original gods until I met you and learned about the old gods."

"They were not birthed, but molded from the materials of the old gods. Created in their images, but dark and twisted, lusting only for power."

Vitania drew her fingers up from the water, forming it into a dark shadow with a single glowing eye. A vortex of darkness swirled at its feet.

"Oh my god." I stared at it. "I've seen that before."

"This is the spirit form of Xanatos, also called Xanos or Xanomiel." Vitania formed several figures in the water next to the first. One resembled a great black spider with a single red slit for an eye. The others looked more humanoid. She pointed to each in order. "Araxos, Kathazal, Posthanied, Couriondral, Zon."

"Vallaena Slade told me that Xanatos was an Abyssal demon."

Vitania nodded. "Yes, that is how they are now known. Few alive today know of the Apocryphan. They believe they are simply demons, which is not too far from the truth."

"Why are you telling me all this?" It was interesting, but all it did was make me feel smaller and more insignificant in the grand scheme.

"The creator of the Apocryphan saw the error in the original plan to start over. One powerful creature could not undo life. It would take many more to accomplish that task." Vitania took my hand and led me to another conch shell. It unfurled, and the cocoon inside began to peel back.

Inside was a woman. Damp, green hair hung around her shoulders. Aside from that oddity, she looked rather ordinary.

"Eve will never stop trying to kill all sentient life so long as she remains a goddess." Vitania squeezed my hand. "She unleashed Bort. She created the Apocryphan. Only you can remove her godhood and end her madness."

I was too shocked to say a word. Eve was a very plain looking woman, but the family resemblance to Mum was unmistakable. I didn't know if I was more surprised to see an imprisoned goddess, or to see a goddess that wasn't gorgeous.

"That's Eve?" I shook my hand loose from Vitania's. "She looks like a middle-aged mum, not an all-powerful goddess!"

"End the madness, child." Vitania took my hands again. "Remove her godhood so we can all live in peace."

I shook my head. "How in the bloody hell am I supposed to do that? She's a goddess and I'm—I'm just a twenty-something woman with school loans."

"And the powers of the goddess." The Siren led me closer. "Just try, child. It is all I ask."

I stood frozen with indecision. Part of me couldn't believe this was really Eve, the mother of humankind. Another part was absolutely terrified to touch her. "This isn't possible. How did you imprison a goddess?"

"After we captured Bort, our alliance knew the only chance to end Eve's war on existence was to capture her or die trying." Vitania stared at the goddess with a blank expression. "We could not find her. Over two centuries later, the Apocryphan descended Mount Olympus and subjected us to their rule. Long after we defeated them, I found Eve again, but she was too powerful for us to imprison, even with all the species united. So I befriended her and waited patiently, hoping and praying she did not try to destroy us again."

I couldn't stop staring at Eve. *This can't be real.* How had I gone from demon banisher to god killer? Was Eve really so twisted and cruel? How could a mother unleash monsters on her offspring?

"So she stopped trying to kill everyone after that?"

"Perhaps. For all we know she turned her attention to the other realms and left Eden alone." Vitania shivered. "When she came to us with your mother and aunt, Eve was weak as a babe. Why she was so weak, I do not know. But I took advantage of it and imprisoned her. Even then, it was difficult overcoming her with the song of sleep."

Vitania offered me a gentle smile. "It is a constant strain keeping her here. If you remove her godhood, then all the realms will be safe from her madness."

I stared at my grandmother for a long time before answering. "No." I shook my head. "I won't do anything unless I can speak with her."

"Impossible." Vitania gripped my shoulders and shook me. "If we wake her, she will escape. Even now she subconsciously seeks her freedom. We do not know how much longer we can keep her here."

"Maybe she's just misunderstood." I tried to free myself from Vitania's grasp. "There must be some explanation!"

She shook me like a scolded child. "You must do this, girl. You must strip her godhood now!"

Can I even do such a thing? I certainly couldn't tear it from her and let it evaporate into nothingness. But to steal such power and make it a part of me seemed terribly wrong. I summoned lycan strength and freed myself. "No, Vitania. I won't do it unless I can talk with her. This doesn't feel right."

The Siren composed herself. Wiped the tears from her cheeks. "You have already done a great service by castrating Bort. I will find a way to allow communication with Eve without waking her so you can soothe your conscience."

"Thank you, Vitania."

"I would not lie to you, child." The Siren stepped out of the lake. Water misted from her dress and sprinkled back into its source. "It is vital Eve be stripped of power. Should she ever escape, all our lives would be in danger."

I followed her out. My wet shoes squished, and my clothes were soaked from falling down earlier. But Vitania seemed too preoccupied to think of drying me out. I wanted to ask her if she would but felt guilty for denying her request.

"Is this the real reason you decided to teach me?" I asked. "So I would take away Eve's powers?"

"Your powers were impressive, but not godlike when you arrived." She didn't look back at me as we walked to the great tree. "Rift magic is incredibly demanding. Even one with powers such as mine can open only a small rift and hold it for seconds." She stopped and faced me. "I needed to see what you were capable of, and you did not disappoint. The singular act of opening that massive rift strengthened your magic exponentially."

"Like working out at the gym?" I said.

She paused, as if translating what I'd said. "Yes, like exercising muscles. Even magical ability atrophies if not used. That is why your first act of opening such a large rift was so amazing. It means you have depths of power barely untapped." The Siren turned again and proceeded to the tree. The wind swept us up near the top where we climbed the branches back into the house.

This was the earliest we'd come back, and I found myself at a loss for what to do. I hoped Tyler decided to come back early.

"I have a gift for you, child." Vitania handed me a tiny brown shell. "This contains all the coordinates for known realms and brief descriptions. But be careful, for some realms are not hospitable to life."

"Oh my. This is amazing!" I hugged the Siren.

She patted my back awkwardly. "Simply grasp it and will it to activate."

I released her and tried it. Water misted from inside the shell, forming symbols and descriptions. Unfortunately, most of it seemed to be in Cyrinthian. "Please tell me there's a translate function."

"Will it to be in English."

I willed it and so it came to pass that the descriptions morphed into English, leaving the actual realm codes in Cyrinthian. I wasn't sure I had the bravery to try any of them. "What if I went through a rift and trapped myself on the other side?"

"Use the Eden code, child." Vitania swiped the air and the list scrolled down to the code for Eden. "You may also use the code of the realm you're in to travel to other places within the realm, provided you know exactly what it looks like. You must be extremely careful with this. If you cannot picture the destination precisely, a rift to the Void may open. It is imperative that not happen."

"The Void?"

"The details are in the shell I gave you. Study it if you desire. I have a more pressing problem to solve." She walked to the doorway and paused. "If I find a way to allow communication with Eve, I will let you know."

Once I was alone, I sat down at the table and poured myself a glass of what looked like white wine. It was sweet and definitely fermented. Then I started scrolling down the list. Every realm had the code, its name, and a brief description. If I touched the code, the water would mist into an in-depth essay about the realm.

I found myself sucked down the rabbit hole, reading about realms of all kinds. Some with nothing but lifeless desert, others thick with jungles and monsters. Vitania, it seemed, had really gotten around over the past few thousand years. There was even a section on the Abyss.

The front door opened before I could read more, and the most delicious sight walked through. Tyler had grown a beard, and his jade eyes sparkled with confusion when he saw me.

"Oh, Tyler!" I pocketed the seashell and leapt into his arms.

"Happy to see me?" He pressed his lips to mine and came up gasping for air a moment later.

"Does that answer your question?" I bit his lower lip and felt an immediate reaction.

"In the best way possible." He carried me into the bedroom and threw me down on the bed.

We had so much fun, we only left the room for a quick dinner. Lumia and Vitania were nowhere to be found, so we went back to the bedroom and continued our little romp. I meant to tell Tyler all about the bizarre excitement of the day, but a gentle melody drifted through the house and I forgot what I was going to say.

Tyler seemed just as mesmerized as I was. His face went slack, and he drifted to sleep in seconds. That was when it hit me.

That's a Siren song. It's putting us to sleep!

I fought the urge to close my eyes and pressed hands to my ears. It did nothing to quiet the song. It seemed as if emanated inside my very mind. I staggered to my feet and bit my tongue hard enough to hurt. Even that had little effect. The song grew more insistent, dragging my conscious mind into the murky depths. I fought back, swimming for the surface, desperate to get another breath of wakefulness.

I opened the door. Pulled myself into the hallway. Vitania stood at the far end, staring at me as she tried to sing me to sleep.

CHAPTER 31

"What are you doing, Vitania?" I put a hand on the wall to steady myself. "Why are you doing this?"

Her answer flowed past, an undercurrent to the singing. "Rest, child. There is no reason to worry."

"Stop!" I tried to shout, but my lips didn't want to move. I felt as if my mind was leaving my body. No matter what I tried, there was no escaping the song. I had only one hope to end the madness. Hands gripping the living wood of the wall, I pulled myself toward Vitania. The song rippled against me like a physical force, pushing me back.

It was a terrible risk, but I closed my eyes and dipped inside for the lycan aura. I didn't care about controlling it, I simply knew that I desperately needed it. A fresh rush of adrenalin burned into my veins. Instinct snapped me awake like smelling salts. A low growl rumbled in my throat.

For the first time, Vitania looked alarmed. She backed up a step. I sensed fear, and it invigorated me. With a howl, I sprinted down the hall even as the sonic waves grew strong enough to physically hurt. Claws grew from my fingertips. They dug into the wooden walls, leaving long marks. The waves pounded me like the ocean tide. But I dragged myself closer to my target.

If I had removed the aura from a lesser god, surely I could remove Vitania's. I hated to do it, but I had no choice.

"Stop this madness!" My lycan claws raked the wooden walls. I felt my human form slipping away from me. "I don't want to hurt you, but I will!" My voice grew animalistic, barely human.

Consciousness began to lose its grip on my mind again. My body didn't seem to know what to do. Tufts of fur grew and receded. Claws extended and retracted. I had so little experience as a lycan that losing control of my mind had cast my body into metamorphic chaos. I threw all my physical strength into crossing the last ten feet between me and Vitania.

Her mouth opened inhumanly wide. A scream unlike anything I'd ever heard rippled through the air. It slammed into me, a physical barrier of sound, and threw me down the hallway. My head bounced off the wooden walls more times than I could count. Even the lycan toughness didn't shield me from the pain.

As I lay bloodied and wounded on the floor, the song of sleep continued unabated. I tried to get up. Tried to fight it. But light receded and darkness swallowed me whole.

"I'm still awake." My voice echoed in the void. I saw a humanoid shape in the darkness. It glowed gently, a silhouette in the pitch. I made as if to walk toward it, and suddenly I stood inches away.

I gasped. It was Timmy! His eyes stared blankly, catatonic. I snapped my fingers, but he didn't look at me. He looked like a pale ghost of the man I'd stolen the lycan aura from.

That was when the truth hit me. "You're not Timmy." It was a subconscious representation of his stolen aura. That meant—"I'm inside myself.

I'm trapped in a waking dream." And somewhere out there, my body lay on the hallway floor, vulnerable to whatever plans Vitania had for it.

"Why are you doing this?" I screamed.

A voice echoed from the void. "There is no other way, child. Eve must be dealt with."

"By putting me to sleep? You can't force me to help you."

There came no reply.

I tried to sense my body but closing my eyes and concentrating didn't help. My mind was somehow cut off from the rest of me. I inspected my hands, arms, and legs. Like Timmy's aura, I glowed gently, my form translucent.

"Am I a ghost?" I pinched myself and sensed the pressure, but it didn't hurt. Another possibility occurred to me. This might be my spirit form, somehow consciously manifested. Though my body slumbered, I felt perfectly awake. But aside from the lycan aura, darkness pressed in on all sides, smothering me like a blanket of pitch.

Where was I? Was I trapped deep in the subconscious of my own body, or had I been transferred somewhere else?

I felt closed in, claustrophobic. Trapped. Anxiety wound through my chest and tightened its noose. I took deep breaths and hovered close to the glowing lycan aura. *Do not freak out. Remain calm.* There wasn't a floor beneath my feet, or walls, or a ceiling. Just a vast endless void. *You're not closed in. There's plenty of space!*

It was almost funny when I thought about my predicament—a spirit having an anxiety attack! It was so funny, I began to cry hysterically.

After I cried it out, I noticed two things. One, sound didn't echo in this place, and two, despite my spirit or ghost form, I was having physiological reactions. Spirits didn't have tear ducts, or hearts, or any of the components of a living body. Those seemed like insignificant details, but it made me think back to something Tyler once said.

Demons don't have to be caustic forever. We're spirits, after all, only trapped by our own limited perceptions about who we are and of what we're capable.

It was possible I wasn't in spirit form. In fact, it seemed more likely I was asleep and simply dreaming all of this. But maybe, just maybe, all the practicing and stretching my magical muscles had strengthened me in other ways. It was possible I'd remained conscious by transferring over to my spirit form.

Unfortunately, I knew next to nothing about this part of me except I somehow used it to nick auras from naughty supers. Perhaps there was more to it. Perhaps I could somehow use it to wake myself, or perhaps even have an out-of-body experience

I paced in a circle around Timmy's aura hoping for an epiphany that might offer a way out of this void. My spirit form could obviously leave my body at least partially. That was how it did its business. But the only way it had worked in the past was by me physically touching someone else. This place cut me off from my body. I could be touching someone right now in the real world and not even know it.

Pacing in circles accomplished nothing, so I sat down and closed my eyes. Opened my senses. Tried to reconnect with my flesh and blood. Instead, I sensed something else. The sound of ocean waves. The taste of salt in the air. The great blue-green ocean swam in my mind's eye.

I'd just glimpsed Vitania. That meant she had to be close. I sensed other auras, but they were muted and distant. One of them pinged stronger than the rest, so I focused on it. It remained just out of reach. I imagined myself, fingers outstretched, trying to reach for it, grasping hand getting closer to the goal.

And then I had it. A black orb rotated in the dark of space, its surface traced with glowing orange lines and volcanic eruptions. The rocky surface was barren and lifeless.

I gasped and lost my grip on the aura. "My god." Had I just sensed a being who destroyed worlds? Judging from the number of other auras pressing against my senses, it was obvious Vitania had taken my body to her prison. I was now among the ancient monsters.

"Why did you bring me here, Vitania? What did I do to deserve this betrayal?"

No answer.

Either she ignored me, or she couldn't hear me. It was possible I'd spoken to her with my real mouth and heard her reply through my ears before completely falling under her spell. Because if she could have spoken to me in this state, it meant she could speak to Eve as well.

Eve!

My long-lost grandmother might be near my physical body. I wondered if Vitania put me near her, or if I was somewhere farther back. I cursed myself for not having noticed the auras in her prison before. As my abilities had grown, so had my tendency to filter out signals. They'd become background chatter in a crowded room.

But it seemed these cocoons also muted the auras. Perhaps I only felt them now because I had no other external stimuli. Perhaps I could make contact with Eve. Together we might find a way out.

Then again, if a goddess had been unable to escape this trap, what possible assistance could little old Emily provide?

It didn't matter. I still needed to try. I sat down, crossed my legs, and made like a monk meditating. Naturally, the first thing I thought about was Tyler. I wondered where he was and if he was okay. When I cleared thoughts of him from my mind, I wondered how dragons blew out candles.

Quiet your mind, you little fool!

I had to make sense of this. It seemed that this void was inside my physical body—my mind perhaps? And I was consciously controlling my spirit form, but unable to leave the confines of my flesh and blood. Every aura I sensed was somewhere near my body.

I latched onto the world-killer's aura as an anchor to get my bearings. I didn't know the orientation of my physical body, but it felt as if the sensation came from behind and to the left of me. I reached out to the next aura. It felt much weaker but didn't seem more distant than the last.

The smell of spring and forest tickled my nose. Animals crowded a moonlit glade. It seemed similar to what I'd sensed with Lumia, but different enough to make me suspect the prisoner wasn't a Fae. I connected the dot and moved to the next. The next two auras burned cold like ultraviolet suns. Even though they were virtually identical to Nightliss's aura, they seemed stronger, richer, and more ancient.

How in the hell did you trap such powerful beings?

Vitania was certainly no one to be trifled with. I understood her desire to neuter such dangerous beings. But I couldn't simply be her executioner without knowing everything about these prisoners. Was Eve as evil as she said, or simply misunderstood?

A map formed in my mind. While I couldn't precisely gauge distance, it seemed the world killer was closest to me, with the two Seraphim and the woodland entity forming a semicircle behind me. Vitania stood in front of me, but it seemed her aura was fading with distance.

I concentrated hard, focusing on her aura. She must have stopped moving, because it remained static. The only reason for her to stop right now was perhaps to look at the one being she most wanted to serve justice to—Eve.

But try as I might, I couldn't sense a powerful aura near her. Fainter sensations touched the outer boundaries of my psychic radar, but where Vitania stood, there was nothing but her. If anything, I only glimpsed myself reflected back at me.

I had never detected anything special about my mother or Lydia. In fact, my senses hadn't even detected Olivia when she was feet away from me. Did that mean Eve was also invisible to me? I threw up my spirit hands.

"Fuck!" I might as well be fishing for water. There was no way for me to detect Eve because something about her powers made her undetectable to others like her.

Vitania's plans for me to remove Eve's powers wouldn't have worked in the first place because I couldn't find Eve's aura. It made me wish I'd at least tried. Maybe then the Siren wouldn't have gotten mad at me and thrown me in her prison. Or perhaps she would have since I was the only person besides her who knew about this place.

I wondered why she'd even let me come back to the house. Perhaps she knew it was best to take me and Tyler at the same time. Or maybe she was unsure about taking me and finally made up her mind.

My senses lingered on Vitania. She still hadn't moved from her spot. When I focused on the area around her, I saw nothing except glimpses of myself bouncing back. Which seemed awfully strange.

Why do I see myself?

I focused on the unsettling sensation and took a closer look. It was indeed the pale ghostly form of myself, but curled up in a ball, sleeping peacefully. Except, I wasn't sleeping. The harder I looked, the more I felt as if I were looking right back in on myself. But that was only because the aura was nearly identical to mine. But it wasn't me unless I'd figured out how to sleep in the fetal position and sit cross-legged at the same time.

The aura had a gentle golden halo around it. If Tyler were here, he'd certainly quote Sherlock Holmes again. He'd tell me that even though it seemed completely improbable, perhaps Eve's aura was so in synch with my own, that it was nearly invisible to me. It was like seeing myself in a hall of mirrors.

It explained why I'd never sensed Mum, Lydia, or Olivia. We were all so similar that my ability ignored them. I resisted the urge to clap my hands and cheer. Holding onto this glimpse was harder than usual, probably for the same reason it was so hard to find it in the first place.

I opened my eyes to the void and saw the same ghostly shape, as if it occupied the same dark place as me. Looking around, I saw the other auras I'd sensed, each one hovering in place at what I imagined was their relative physical position from me.

"Oh my god." I stood and turned in a circle, stunned by the sight. I hadn't taken these auras and made them part of myself, but I could see them—a map to the real world. Even Vitania's blue-green ocean hovered only a few feet from the ghostly sleeping form.

If the figure I saw was Eve, she seemed to be over a hundred feet away. From this distance I couldn't clearly see her face. Her form and figure looked so much like mine or Mum's that without more details I would never have known the difference.

I didn't think it would work, but I tried anyway. "Eve!" I shouted across the void. "Eve, wake up!"

She didn't so much as twitch. I wondered if the cocoon put her into such a deep sleep that even her subconscious couldn't resist. Did that mean I wasn't in a cocoon yet? Or had I somehow remained awake?

Vitania's aura drifted another foot away from Eve and abruptly vanished. I didn't think she'd left my range, but it was possible. I called out for Eve over and over again, but she didn't stir. I wished I could just go over to her and shake her awake. In a heartbeat, I stood right next to her. Her plain features became clear. It was definitely the same woman Vitania had shown me earlier. I knelt and reached out to touch her, but an invisible barrier blocked my hands.

"You've got to be kidding me." I pounded on the unseen wall and shouted, "Eve, wake up! Eve!"

Still not a twitch. Nothing.

Vitania's aura blipped back into view. Something blurry hovered next to it. I focused on it and felt the odd sensation of my glimpse reflecting back on me. The blur resolved into shape and form, ghostly, but all too recognizable. The face was one I'd seen a million times in the mirror, but the hair was short and pale.

"Oh, shit." I didn't know how, but I certainly knew why.

Olivia was here.

CHAPTER 32

Olivia's ghostly shape seemed to look right past me and Eve. She seemed as blind to us as I had been to her. Her lips moved, but I couldn't hear what she said. She displayed a wicked grin and clapped her hands, but again, I heard nothing. It seemed her spirit form mimicked whatever her physical body did, but since my physical body was bound up in a cocoon, I couldn't hear her.

"That's bloody confusing." I'd been tossed into the deep end of the god pool, and all I could do was float on my water wings and pray I eventually drifted close enough to the ladder to climb out.

I ran a ghost hand across my ghost face and forced myself to think. But no one had prepared me for this. This was one of those instances where I had to completely wing it. So I asked myself, "What have you learned about this place so far?"

First, I somehow willed visual representation of nearby auras to be here with me. Second, I could travel instantly across this void. I wished myself closer to the planet killer's aura and instantly stood less than a foot away. There was no odor, but I imagined the sulfurous stench rising from the volcanoes along its surface. My outstretched hand found another invisible barrier preventing me from touching it.

Third, I now knew that even though I could travel closer to the auras, something stood between me and them. It was possible I only perceived myself being closer when, in reality, I was not. Number four was more theory than fact. My spirit form was still trapped in my body. It was possible that my own flesh was the invisible barrier. My body wasn't actually touching the owner of the other auras.

So what did that mean?

Light poured in from overhead. Before I could react, I flew through a brilliant tunnel and into a burning sun.

A scream erupted from my throat—my real throat. Light stung my eyes. I blinked away the pain and focused on the gloating face of my half-sister. She and Vitania stood in front of me. I tried to move, but a cocoon held me from my shoulders down.

"Bloody hell, you're alive." Olivia's eyes shone with delight. "Vitania just told me the most amazing thing, Emily. You're not my cousin. You're my fucking sister!"

"Half-sister," I croaked.

Olivia laughed. "My god, you were disguised right in front of me and I didn't even know." She clapped slowly, mockingly. "Well played, sis. Domathus jizzed in his demonic pants when he heard the news of your death. He lost a lot of street cred after you busted his nuts and sent him back to Hell."

"Why do you work for demons?" I asked. "Why would you want me dead?"

"Simple." She pulled a lollipop from her red leather jacket and peeled off the wrapper. "I was tossed to the wolves when I was a babe, and you got the good life. I survived by doing whatever my wicked foster parents wanted." Olivia gritted her teeth and loosed an animalistic snarl. "You don't even want to know what I did to survive. You don't know half the shit I went through before I was even twelve."

"I'm sorry, Olivia." I felt horribly guilty even though it wasn't even remotely my fault for her life. Another part of me didn't care about the guilt. It wanted to punch Olivia in the throat.

She ignored me. "But then I realized I had abilities. I discovered demons and realized even the caustics were better than most humans."

I looked at Vitania. "How did you find her? And how did you bring her here so fast?"

"I sought her out with song the day after you arrived, child." The Siren didn't look the least bit sorry. "I knew one of you could neutralize Eve and keep us safe."

"Did you open a portal to bring her through?"

"Of course." Vitania turned to Olivia. "You have spoken with her as agreed. Now will you remove Eve's godhood and let it dissipate?"

A crooked grin lit Olivia's face. "Of course, babe. But I want Emily's powers too."

"That was not agreed upon." Vitania's lips flattened into a line. "Your sister will remain here for a time, and then I will release her."

"Why, because she's all sweet and innocent?" Olivia's eyes narrowed as if something else occurred to her. Whatever it was, she didn't mention it to Vitania. "All right. Let's get this over with."

"Very well." Vitania lowered her hand. Before I could say anything, darkness swallowed me once more and shoved me into the void.

I didn't trust Olivia not to make a play for my aura once she was done with Eve. I also didn't trust Vitania to release me. She'd had no reason to keep me here in the first place if she planned to ask Olivia for help. It meant her plan had more layers to it, and I was important to them somehow.

The lycan aura was visible in the distance, but all the others I'd sensed earlier were gone. I didn't see any reason to relocate them, so I focused on Eve, Olivia, and Vitania. I found them quickly and formed visual representations of them in the void. Olivia's arms waved in complex patterns. She wore a frustrated look on her spirit face.

Vitania's aura was a sphere like many others. I wished she had a spirit form I could observe but trying to make her aura take another shape didn't work. I watched Olivia work for a moment. She seemed to be trying variations of Cyrinthian symbols. I studied them, trying to make sense of what she was doing.

Apparently, Olivia hadn't developed her aura-stealing powers in the same way I had if she had to use symbols to do it. She seemed to hit upon something at last, and began sliding her hand through the air, like a veterinarian reaching into a cow's anus.

What an awful analogy!

The power symbols glowed ever so slightly on the spirit plane. The last four were mirror images of some of the symbols Vitania taught me. I didn't recognize the first few, but I practiced drawing them as well. Olivia abruptly jerked back her hand and clenched her fists.

"You're getting frustrated, aren't you?" I grinned. "Maybe you don't know what you're doing." Olivia had demonstrated she could sense auras. She'd known Tyler was a jade spirit, and that George was a Custodian. But she didn't seem capable of simply reaching in and taking an aura. Maybe she'd never tried.

Olivia looked to the side. Her mouth moved. She was probably talking to Vitania. I wondered if she was asking how I removed auras. My half-sister stood still for a moment, then turned and stared at Eve. Her arms stretched out and reached for the slumbering spirit form of the goddess.

"Oh, shit." I willed myself closer and instantly stood at the invisible barrier between myself and Eve. I pounded on it. Screamed her name over and over. But the goddess didn't stir.

Olivia's outstretched hands lay flat, seemingly against the same barrier. She hadn't yet been able to reach inside and grasp Eve's aura.

I closed my eyes and let my senses reach out, just as I did when touching other auras. I imagined my hands gently caressing Eve's aura. Maybe I could bring it inside my subconscious and keep it safe with me. But no amount of concentration of willpower allowed me to push through the barrier. Just as it had been with the planet killer's aura, I couldn't do anything in this form.

"It doesn't make any sense!" I leaned against the invisible wall and watched helplessly as Olivia's hands slowly reached closer and closer to Eve's aura. "If I'm in spirit form, I should be able to go through my flesh."

Then again, my spirit might be anchored to my flesh. Maybe it couldn't unchain itself and drift across the physical divide. Another idea occurred to me. It probably had zero chance of success but trying anything would be better than sitting here helplessly.

I recalled the symbols I'd learned so well. I traced the first one in the air and willed it to remain. It flashed and dimmed. I went through the first few symbols and held them in place, then finished with the last four.

Avin, xhi budi tuan zot. Avin, I will to be a rift.

I fixed the precise location in my mind and willed the rift to open large enough for me to fit through. The air ripped vertically and widened a window to darkness. "I hope this doesn't break the universe," I said, and stepped through.

The darkness warped and snapped back into place. I felt a horrific wrenching, as if someone gripped my insides and tried to yank them out, but like a rubber band, they snapped back into place. I gagged and lurched. A funnel of light sucked me out of the darkness and my physical eyes opened.

I lay inside Vitania's library; a place I'd memorized from my many hours of practice. I gagged and retched up a puddle of white goo. It was so disgusting, I nearly threw up again. My legs felt weak and my arms could barely push me up off the floor. I didn't have much time to lose, so I slid on the lycan aura.

Strength bolstered my limbs and savage bloodlust crowded my conscious mind. I heard birds chirping and forest animals rustling in the forest outside the library. The urge to sniff them out and hunt was almost irresistible. I forced my conscious mind back to Eve. Back to my escape from Vitania's cocoon.

It seemed I could do rift magic in spirit form. Since my body and spirit were chained together, I'd dragged my physical body through the rift after me. I wondered if Vitania and Olivia realized what had happened, or if I'd been closed up inside the conch shell, unseen by them.

There was only one way to find out.

I sneaked to the open clamshell leading into the underground prison and followed the coral tunnel until I reached the entrance to the cavern. Olivia stood in front of Eve, brow furrowed in concentration. Vitania watched with great interest. Both stood in profile to me, so unless they looked to the side, they wouldn't see me.

Unfortunately, there still wasn't anything I could do to rescue Eve. If I stormed in there, Vitania would simply sing me back to sleep. Even if I were fast enough to dash in and slide Eve from her cocoon, I didn't know where Tyler was. Leaving him at Vitania's mercy wasn't a good idea.

Then again, I had this wonderful new magic at my disposal. Could I somehow create a portal and yank Eve to safety before the Siren could react?

I'd only have one chance with this one. I hoped I could create another rift and still have the strength to rescue Eve. I visualized the cocoon. Despite having just seen it, the image wasn't crisp and clear. That meant I'd have to have line of sight. I sneaked back down the stairs and peered into the cave. If either Olivia or Vitania looked my way, they'd see me. I wanted to burn the image into memory, but my mind was frazzled, and

I couldn't concentrate. Opening the first rift had exhausted me. I'd be lucky if I could even open another one. My best chance would be to make the attempt from right here.

"Yes, I've got it!" Olivia cackled with glee. "I'm getting through." Ghostly hands reached from within her physical ones and into Eve.

Time had just run out.

Lycan strength surged into me. I drew the symbols and willed a rift to open right next to Eve. The air ripped open. I saw Olivia's outstretched hands just inches from me. She shouted in alarm and her arms jerked back. I rushed through the slit in the air and yanked Eve's entire cocoon out of the unfurled shell.

Vitania's mouth dropped open. Olivia lunged for me. I leapt back through the rift and swiped away the symbols to close it. Lycan strength made Eve feel light as a feather. I slung her cocooned form over my shoulder.

"She's on the god damned stairs!" Olivia shouted. I looked back and saw Olivia racing toward me at normal human speed. She hadn't summoned a demon to give her strength yet, so I took advantage and sped up the stairs. The library blurred past me. I dashed outside and raced toward the great tree. Forest animals scattered in all directions, but for once I didn't feel the impulse to chase every squirrel I saw.

A gust of wind hurled me skyward when I reached the base of the tree. Limbs blurred past and I landed lightly at the top. Despite my adrenalin, I couldn't stop thinking about Tyler. I prayed Vitania wouldn't harm him. I also prayed Eve wasn't the total monster she'd made her out to be, or I might have made a terrible mistake.

I climbed through the hole in the sky and emerged back in the house. White slime from my cocoon and Eve's dribbled down my clothing. It was freezing outside, and my wet clothes would only make things worse, but I had to get to the car. On impulse, I decided to check the bedroom just in case Vitania left Tyler sleeping in there.

But I never got there. The moment I passed through the kitchen, the walls came alive. The doorways vanished, and the room closed in around me. A figure seemed to melt through the wall, but I realized it was simply the living wood making way for her.

Lumia shook her head. "I cannot let you go, child."

CHAPTER 33

Vitania had beaten me and I had little doubt Lumia could overpower me in a house made of living wood. She could probably throw her fairy dust in my face and knock me out too. I didn't have time to form another rift, so I pounded on the wall with all my lycan strength. The wood cracked. Sap leaked from the scars. More wood grew over the wounds, reinforcing it.

Encumbered as I was with Eve, I couldn't use both hands to claw through the walls. Even if I tried, Lumia would probably restrain me. Trying to talk her out of this wouldn't help, and I certainly didn't have much time before Olivia and Vitania caught up to me.

So I did the only thing I could. I gripped the cocoon and ripped it completely open. Hundreds of tiny spines in the walls of the slimy shell slid out of Eve's flesh. I gagged to think those things had been in my skin as well. I rolled Eve out of it and hurled the cocoon at Lumia. It smacked wetly against a branch that sprung out to intercept it.

Eve sucked in a ragged breath and just as suddenly projectile vomited white goop across the room. She rolled over and pushed up to her knees. Her head rose, eyelids fluttered opened. She looked up at me with big brown eyes. Then the goddess rose unsteadily on trembling legs.

"Eve." Lumia clasped her hands like a priest seeking forgiveness. "Let me explain."

The goddess stumbled and leaned on me. She held up her hand and inspected it. "What is wrong with me?"

"Vitania put you in a deep sleep for over forty years." I helped her stand. "Her and my crazy half-sister are chasing me, and Lumia blocked us in this room."

"Eve, please don't be angry." Lumia's face blanched. "Vitania convinced me it was for the good of the world."

Eve held out a hand and the walls shifted back to their original shape.

"Thank you for moving the walls." I steadied the groggy goddess. "I need to find Tyler."

But Eve looked confused, as if she didn't know what was going on. "I did not do that. Why do I feel so weak?"

"I'll tell you why," Olivia growled from behind us.

I spun around as Olivia and Vitania stepped into the room.

Olivia's eyes sparkled and glowed golden. A halo of yellow sunlight basked her skin. She bared her teeth. "I took your godhood."

"Oh, shit." I went weak in the knees and stumbled back against Eve.

"Impossible." Eve leaned on me for support. "Only another god could do such a thing."

"Well, I guess I'm a god." Olivia cupped her hands. Orbs of golden light coalesced. Her body levitated off the floor and her hair blazed like fire. She looked so magnificent I wanted to punch her in the face.

"You kept it?" Vitania reeled back. "You were to let it dissipate, child!"

Olivia gripped Vitania by the throat. "I'm sick of you calling me a child!" She flung the Siren across the room. Vines grew from the walls and cushioned her impact. Claw-like branches shot from the walls behind Olivia, completely enclosing her in wood. Smoke rose from within. Wood crackled, burned, and exploded. Sparks and ash rained down on us. I grabbed Eve and dragged her across the room towards Lumia.

"You can't hurt me." Golden tears streamed down Olivia's face. "No one can hurt me anymore." She blurred across the room and slammed me aside. She grabbed Eve by the shoulders. "Can I go back in time and change things?"

Eve shook her head. "You cannot change that which is done. Create, destroy, or maintain. That is all the present allows."

"Olivia, let her go." Even with the lycan aura, I was still stunned from the tremendous blow. "You shouldn't have her powers. You'll destroy everything."

"You're so right, sister." Olivia laughed and sobbed at the same time. "Not even the fucking Netherlord can touch me now." She gripped Eve by the neck and squeezed. Bones cracked and the goddess went limp.

"No!" I screamed. "You killed her!"

Olivia grabbed my neck. "I'm going to turn your life to absolute shit, Emily. Maybe if you're lucky, I'll kill you later."

"Heal her." I gasped. "Please."

Olivia wiped the tears from her face. "God, you're pathetic. You had family. A good life. You're weak and pathetic."

"I don't care what you think of me. Just please help Eve."

"She's dead." Olivia dropped me like a sack of garbage. She slashed the air and a rift opened to a rundown apartment complex. A blackened sign in front read *Armitage Apartments*. "And I've got some scores to settle."

I grabbed the hem of her skirt. "Please save Eve!" I didn't know the woman at all, but she was my grandmother. I had so much to ask her, and hopefully just as much to learn about my powers.

Olivia booted me away and walked to the rift. She stopped and looked back. "You know what I hate the most about you, Emily? I wish I was you. I wish I had your life." She stepped through the rift and it closed behind her.

Lumia dropped to her knees next to Eve. She rubbed her hands together and conjured glittering dust around her hands. Then she gently stroked the back of Eve's neck. Bones popped and the ghastly shape of her neck corrected itself. Eve took a shuddering breath. Her eyes flared open.

Tears flowed down my cheeks. "You saved her!"

Lumia shed tears of her own. "If she had gone without breath another moment, it would have been too late."

Vitania huddled against the far wall. Her usually flowing hair hung lank around her shaking shoulders. "What have I done?"

Eve looked at Lumia. "It would have been better if you let me die."

"Why?" I said. "We have to stop Olivia."

"I have done my best to be a mother and a friend. But I have failed everyone." Eve began to cry and that just triggered another flood of my own.

"No, you haven't failed anyone." I didn't know this woman at all, but I'd seen this look before in the eyes of my own mother, and mothers everywhere. "We're the ones who failed you, Eve. It's our fault."

She smiled and caressed my cheek with a trembling hand. "Thank you, daughter."

I wiped my face. "For what?"

"For saving me, of course." She sat up and winced. "My head hurts."

"Your neck was broken. It will hurt for some time." Lumia wrapped her arms around the fallen goddess from behind and hugged her. "Forgive us, old friend. I told Vitania you meant us no harm."

"Harm?" Eve leaned back into the embrace, her back against Lumia's chest. "What do you mean?"

I walked over to the weeping Siren and held out my hand. "I could use a spot of tea and a heartfelt apology."

Vitania looked up at me with miserably red eyes. She looked like a little girl who'd lost her balloon and her puppy. She took my hand and nodded. I helped her up easily with my lycan strength. The Siren wrapped her arms around me and kept crying.

I was furious with her. At the same time, I pitied her. The woman had thousands of years on me and it seemed she was every bit as fallible as anyone else. I pushed her off me gently and asked, "Where's Tyler?"

"The bedroom." She led me there and released him from the song.

Tyler jerked awake. He grinned up at me, then flinched when he saw Vitania.

"Oh, man. Did we just have a threesome?" He sat up. "What happened?"

I laughed and threw myself into his arms. "Vitania imprisoned me. Olivia stole Eve's godhood and is probably on her way to end the world right this moment. But I'm glad you're okay."

Tyler stared blankly at me. "Babe, are you being serious? We were just having sex and then—"

"Yes, yes." I took his hand and pulled him off the bed. "We're about to cover everything." I glared at Vitania. "And I mean *everything*."

"Yes." The Siren turned and left the room.

I pulled Tyler after me.

"What in the hell is going on, Em?" He caught up to me. "I don't remember anything!"

"Don't worry, babe." I took his hand. "We'll get you caught up."

We sat down for some blue tea and then gave Vitania the floor so she could express how terribly remorseful she was. She told Eve everything. About how she thought Eve wished to destroy humanity with Bort and later the Apocryphan. About her decision to imprison Eve for eternity to preserve the world. About my appearance and the realization she could render Eve powerless and then set her free.

Just in case I wasn't up to the task, she used the song of seeking to find Olivia and spoke with her several times. When I refused to remove Eve's godhood, Vitania decided to keep me out of the way so Olivia could finish the job.

Olivia had done the job, all right. But now we had a crazy killer goddess on the loose. Judging from my encounters with her, she wasn't emotionally stable enough to handle that kind of power. Eve looked shocked when Vitania told her Olivia and I were descended from the twins, but she didn't interrupt.

When Vitania ended her story, she turned to Eve. "I would ask your forgiveness, but I could not in good conscience allow you to wipe the world of sentient life simply so you could start anew."

Eve drank her tea with shaky hands and set it down. "Bort was not made to destroy the world. He was made to end the wars between the ancient kingdoms of the world. Sirens and Seraphim warred constantly. The Fae supplied the Lyrolai with enchanted weapons to conquer the Nazdal. I sought peace for over a century but found nothing but blood. So I let the kingdoms have true blood. True savagery."

Tyler whistled. "Wow, that's some *Art of War* logic right there."

"You nearly destroyed the Fae," Lumia said. "I narrowly escaped the bloodbath at the Battle of Crimson Falls."

"The kingdoms did unite," Vitania said. "Bort was too strong for us to kill, so we created a special prison for him. He remained there until the Sundering forced us to move him."

"But the unity did not last," Lumia said. "The Sirens and Seraphim returned to war."

"And so I birthed the Apocryphan." Eve took another sip of tea. "Bort was an attempt to unite enemies against a greater enemy. The Apocryphan were meant to take power and unite by force."

"How'd that work out for you?" Tyler asked.

"Not well." Eve sighed. "I took genetic material from the other gods and used them to create the Apocryphan. This made each one uniquely powerful. But as they aged, their powers grew out of my control. They stopped listening to me."

"Spoken like a true mother." Tyler shrugged. "I've seen life from more angles than I can remember. Kids never grow up like their parents planned. Giving kids godlike powers is like handing the keys of a Ferrari to an eighteen-year-old boy and telling him not to speed."

"Why didn't you stop them earlier?" I asked.

"Together, they were too strong for me to overcome. Creating them also left me very weak. It took me decades to recover."

"That's weird," Tyler said. "You're a goddess. Shouldn't you recover instantly?"

"Even gods have limits." Eve looked into her tea. "If we draw on great amounts of power, it is physically and spiritually taxing."

Vitania's lips pressed into a line. "Creation did not go as planned, so you tried to indirectly control it." She lowered her head. "You petitioned us many times to stop the bloodshed, but you also pledged not to take sides, so we ignored you."

"And paid a terrible price." Lumia shook her head sadly. "So many died in the Sundering. Bort did not kill nearly so many as the Apocryphan."

"You are the children of other gods, but I am proud of how you stopped the Apocryphan." Eve swished the tea around in her cup. "The Sundering separated the kingdoms. That, at least, brought peace."

"Basically, you sent all the kids to their interdimensional rooms," Tyler said. "They can't fight if they can't see each other."

Eve smiled. "Yes. And some species have thrived better than others. I am most disappointed in my own children, in humanity. They multiply as if the gods demanded it and overwrite the rest of creation with little regard for the realm."

Vitania loosed a long sigh. "I do not approve of your methods, but I was wrong to imprison you, Eve. Please forgive me."

Eve got up and walked to Vitania. She took her hands and nodded. "I forgive you, old friend. Please forgive me." She turned to Lumia. "I would ask your forgiveness as well, Queen Lumia."

The Fae wiped tears from her cheeks and walked over. Then the three women hugged and laughed like old friends who'd just ended an argument.

Tyler leaned over to me. "A Fae, a Siren, and a goddess walk into a bar…"

I rolled my eyes. "Perhaps the most momentous thing in all of history is happening right before our eyes, and that's what you come up with?"

He chuckled. "I'm just trying not to freak out right now. Eve is the freaking mother of all humanity and we're in the same room as her." Tyler squeed like a fan-girl and hugged me.

I'd been so embroiled in my own emotions that I hadn't really thought about it that way. Now that Tyler made me think of it, I felt anxiety swelling in my chest. But there were many more reasons for a panic attack than being in the same room as the first mothers of three races.

My mentally unstable half-sister had Eve's powers and there was no telling what she'd do next.

The three women finished their group hug and sat at the table. The tabletop grew to accommodate more people, and more mushroom stools sprouted.

Vitania turned to me. "How did you escape the cocoon, child?"

My mind was so filled with terrible thoughts of Olivia that it took a moment for me to think of the answer. "I opened a rift to the library."

The Siren frowned. "But you were unconscious."

"My physical body was, but my spirit or subconscious was still awake." I shrugged. "I was in the same void where the lycan aura resides."

Eve regarded me. "I culled the powers from the twins, and yet you have soul powers."

"Yes." I leaned my elbows on the table and watched her reaction to my next question. "Why did you have Lydia and Victoria?"

CHAPTER 34

E ve hesitated, as if ashamed to answer.

"Were you making more kingdom-uniting world-killers?" Tyler asked.

Eve shook her head. "I was at a very low point in my existence. I was ashamed of the savagery and evil my children inflicted on one another, so I went among the mortals to try to understand them better. I witnessed horror and heroism. I met people from many walks of life. I met people both good and evil. But what gave me true joy was experiencing love.

"I desired to be young again. To enjoy the simple desires of life and forget the eternity of boredom. So I blocked my memories of being a goddess and made myself mortal. I met a man. One night of fun turned into a week, and that into months. I had found joy and love again."

Tyler's eyes flared with almost comic surprise. "You got a boy toy and lived with him?"

"I found a good man and enjoyed life." She wiped a tear from her eye. "I had willed myself sterile before blocking my memories. But I must have subconsciously changed my mind, because I became pregnant. When I was only a few months along, my love was murdered. In my grief, I remembered who I was and what I was capable of. I avenged him and reveled in the grief of love lost."

"Damn, that's dark." Tyler grimaced. "So you kept the babies?"

"I nearly ended the pregnancy but could not bring myself to do so." Eve sighed. "I came to Vitania and Lumia to give birth to the babies. Soon thereafter, I culled the powers from them so they would fit in among mortals. And that is the last thing I remember."

I slapped the table with my palm and glared at Vitania. "I knew it! Tell me how those babies ended up at Little Angel Orphanage."

Vitania and Lumia flinched and looked down at the table. Vitania finally looked from me to Eve and answered. "The Anagnos were a normal mortal couple who lived next to us. We never gave them the babies because we didn't know if they might manifest abilities later. So we found an orphanage that specialized in supernatural children, and the lycan came and picked them up. I told him our last name was Anagnos."

"Holy flaming hell!" Tyler's mouth hung open in astonishment. "You imprisoned Eve and tossed her babies to the wolves? What kind of sick fucks are you?"

Tears poured down Lumia's cheeks. "We did not know the orphanage was such a terrible place. We thought that was their best chance for a normal life!"

"We could not care for them, and if they developed powers, they could not remain with mortals." Vitania's stony expression didn't waver. "We did what was best for the children." She looked at Eve. "And I could not allow you to continue your quest for genocide. Imprisoning you was the only answer to keep you from birthing another monstrosity that threatened existence."

"It is in the past," Eve declared in a voice that was almost godlike. "All is forgiven, and we will move on."

Vitania nodded. "As you wish, Eve."

"Thank you." Lumia wiped her eyes.

"Really?" Tyler looked back and forth. "That's it? These women gave away your babies and threw you into a cocoon prison, but you forgive them in a heartbeat?"

Eve's heavy gaze settled on Tyler. "I birthed humanity. What are two more children out of my billions?" She sighed as if the weight of existence settled on her shoulders. "I have done terrible things that make anything Vitania and Lumia have done pale in comparison."

"And you're not the least bit upset?" Tyler said.

"What is the point?" Eve's shoulders slumped. "Sometimes, I think there is no point to existence."

"That's not reassuring at all, coming from the original goddess." Tyler looked worried. "You need therapy."

I agreed with Tyler's assessment, but Eve had been around since the beginning and she had some serious mental issues going on. I decided to change the subject, because there were more important things to discuss. "Eve, why do I have powers if you culled them from your children?"

"I must not have finished the task before Vitania put me to sleep." Eve furrowed her brow in concentration. "When I blocked my memory, I also made myself mostly mortal. I had not yet regained all my powers when I gave birth and removed the powers from the babies. That is why Vitania took me so easily."

"It was the only way I could have ever taken you," Vitania said.

Eve regarded me with her brown eyes. "You should not have soul powers. And yet, it seems you do. You risked everything to save me even though you know almost nothing about me. You are a good person, Emily, and I am proud of you."

A lump formed in my throat and I couldn't stop the tears. "I'm glad to hear that, Grandmother."

Eve laughed. "Yes, child, I suppose I am your grandmother."

I looked at her uncertainly. "Can I hug you?"

Another laugh. "Yes." Eve stood and wrapped her arms around me.

It almost felt like hugging Mum again. This woman was strong even without her godhood. Like any mother, she did her best. Sometimes she succeeded, and other times she failed. But she'd done everything she could to make life better for her children. It wasn't her fault most of them were assholes intent on destroying the world.

I didn't want to let her go, but I didn't want to make things awkward, so I backed away and sat down again. "I think you would've been proud of Mum, too. Lydia, not so much."

"Perhaps I will meet Lydia." Eve clasped her hands. "My newfound mortality will make the rest of life interesting."

"About that," I said. "We can't let Olivia keep your powers. We've got to get them back before she blows up a city or the world."

"I can do nothing about that, child." Eve put her hand on mine. "You and the others are the only ones who can stop her."

"Stop a mad goddess?" Tyler grimaced. "I want to help, but I'm just a dude who's a demon."

"I unleashed the child on the world." Vitania shook her head. "I will do everything I can to stop her."

"Maybe we can capture Olivia like you caught Eve," I said.

"Eve was exhausted and unconscious." Vitania looked away from Eve. "Birthing demigods and removing their powers made her vulnerable. I do not think we can count on Olivia doing the same thing."

Eve stared at Vitania for a moment but didn't rehash the subject. "Our only advantage is that Olivia lacks experience."

"We will have to catch her unaware," Vitania said. "It is the only way."

Lumia nodded. "Perhaps a magical snare will do the trick."

Tyler frowned. "How did you catch all the other super villains in your basement?"

"Despite their powers, they all had weaknesses." Vitania clasped her hands. "I also had powerful allies and seldom caught them by myself."

"Can we round up your allies?" Tyler asked.

"They are scattered throughout the realms." Vitania shook her head. "Even with the song of seeking, it would be difficult to find them."

"We need to strike while Olivia is still new to her powers," I said. "She might be strong, but she'll be just like I was when I got the lycan aura."

Tyler scoffed. "Didn't look like she needed much experience the way she opened a rift. She grew up on the streets. Had all kinds of nasty things done to her. You can bet she knows how to fight."

"She already knew how to open rifts to Haedaemos," Vitania said. "I showed her the symbols for travelling in Eden when I brought her here. She seemed very nice and willing to do whatever I asked when I met her."

It was my turn to scoff. "Because Olivia knows how to play people. She grew up like Oliver Twist, while I had the perfect nuclear family."

"So she can open rifts and is super strong, but she can't use your advanced abilities?" Tyler said.

Eve shrugged. "You cannot simply use my powers without under-standing them. Even I am bound by the laws of physics and magic."

"How much does she need to know to kill people?" Tyler said. "Probably not much. And who can blame her for wanting revenge?"

"Well, we can't just sit here." I smacked a hand on the table. "We've got to try to stop her right now."

"Subterfuge is key," Lumia said. "We must take her by surprise."

"She'll sense our auras before we're close enough." Vitania frowned. "Even masking ourselves will be ineffective against her new power."

Tyler pursed his lips. "Actually, I think we should consider a full-frontal attack."

"Attack her directly?" Lumia's forehead scrunched. "Are you mad? She would incinerate us before we reached her."

Tyler wore a confident grin. "Just hear me out."

We did. Afterward, we agreed his plan was mental and probably wouldn't work. Well, all of us except Eve. She seemed to think Tyler's was the least terrible idea out of the other ones we put on the table. It was also the one that we could enact right away. If we gave Olivia time, even a day, she might learn enough to become unstoppable.

Vitania tried to offer me some comforting advice before we left. "Eve's power dwarfs your own, child, but you are stronger than you think."

I felt like a little girl going up against a playground bully who also happened to be eight feet tall, two hundred pounds of pure muscle, and a karate master. "I'll do my best."

Unfortunately, I was still quite weak and shaken up from my earlier escape. Opening the rift that pulled my physical body from the cocoon had drained me, and I still wasn't fully recovered from days of rigorous training. The only thing I had going for me now was the lycan aura.

We'd seen where Olivia went, so opening a rift wasn't hard for Vitania. The gateway opened to the Armitage Apartments and we stepped through. A grimy brick building five stories high sat on a plot of muddy earth, bordered on all sides by a five-foot brick wall. Boarded up businesses and dirty old buildings seemed the norm in this part of town. A quick glance at my arcphone map told me we were in Peckham, London. It was the same place mentioned in Olivia's state records.

A badly burnt body lay on the sidewalk outside the apartment building. Tendrils of greasy smoke still rose from blackened flesh. At first glance, the entire block looked deserted, but I glimpsed people peering around the corners of buildings or huddled behind cars.

"It seems Olivia made quite an impression already," Tyler said.

"I guess she went inside." I looked at the building for other signs of fighting. "We've got to draw her out."

We took cover at the brick wall and peered toward the entrance.

"Maybe if we call her name," Tyler said.

A man smashed through a window on the fifth floor and screamed earthward. A blur of gold streaked after him and caught him just before he hit the ground. Olivia hovered in the air, holding her prey in one hand. Gold flames danced in her hair and her eyes burned like the sun.

"Now do you remember me, you fucking pervert?" Olivia shook him like a rag doll. "Do you remember what you did to me?"

"Let me go, bitch!" the man shouted.

"I begged you to let me go. I was just a little girl!" She gripped his crotch. Smoke billowed and an agonizing scream tore from the man's throat. Olivia ripped off his pants, revealing a burnt and cauterized crotch. "Enjoy your life, you fucking filth." She dropped him the final five feet and turned back to the building.

"Damn." Tyler blew out a breath. "Maybe she's doing god's work."

"I can't disagree," I said. "But what happens after she's done dealing justice to everyone who wronged her?"

Olivia rose in the air, levitating on golden flames. Tears of fire dripped from her cheeks and sizzled on the ground. She slowly turned to face the building. I saw dozens of terrified faces peering out from the windows. One of them would be the next victim.

"All of you stood by and did nothing!" Olivia screamed. "You're all as guilty as he is!" Her body blazed into an inferno.

"Oh, shit." Tyler gripped my arm. "Here's the part where she goes crazy."

Olivia streaked toward the building and smashed into it dead center. Brick melted into lava, leaving a hole a story tall. People inside ran away screaming. Olivia vanished into the structure again, leaving a fiery trail of destruction. The entire building trembled. A gout of fire erupted from the top. Glass and ash exploded from the sides.

Frantic tenants flooded from the front doors and clambered down emergency stairwells on the outside. Olivia pounded on the building again and again.

"We've got to help them!" I said.

But it was too late. With a terrible roar, the building crumbled and collapsed. Drifting dust swirled into a whirlwind and was swept away. Olivia hovered above the destroyed building, a golden mote in a gray sky. Her laughter sent terrible chills down my spine.

Injured people, bloody and covered in dust, staggered across the muddy lawn. Golden beams streaked from Olivia's fingers, incinerating the survivors before they made it even a few feet.

Tyler gulped and put his back to the wall. "I don't think my plan is going to work."

I squeezed my eyes shut. "My god, she just killed all those people. We've got to confront her now."

"She is so preoccupied with revenge, she doesn't sense us," Lumia said. "Striking now is our only chance."

"Agreed." I pointed across the street. "Eve, go take cover somewhere."

The goddess shook her head. "I will not hide like a coward."

"You've got no powers," I said. "Hide like someone with common sense."

She frowned and looked ready to argue, but Vitania gave her a stern look. "Don't give us that indignant look. You're not a goddess right now."

Eve narrowed her eyes but acquiesced and walked across the street.

Tyler cracked his knuckles and took a deep breath. "Let's do this."

Lumia summoned an orb of glittering dust and blew it onto Tyler. He held his breath and waited a moment before stepping to the side and out of the dust. "Wow, that's cool."

"Let's put it to the test." Tyler wiggled his fingers and jogged in place. "Yeah, this is gonna work." He dashed around the corner, waving his arms. "Hey, ugly!"

Olivia streaked toward him like a meteor and stopped twenty feet diagonally above him. "What did you say, mortal?"

"I said you're ugly, bitch!"

She unleashed a torrent of golden fire right on top of him. Tyler screamed piteously and ran in circles, before collapsing. He lifted a burning finger and flipped her off. Olivia snarled and doubled down with even more fire.

The real Tyler blinked as if out of a trance. "Whoa, that was trippy. It was like one of those virtual reality games that Jack showed me."

Lumia dusted Tyler and me. We let the dust settle on us and then stepped aside. A male and female with no resemblance to us stood where we had. Olivia would consider them noms, or so we hoped. I reached out and touched the female. It was like touching the tip of a fine paintbrush.

"What are these things?" I asked.

"They are solid illusions, but only last for a short while." Lumia looked towards my mad half-sister who was still scorching the earth where Tyler's illusion perished. "I certainly hope she is growing weaker."

"Me too." I closed my eyes and shifted into the perspective of the illusion. Then I ran in place and it ran forward. I turned and it ran around the wall and toward Olivia. I mouthed the words I wanted it to say and it repeated them.

"You insane bitch! You killed everyone!"

"Apparently not everyone." Olivia turned her burning gaze on the illusion, but with the first-person perspective it felt like I was really staring down a mental patient with godlike powers.

"I'll kill you!" my illusion shouted.

Olivia snarled and lifted a hand. Then she stopped and looked around as if suddenly sensing something. Her snarl turned into a malicious grin. "What sort of stupid game is this?" She slashed her hand and the view from the illusion vanished. I heard an awful clatter. Lycan reflexes leapt me out of the way as the brick wall collapsed and sent us scattering.

Tyler dove to the side and rolled away. A nearby car provided him with a hiding spot, but Vitania and Lumia were caught in the open.

"Bloody idiots. Did you really come after me?" Energy gathered in Olivia's hands. "I was going to let you live, but I can't help it if you want to commit suicide." She hurled a miniature sun at the Fae and Siren.

"No!" I froze in place. There was nothing I could do.

Lumia cast a veil of dust around them. It solidified into a curtain of water. Steam billowed into the air as the water bore the brunt of the attack. Olivia unleashed golden beams from her fists. The water vaporized, but the Fae and Siren were nowhere to be seen.

I saw them leap from a rift a block down the street. Olivia saw them too. "Do you really think you can beat me? I'm a goddess now!"

The plan had been simple. Make Olivia burn through her energy by attacking illusions and chasing ghosts. Her body wasn't used to godlike powers, so we hoped she'd tire quickly. Despite all the destruction, all the incredible energy expended, Olivia remained as energetic as a child in a toy store. Now the world was her plaything, and we'd be lucky to escape alive.

"Fuck this city." Olivia dropped to the ground and slashed a pattern. Her hand clawed the air, slashing open a rift. The odor of brimstone filled the air. Yellow mist streaked out. "Fuck every god damned human. Eve was right. They deserve to be wiped out."

Olivia furrowed her brow in concentration and funneled the mist into a biped with the top half of an octopus. Its massive tentacles writhed like giant snakes. Olivia funneled another demon spirit into a humanoid with four arms and a shark head. The last took the shape of a black scorpion the size of a horse with four human heads rising on serpentine necks.

The dry demonic heat I felt from possessed people was nothing compared to the boiling sulfurous sensations emanating from these monstrosities. It was like standing in the steam from an erupting geyser.

Tyler dashed across the road and took cover behind a car with me. "She's summoning demons into physical form without a pattern." His face paled. "That shouldn't be possible."

"Maybe not for a human who can't utilize quantum tunnels." I clenched my teeth. "There's nothing we can do to stop her."

"Those are no ordinary demons." He wiped sweat from his forehead. "They're deep ones. Octolon, Hydranis, and—well, I don't remember shark boy's name."

"Deep ones?" It sounded like something he'd just made up. "Are those their true names?"

"Maybe, maybe not," Tyler said. "Some demons take names that have nothing to do with their true names."

Unfortunately, touching these monsters was the only way for me to find their true names and banish them.

The demons shrieked, roared, and plowed through the remnants of the brick wall. Hydranis and the shark man headed for Vitania and Lumia. Octolon came for us.

"How are we supposed to fight this thing?" I said. "I don't even have a knife!"

"No, but you've got wolf claws." Tyler looked around. "I don't see a hardware store. I'd give my eyeteeth for a damned hammer right now."

I hadn't shifted into full wolf form yet. I didn't even know how to, and I certainly didn't want to give in to instinct right now. So I concentrated on my hands and imagined growing claws. Fur sprouted from my hands and razor-sharp claws stabbed through the tips of my fingers, even as they turned into paws. My scream of pain turned into a howl.

My howl turned into a yelp when a tentacle snatched me off the ground and pulled me toward a gaping maw of sharp teeth. I slashed the tentacle with a claw. The skin was tougher than it looked. Green ichor dribbled from the wound. I clawed furiously at the slick flesh, desperate. The demon shrieked. I shrieked too as I came closer to that terrifying mouth.

I'd transformed halfway into a wolf, still humanoid, but with claws and fur. I felt like a cornered animal, lashing out in one last attempt to save my life.

The demon's true name and pattern flashed into my head, only marginally different from the name Tyler told me earlier. "Octolonagresh, I banish you to Haedaemos!"

But Octolonagresh just laughed. "I'm here in the flesh, mortal. Only my summoner can control me."

My god, I can't banish this thing?

If I couldn't use my greatest power on these things, that meant we had to fight them. It meant there was nothing we could do to save ourselves or the city.

CHAPTER 35

U nable to rely on my demon-banishing ability, I redoubled my efforts. I rammed my foot against the demon's lower half to keep it from pulling me into its giant mouth. I hacked and slashed with everything I had. The limb finally severed, and I dropped to the ground on furry hind legs.

But Octolon had plenty more tentacles in play. As if that wasn't enough, the one I'd hacked off slowly grew back to full length even as the severed part flopped on the ground.

How in the hell was I supposed to get rid of this thing if I couldn't banish it? I leapt away from the flailing tentacles. Tyler emerged from a rundown food mart with a big knife in hand.

"That won't do anything!" I said. "It just regrows its limbs."

"We've got to get it back in the demon portal." Tyler pointed to the fiery rift. "That's the only way to get rid of them since they're here in physical form."

Olivia still stood near the rift, her face taut with concentration. I backed away as Octolon stalked closer.

Tyler's gaze locked onto Olivia. "I don't think she's done this before. She obviously didn't realize how hard it is to maintain physical demons without a pattern."

"She's straining herself?" I said.

"Not even the most skilled demon summoners could summon a demon without a pattern."

"Then we've got to keep up the cat and mouse as long as possible." I ducked beneath a swinging tentacle and tried to find Vitania and Lumia. The scorpion demon and his companion were two blocks away, throwing cars around as if they were toys, but the Fae and Siren were nowhere to be seen.

"I've got a better idea." Tyler dodged to the side as Octolon tried to grab him. "Since there's no pattern, Olivia can't release the demons. She'd have to recall them and put them back through the portal. So as long as they're here, they're a heavy burden on her new powers. That means she's vulnerable. You've got to try to take back Eve's powers now."

"And leave you alone with the demon?" I said.

Tyler flashed a grin. "This idiot can't catch me."

The demon shrieked. "I will devour you, fool!"

Tyler shooed me away. "Go. I'll be fine."

I didn't like it, but I didn't have a better idea. I dodged around Octolon, but it wasn't ready to let me go. It turned to chase me. Tyler flashed in behind it and stabbed the knife into one of its human legs. It shrieked and spun back to face him, leaving me free to run away.

Olivia might be straining to maintain the demons, but I didn't dare run headlong into her. Surprise was the best option. So I circled around the remnants of the brick wall and came at her from behind.

I had to touch her to reclaim the goddess aura, which would put me right in the kill zone. If removing the aura from Bort had been challenging, I couldn't imagine how hard it would be to take it from Olivia. Strained as she was, Olivia could probably still kill me on the spot. The moment I touched her, she'd fight back. My only hope was that the demons kept her distracted long enough for me to claim the goddess aura.

Stopping a short distance away, I closed my eyes and glimpsed her. As before, it was hard to see her. But when I did, it was almost like seeing double. A pale ghostly form seemed halfway merged with an identical golden silhouette. I wondered if the goddess aura operated the same as the lycan one, or if it was actually becoming a part of Olivia's primary aura.

With the glimpse firmly fixed in my mind, I opened my eyes and sneaked up behind my half-sister. The flames in her hair had died down, and the golden glow around her body had dimmed slightly.

Please be tired!

Just as I reached out a hand to touch her, she spun and faced me, a malicious grin on her face. The golden halo brightened, and flames once again danced in her hair. "Foolish little Emily. Did you really think you could sneak up on a goddess?"

It's do or die!

Hesitating meant death, so I took the only option available.

I lunged across the last two feet separating us and wrapped my arms around her. My spirit grasped at the aura and yanked. Olivia cried out in surprise. Apparently, she hadn't been ready for such a desperate move. I closed my eyes and concentrated with everything I had on removing Eve's aura.

Unlike Bort's aura, it wasn't like a stone stuck in the mud. In fact, it slid out smoothly and into my embrace. It might have been because the aura was stolen and not part of Olivia, or it might have been because Eve's aura was so similar to mine that it didn't resist.

But Olivia refused to give up the ghost. Her spirit form gripped the goddess aura and pulled back. My lycan strength didn't aid me in the spiritual tug-of-war. Apparently, it all came down to the abilities we'd inherited from Eve. I strained with everything I had, but Olivia still had god strength, and I didn't.

That was when my physical ears heard the awful roars. I risked a peek with my real eyes and saw the demons rushing straight for my half-sister. In our struggle against each other, she'd stopped controlling them and now they were turning on their master.

Olivia sensed it too. She screamed in outrage and flung out a hand. An invisible force swept the demons back into the hell rift. The gateway sealed shut. That instant of diversion allowed me to yank the goddess aura ever so slightly from Olivia's grasp, but still not enough to remove it.

Sonic waves rippled the air. They pressed against my skin like the relentless ocean tide, carrying with them the song of the Siren. Lumia flew overhead on gossamer wings. Fairy dust rained down on Olivia, quenching her flaming hair and trying to lull her to sleep.

"No, no, no!" My half-sister stomped a foot and the ground cracked. The boarded-up building next door cracked and imploded. The next two buildings in a row crumbled and collapsed. "Leave me alone!" A desperate scream crackled like thunder. The front of my body felt as if it kissed the sun. An explosion threw me back with such force, I expected to smash into something solid and die instantly, even with the lycan aura.

Something cushioned me. Strong arms wrapped around my torso and I skidded several feet through the mud. I wiped the grime from my eyes and saw Tyler lying beneath me. His eyelids fluttered but didn't open. The impact seemed to have knocked him out.

"Baby, are you okay?" I slapped his cheek. He moaned. I wanted to make sure he was okay, but I couldn't spare another second if we were going to stop Olivia.

I glanced back and saw Olivia staggering beneath the onslaught from Vitania and Lumia. The golden flames around her flared and dimmed repeatedly like lights during an electrical shortage. I tried to stand, but agony seared my flesh. My hands were blackened and seared. My face felt as if it had been charbroiled.

It hurt so much I could barely stand it. Even the lycan aura couldn't compensate. It didn't matter. Even if it was the last thing I did, I had to reclaim Eve's aura. If it meant I died or was horribly scarred for life, so be it.

Moaning with pain, I limped back toward the battle. My skin cracked and wept fluids with every step. My hands could barely move. I felt charred down to my very core. This was it. My true moment to die. But I was the only one who could stop Olivia and save the world.

I laughed hysterically at the image. *Save the world? I'm such a drama queen.*

Olivia turned her furious gaze on me as I closed in. "You look awful. Guess I'll put you out of your misery, sis."

Before Olivia could summon another blast, Vitania's mouth dropped open inhumanly wide and unleashed a brutal sonic wave. I screamed and leapt the final few feet, carried only by lycan strength. I slammed into Olivia and clawed at her face. Crimson trails stained her cheeks. My spirit arms caressed the goddess aura and pulled.

Olivia cried out and dropped to her knees.

I brutally tore the goddess aura from her with everything I had.

It slid into me. Every ache and pain faded. I used the rest of my strength to leap away from Olivia so she couldn't retake the aura. But she was done for. My half-sister collapsed. Lumia and Vitania relented.

"She will not wake for some time," Vitania said. "I will put her in my prison."

Power surged through every atom of my being. The lycan aura was but a candle compared to a burning sun. My new vision painted the land in vibrant colors and hues I couldn't name. I sensed odors and heard sounds no human could hear. My burnt skin healed before my eyes and began to glow golden as a summer day.

I looked up and willed myself higher. My body soared on golden flames and I kissed the blue skies. Then I looked down on beautiful creation and saw the death and destruction. Sadness dampened my spirits. My eyes found a lone figure still lying on the ground. The elation of godhood vanished, replaced by fear and pain.

I swooped to the ground and knelt next to my love. I pressed a hand to his chest and closed my eyes. I sensed great trauma—broken ribs, punctured lungs, and internal bleeding. He coughed and crimson foam stained his mouth. "He's dying!" I focused on the damage and willed him to heal, but nothing happened. Tears trickled down my cheeks and sizzled in the mud. "Please, help me save him!"

But no matter how hard I willed his body to repair itself, nothing happened. My own healing was automatically done by the goddess aura, but it didn't work that way for healing others.

"You must weave it together." I flinched and turned around. Eve stood behind me. She moved her fingers in precise patterns. "Weave the bone and flesh. Mend it as you would torn fabric."

I did as she showed me, and golden filaments began to knit broken bone and torn flesh. "What about the internal bleeding?" I asked.

"Unweave it." She showed me another simple pattern.

I followed it and the blood in his lung dissipated. I patched the last broken rib that had punctured the lung.

"You wasted a perfectly good rib," Eve said. "We could have used that to make a woman."

I blinked and stared at her.

Vitania rolled her eyes. "You and your biblical humor."

Lumia laughed. "I love it."

Tyler coughed and his eyes fluttered open. He looked up at me and smiled. "Did I save you?"

I laughed and buried my face in his chest. "Yes, you did, you wonderful man."

"You hit me like a bull." He traced my cheek with a finger. "Why are you glowing?"

I sat up and smiled. "We did it. We beat Olivia." I looked at Eve and jolted to my feet. "Oh, I'm sorry. Let me—"

She shook her head. "Why don't you enjoy it for a moment? Perhaps give your hero a celebratory flight?"

"You can fly like Olivia?" Tyler grinned. "I get to be your Lois Lane?"

I giggled. "Just this once, hot stuff." I cradled him in my arms and jetted into the sky on golden flames.

Tyler whooped with glee and looked down at the destruction and the crowds gathering blocks away from the former battle. "The Custodians are going to be pissed!"

"I hope George is in a forgiving mood." I sighed. "It's not every day you have to fight a goddess."

"Or get to be one." Despite being carried like a child, Tyler still managed to look as manly as ever. He kissed me on the lips. "Think we could get it on up here?"

"Is that all you ever think about?"

"What can I say? You light my fire, baby." He traced a finger across my back.

I giggled and carried us above the low-hanging clouds. A golden sphere enveloped us, keeping us warm and dry. "In that case, let's give it a try."

Surprisingly, flying sex worked out quite well. It seemed as a goddess, I could give Tyler orgasms he'd never dreamed of. When we returned to ground twenty minutes later, I set Tyler down on unsteady legs.

He clung to me for support. "Man, that was amazing!"

Eve looked relieved to see me again.

I walked over to her. "I didn't run off with your powers." I smiled and hugged myself. "But I really love them so much."

"Perhaps you'll grow into your own someday." She took my hands. I closed my eyes and glimpsed her. A pale spirit still resided in her. It looked like Olivia's but was dimmer, less substantial. It didn't seem strong enough to grasp the goddess aura, so I gently pushed it out of me and into her.

My body sagged and the weight of mortality settled on my shoulders. I almost wanted to cry. Eve gasped and shuddered. She hugged me and kissed my cheek. "I am proud to call you granddaughter."

I blinked back tears. "Thank you."

"How sweet it is to taste the food of the gods." Lumia looked at me with sympathy. "How bitter to be allowed only a taste."

"If I feel bad, imagine how Olivia's going to feel when she wakes up." I looked past the rubble, across the muddy field where she lay, arms askew, blond hair muddy. Despite what she'd done, I felt terrible for her. That a little girl had been so abused and used. Her only friends had been demons. The real evil of the situation was that Lydia had cast her aside without ever making sure she had a good life.

Crowds of people began to converge on the demolished building. The entire area resembled a warzone. Burnt corpses littered the ground, and there was no telling how many lay beneath the rubble. As usual, many innocents had paid the price for the crimes of a few.

"It's time to go," Vitania said. "No good will come from remaining any longer."

325

Spots of dry heat pinged against my senses—too many to count.

"Demons," Eve said. "Nearly a hundred possessed bodies."

"Demons?" Lumia frowned. "But how?"

"Because they want Olivia!" I raced around the rubble to reach her, but it was too late. The mob swept toward us and Olivia vanished in the mass of bodies.

"We should go," Lumia said.

"But we have Eve," I protested. "We can fight."

"There are mortals in the crowd," Eve said. "We would only harm them if we fight."

"Then sing them to sleep," I said.

Eve slashed the air and an invisible force pushed us through a rift. The world stretched and snapped back into place. The rift closed and we stood back in Vitania's house in Iceland.

"Why'd you do that?" I spun on Eve. "We could have taken Olivia back!"

"There has been enough war for the day." Golden light burned in Eve's irises. "I will not see more bloodshed."

"But Vitania could have sung them all to sleep!"

Eve shook her head. "Not those demons. I sensed rubies among the possessed. They are resistant to Siren song."

"It is true, child." Vitania scowled. "It seems Domathus values his prize mortal."

"Fuck!" Tyler clenched his fists. "That means it's open season on Emily again."

"It means your old life is over, I'm afraid." Lumia caressed my cheek. "It is time to leave behind your mortal roots and begin a new journey."

"You mean give up my friends? Tyler's companies?" I shook my head. "I'm not going to let a demon overlord bully me into hiding!"

"Em, maybe it's for the best." Tyler squeezed my hand. "Nothing in the world matters as much to me as you."

"Demon assassins be damned." I tugged my hand free. "I won't let them rule my life."

"We'll just have to be more careful." Tyler ran a hand down his face. "Besides, you'll be up to your ears in work for Fjoeruss."

In all the excitement, I'd completely forgotten about it. "Lovely. I went through so much trouble, and now I'm back to square one."

Once again, demons would hunt me.

CHAPTER 36

"Perhaps I can give you a brief respite from your troubles." Eve traced a circle in the air around my head. "That will make you invisible to demons for a time. Perhaps long enough for you to come into your own powers."

I clasped my hands imploringly. "You can't give me a power boost?"

"No, but I can give you something even more valuable." She took my hand and marked a pattern in the air. "We will return soon." Then she pulled me through an invisible rift.

We stood on a desolate plane. Crooked mountains rose in the distance. Dead trees and scrubby bushes dotted the landscape. A red sun hovered low on the far horizon. Lightning struck, illuminating ghostly figures in the shadows of the mountains.

"Where are we?" I shivered even though it was neither cold nor hot.

"Nowhere." Eve held out her hand and closed her eyes. "A very special place where the physical and spiritual coexist." She smiled. Her fingers formed precise patterns as if weaving an invisible tapestry. Pale mist drifted closer, taking humanoid form and coalescing into solid shape.

Dark hair spilled across shoulders, and a face I missed terribly smiled back at me.

"Mum? Is it really you?"

Mum teared up. "Yes, Emily, it's me."

I grabbed her and hugged her, daring to believe this was real. She felt solid. Felt just like I remembered her. She even smelled the same, like leather and lavender. Dad told me it was because of the oils she used on her arrows.

Mum hugged me hard and stepped back. She gave Eve an appraising look. "Are you related to me?"

Eve nodded. "I am your mother, dear."

"How did you call me here? Where are we?"

"She's Eve, the mother of humanity." It sounded like something a crazy person would say, but Mum didn't bat an eyelash. "We're in Nowhere. It's a middle ground between life and death."

"Precisely," Eve said.

Mum nodded. "I've tried to learn as much as possible about the afterlife from other souls, but it's been difficult."

"It's just like you to interrogate even the dead." I smiled. "You haven't changed a bit."

"Why should I?" Mum looked from me to Eve. "There is quite a family resemblance."

I changed subjects. "Was that really you talking to me in my dreams?"

Mum nodded. "Somehow, I'm still connected to Lydia. I haunted her dreams and discovered a dark secret. She has a daughter that she abandoned." Pain pinched her forehead. "She tricked Patrick into impregnating her."

I knew it probably hurt her more than she let on, but I didn't call her out on it. "In hindsight, I understand what you were trying to tell me."

"The only reason I found out was because I have a connection to her just as I have to you. That was how I located the girl, discovered her name, and learned that she consorts with demons." Mum sighed. "I've tried to watch you, but it's very difficult peeking into the living world, even with you as a link."

A painful lump rose in my throat. "I miss you so much. I wish you could come back with me."

"I wish that were possible," Eve said.

"We can see each other again, just not on the mortal plane." Mum kissed my cheeks. "I couldn't be prouder of the person you've become, Emily. And I will always have your back."

I looked at Eve. "How much time do we have?"

"All the time in Nowhere." She smiled. "I will be nearby when you're ready to go."

Time seemed to pass differently in the strange realm. I caught Mum up on everything, although she seemed to know a shocking amount for someone who was dead.

"What's the afterlife like?" I asked.

"It's boring as bloody hell." Mum shuddered. "I've dedicated most of my time to finding lost souls in Nowhere and trying to redeem the devoured, but I haven't found a way into the Hell pit yet."

I flinched. "You're risking your soul to get into the Hell pit?"

"The afterlife consists of different realms much like the physical world. Most people go to what you might consider Heaven, but it's nothing like the bible." She shrugged. "Then you've got Haedaemos with its thirteen levels, the Hell pit, and Abyss down at the very bottom. I'm still exploring, of course, but I think there's a way to redeem the devoured souls trapped around the lake of fire."

"I've seen the lake of fire in visions." I shivered. "It's horrendous."

"And it's all connected—one big circle." Mum sighed and looked at the red sun. It hadn't moved in all the time we'd been here. "You need to be careful. There's a much larger force at play right now, and Olivia is at the center of it."

I nodded. "Some Templars think there's a big war coming." I recalled what I'd heard from Thomas Borathen. "A Seraphim named Daelissa wants to take over Eden."

Mum nodded. "I tracked down rumors of badly drained souls entering the afterlife. It seems Daelissa feeds on the light from human souls. But I don't think she is the true danger. Something else is brewing, and I feel it emanating from Haedaemos."

"Maybe we should ask Eve," I said.

Eve had wandered far across the barren plane, but when we called her, she appeared next to us almost immediately. "Are you ready to go?"

"Almost, but first we have some things to talk about." Mum told Eve about her suspicions.

Eve sighed. "There are always plans and plots and deeds. It seems my meddling in human affairs only made things worse." She shook her head. "So much so that even the mothers of mighty races wished to lock me away forever."

"This is different," Mum said. "I think demon overlords want to make another major play for Eden. Maybe even the other realms."

"It will not be the first nor the last time." Eve caressed Mum's cheek as if she were a child. "Daughter, I cannot be the protector of the realm. That is up to you and Emily. I will help in small ways if I can, but my interference has caused only grief."

"Damn it, Eve, you can't just abandon humanity." Mum jerked her cheek from Eve's hand. "Humanity needs its mother."

Eve laughed and shook her head. "I'm afraid the babe left the nest long ago, as did you." She sighed. "If I could restore you to the mortal plane, I would. Eden lost a valuable protector when you died. I am proud of you."

Mum blinked rapidly and took a deep breath. "Thank you."

It was obvious Mum was trying to act detached, but when your mother says she's proud of you, it's no small thing. I hugged my mother. "I'm proud of you too. I'll tell Dad you said hello."

Tears trickled down Mum's cheeks. She smiled. "Lydia's betrayal has probably filled him with guilt. Tell him he is blameless in my eyes. Tell him he should find another good woman to get him through his final days. Goodness knows every man needs one."

I laughed through my tears. "Dad's been throwing himself into action since you left. I think he's eager to join you."

"Don't let him, Emily." Mum kissed my forehead. "Tell him that I insist he live life to the fullest. Because I will put him to work the moment he dies."

I hugged her with everything I had. "I'll tell him."

Mum kissed my cheeks and forehead again. "I love you, dear. Now go. Return to the living world and protect it."

"Yes, Mum." It was so hard to let her go. I had so much I still wanted to tell her. So many things I wanted to apologize for. But she was proud of me and that gave me more strength than even the aura of a goddess.

Eve led me back to Eden. Tyler stopped pacing when he saw me. "Where did you go?"

"To visit Mum." I wiped the tears from my face. "She says hi."

Tyler stared at me blankly for a moment. "You literally saw her?"

"In the spirit," Eve said. She walked over to Vitania and Lumia at the table. They regarded her warily. She'd forgiven them while mortal, but would she do so as a goddess?

"Are you certain all is forgiven?" Lumia said.

Vitania stepped in front of the Fae. "If you wish to punish anyone, it should be me. I pressured Lumia into helping me."

"I made my own decisions, Vita." Lumia gave her a stern look. "You do not have to protect me."

Eve sat down. "I am only here to visit and have a cup of tea with friends."

Tears trickled down Vitania's cheeks. She wiped her eyes and managed a smile. "I did not think you would truly forgive me."

The goddess put her hand over the Siren's. "I am the one who needs forgiving, friend. I interfered with creation. If I had left it alone, the kingdoms might have found peace on their own."

"That's called being a hover mom," Tyler said.

I elbowed his rib. "Shush."

Eve reached across and touched Lumia. "Gentle friend, I know this has been hard on you."

"I don't like violence," Lumia said. "This has been quite taxing."

"Perhaps we should go on a retreat then." Eve poured herself a cup of tea. "I have some amazing realms I'd like to show you."

I dearly wished I could go on vacay with them, but I had to report to Fjoeruss the next day.

Tyler snapped his fingers. "Hey, maybe Eve knows what this thing is." He vanished and returned with the tridecagon.

Eve's eyes flared. "Where did you get that?"

"It was with my Mum when she was left on my grandparents' doorstep."

I rubbed a hand on the smooth metal. "I hoped you'd know what it was and where it came from."

"It an infernal key." Eve touched it. "I thought we had destroyed them all after Hades forged them to create the netherworld."

"That would explain why I've never seen it," Vitania said. "What does it do?"

"Hades wished for his creations, the demons, to roam freely between Earth and Hell, but they wreaked havoc, so we banished them and made him destroy the keys." Eve shook her head. "Its power comes from the infernal fount, so only Hades and his overlords had the power to use them."

"Uh, this thing follows Emily around like a puppy," Tyler said. "And she's definitely not an overlord."

Eve's forehead pinched with obvious confusion. "But her powers are divine, not infernal. It should not have bonded to her."

"Can you destroy it?" I asked.

Eve shook her head. "Only Hades could, and he left this place long ago. Perhaps we should lock it away somewhere."

"I have the perfect place," Vitania said.

Eve nodded. "Perhaps we should discuss your other prisoners. I would know who else you keep in that dungeon."

"As you wish," Vitania replied.

Tyler grinned. "What Eve didn't realize was that when Vitania said 'as you wish', what she really meant was, 'I love you.'"

I was the only one not confused by the *Princess Bride* reference. "You're incorrigible."

"Thanks, babe." Tyler kissed my forehead.

I stared at the infernal key, wondering if I somehow had it in me to activate the thing. But why would I want to go to Hell? "Does the key still work even though Hell blew up along with the rest of the world during the Sundering?"

"I do not know and do not care to find out." Eve nodded at Vitania. "Let us lock it away forever."

I sighed. "Well, that was kind of a letdown. I thought it was something from my mysterious grandmother."

"I'm afraid I have no idea why it's attracted to you." Eve patted my hand. "Your bloodline is divine, not infernal."

"God, I wish I could spend more time with you. I wish I didn't have to work for Fjoeruss tomorrow." I hadn't even left and already I felt sad.

Tyler kissed my forehead. "I'm sorry, babe. I wish things had worked out better."

I shook my head and laughed. "Everything worked out far better than I hoped. I saw Mum again. I found my real grandmother. I finally feel like I know where I'm from and what I have to do."

"And what's that?" Tyler asked.

I stood on tiptoe and kissed his lips. "Save the world, of course."

Tyler grinned. "Looks like I'm the sidekick now, but I'm with you every step of the way."

The cruel world had twisted my half-sister. Now she was the right hand of the mysterious Netherlord who wanted to control it. But I had news for them. Emily Glass was alive and kicking.

And no demon would conquer the world on my watch.

EPILOGUE

Fiery claws seared flesh. Olivia screamed in agony. "Please, stop. Please!"

The ruby demon sighed, almost sympathetically, but he sank his burning claws into her thigh, her arm, the bottom of her foot. Her throat went raw from screaming. Then he vanished into the darkness of the room.

Olivia sagged with relief. Her eyes settled on the intricate patterns burned and blooded into the concrete floor of the warehouse. Many souls had been devoured to create this gateway that allowed demons access to the mortal plane. Domathus had once used it to communicate with her. He had charged her with killing Emily for destroying the demonicus that would have allowed him physical passage into Eden.

But the demonicus gambit cost him dearly. His forced banishment burned through his essence, weakened him. That had given another powerful demon the opening he needed. The same demon who'd originally mapped out the demonicus gambit only to have it stolen by Domathus's minions.

The pattern flickered and a tall man with a thick beard formed. A tattoo covered his muscular chest. Olivia had seen the pattern enough times to know whose it was. It was the true name and pattern of Domathus. The new overlord wore it as a token to remind all others who truly ruled the netherworld.

"I'm sorry for this pain, dear." The Netherlord stopped before the metal chair. "But you made a terrible mistake not coming to me the moment you stole Eve's powers." He sighed. "It would have made things so much easier."

Olivia shivered. "Please, my lord. I will redeem myself."

He stroked her cheek, her hair. "I know. I'm working with a mortal who thinks it's possible to create golem bodies for demons. I believe your particular expertise will push his research over the edge."

"Create bodies?" Olivia didn't understand. "But there are humans every-where. Bodies for the taking."

"Yes, but not quite like this." He grinned, displaying perfect white teeth. "He calls them infernus. Imagine cloning anyone we wanted to and controlling them."

She gasped. "You could control the world without a war."

"For a start." He sighed. "God powers would have been so nifty to have. I don't think you realize how hard you made this on me."

"What is it you desire, my lord?"

"Why, to rule everything, of course." He smiled. "While the Overworld battles Daelissa, I will sink my fingers into every pie I can reach. I have been planning this for so long, my dear." He leaned down and kissed her cheek.

Heat seared her flesh. Olivia cried out until she was hoarse with agony.

"You'll be a good girl and get me those powers again, won't you?" He licked her cheek. The pain vanished, replaced by numbing ecstasy.

Olivia knew this was how she'd been controlled before. Terrible pain.

Blissful relief. But she couldn't run from the Netherlord. He was too powerful. Even Domathus in his prime was an ant compared to him. "Yes, my lord."

He chuckled. "Domathus thought he was so clever when he stole my plans for the daemonculus. He didn't even realize until the very end that I wanted him to make a play for Earth. He was a test to see how the mortals would react to an incursion."

Olivia gasped. "You tricked an overlord?"

"Not the first time and not the last." He gave her a devilish grin. "I have manipulated even the old gods into fulfilling my will. So the next time you come into god powers, you remember that."

The Netherlord unstrapped her from the chair. He helped her stand and gave her a gentle hug. To Olivia it felt as if he were her savior even though he was also her tormenter.

"Can you stand, darling?" He backed away.

Olivia stood on wobbling legs. "Yes, my lord."

"I have to admit, I'm a bit disappointed how you and your sister turned out." He circled her, a man inspecting a prize horse. "I hope your own abilities grow into something more powerful."

"I will prove myself to you, my lord."

The Netherlord sighed and flicked his hand as if batting away an annoying fly. "Let's get rid of the formalities, shall we? From now on, you can call me Dad."

She looked down. "Yes, Father."

He laughed. "Defiant. I love that about you." The Netherlord made a shooing motion. "Now go and have fun. Get into trouble like kids do."

"Yes, Father."

In an instant, he stood nose-to-nose with her. He gripped her neck and lifted her off the ground. His voice channeled the chorus of a thousand damned souls. "And get me Eve's fucking powers. Do you know how hard it was to trick that bitch into falling for a mortal? Do you know how fucking hard it was for me to impregnate her without her knowing?" He threw Olivia to the ground. "If I had known she was still in Eden, I would have used you to steal her powers sooner. But you squandered everything!"

Olivia curled into a ball. She had no more tears to cry. No more apologies left to offer.

"Get the fuck out of my sight." The Netherlord walked back into the pattern. His body flickered and vanished.

Bones aching, skin burning, Olivia climbed to her feet. She bore no physical wounds from the infernal claws. The only scars it left were on her soul. A few scrapes and bruises from the straps and floor were all that remained. She took a deep breath and steeled herself. If she ever got Eve's powers back, she would castrate dear old Dad. He might be formidable, but she would find a way.

The Netherlord thought he was the smartest fucking demon on the block. But Olivia knew his real name. She just lacked the power to do anything to him. But one day, the bastard would pay for this.

Fuck you, Baal.

ABOUT THE AUTHOR

John Corwin is the bestselling author of the Overworld Chronicles. He enjoys long walks on the beach and is a firm believer in puppies and kittens.

After years of getting into trouble thanks to his overactive imagination, John abandoned his male modeling career to write books.

He resides in Atlanta.

Connect with John Corwin online:
Facebook: http://www.facebook.com/johnhcorwinauthor
Website: http://www.johncorwin.net
Twitter: http://twitter.com/#!/John_Corwin

www.johncorwin.net
john@johncorwin.net

BOOKS BY JOHN CORWIN

THE OVERWORLD CHRONICLES

Sweet Blood of Mine

Dark Light of Mine

Fallen Angel of Mine

Dread Nemesis of Mine

Twisted Sister of Mine

Dearest Mother of Mine

Infernal Father of Mine

Sinister Seraphim of Mine

Wicked War of Mine

Dire Destiny of Ours

Aetherial Annihilation

Baleful Betrayal

Ominous Odyssey

Insidious Insurrection

Utopia Undone

Overworld Apocalypse

Assignment Zero (An Elyssa Short Story)

OVERWORLD UNDERGROUND

Possessed By You

Demonicus

Infernal Blade

OVERWORLD ARCANUM

For the latest on new releases, free ebooks, and more, join John Corwin's Newsletter at www.johncorwin.net!